Wishing on Willows

"Have you ever been through a painful season in life and wished for something new, something fresh, or even something healing to come along? Take this journey with Robin Price, a widow and single mother with a big heart and passion for those closest to her, as she wades through trying to live, let go, and love again. *Wishing on Willows* is a story of hope that will find you stepping up to the willow tree and daring to make wishes."

—CHERYL MCKAY, coauthor of *Never the Bride* and author of *Finally the Bride: Finding Hope While Waiting*

"What I've come to admire about Katie Ganshert's writing is how skillfully and compassionately she creates memorable characters and weaves into their lives authentic struggles. From the very first line, "The first time I lost my husband…," to the last line, "The whispered words came without fear or guilt or hesitation," we are given the gifts of grieving and letting go told with humor; realistic trials; characters I want to go on telling their stories; and the longings of the human heart. This is a fine, fine novel."

—JANE KIRKPATRICK, *New York Times* best-selling author of *Where Lilacs Still Bloom*

"Just like a willow tree, *Wishing on Willows* evokes grace, humility, and beauty. A well-penned story of sacrifice, second chances, and love, Ganshert's second novel is as poignant as her first. This is a must-read for any reader seeking to find comfort beneath their own proverbial willow."

—BETSY ST. AMANT, author of *Addison Blakely: Confessions of a PK*

"In *Wishing on Willows*, Katie Ganshert delicately weaves together a story of healing and renewed hope. Will young widow Robin Price choose to fight for what she had or to relinquish the past for the chance to love again?

Ganshert deftly writes of grief and wounds that leave us shattered, pointing her characters—and her readers—to the One who provides the strength to embrace life again."

—BETH K. VOGT, author of *Wish You Were Here*
and *Catch a Falling Star*

"Katie Ganshert's *Wishing on Willows* is rich in symbolism but as down-to-earth as its Midwestern heroine, a young widow juggling the roles of single mom, business owner, and ministry volunteer. I was thoroughly drawn into her changing seasons of love and loss, memory and hope. Like a May basket left at a neighbor's door, this is a generous story filled with charm and surprises."

—MEG MOSELEY, author of *When Sparrows Fall*

"Katie Ganshert has created an interesting cast of characters that are likable yet flawed. Fans of inspirational romance are sure to enjoy this novel."

—KATHRYN CUSHMAN, author of *Almost Amish*

"Katie Ganshert is a fresh and powerful new voice in contemporary Christian romance. Her writing wraps itself around your heartstrings and refuses to let go."

—ERICA VETSCH, author of *A Bride's Portrait of Dodge City, Kansas*

WISHING
on
Willows

Enjoy!

Katie Ganshert

WISHING on *Willows*

A Novel

KATIE GANSHERT
AUTHOR OF *Wildflowers from Winter*

WATERBROOK
PRESS

WISHING ON WILLOWS
PUBLISHED BY WATERBROOK PRESS
12265 Oracle Boulevard, Suite 200
Colorado Springs, Colorado 80921

All Scriptures quotations and paraphrases are taken from The Holy Bible, English Standard Version, copyright © 2001 by Crossway Bibles, a division of Good News Publishers. Used by permission. All rights reserved.

The characters and events in this book are fictional, and any resemblance to actual persons or events is coincidental.

ISBN 978-0-307-73040-4
ISBN 978-0-307-73041-1 (electronic)

Cover design by Kelly L. Howard; cover photography by Jacques Loic, Photononstop; author photo by Kinsey Christin Photography

Published in the United States by WaterBrook Multnomah, an imprint of the Crown Publishing Group, a division of Random House Inc., New York.

WATERBROOK and its deer colophon are registered trademarks of Random House Inc.

Library of Congress Cataloging-in-Publication Data
Ganshert, Katie.
    Wishing on willows : a novel / Katie Ganshert. — First edition.
        pages cm
        ISBN 978-0-307-73040-4 — ISBN 978-0-307-73041-1 (electronic)
    1. Widows—Fiction. 2. Single mothers—Fiction. 3. Real estate developers—Fiction. 4. Right of
property—Fiction. I. Title.
        PS3607.A56W57 2013
        813'.6—dc23

Printed in the United States of America
2013—First Edition

10 9 8 7 6 5 4 3 2 1

For Brogan, my dinosaur-loving, adventure-seeking,
laughter-inducing little man.

When your dad and I saw those two lines in New York City, we had no idea
they'd become our entire world. You make life so much fun.

෨

D'APERTURA

The first time I lost my husband, we were in Italy on our honeymoon. For the briefest of moments, as he walked toward me with our train tickets tucked in the back pocket of his jeans, the sunlight swallowed him. Even though he came back into view not more than a second later, my breath caught. I had this terrifying thought that something could happen. That moments were fleeting, and with the snap of a finger, he could be gone.

Before the idea could settle, Micah wrapped his arm around my waist and we boarded a train that took us up the coast to Cinque Terra—a cluster of five towns precariously built atop cliffs rising from the sea. With Micah's warmth beside me and our train window framing a fire-burning sunset over the Mediterranean, life felt so intensely beautiful and limitless and vibrant that my heart ached. I understood why my mother had never wanted to vacation anywhere else.

We stayed at a bed-and-breakfast in the town of Riomaggiore. The next morning, instead of joining the tourists walking the main road, Micah and I went exploring, holding hands while a gentle breeze carried the scent of baking bread through the streets and church bells chimed in the distance and multicolored clothes danced on lines outside opened windows.

That's when we discovered Caffe di Luca.

It was small and squat, and not nearly sturdy enough to support the jumble of buildings stacked on top. But happy chatter lured us inside and we ordered in broken Italian. Then we sat by the window and drank the world's best coffee, wondering out loud how anyone could tend and harvest vineyards that grew on vertical hills. We stayed through another two cups until we were giddy with caffeine.

Discovering Caffe di Luca was like finding a pearl in the belly of a clamshell—wonderful and unexpected. Like dedicated pearl divers, we spent the rest of our honeymoon searching for more, making a game of who could order in the best Italian, and later, French. Sipping café au laits. Eating pasticiotti and macarons. Taking silly pictures and dreaming about the children we would have and the memories we would collect with each passing year.

Ending such a magical time in Paris felt too cliché. Too American. So instead, Micah picked the second largest city in France. Which is how we wound up in Marseille at Café de Petit, an inconsequential establishment hidden behind a pair of olive trees.

In what I still claim to have been impeccable French, I ordered coffee—black for me, a double shot of espresso for Micah—and chocolate brioche to share. We took our treat outside and sat beneath one of the trees.

Even now, eleven years later, I can still taste the flaky brioche melting over my tongue. I can hear the canopy of leaves rustling with the warm breeze. I can still feel Micah's arms around me as I rested my head against his shoulder.

"We should do this." His chest vibrated with the words.

"Do what?"

"This." He motioned toward the doors behind us, his arms tightening around my body. "A café."

I laughed. "You're nuts."

"No, seriously." His lips brushed my temple. "I've seen you fall in love with every single one we've gone to. Your eyes light up. I'll miss seeing that when we go home." He turned me around and kissed my nose, ran his knuckles across my jaw. "I want you to have a café, Robin."

I leaned into his touch.

"Plus, you'd be the world's sexiest café owner."

He kissed my lips then. Long. Slow. Delicious. One of a thousand delicious kisses he'd given me over the last three weeks. And this magical, light, tantalizing feeling captured me—that even though we would soon be leaving, even though our honeymoon was drawing to a close, this was just the beginning. Micah and I had the rest of our lives to plan. To have children. To open a café. To come back here when we were old and gray, to Marseille and Cinque Terra and every other town we stopped at along the way. To celebrate the life we would build. The life we would share together.

ONE

Amidst a pile of discarded tops, inside a closet she used to share with her husband, Robin Price deliberated between high heels and flats, but her mind was on her house, a disaster zone of plastic dinosaurs, old maid cards, and Thomas the Tank Engines littering a path from Caleb's room to her own. Unfazed by the chaos, or perhaps just accustomed to it, Robin's sister-in-law held pendant earrings by one ear, gold hoops by the other. She seemed more her old self each day.

"These would look great with your black top," Amanda said, jiggling the hoops by her left ear. "But these really match the blue one." She held the pendant earrings up to her right.

Behind her, clomping around in a pair of high-heeled brown boots, his beloved John Deere toy combine clutched in his fist, Caleb looked so much like Micah with his flyaway cowlick and those big hazel eyes that it stole a little of Robin's breath. "Look, Mommy," he said. "I'm a cowboy! And I'm gonna get those bad guys with my shooter." He raced down the hallway as fast as the too-big shoes allowed.

Amanda held the earrings up higher. "So what do you think?"

"I think we're overthinking this." Robin plopped onto the bed and brushed wisps of hair from her eyes.

"Your first date in over four years? Impossible."

"You have to stop calling it that." Robin's palms were clammy enough at it was. Not to mention her stomach hurt and her nerves were messier than the house. "It's not a date."

"A single man asked you to dinner. I hate to break it to you, but that's a date."

With a groan, Robin fell back onto the mattress. "I'm an awful, horrible woman. Somebody should lock me up and throw away the key."

"Wanting to get back out there does not make you awful."

"But that's just it. I don't *want* to get back out there." In fact, the only living male Robin had any interest in spending time with was currently wearing her high-heeled brown boots—and those dates usually entailed her flannel pajama bottoms, heavily buttered popcorn, and the umpteenth viewing of *Pete's Dragon*. She flung her arm over her eyes and shook her head. "This whole thing was one giant misunderstanding."

"What are you talking about?"

"Kyle mistook my suggestion. He probably thinks I was fishing for a date, but I honestly just wanted to chat about the meet and greet on Sunday." Kyle was the new director for One Life, a beloved storefront ministry attached to Sybil's Antique Shoppe. One Life did everything, from delivering meals to equipping the unemployed to offering free after-school programs to hosting a support group for people battling addictions. It was located next door to Robin's café, which meant she could bake to her heart's content, because whatever she didn't sell for the day, she'd bring over to One Life, where the food never went to waste. Yesterday, when she dropped off some apple fritters and mentioned they should find a time to discuss the event, he'd said, "How about tomorrow night over dinner?" and in the midst of her shock, she said yes. She said yes! "Oh my goodness, I'm leading him on. I am a leader-on-er."

"You are not." Amanda dug through an opened jewelry box on the dresser. "For all you know, you could totally hit it off."

Robin blinked at the textured ceiling and the layer of dust on the wooden fan blades. Two of the three light bulbs in the fixture were burnt out. She would wait for the entire room to go black before she took the time to change them. It had been one of Micah's pet peeves. Robin could picture him standing on their bed, faded blue jeans slung low around his hips, twisting in a fresh bulb. *"What would you do without me?"* he'd always ask. *"Go blind from squinting,"* she'd say. As it turned out, she did not go blind, but the house was dimmer. She frowned and sat up.

Amanda pulled something black from the pile of clothes in the closet. "Caleb's just getting over his cold."

"Your son will be fine. That's one of the perks of having me as your roommate. Built-in baby-sitter." Amanda set the gold hoops on Robin's knee. "Black top. Gold hoops. It's too late to cancel now."

As if on cue, the doorbell rang.

The sound made Robin jump up from the bed, her nerves swooping and twisting—not the excited kind of nerves she'd had on her first date with Micah either, but the nauseous ones. She pulled the black top over her camisole, put the gold hoops in her ears, slipped her feet into a pair of black flats, and hurried down the steps, Caleb chasing behind her with an empty squirt gun.

She placed her hand over the doorknob and took a deep breath. *Inhale*—this was not a date. *Exhale*—this was not a date. Amanda was making a bigger deal out of this than it was. Forcing her lips into a smile, she pulled open the door.

Kyle stood on her front stoop with neatly trimmed hair, a navy-blue polo, and a single red rose.

This was totally a date.

"Wow," he said, holding out the flower. "You look great."

Her stomach didn't swoop. Her heartbeat didn't quicken. But she thanked him and took the gift. "Come on in."

As soon as he stepped inside, he crouched down to toddler height and stuck out his hand. "You must be Mr. Caleb, the man of the house. My name's Kyle."

Caleb pressed his face against Robin's hip and made a sound that was half whine, half huff. A wordless "I don't wanna." Her boy wasn't shy and he certainly was not a brat. So why did he choose now to act like it? "Caleb, when somebody says hi, the polite thing to do is say hi back."

He made the sound again and wrapped both arms around her thigh. *Oh, good grief.* She was not going to have a power struggle with her child in front of this man before her first accidental date in four and a half years.

Kyle straightened to his full, lanky height and waved his hand, a gesture that said not to worry, he wasn't offended. Robin moved to get her purse but Caleb wouldn't let go of her leg. She looked at Amanda. "Don't forget to give him his medicine. It's the pink bottle in the fridge. Dr. Dotts was very clear that he needed to take it for the full ten days, even if all the symptoms are gone."

"I know. I know. Stop worrying and have a good time."

"I want to come with you," Caleb said.

Handing the rose over to her sister-in-law, Robin peeled away Caleb's arms. "Honey, you're going to stay and play with Aunt Mandy."

"But I wanna come with you." He stuck out his bottom lip and grabbed onto her leg again, but Amanda grasped his shoulders and pulled him away. Caleb was having none of it. He dug his feet into the carpet and began to cry.

"We can watch the dragon movie," Amanda said.

"I want to go with you!" His cry turned into a full-fledged wail.

Heat rushed into Robin's ears. Caleb—her wonderful, kindhearted, happy-go-lucky, almost four-year-old boy—was throwing a temper tantrum that would rival the most terrible of two-year-olds. Robin stared, completely mortified, until Amanda wrapped her arms around her traumatized son and mouthed the word *go*.

So she did. With the sound of Caleb screaming behind her, she stepped outside and closed the door and smiled at Kyle, feeling lonelier than she had in a long, long time.

∾

Her favorite canvas hung slightly off kilter, tilting to the left, as if trying to slip away from the chaos in the café. Despite a broken appliance and an employee who had called in sick, Robin breathed in the steam rising from her coffee and smiled, because it was *her* chaos. And nothing could ruin Saturday mornings. Not even the empty table next to the counter where Mayor Ford usually read the newspaper while enjoying a white chocolate caramel latte and homemade cinnamon roll.

A loud sound, like a hammer on pipes, clanged from the kitchen.

The chatter of her three table mates paused, then resumed.

Robin needed to corral the grief support group's conversation toward more productive things, like who would visit Jed Johnson and take him meals throughout the month. Instead, she twirled her wedding ring, relishing each of the ladies' smiles—especially Linda's. A year and a half ago, the woman hadn't wanted to take another breath, let alone go out in public. Now here she sat, appetite back, ready to support those whose grief was a little more fresh.

Robin took a sip of her coffee, contentment resting in her chest. She was so proud of everyone's progress.

"So…" Cecile Arton's face lit like a Christmas tree. She wore a loose-fitting pink track suit embossed with rhinestones and her gray roots gave way to teased, bottle-blond hair. "How was your date last night?"

Robin's attention snapped into place. "My date? How did you hear about that?"

"Richard saw you at Shorney's Terrace with a certain someone."

"Sorry to disappoint, but that certain someone is only a friend."

Cecile folded her hands beneath her chin. "Shorney's isn't exactly the kind of place you bring a friend."

Robin was well aware of that fact, especially after spending an entire meal surrounded by smitten high school couples bedecked in prom clothes. Nevertheless, she had cast aside the awkwardness and used the opportunity to get to know the new director of One Life. Robin loved his passion for the ministry, but even in her unguarded moments, when she made herself consider the possibility of something more, she only missed Micah. "We were discussing the meet and greet on Sunday. That's all."

The kitchen door swung open and out came Lenny, her trusty repairman, a tool belt slung around his waist. Caleb trailed close behind on his tiptoes, arms folded up to his chest like a T. rex. When he woke up this morning, the fiasco from last night had been completely forgotten.

"Just need to grab something from the van," Lenny said, saluting Robin and the ladies with her. Caleb mimicked the salute.

"Hey, Wild Man, why don't you come over here and color for a few minutes while Lenny fixes the oven?" Robin said.

Caleb let out his best dinosaur protest—something between a growl and a roar. Linda chuckled and took a sip of her herbal tea. She'd watched Caleb since he was old enough to crawl, which meant she knew better. The kid had no interest in coloring. Or anything that involved sitting still. Not when there were dragons to slay and monsters to chase and bad guys to capture.

"That's okay, Robin. He's a good helper." Lenny tousled Caleb's dark hair and opened the front door wide. Shafts of early-morning sun poured across marbled flooring. "We should have your oven up and running in no time."

As soon as the pair disappeared outside, Cecile took a sip of her mocha, lipstick staining the mug rim. "That Lenny's a nice-looking fellow."

"I don't care if he's cute or covered in warts," Bernie said, "as long as he fixes that oven so I can have my cinnamon roll." She poked at the day-old rhubarb muffin in front of her. Exactly like the rhubarb muffins Cecile and Linda had eaten without any complaint. "It's the only thing I look forward to eating anymore."

"A nicer guy you couldn't find. Strong shoulders. A decent head of hair." Cecile took another drink and peered at Robin over the top of whipped cream and chocolate sprinkles. "What do you think about Lenny?"

"I think he's an excellent repairman. I also think we should be back on track."

"You're avoiding," Cecile said.

"Avoiding what?"

"The question." She dabbed the corners of her mouth with her napkin, leaving her lips paler. "Just because sparks didn't fly last night with Kyle doesn't mean they won't with Lenny. You have to keep trying until you find the right guy."

Robin had found the right guy. Losing him didn't mean she should go looking for a backup.

"Caleb sure seems to have taken a liking to him."

"Caleb takes a liking to anyone who lets him hit things with a hammer."

Cecile placed each of her ringed fingers against her chest, dimpling the skin above her zippered top in four different places. "All I'm saying is you could do a lot worse than Lenny."

Bernie muttered something about doing a lot better too and massaged the tops of her knees.

Robin chuckled. "How about this? If I'm ever in want of a matchmaker, you'll be the first to know."

"Speaking of matchmaking"—Cecile turned her attention to Linda— "how did *your* date go last night? Was he as charming as I promised he'd be? Did he take you to Val's Diner? I told him to spring for something nicer than Val's."

A slow blush crept into Linda's cheeks.

Robin looked at Cecile. "You set her up?"

"With that handsome fellow who runs the Laundromat."

Linda's blush deepened. "It's okay, Robin. Really. We had a nice time."

Cecile's eyes glittered. "I knew you would."

"He's taking me line dancing next week."

A puff of air escaped Robin's lips. She leaned back in her chair and studied Linda, trying to ignore the odd sensation of being lapped.

"Can I have that?" Cecile pointed to Bernie's uneaten muffin. The old woman scooted her plate over and scrunched her nose, like Robin had served them rotten fish. "I'm so glad you're letting go, Linda. Moving on. Living your life again."

Robin's muscles tightened in her chest. Then in her arms and legs. *Letting go. Moving on.* Why should dating be the proof for either of those things? And how could Cecile make it sound so easy when she didn't have a clue? Cecile had lost a sister and Robin had lost a husband. While both devastating, they were not the same.

The front door swung open. Lenny and Caleb marched inside, gave them another salute, and made their way into the kitchen. The sight of her son loosened Robin's muscles. If Linda wanted to get back out there again, good for her. Robin didn't need to feel left behind, not when it was a race she had no desire to run. Her attention wandered toward her only customers—a middle-aged couple finishing coffee and conversation.

The woman stood and hitched her purse over her shoulder while the man brought both cups to the counter. "I'll be right back, ladies," Robin said.

She processed the couple's payment and watched them walk toward the door. Their clasped hands and matching gait stretched something inside her, but she pushed the sensation away and pinned her gaze on the mayor's vacant spot.

"Does anybody know where Mayor Ford is?" she asked, coming around the counter.

"He won't be here today." Cecile swallowed a mouthful of muffin and paused, long enough to make Linda lean forward in her seat. "Richard says the mayor's working. We all know that man can't read the comics when he's in work mode."

"Working on a Saturday?"

"I guess he's preparing for a lunch meeting with a developer. Something about building condominiums in Peaks."

Bernie laughed. "Why in the world would a town the size of ours need condominiums?"

"Didn't you hear? That software company—Fixtel? They confirmed last week that they're going to build outside of town. Mayor Ford is ecstatic. He's hoping for a population boom."

"Population boom?" Robin sat down, a little too hard. "In Peaks?"

Cecile's bobbing head made her earrings jiggle. "Richard's been swamped lately. Town council's been working on a development plan. Something about revamping parts of the business district. Heaven knows the place could use a facelift."

Robin frowned.

"It's supposed to be the topic of our next town meeting. Condominiums will be great for business. At least for those still around."

Something about Cecile's ominous tone made Robin sit up straighter. "Your jewelry store's doing all right, isn't it?"

"If you consider all right ending each day in the red, then sure. We're doing just fine." The woman rested her chin in her palm and sighed. "Richard put a For Sale sign in the window this morning."

"What?" Arton's Jewelers was one of the oldest businesses in Peaks. If they closed their doors, it would leave Willow Tree Café sandwiched between an abandoned jewelry store and a run-down antique shop. Not exactly good for business. "Why haven't you said anything?"

"We're ready to retire, especially now that he's so busy with council. And since none of our children are jumping in to take over, we thought it was time. We made the decision last night."

"I know things have been slow." Robin looked around her empty café. The problem was not unique to the jewelry store. "But are you sure you're not jumping into this too quickly?"

"Honey, you're our only regular customer. And all you ever do is polish that ring." Cecile examined Robin beneath overly plucked eyebrows.

Robin checked her watch. The big hand crept past eight and they hadn't accomplished any of the things they normally covered during their meetings. "We should probably discuss Jed Johnson before I leave."

Bernie fixed her steel-gray eyes on Robin. "What about him?"

"He's not doing well. I visited him yesterday and he looked terribly thin. I thought we could arrange some more meals for him this month. And if somebody could go check on him today, that would be great." More clanking sounded from the kitchen, followed by a round of Caleb's giggles. If only Robin could bottle that sound and sell it on eBay, she'd be able to fix the entire town's financial woes. "I'd be happy to do it, but I promised I'd help set up for my brother-in-law's birthday. Caleb can't wait to get out to the farm."

"Jed's wife passed away four months ago," Bernie said.

"Yes." Robin drew out the word. What was Bernie getting at?

"How do we know he's not playing this out to get free meals?"

Robin blinked at the old woman. "Playing it out? Bernie, there's no timeline on grief. If anyone should understand that, it should be us." Four months after Micah died, Robin was a complete wreck. If she hadn't had her friend Bethany urging her to eat, who knows what would have happened? Especially to Caleb, who had been growing in her womb and depended on her for nourishment.

Linda patted Robin's hand. "I'd be happy to visit him today."

The kitchen door swung open and Lenny came out with Caleb. "The oven's fixed."

Robin exhaled. "You're a lifesaver."

"Now before you go getting too happy on me, the prognosis isn't good. You need a new oven. Either that or update the electrical. Perhaps you oughta do both. Because those two together will keep short-circuiting and if you don't do something about it soon, I swear this place is going to catch fire."

"Just as long as it doesn't catch fire tomorrow."

The front door chimed. Amanda breezed inside, her hair swept up in its usual perky ponytail. Robin met her halfway and wrapped her in a hug. "You're a Lenny. Or a Linda. Either one works."

"What?"

"You're a lifesaver."

"And you're lucky I love you so much."

"I'm so sorry to ask you to do this. It's just that Joe called in sick this morning and you know Caleb will be unbearably cranky if I stay and work." She looked over at her son, who was talking with great animation to a very attentive Lenny. "Molly should be here by eleven to take over. I really need to get to the farmhouse and make sure Bethany isn't concocting any unholy mixtures with her cake baking."

"Please hurry."

Robin grabbed the empty plates from the table. "I'm sorry I have to cut this short today, ladies. I'll go put those cinnamon rolls in right now. Bernie, you make sure and take two before you leave."

She made her way toward the kitchen, stopping twice. Once to straighten the crooked canvas—a picture Micah took outside Café de Petit eleven years ago. Again to remove the newspaper she had laid out on Mayor Ford's table.

She wasn't eager to see her town lose any of its small-town charm, but perhaps the new residents would bring more customers to her café. Sharing the place she loved with more people could only be a good thing. Robin dusted her hands and pushed through the door into her kitchen.

Condominiums in Peaks.

She wondered where they would build them.

TWO

Ian McKay found himself in the real-life version of Andy Griffith's Mayberry, with paint-chipped streetlamps and mulberry trees forming a crooked line on either side of Main Street. A bike path meandered through a riverfront park, and well-worn businesses boasted faded awnings and an assortment of window displays. He half expected all color to fade to black and white and Barney Fife to make an appearance.

He welcomed the change of scenery. Something about being out of Peoria in this small Iowa town, away from the mess of his past, bolstered his spirits and filled him with optimism. He speed dialed his father and stuck his free hand in his pocket.

To his right, a For Sale sign hung in the door of a jewelry store fresh out of the nineteenth century, and to his left, an eyesore disguised as an antique shop bookended the business district like a pathetic caboose ready to collapse on top of itself. Sandwiched between the two, Willow Tree Café possessed a charm the other places lacked. But the lone Honda Civic in the otherwise deserted parking lot told him all he needed to know.

"That was quick." Dad's voice lost none of its vibrato through the phone line.

"Traffic was light."

Dad chuckled. "What do you think about the location?"

Ian peered at the sign hanging in the window of Arton's Jewelers. One of the businesses was already closing shop. Judging by the looks of things, the other two weren't far behind. "Mayor Ford was right. The area could definitely use some improvements."

"We have a lot hinging on this."

Ian plucked the cuffs of his sleeves and pictured his father, dressed in his Saturday khakis, poised behind the mahogany desk in the study while he drummed a pen against his knee and examined the framed picture taken last Christmas, the one of Ian and his mother. He could almost see the stubborn set of Dad's jaw, as if enough determined belief in his son would restore what had been lost.

"I believe in you, Ian. I wouldn't have given you the deal if I didn't."

The bloated words sat on Ian's shoulders. Dad had made it clear—this would be the biggest deal of the year. Big enough to chase away the threat of downsizing that hovered over all of their spirits, Dad's most especially. He was a good boss. He cared about each of his employees and didn't want to lay off anyone. With everything going on, after all that had happened, sparing him from the burden was the least Ian could do.

"Can we expect you for dinner tomorrow evening?"

"I think I'll stick around Peaks for a while."

A drawn-out pause lingered over the phone line. Ian scuffed his shoe against the ground and connected with a small rock. It skittered across the cement and landed in a flower bed. "Is that a problem?"

"Your mother—"

"Will be fine." He rubbed the back of his neck and eyed the ramshackle shutters hanging on either side of the antique shop windows. "Look, I'll be back for the meeting on Wednesday, so it's not like I'm going to be gone very long."

"Will you be ready to present your plans?"

"Of course."

"I'll see you on Wednesday, then."

They said their good-byes and Ian pocketed his phone. Mom would be fine. Dad would make sure of it, just like he made sure of it last time. And while his father took care of his mother, Ian would take care of the family business. He might not share Dad's passion, but he was good at what he did. He'd earn back the respect he'd lost. Prove to himself and everybody else that he deserved to wear the last name McKay.

A breeze ruffled his hair, and a rusted-out pickup with a faulty muffler grumbled down the two-lane road. He peeled his gaze away from the For Sale sign and strode through the front doors of Willow Tree Café.

"Oomph!"

Hot liquid splashed against his chest and soaked through his button-down shirt. He yanked the fabric away from his skin and reached out to steady the woman he'd smashed into.

She tottered before him, her hand wet with spilled coffee, light brown hair swept into a loose ponytail. Her eyelids fluttered like two hazel strobe lights. She captured her bottom lip between her teeth, her attention stalling on his chest.

"Are you okay?" Ian asked. "I didn't mean to run into you."

She pointed to the mess down his front—lavender fabric turned rotten plum. "Please tell me that's not a new shirt."

"Define new."

She slapped her palm over her eyes and groaned.

Ian smiled. "The good news is I own more than one shirt."

"I am so sorry."

"Really, it's not a big deal."

Her hand slid down her face and stopped over her mouth. "Let me go get you a towel." Her palm muffled the words as she took two careful steps out of the puddle. "And something to clean up this mess."

Ian watched her go, wiping at his ruined shirt. Classic jazz music and the smell of cinnamon and fresh coffee grounds floated in the air as he walked toward a row of marble-topped tables and studied the canvases hanging between the windows—black-and-white photographs of what looked like European cafés. The photographer had toyed with the focus and the zoom to give each picture an artsy look. His attention roamed up the tightly spiraled metal staircase to a small loft overhead, then returned to the main floor and landed on a shadowed instrument in the front corner of the room, flanking one side of the counter.

A baby grand piano.

The squeaking wheels of a mop bucket interrupted his inspection. The young woman handed him a wet towel and got to work mopping the brown puddle off the floor. "Did you decide what you wanted? We've got cinnamon rolls. Iced coffee cake. The best espresso in the Midwest. Anything you want. On the house."

How about a blueberry scone and the café to go?

He bit the inside of his cheek and followed her and her squeaky mop bucket to the counter. "I'll take a chai tea and I insist on paying."

"I'm not taking your money." She eyed his shirt and reclaimed the towel. "Trust me, Robin would kill me if I made you pay."

"Robin?"

"The owner."

"You're not the owner?"

"Are you kidding? I'm not even an employee. Not technically. I'm Robin's sister-in-law. Or roommate." A frown flickered across her brow. "I only help when she's desperate."

He removed his billfold from the back pocket of his slacks and handed over a crisp five-dollar bill.

She ignored it and pushed some numbers on the cash register. "One chai tea, courtesy of Willow Tree Café. Can I get you anything else?"

The owner. In a good mood. Preferably open to a career change. "I think I'm good for now, thanks."

She plucked a to-go cup from a stack. "If you don't mind me asking, what brings you to Peaks? It's not every day we get a stranger in town." Her eyes roved over his apparel. "And I mean this in the most flattering way, but you sort of stick out."

"I do?"

She traced circles along the countertop with the pad of her thumb. "You're very fancy."

A low chuckle rumbled in his throat. "Is the owner by any chance coming in today?"

"You're not going to complain about the service, are you?"

"I wouldn't dream of it."

"Then you can catch her this evening. She comes in on Saturdays before close and plays a few songs. It's the only night the café's open."

"Plays?"

The woman wiggled her fingers in front of her, as if playing an imaginary keyboard.

Ian reexamined the instrument he'd noticed earlier, a hint of uncertainty stirring in his gut. "I've never seen a piano inside such a small café before. Jazz clubs maybe, but not this."

"That's because you've never seen this café. Music is ingrained in Robin's soul. She loves it. Almost as much as she loves this place."

His uncertainty grew, sticking to his insides like a heavy meal of pancakes and syrup. "Can I take a rain check on that tea?"

"Sure. Just tell whoever's working that Amanda spilled coffee all over you and she promised you a free drink." She cupped one hand to the side of her mouth and whispered, "I don't think anybody will be surprised."

His chuckle returned. "Great, thanks." He gave the counter a knock and walked toward the door. Hopefully this Robin would be as eager to help as Amanda.

∽

Forty-five minutes inside Sybil's Antique Shoppe and Caleb finally found the perfect birthday present for Uncle Evan—a model John Deere tractor with a missing front wheel. As they stepped away from the cash register, Caleb held it over his head. "Can we get dinosaur paper?"

"I'm sure Aunt Bethy has wrapping paper we can use at the farm."

"Did Daddy love dinosaurs like me?"

The thick cloud of incense Sybil insisted on burning made Robin's eyes itch and her brain fuzzy. She hurried her son toward the exit, eager for fresh air and sunlight. They couldn't have ordered more perfect weather for Evan's birthday, and the promise of an entire day spent with family sounded glorious. "Grandma says they were his favorite toy when he was your age."

"And tractors too?"

"Tractors and dinosaurs. Just like you." Threading her fingers with his, she batted aside the strings of beads that hung like cobwebs in the entrance, ushered Caleb outside, and almost plowed into a wall. Scratch that. A person. She stepped back and shielded her eyes from the low-hanging sun silhouetting the man in front of her.

He was a stranger. With dark blond hair and light brown eyes and a giant stain on his shirtfront. Fresh, by the looks of it.

"I'm sorry. I shouldn't have come barreling out of the door like that."

"No worries." He stepped out of the way and motioned to his shirt. "I'm starting to suspect I'm the problem."

"I'm not used to anyone coming into Sybil's." Her cheeks flushed. Hopefully the combination of distance and age would keep Sybil from hearing the thoughtless words. "Not that there's anything wrong with the store. It's just…out of the way. I guess."

The man's smile crinkled his eyes and showcased teeth that were white and straight—a walking advertisement for orthodontia.

It was the kind of smile that made her stomach dip, like she accidentally skipped that final stair leading down to her basement. The silly feeling left her flustered. "She'll be glad you're here. There's, um, lots of great stuff."

"I'm sure there is." He removed one of his hands from his pocket and stuck it out. The sleeves of his dress shirt were rolled up to his elbows, revealing tan forearms and a nice-looking watch. "I'm Ian."

She hesitated long enough for Caleb to tug on her arm. "C'mon, Mommy. Let's go."

Quite often her son made carrying on a conversation impossible. At times, his impatience crawled under her skin. Today was not one of those times. She let herself be tugged away from the man's outstretched hand. "He's right. We're late. It was nice meeting you."

"Don't I get to know your name? Or will I forever have to refer to you as the woman who almost knocked me over outside the pawn shop?"

"Antique."

"Excuse me?"

"It's an antique shop." She pointed to the sign.

"Oh, right." He stood with his hands in the front pockets of his slacks, thumbs out, completely at ease, his eyes still crinkled as Caleb pulled her farther away. "So do you have a name?"

Robin batted away her discomfort. There was no harm in sharing her name with a stranger. So why did she have the silly urge to lie? Maybe it was the way the man's attention kept flitting to her son. "My name's…Janet."

Caleb stopped tugging, his forehead scrunching in massive confusion. She squeezed his hand and stepped toward the car before he could blow her cover.

"Nice meeting you, Janet."

"You too." She gave him a halfhearted wave and turned around. "Take a deep breath before you go inside," she muttered.

"What did you say, Mommy?"

"Oh, nothing. It was nothing." She ushered Caleb toward her car and resisted the urge to look over her shoulder.

THREE

Caleb sprinted toward the John Deere tractor parked outside the machine shed, Spider-Man tennis shoes kicking up droplets of mud from the soggy ground.

"Don't climb on that tractor," Robin called after him. She looped her fingers through the handle of a plastic bag in the backseat of her car, tucked her free arm beneath a platter of fruit and cheese, and emerged from her vehicle. She checked that Caleb wasn't climbing and walked along the gravel path toward the farmhouse when the smell of smoke curled up her nose.

She jogged the last several paces and struggled to open the screen door with both of her hands already occupied. She fumbled with the handle, then nudged the door the rest of the way with her foot. Its hinges squealed and the door slammed shut behind her. Smoke decorated the ceiling while Bethany stared morosely at the charred cake smoking on the countertop, her long hair tied up in a messy knot. "How is it that I can design buildings, but making a cake is a complete stumper?"

Robin set down the cheese tray and flapped the black haze out the opened window. "How in the world did you burn it so badly?"

"I was preoccupied."

"With what? Plowing a field?"

"Trying to squeeze an entire day's worth of work into an unpredictable nap time."

Robin plucked the cake mix box from the counter and held it away from her like a dirty sock. "You'll accept Betty Crocker's help but not mine?"

"I'm his wife. I bake the cake."

Right. So where did that leave Robin? Cakeless, that's where. She feigned interest in a nearby spatula and manipulated her features into something less conflicted. "So because you're Evan's wife, we all have to suffer?"

"I baked one last year."

Robin's lips twitched. "Is that what that was?"

"Evan said he loved it."

"That's because Evan loves you. And you were pregnant."

"How am I supposed to do anything when I'm getting two hours of sleep at night?" Bethany plopped her elbows on the counter and rubbed her eyes. "Evan is already talking about having more. Four, Robin. Last night he actually said he wanted four kids."

"Elyse isn't sleeping any better?"

"She's three months. Caleb slept through the night when he was three weeks."

"Every kid is different." And Caleb had come into Robin's life like a bundle of grace. Back then, during the days of Desitin and Johnson's baby shampoo, her grief was still so jagged. If God had given her a colicky baby, she might have curled up on the floor and cried them both to insanity. "I promise it won't last forever."

If God had taught her anything over the past four years, it was that life came in seasons. Elyse's poor sleeping habits were no different. Robin peeked out the kitchen window and spotted Caleb sitting in the dirt by one of the tractor tires, making explosion noises as he rammed his toy combine into the treaded rubber.

"Maybe I should go wake her up. Do you think I let her sleep too much during the day?"

Robin threw the box in the trash and handed Bethany the plastic bag of groceries she'd brought. "You let Elyse sleep and I'll go check on Caleb. When I get back, we can bake a real cake."

Bethany pulled out eggs and flour and other various cake ingredients, the plastic crinkling. "I should be insulted."

"You should be thankful." Robin set the smoldering cake outside in the mulch and made her way toward Caleb. "Hey, Bugs, why don't you come inside with Mommy and Aunt Bethy?"

He raced to her side and placed his chin against her hip, his large hazel eyes pleading through dark, thick lashes. "Can I play by the tractor? Please, Mommy?"

Robin feathered her fingers through his hair. "I thought you wanted to wrap Uncle Evan's birthday present."

He eyed the green machine with such longing that she had to laugh. The boy was tractor-obsessed. "Make sure you stay where you can see me through the window." She held up her finger and gave her little man a stern look. "And no climbing."

He bobbed his head and raced away. Robin returned to the kitchen, where Bethany had lined up all the ingredients on the counter and was drying out a steel mixing bowl. "In case I forget to tell you, thanks for doing this. You know how much Evan loves his cake."

"Thanks for agreeing to help me with the meet and greet tomorrow."

"Of course."

"And thanks for not asking about last night."

"Amanda already warned me." Bethany gave Robin a sympathetic smile and ruffled through the empty bag. "So where's the recipe?"

"Now it's my turn to be insulted." Robin took the bag and tossed it in the garbage can. "You know I hate asking, but do you think you could work a couple short swing shifts this week?"

As a freelance architect, Bethany had the flexibility to work a few odd shifts at Willow Tree whenever Robin found herself short-staffed. They set up a Pack 'N Play in the back room for Elyse, who would either sleep or enjoy some tummy time. Not something they could do once Baby Girl got older and more mobile.

Bethany scratched at an imaginary stain on the counter. "This week might be tough. I received two phone calls from potential clients yesterday. One for a home renovation and the other for a new restaurant in Le Claire.

The restaurant will be my first big project post-baby. I'm hoping it'll get me back into the swing of things."

"That's great."

Bethany gave her a look—one that said she wasn't buying it. "Great for me, but what about you? You can't be at your café 24/7. It's not healthy."

Robin rolled up her sleeves and spooned flour into a measuring cup. "Maybe I can beg Amanda to help."

The screen door shut behind them. "Help with what?"

Robin looked over her shoulder. Amanda stood in the doorway with a six-pack of pop.

"Picking up a couple shifts this week."

"I do have a real job, you know. I'm the one who balances your café's bank account." Amanda slid a can from a plastic ring and cracked it open. "And anyway, I think your café works better without me. I shouldn't be allowed to carry drinks."

Robin's hand froze, the cup of flour poised in midair. "What happened?"

"You always jump to the worst conclusion."

"Amanda."

"I spilled coffee on a customer." Amanda took a sip and scrunched one of her eyes. "No, *customer* can't be the right word. He didn't actually buy anything."

Robin pictured the gentleman with the tan forearms and the mischievous smile and the giant coffee stain down his front, the one she'd met outside Sybil's Antique Shoppe. He'd been in her café? Bethany reached out and overturned Robin's hand. The flour plopped into the mixing bowl, kicking up a puff of white.

"Don't freak out. I offered him anything he wanted from the menu for free." The pop cans clanked as Amanda set them on the kitchen table. "Have you ever considered your financial problems with Willow Tree might have something to do with your tendency to give things away for free?"

"There's nothing wrong with generosity."

"Well, Miss Generous, he seemed very interested in meeting you."

Robin's brow puckered. "I think I already met him."

"Where?"

"I ran into a guy with a big coffee stain on his shirt outside Sybil's. A little shorter than Evan? Blond hair?"

"A total hunk?"

Robin rolled her eyes. "He's probably an auditor."

"He was way too cute to be an auditor. And polite." Amanda poked her finger into Robin's arm and wagged her eyebrows. "And he was asking about you."

Robin dipped the measuring cup into the flour bag. She liked that Amanda was coming back to her jocular self, but she did not want her playing Cupid. Cecile Arton had that position covered and Robin didn't need two in her life. She didn't even need one. Last night was proof. "Like I said, he was probably an auditor. And you spilled coffee on him."

"Well, I promised the auditor something for free. He took a rain check, which means he's coming back. Don't say I didn't warn you."

"Why would I need to be war—"

A high-pitched scream sliced off the end of her question. A horrifying sound capped with a sickening thud. Robin's nerve endings shot through her skin. Everything seized. Her heart. Her lungs and mind. It all halted in a painful standstill. Until her son's cry sliced through the frozen imbalance and hurled Robin into fast-forward. She tossed the measuring cup aside, and with a thousand horrendous thoughts spiraling through her mind, sprinted toward her son crumpled in the grass.

FOUR

The large Victorian home sat back from the road, peeking over a squat insurance building and an old-fashioned barber shop. Pale blue siding wrapped around a front-facing gable and climbed toward a steeply pitched roof. Ian shaded his eyes from the sun and squinted at the sign near the walkway.

Bernie's Bed-and-Breakfast. His sister would appreciate the alliteration.

He slammed his trunk shut and wheeled his travel suitcase up a shaded walkway lined with ugly garden gnomes. A chime jingled as Ian stepped into the dimly lit foyer, wide enough to accommodate a tall cherry desk with a computer, upon which sat a chipped mug and a silver bell. Behind the desk a plant grew out of an actual toilet bowl, porcelain painted the color of butter, and a wide-set staircase climbed to the second floor. Muted voices from a television filtered down the steps. He wiped his shoes on the welcome mat and stepped forward, the wooden floorboards creaking beneath him. "Hello?"

Footsteps padded down the stairs and a lady emerged—Bernie, he assumed—looking much too old to run a bed-and-breakfast on her own. She stepped behind the desk, brushed at a few scattered crumbs circling the coffee mug, and squinted at his stained chest.

Ian fished his billfold from his back pocket and gave her his most charming smile. "It's not the best look for me, I admit. I usually take my coffee in a cup."

She didn't smile back.

He cleared his throat. "Do you have a room available?"

If she turned him away, he would have nowhere to stay and back to Peoria he would go. In the small town of Peaks, this was his only option.

"We have three."

"I'll only need one."

Nope. Not a crack. He ran his finger beneath his collar. "The biggest is the room next to mine," she finally said.

"I'll take it."

"Do you snore?"

He blinked. Usually, a place of lodging took a person's name. He almost chuckled, but the look on her face made him swallow the sound. This was not a joke. Bernie was very serious about the snoring. "Only when I have a cold. I'm very healthy at the moment."

"Do you talk or laugh in your sleep?"

"Laugh?"

"My husband used to laugh in his sleep. I'd have to whack him with my pillow to get him to stop and then I'd never get back to sleep again."

"I don't believe I laugh or talk."

"No guests past nine. No music or TV past then either."

He slipped his hands in his pockets, dipped his chin and leaned forward. "What if the TV is muted?"

Bernie gave him a heavy-lidded stare. "If you come in after nine, do your best to avoid the squeaky stair. It's the fifth one from the top. I'm a terribly light sleeper and it gets worse with old age."

"Have you tried ear plugs?"

"I don't trust them."

"Of course not." A smile tugged at his lips. "My name's Ian McKay, just so you know."

She pecked at her computer keys. "How many nights?"

"I'll be here on and off for the next couple weeks." The sooner he had this deal under wraps, the better everyone at McKay Development and Construction would feel. He dug out his credit card and handed it over.

She snapped the plastic onto the desk, typed his information into the computer, and slid his card back. "Upstairs. Follow me."

His room—apparently the big one—was barely big enough to fit the full-sized bed, an armoire, and a small desk. As soon as they stepped inside, Bernie held out her hand. Ian dug into his pocket for a couple stray dollar bills.

"I do not want a tip, Mr. McKay. I'm waiting for your shirt."

"My shirt?"

"Somebody needs to treat that stain."

Ian set his luggage on the bed, which let out several creaks, then unbuttoned his shirt and handed it over. Bernie arched her sparse eyebrows at his undershirt. He glanced down. It was equally soiled with dried coffee. "Oh. I'll just throw this away."

"It's a perfectly fine undershirt."

Heat crept up Ian's neck. He couldn't remember the last time a woman made him blush. But seriously, he was not about to strip down to his skin. This was a far cry from playground basketball.

"I'm eighty years old, Mr. McKay. I promise I won't see anything I haven't seen before."

He hesitated, then pulled the undershirt over his head. Bernie appraised his bare chest with those same heavily-lidded eyes and draped the shirt over her arm. Ian wasn't sure if he wanted to laugh or cover himself. She grumbled something about trouble, then turned and left.

His laughter escaped like a squeak. So far, the people of Peaks had been far from dull. He unzipped his suitcase, pulled out the shirt on top, and gave it a good shake. Something drifted into the air and dropped to his feet. The whiteness of the returned alimony check stood out against the mahogany floor. Ian stared at it, his smile fading as he recalled the angry red words Cheryl had scrawled on the attached note.

I don't want your money.

He crouched down and tore the check in half, in fourths, in eighths. A scrap slipped between his fingers and floated beneath the bed. He got down on his belly to grab it and found his reflection in the full-length mirror beside the dresser—grim-faced, prostrate on the floor. He looked away. The reflection was painfully symbolic, reflecting so much more than his physical position. Especially these days. Ian walked over to the garbage can beneath the small desk and let the tiny scraps flutter from his hand like wrinkled confetti.

∽

Ian stepped inside Val's Diner at half past noon to the smell of bacon and syrup. The aroma stirred up long-ago memories of Saturday mornings, when he and Dad would make chocolate chip pancakes in their pajamas while Mom slept in.

A group of teenage boys sat in a corner booth, shooting spit wads at one another through straws. A heavyset man ate a piece of pie at the counter while a waitress filled his cup with coffee. She was petite with frizzy hair pulled back into a low knot and a baby face that made guessing her age impossible. When she spotted Ian in the doorway, she kept pouring until the man yelped and a bit of coffee spilled over the rim. She dabbed at the mess with some napkins and came around the counter sporting a black shirt that said Poetry Is Life. "Can I help you?"

"Is the food as good as it smells?"

"Nobody ever complains."

"Then count me in."

She led him to a booth on the empty side of the diner, smoothing her fingers over her hair and pulling her frizzy knot tighter. She smelled like a library. He slid into the cushioned seat while she took a small menu from the front pocket of her apron and stared at him like she wasn't sure if he was real. "Would you like something to drink?"

"Do you have iced tea?"

"Yeah."

"Then that's what I'll have. With a lemon, if you have them."

"We have lemons." She smoothed the hair over her ear again and looked at the front doors. "Are you eating by yourself?"

"I'm meeting with the mayor. He should be here shortly."

"Oh. Okay." She hurried to the counter and knocked on the window ledge opening to the kitchen. "Fry up some onion rings, Harry. The mayor's coming."

Ian took a deep breath and braced himself in the booth. This was it. Dad's company. People's jobs. Ian's reputation. All of it hinged upon today's meeting.

The front door opened and a man with a shiny head and stooped shoulders stepped inside, scanning the diner. Ian recognized him from the picture on the town's website. He stood and waved. Mayor Ford walked over to the table and pumped Ian's offered hand. "You must be Mr. McKay."

"I'm afraid Mr. McKay is twenty-five years my senior and much better looking."

The mayor's laugh escaped like a sharp bark—the sound didn't at all coincide with a bald Mr. Rogers. "Ian, then."

"It's a pleasure to meet you, sir. This is a very charming town you've got here."

The mayor slid into the booth. "We like to think so."

Ian resituated himself in his seat while the waitress set his iced tea on the table and scooted a mug of foam-topped soda toward Mayor Ford.

"Am I that predictable, Megan?" he asked.

"Harry's frying up your onion rings."

"I guess you know I want the french dip, then?"

Megan winked and pointed her pen at Ian. "Are you hungry?"

It was a funny question, seeing as he was sitting in a restaurant at lunchtime. "I'll have whatever the mayor's having."

This seemed like the right suggestion because the mayor barked again. When Megan left, Mayor Ford grabbed the saltshaker and twisted it in a slow circle. "I'm so glad you could meet me on a Saturday. I sure appreciate the flexibility."

"Of course."

The glass shaker scraped against the laminate tabletop—a steady, hypnotic sound. "I've been talking with the council members ever since Fixtel made their announcement."

"Looks like Peaks will be seeing some changes soon."

"We sure are hoping." Mayor Ford stopped his salt-twisting and leaned over the table, as if the boys across the diner might hear or care. His cheeks glowed like two shiny cherries. "For years I've been wanting to implement a development plan for our downtown, but improvements are hard to make without tax revenue."

"A population boom would make for an expanding tax base."

"Exactly. Which is why we need to woo potential residents. We can't reap the benefits of an expanding tax base unless the employees of Fixtel choose to make Peaks their home."

Ian folded his hands over the table and mirrored the mayor's posture. "I hope that's where we come into play."

"The council members and I are pleased with what we've heard about your business. You're a smaller development company, to be sure, but you have a solid reputation."

"McKay Development and Construction is committed to excellence." It was one of his father's mottos. *If you're going to do something, son, you do it right and you do it well.* Dad managed to live by it in all aspects of his life—as a businessman, as a father, as a husband.

"Which is why we're hoping you're interested in the job."

They were hoping *he* was interested? "We're more than interested, sir."

Megan set a steaming basket of onion rings, a side of ranch, and two plates in between them. Mayor Ford scooped a handful onto his plate and pushed the basket to Ian. "Eat 'em while they're hot."

Ian no longer cared about the food, but he pulled apart one of the rings. Trapped steam spilled from the fried batter while the mayor poured some ranch on his plate and sprinkled his food with pepper. "What did you think about the location I suggested?"

"We know the type of people who will be moving in to work for Fixtel. We've built condos for them before. They're definitely looking to live downtown."

"It's a perfect situation, really. They get their downtown and we finally get to develop the south end." Mayor Ford dunked a ring into ranch dressing and took a big bite.

"Are the businesses there open to selling?"

"Richard Arton's on town council. He and his wife just put their jewelry store up for sale, so he'll be thrilled." Mayor Ford brought another bite beneath his chin. "And between you and me, I've been looking for an excuse to get rid of that antique shop ever since I became mayor. Talk about an eyesore."

Ian took a sip of iced tea. "What about Willow Tree Café?"

The mayor stopped chewing, worry lines crowding around his eyes. "I do wish we could leave Willow Tree Café out of the mix. Robin makes a killer latte. She's a nice woman. Very passionate about what she does."

"The place looks well loved," Ian said.

The mayor drummed his thumb against the tabletop and stared hard at the black-and-white checkered flooring. "And then there's One Life to consider. The ministry attached to Sybil's."

Ian sucked a drink from his straw and let the mayor work out the conundrum in peace. He didn't care where the condos were built. He only cared that McKay Development and Construction built them.

Mayor Ford continued his drumming. "Some of the townsfolk won't be happy to see that go."

"What about the north end? Would it be better to build there?"

"We just updated it last year, plus the buildings on that end are protected by the historical society. We'd never get away with it. And besides, with Arton's already selling and the place in need of renovating, it really is an ideal location."

Ian couldn't argue. "The park on the south end is an added bonus. Easy access to the bike trail too."

"These condominiums. They'll boost the economy, right? Bring in more business. Open up jobs for the unemployed."

"That's usually the case."

"One Life's ministry has been a much-needed Band-Aid these past few years, but this development will get at the root of our problems. As mayor, I have to do what's best for the entire town."

"Times are tough right now." Ian knew. So did Dad.

The drumming stopped. Mayor Ford's worry lines lost their sharpness and his cheeks took back some of their glow. "I'd shake your hand right now if I could, but we'll have to convince the taxpayers first. Let's hope the majority's in favor of your condominiums."

Ian held up his iced tea. "To hope."

The mayor tapped his mug of cream soda against Ian's glass. "To Peaks."

FIVE

Robin tiptoed around the mess of dinosaurs on the floor and groaned against Caleb's weight as she laid him beneath the tractor-covered bedspread. She blanketed his chest, brushed her fingers over the scrapes on his cheek, and kissed his forehead. No doubt he'd end up in her bed before the sun rose the next morning—a habit formed the very first night Caleb slept in his big-boy bed. She had lain awake, listening to the crickets outside her window, overwhelmed by all the milestones Micah had missed, when tiny footsteps pitter-pattered down the hall. Perhaps she should have put a stop to it then and sent him back to his bed. But at the time, she needed him as much as he needed her. So she rubbed his back and fell asleep with his warm body tucked to her side.

Inhaling the scent of his cucumber-melon shampoo, Robin kissed her boy one last time, flicked off the light, and crept down the stairs. Amanda sat on the very edge of the sofa, staring intently at a stack of envelopes.

"Hey."

She slid the stack under her knees, as if she didn't want Robin to catch sight of the mail. "Hey to you. How's Caleb?"

"Sleeping like a rock." Robin set her hand on the top of her head and blew out a great big puff of breath. The day had completely derailed. What was supposed to be a Saturday spent celebrating Evan's birthday ended up being a Saturday spent in the ER. She shuddered. It could have been so much worse.

"Okay, so next question. How's Robin?"

"A little rattled, but okay."

"You sure?"

"I feel bad that Evan's birthday was ruined."

"My brother has had thirty-six birthdays." Amanda fingered the envelopes. "They start losing their sparkle after twenty-one. And besides, we have the picnic next weekend. We'll celebrate then."

Tears welled in Robin's eyes, just as sudden and unanticipated as Caleb's accident. She meant what she said. She was okay. So why this ache for Micah's strong arms to hold her? It was a droning hum. A hopeless longing. An unexpected visitor overstaying its welcome whenever life turned prickly.

Amanda frowned. "Why don't you drive over to Willow Tree and close up? It'll give you a chance to unwind."

"I'm not going to leave Caleb two nights in a row."

"Robin, he's sleeping."

"What if he wakes up asking for me?"

"The doctor pumped him full of pain meds. The kid's in la-la land."

The idea of escaping to the cafe and pounding out her worries and praises on the piano twined its fingers around her heart. Maybe it wasn't too late to catch the Crammers before closing. She would serve them each two cups of piping-hot coffee—decaf, of course—and whatever cinnamon rolls she had left over. Carl and Mimi had come to listen to her play every Saturday evening since she opened Willow Tree four years ago. Apart from the café, she probably wouldn't know them.

"It's not like I have anything planned," Amanda said.

Robin picked at the banister. Caleb was sleeping and the doctor had given him pain meds…

Amanda waved her hand. "Get outta here already, would you?"

Something heavy and light—a familiar contradiction—flooded Robin's soul. What would she do without Amanda? Or Bethany and Evan? Before the moisture in her eyes could thicken, she slipped on her shoes and joined the cool humidity lingering on her front step.

∾

Ian spun his car keys around his finger and walked toward the café, cicadas singing backup as he whistled a tuneless melody. He checked his watch:

8:15 p.m. A faint glow filtered out the front windows of the café, ran along the tops of the boxed bushes, and cast elongated shadows over the cement.

A smile stretched away his whistling. Lunch with Mayor Ford couldn't have gone any better. Now if he could talk Robin and the antique store owner into selling, he would have this deal under wraps before he left on Wednesday for the development meeting.

He approached the glass doors and peeked over the Open sign. A leathery-skinned man wearing stained overalls sat across from a lady in a faded flannel shirt. The only patrons in the café, the pair huddled over a table, sipping from off-white mugs. Ian followed their stare and saw the slender backside of a woman perched on a piano bench, dark hair cascading down her back, hands poised over the instrument.

Intrigued, he slipped through the doors and eased onto a chair at the table closest to the exit. The woman's shoulders rose and fell. Her fingers grazed the keys and she started to play. So soft at first the notes tickled his ears, then slowly gathering power and momentum until the music grabbed his full attention and refused to let go. He sat up straighter, unable to look away from the woman's hands, captivated by the passionate, almost choreographed way they moved.

"Can I get something for you?"

Ian jumped.

"Sorry. Didn't mean to scare you."

A woman stood beside him, an apron tied over clean but faded clothes, stringy hair tucked behind ears that stuck out from her head. The lines around her eyes didn't match her youthful face. It was as if worry, instead of age, had etched them there. She nodded toward the piano. "It's beautiful, isn't it?"

Beautiful. The word felt inadequate, but he nodded anyway.

"Can I get you anything?"

He eyed the pianist. "I haven't decided yet."

"Come on over to the counter when you've made up your mind." The woman smiled and walked away.

Trying his best to ignore the music, Ian surveyed the empty chairs. The residents of Peaks wanted to sit at the counter of Val's Diner, sip on refills of Folgers, and chew the fat. They weren't interested in a classy café or gourmet coffee or soul-stirring piano music. His developer experience told him that Peaks wasn't ready for Willow Tree. Perhaps business would improve after Fixtel opened, when a more savvy clientele moved to town, but by then it would be too late. The café would be gone.

The woman's hands fell into her lap and the worn-out duo broke into applause. She stood gracefully from the bench and approached them. Something about the shape of the woman's body filled him with an odd sense of déjà vu. He shifted forward in his seat and eavesdropped on the conversation.

"Our boy Jake's always trying to get us out to Chicago so we can hear him play in one of them fancy concerts of his." The man's voice had a distinct rasp to it, as if gravel paved his throat. "But Mimi was just saying how it can't be much better than what we hear at this café every Saturday night."

"You sure know how to flatter a girl, Carl."

"It's not flattery when it's the God-honest truth."

The pianist, who must be Robin, brushed her hands over the backs of her thighs. "Well then, how about some more coffee before you head out, on the house? It's the least I can do for my two most loyal listeners."

The man's grin revealed a mouthful of crooked teeth. He held out his mug. "You know we aren't too proud to accept something for free. Not from you anyway."

Mimi, his flannel-clad wife, cradled her mug. "I'm not sure, Carl. She sure gives us an awful lot of free stuff."

Robin batted her hand. "It's my pleasure."

Mimi looked doubtful.

"How about this? You let me introduce you to the new director of One Life at tomorrow's meet and greet, and we'll call it even."

Mimi pursed her lips, but Carl bent the bill of his well-worn hat and chuckled. "You're as determined to get us in the doors of One Life as Jake is to get us to that big city he ran off to."

"I'll be right back with one last cup of coffee." Robin curled her finger under the handles of the two mugs and turned around. And in the turning, he saw her face.

His eyes widened. Because Robin, the pianist and café owner, was... Janet, the frazzled, pretty woman who almost ran him over outside Sybil's. She stopped, the smile on her face slowly melting away. Ian crossed his ankle over his knee and waved. She turned around, the porcelain mugs clinking together as she hurried to the counter. Now this was an interesting turn of events. Why would this woman tell him her name was Janet?

She dropped the refills off with Carl and Mimi and approached his table, her steps slow and uncertain. "May I help you?" she asked.

He clasped his hands over his knee. "Either you have an identical twin, or your name isn't Janet."

Her face turned red.

"Or maybe Janet's a nickname?"

"I..." Her voice faltered. She glanced over her shoulder at the display counter, filled with an assortment of pastries, then at the wall clock hanging behind it.

"Your music..." Really, what could be said about her music? Unlike Carl and Mimi, he'd been to his fair share of concerts. He grew up with a younger sister who loved Chopin and Brahms. Yet he'd never heard anyone play with such passion. It had been palpable. Contagious, even. He draped his elbow over the chair's back. "What song did you play just now? I didn't recognize it from anywhere."

"I write my own."

"Impressive."

She pulled at her earlobe. "We're closing soon. Would you like something to go?"

He nodded toward the older couple. "Their coffee wasn't to go."

The red came back. It made him smile.

"You were here earlier, weren't you?" she asked.

"You serve very hot coffee."

She set her hand on top of the chair across from him. A diamond caught the light and sparkled on her finger. He hadn't noticed it this morning. "Amanda mentioned that you wanted to speak with me," she said.

He could have told her about his plans but something held him back. Maybe it was the aftereffects of her music, or the rich scent of coffee in the café, or an instinct he'd inherited from his father. He simply knew now was not the time. "Just wanted to compliment the owner."

Her forehead wrinkled. "An employee spills coffee on you and you want to compliment the owner? You do realize that's not a typical response?"

"Maybe I'm not a typical guy." He leaned across the small table and stuck out his hand. "Ian McKay. I'm in Peaks on business."

She twisted the ring around her finger. "Didn't we already do this?"

"I don't recall meeting any Robins today. A nice lady named Janet who tried to warn me about the hazardous cloud of incense in Sybil's Antique Shoppe, maybe. But no Robin."

An uncomfortable laugh escaped her lips as she reached out and shook his hand. Her movement was soaked in hesitation.

∾

Robin flipped the sign from Open to Closed and eyed Ian as he strolled down the walk and disappeared into the night. Her nerves fizzled and popped like carbonated foam. She'd come to the café to unwind. She'd been doing well too, until she turned around and saw the gentleman she'd met outside Sybil's.

Her heart beat in a series of short, detached notes. Why had she fibbed about her name? Of all the uncharacteristic, idiotic things. That wasn't like her at all. And then to be caught in the lie? Her cheeks warmed at the memory. Their entire interaction had caused the day's tension to rebound with renewed fervor. She snatched the rag from her back pocket and joined Molly. "You can get out of here if you want. Get home to those adorable children of yours."

"Are you sure?"

"So long as you're back tomorrow for the meet and greet."

"Of course. I need the extra shift." Molly clocked out on the cash register and shuffled toward the doors. "Who was that guy that was in here? Did you know him?"

Robin stopped midwipe and scratched the back of her neck. No, she didn't know him. Nor did she know why he made a point to come to her café twice in one day. "I just met him today."

"He's pretty good-looking. And nice. I hope he comes back." Molly grabbed her keys from her purse and stepped outside.

A cool breeze swept across the floor and swirled around Robin's ankles. She blinked down at her shoes, then scoured the table with matchless ferocity. Molly and Amanda needed to get together and form a fan club. One she would not be joining. The guy looked nothing like Micah. Her husband, like all the Price brothers, had a ruggedly handsome, down-to-earth look about him. This man—Ian Whoever—came straight from a *GQ* magazine. Robin would take down-to-earth over model boy any day.

Once she finished her table-scrubbing, made a quick sweep of the floor, and balanced the cash register, Robin flipped off the lights and stepped into the darkness.

Voices filtered up the cement stairs. One a breathy soprano. The other a familiar baritone. She locked the doors and peered toward the lit street below. It was Ian McKay, talking to someone she couldn't make out in the dark. She hiked her purse strap over her shoulder and crept down the stairs, keeping her elbows tucked in and her head down, as if a diminished posture might hide her. Maybe, if she walked quietly enough, she could slip past undetected. After her time at Willow Tree, she was ready to get back to Caleb and make sure he hadn't woken up.

"Hey, Robin!" The breathy soprano thwarted her escape.

The yellow glow from the streetlamp played across Ian's face, casting shadows beneath his cheekbones. He stood with his hands in his pockets, a waitress from Val's Diner beside him.

"Hi, Megan," Robin said. "This is a late night for you, isn't it?"

"I was just walking home. I worked a double shift. Trying to earn enough money to go to a writers' conference next month." Megan had graduated from college last year with a degree in literature. As far as Robin knew, she lived in her parents' basement and spent her free time writing poetry. She didn't seem like the boy-crazy, fan-girl type, but she ogled Ian like he was a superhero. The third member of the Ian McKay fan club. "Ian said he stopped in Willow Tree for a late-night coffee."

"You two know each other?" Robin asked.

"He came to the diner today and ate lunch with the mayor."

Robin snapped her fingers. "Hey. You're that guy Cecile was talking about. The developer who wants to build condominiums in Peaks."

Ian rocked back on his heels, his face falling into shadow. "Word gets around fast."

Megan leaned toward him like an uprooting tree. "How long are you staying in town?"

"Depends on how fast I can wrap things up."

"Maybe it will take a long time." Megan spoke in hope-drenched syllables.

Robin wanted to pull the poor girl aside and give her a lesson in subtlety. Instead, she faked a yawn. "It's late. I should get home." She stepped around the pair and fished out her car keys. "Have a good night."

It took her half the drive before the puzzle piece clicked into place. The condominium man had stopped by her café twice today and both times, he hadn't ordered anything. Robin pressed down on the gas pedal, as if the speed might carry her far away from the ominous weight sinking into the pit of her stomach.

SIX

There was never a time in my life when I didn't play the piano. At least none my memory can recall. When most kids were focusing on the alphabet and counting to ten and staying dry overnight, I was sitting on a piano bench, feet dangling above the ground, snuggled up to my mother's side as she wrapped us in a cocoon of beautiful music.

It was my mother's love language.

She wrote songs for my dad. She wrote songs for my grandparents. She wrote songs for me. And at the very end, she wrote songs for Jesus. It was an odd shift, especially since we weren't a religious family. We never went to church on Sundays. Not because we didn't think God existed, but simply because it had never been a part of our life. My mother's spiritual awakening in her last days wasn't something that would comfort me until many years later.

Supposedly, she wrote me a song on my third birthday, and when she played it, I pranced around the living room in a pink tutu, flapping my arms like a butterfly. Then I climbed onto that bench and asked her to teach me.

So she did. "Chopsticks" and "Twinkle, Twinkle Little Star" eventually turned into *Für Elise* and the *Hungarian Rhapsody No. 2*. Her love language became my love language—the way we not only expressed our feelings, but processed them. As my mother got sicker and sicker, her music turned lighter and lighter, and mine? It became angry and dark, frantic and loud. Filled with dissonance.

Because I wasn't ready to lose her.

She was supposed to be there for my prom and my high school graduation. She was supposed to help me pick out a college. Celebrate with me when I got engaged. She was supposed to help me plan my wedding and gush over my dress and blot her tears when I walked down the aisle. All my life, I had counted on her being there. I never contemplated her absence. Until radiation stole her hair and chemo stole her energy and all I could do was contemplate it.

Mom didn't try to talk me out of this dark musical period I went through. She sat and listened while I pounded out *Black Mass Sonata* and *Mozart's Requiem* and *Beethoven's Fifth Symphony*. When she finally went, I covered the piano she left to me with a black sheet and didn't touch it for a year. I couldn't bring myself to play, not when she wasn't there to hear.

For a year, my love language ran dry. I thought I'd start playing once it came back. I didn't realize it was the playing that made it flow.

SEVEN

Black sky and moonlight and the rise-and-fall buzz of insects filtered through the opened window in Amanda Price's bedroom. A hint of a breeze lifted the curtains. If she tried hard enough, she might hear the heavy, even breathing of Caleb in the next room.

She lay flat on her back, hands folded behind her head, staring at the spider that slowly crept out from its hiding place and scurried across the ceiling. Her heart thudded out a heavy, monotonous beat as she turned her head and looked at the unopened envelope on her nightstand.

The minute she pulled the stack of envelopes from the mailbox and noticed the return address of the one on top, her breath had whooshed away. An hour and a half later and she wasn't sure if it had come back. After two months of silence, two months of shoving her tattered emotions into a box, he had come back into her life.

Amanda sat up in bed and snatched the envelope. She clutched it in her hand and blinked dumbly at the familiar scrawl. Jason Ainsley. A name that was as familiar to her as the moon outside her window. A name that used to encompass her future. A name that turned sour two months ago, when he ruined everything. She hadn't yet gathered the courage to slide her finger beneath the seal and tear open the envelope. She wasn't sure she wanted to read what Jason had to say.

Tiny pockets of hope bubbled in her heart. What if he regretted his decision? What if this was his attempt to resuscitate their tenuous connection before it died altogether? Amanda shook her head. Part of her wanted to tear the thing into tiny pieces and throw them in the trash. The other, bigger part knew if she did, she'd spend the rest of the night piecing them back together with tape and desperation.

The only option was to open it. To face whatever he had to say. He'd wrecked her heart two months ago. Really, how much harm could be done by a small aftershock? Before she could change her mind, she opened the envelope and removed the letter.

The slant of his writing unfurled the ache she tried hard to ignore. But the actual words stirred up anger that had been simmering beneath the ache for the past sixty days. The more she read, the more the anger grew, until she reached the end and the ache was overwhelmed.

He missed her? He hoped she would forgive him? *All my love, Jason*? She crumpled the letter and glared out her window. He had no right to say those things. He made his decision and it wasn't her. Instead of proposing, he went to Nairobi. Not for a week, or a month, or even a year, but indefinitely. He told her he prayed. He told her not going would be an act of disobedience. Effectively stealing away any arguments or protests. Because who could fight words like those without sounding selfish and unchristian?

Well, she had prayed too. Over and over again, she'd prayed. For a man who now resided on the other side of the planet. She thought they'd be husband and wife. She thought they'd live in a house and start a family and go to church on Sundays. Instead, she was here. And he was there.

She didn't understand it. Wanting to be Jason's wife, wanting to have children and raise them to love the Lord…why wasn't that a good enough plan? Why was that any less godly than missionary work?

Amanda flopped back in her bed and searched for the spider, but it was no longer there. She sighed. This wasn't supposed to be her life. She wasn't supposed to be an accountant in Peaks, living with her brother's wife and their adorable son. She uncrumpled the letter and stared at Jason's new e-mail address he had scrawled at the bottom of the page. She wished more than anything he hadn't shared it with her.

~

A steady stream of people filed into the doors of Grace Assembly, an unpretentious brick church nestled behind a line of towering oaks, a fortress of protection from the neighboring Piggly Wiggly. Ian held his breath captive and eyed the steeple, his insides tightening with every inch skyward.

Over the past year, his church attendance had been spotty at best. Partly because he had a hard time interacting with a congregation of people who didn't understand what went wrong. Partly because shame was a powerful thing. The imprisoned air escaped. He brought his forehead to the steering wheel and stared into his lap. He could do this. It was only an hour and nobody knew him here. It was the perfect time to start going back.

Somebody rapped on his window.

"Ian? Is that you?" The pane of glass muffled the words, but the voice was familiar enough. He looked up and came face to face with Mayor Ford, bushy brows knitted together. Ian opened the door and stepped into the sunlight.

"You looked like you were sleeping in there."

"No, I was just…praying."

"I didn't know you were a churchgoing man. What a pleasant surprise." Mayor Ford wrapped his arm around a woman who resembled a contemporary Aunt Bee. "This is my wife, Elaine. Elaine, this is the fellow I was telling you about. The man who's going to help us bring this town back to life."

Ian shook her hand. "Pleasure to meet you, Mrs. Ford."

"The pleasure's all mine, young man."

"My wife is quite the woman, Ian. She's been the president of the high school's PTA for the past"—Mayor Ford puffed up his cheeks and scratched his ear—"what has it been? Twelve years now?"

Elaine nodded.

"Believe it or not, we've had three kids pass through this school system. Condos bringing in the taxpayers—well, you know what that means." He offered his elbow to his wife and turned toward the church. "More revenue for the school district. You'll make winners out of all of us."

Ian fell into step behind the mayor and his wife. *Winners out of all of us.*

He needed to nail this project. McKay Development and Construction depended on it and so did he. Saving the company was his second chance— to do something right, to start over, to see the pride return to his father's eyes. A winner once again. Clutching onto that hope, he followed Mayor Ford through the congested lobby to the sanctuary.

The man shook hands with several people before ushering his wife into one of the pews. Ian pulled at his collar and sat while Mayor Ford removed a Bible from the hymnal rack and handed it over. The book sat in Ian's palm, weighted with words he knew. Words he clung to. Words that were all too easy to forget.

"Elaine and I usually eat brunch at Val's after church. Harry makes one killer stack of hot cakes. Care to join us?"

Ian ran his finger down the Bible's spine. "I'd love to."

Piano music filled the sanctuary. The familiar melody pricked his ears. He looked up from the book and found Robin Price sitting behind the piano, bathed in light in the center of the stage, radiating so much warmth and peace Ian wanted to take some for himself. With closed eyes, she leaned toward the microphone and started to sing, her voice every bit as captivating as her music.

The congregation rose to their feet and joined, but Ian couldn't stand. He stayed seated, and like a deep massage against all-too-tender muscles, the lyrics dug into his knotted-up soul, reminding him of a truth that had become entirely too slippery. God's grace was big enough. For him. And for Cheryl.

When the service ended, he found himself outside in the late-morning brightness, shaking hands with half the congregation, the most recent being a gray-haired string bean of a man named Brian O'Malley and a barrel-chested gentleman named Darrell Maddocks. Apparently, Mayor Ford enjoyed introducing people.

"We hear you've got some plans for our town," Darrell said after taking back his meaty paw. "Chuck mentioned something about meeting soon to discuss the specifics. Brian and I are both council members."

Ian looked to the mayor. "Oh?"

A man tried to squeeze his way between O'Malley and another group congregating nearby, but Mayor Ford called out to him. "Evan, it's been a while. How's farm life treating you? And that pretty young wife of yours?"

The man—Evan—stopped his maneuvering. Mayor Ford had him cornered. "Doing great. She's getting our little one right now."

"Enjoy these days while you can. They slip by so quickly."

"I can believe it."

"I'd like to introduce you to a friend of mine, Ian McKay. Ian, this is Evan Price. Excellent mechanic. You ever have any car troubles while you're here, Evan can fix it right up."

Ian doubted his car would give him any problems, but he shook Evan's hand anyway.

"Ian's in town on business," the mayor said. "His father owns McKay Development and Construction."

Evan seemed to study him from the corner of his eye. "A developer, huh?"

The niggling familiarity plaguing Ian upon their introduction clicked into place. Price. The same last name as Robin's. "Are you by any chance related to the owner of Willow Tree?"

Evan opened his mouth to answer, but before any words could escape, a flash of brown hair and a small body sporting an electric-blue cast catapulted itself into the man's arms. He absorbed the brunt of the impact with a grunt and tossed the small boy into the air. Evan tickled his ribs and the boy squirmed and laughed.

Ian pulled his gaze away from the father-son duo and spotted Robin quickly approaching, wearing the same frazzled expression she'd worn outside Sybil's yesterday morning. "Caleb, you cannot run off like that." She caught sight of Ian and stopped.

"Robin, excellent." Mayor Ford folded his hands. "Allow me to introduce a new friend of mine, Ian McKay. Ian, this is Robin Price and her son, Caleb."

"We've already met," Robin said. "He came to my café last night."

The mayor's eyes widened. "Already? Well, you sure get right to work, don't you?"

Ian cleared his throat and shook his head, but it was too late. Robin glanced around the small gathering, her smile confused. "I'm sorry. I don't understand." Her words came out soft as she turned to Mayor Ford, whose bald head had gone vermillion.

"I assumed... I thought..." His bumbling did not help the situation.

She looked at Ian. "Get right to work on what?"

"I was hoping to talk with you about this later, Mrs. Price." He glanced at Caleb, who was now leaning against his mother, his uninjured arm wrapped around her leg. "Did something happen to your son? I could've sworn he wasn't wearing a cast yesterday."

Her attention flitted to the boy, then back to Ian, her eyelids fluttering like butterfly wings. "What were you hoping to talk to me about later?"

He searched for a way to explain away Mayor Ford's premature words. This was no way to approach Robin about her café—on a Sunday, outside of church, of all places. But she would not be distracted. She rested her hand on her son's shoulder and met his eyes directly. The other men stared too.

"I was going to speak with you about buying your café."

Her face went slack. "Buying my café?"

"For the condominiums we talked about last night."

Robin looked at each of the men, all of whom were fidgeting—Mayor Ford worst of all—and her expression turned suspicious. "Why didn't you mention any of this then?"

"I was—"

"You were what? Spying?"

"No, I wasn't spying." What a ridiculous idea. What was there to spy on?

"Well, I'm afraid I can't give you what you want. I'm not interested in selling."

"I'll make sure you profit from the transaction."

She raised her chin. "I don't care about profit."

Ian turned to Evan. Perhaps her husband would be more rational. "You might want to reconsider."

Evan's forehead broke into wrinkles, so Ian pounced on his uncertainty. "I won't argue with you. Willow Tree Café is a fine establishment. I can tell you've taken great care of it over the years, but you've got a family to think about."

"I think you're mixed up about—"

"Trust me, Mr. Price, I'm not wrong. I've seen plenty of businesses like Willow Tree. Owners hold on too long and end up with outstanding debt. I'd hate for this to happen to you guys. I'm not sure what—"

"You can stop right there, Mr. McKay." Robin's words came out firm, confident. Gone was the vulnerable woman behind the piano. "My business is not about money."

Ian took her in—the stiffness of her posture, the subtle jut of her jaw, the fierce protectiveness burning in her eyes—and his competitive juices started to flow. He wouldn't let this woman cost a bunch of people their jobs. He stuck his hands in his pockets. "Maybe not, Mrs. Price, but it's kind of hard to run one if you don't have any."

EIGHT

How'd we do?" Robin unrolled the napkin from her silverware while Caleb bounced beside her in one of the booths at Val's Diner, making growling noises as two plastic dinosaurs waged war in his hands. The ghost of his toy combine haunted the fun. He had abandoned it on his nightstand this morning, something he hadn't done since he unwrapped the gift for his third birthday last July. Robin rested her chin on her hand and leaned forward. "I have a good feeling about this month."

Amanda tapped papers against the tabletop. "You say that every month."

"Yes, but this month I feel it in my gut."

"You know what I wish you felt in your gut? The desire to keep better track of your inventory. Because it's impossible to keep an accurate tally when your records are about as organized as a junk drawer."

Robin held up three fingers in a Girl Scout's pledge. "I promise to do a better job. I'll make it my personal goal. Now lay it on me. How did we do?"

"Pretty much the same as last month."

A thin layer of disappointment settled over her spirit. Thanks to her mother's inheritance and Micah's insurance policy, Robin didn't pay much attention to numbers. Her café was about community and fellowship, none of which could be measured by a profit and loss report. Still, Ian's ominous warning outside Grace Assembly hovered fresh in her mind.

"Why the frown?" Amanda asked.

"If this keeps happening, I'm going to run out of money."

"That's the beauty of Roy, right?"

Robin exhaled. Amanda was right. And smart. Per her request, Robin had taken out a line of credit from Roy Hodges, her banker, a year after opening the café. It prevented her from dipping into her savings account when a dry spell hit.

"And just be thankful you don't have a mortgage to pay. It could always be worse."

True. She had it better than many businesses along the riverfront, especially on the south end. There was no reason to worry. She'd told Mr. McKay she wouldn't sell. End of story.

Megan set three plates of steaming food on the table. Today she wore a purple T-shirt that said *The Bell Jar.* "A stack of hot cakes, eggs and bacon, and one ham-and-cheese skillet."

The salty-sweet aroma of bacon and syrup wafted up Robin's nose, filling her with renewed optimism. She picked up her fork and cut a tick-tacktoe into Caleb's pancakes while he bounced in his seat. "Thanks, Megan. It smells great."

"Can I get you anything else? Water refills? Coffee?"

Amanda tapped the white mug and saucer set in front of her. "I'll take a refill."

As soon as the waitress left for the coffeepot, Robin leaned over the table. "You do realize you're part of the problem. Even my accountant doesn't mind a cup of overcooked Folgers."

"Hey, if you're genuinely concerned, you know what I think you should do?" Amanda pointed her butter knife at Robin. "Open the café on Sundays. That would help business."

"I was kidding about the coffee."

"I think it's a good suggestion. Worthy of consideration, at least. You could close the café early on Saturday like you do every other afternoon and open Sunday morning instead." Amanda shoved a forkful of ham, egg, and melted cheese into her mouth.

Caleb drenched his plate with blueberry syrup. Robin stopped him before he poured the entire bottle onto his breakfast. "I'm not asking anyone to give up their Sunday and there's no way I'm shuffling Caleb off to day care another day of the week." Her son looked up from his food with sticky lips and round eyes. A glob of pancake fell from his fork and landed on his plate.

"I could watch the little rug rat," Amanda said.

Robin shook her head. Caleb would never forgive her, and she'd never forgive herself.

"I'm just saying. Willow Tree is struggling, and you close your doors on the one day that people are most likely to go out for a relaxing cup of coffee. It's not exactly an intelligent move."

"Sorry. Not doing it."

Amanda lifted her shoulder and speared a piece of ham. "You're opening this afternoon."

"That's different. It's a special occasion. I want to introduce folks to the new director of One Life. If I sneak in a little business while I'm doing it, then that's a double bonus."

"I thought you weren't charging."

"I'm not."

"So how do you figure you're going to 'sneak in a little business'?"

"I'll wow everyone with amazing food and drink, and they'll come back the next time as paying customers."

"Or"—another bite of egg and cheese paused near Amanda's lips— "you could charge your guests today and they become paying customers without you having to lose money first."

Megan stepped up to the side of their table and poured black liquid into Amanda's cup. Robin dipped a slice of buttered toast into her egg yolk and took a bite. The greasy combination slid over her tongue, crunchy and warm.

Pulling at her messy knot of hair, Megan leaned close. "I've never done this before but I've always wanted to. Nine o'clock." She mumbled the words from the corner of her mouth.

"What?"

Megan jerked her head toward the front door. "Nine o'clock."

Robin glanced off toward the left. The food in her mouth lost its flavor. She forced the lump down and watched Ian McKay, looking just as polished as he had an hour ago, stroll through the front doors of Val's Diner. Good grief, the guy was everywhere.

Megan scurried behind the counter. Robin dabbed her lips with one corner of her napkin and turned her attention to Caleb, who had a pterodactyl in one hand, his fork in the other. She saved the plastic creature from the plate of sticky pancakes as a shadow loomed over their booth and Amanda kicked her under the table.

"Fancy meeting you here." The familiar timbre of Ian's voice—rich, deep, cultivated—grated on her. No one sounded that refined without careful practice.

Amanda set down her silverware and brought her cup beneath her chin. "You're looking just as upmarket today as you were yesterday. Even better without coffee dripping down your front."

Ian snapped his fingers. "It's Amanda, right?"

"The one and only."

"It's a pleasure meeting you again."

"Oh, the pleasure's all mine." The steam from Amanda's coffee cup swirled around her chin. "How's your business going? Well, I hope."

Robin rolled her eyes. "He wants to tear down Willow Tree and build condos. That's his business."

"Seriously?"

Robin gave her a yes-that's-right-so-you-better-stop-flirting look. Just because Amanda was newly single didn't mean she needed to fall for this man's charm.

Mayor Ford finished his conversation by the door, seated his wife at a table, and joined them at the booth, looking no more comfortable than he had outside of church this morning. "I sure hope you didn't feel like the rug was being pulled out from under you earlier, Robin."

"It was definitely a surprise." She turned in her seat and addressed Ian. "I'd introduce you two, but you've already met. Amanda's my accountant. And my sister-in-law."

He slid his hands in his pockets and winked, like this whole thing was funny. "So she has insider information. That could come in handy."

The mayor barked. Caleb looked up from the sticky mess he was making with his pancakes. "What's so funny?"

"Nothing, honey," Robin said.

Amanda folded her hands beneath her chin "You two can join us if you'd like."

It was Robin's turn to do the under-table kicking. What was Amanda thinking? They most certainly could not.

"Thanks for the invitation," Ian said, "but we have to finalize some plans for our meeting with town council on Friday."

Worry gathered in the pit of Robin's stomach, ruining a perfectly delicious brunch. "Why do you need to meet with town council?"

"Mayor Ford would like to add the condominiums to the development plan for the south end of the business district."

Betrayal joined forces with her worry. She looked at Mayor Ford—a man who came to the grand opening of her café and had returned every Saturday morning after. "You want to knock my café down?"

His ears turned red.

The visible discomfort made her equally uncomfortable, but she couldn't let him off the hook so easily. "I thought you supported Willow Tree."

"I'm sorry, Robin. It can't be helped. I'm proud of what you've done with the place. It's a fine establishment. It's just in an unfortunate location."

"And One Life?"

"I have an obligation to look out for the town's greater good."

Something strong and fierce pushed aside Robin's worry. Greater good? How could bulldozing a ministry that served people like Molly be for anyone's good? She lifted her chin and met Ian's gaze. "You do know you can't force me to sell, don't you?"

He raised his eyebrow like she was nothing more than a tired child refusing to go to sleep. Like all he had to do was wait and the place that had given her such a sense of purpose over the past four years would nod off into oblivion. "I'm not going to use force."

"Of course not." The mayor gave Robin an uneasy smile and patted his belly. "We'll find a way to work this out. Until then, I'm starving. We should probably get to it, Ian. Robin, I look forward to your meet and greet later today. What a welcoming gesture for the new director."

Heat filled her chest. The mayor complimented her for welcoming the new director of One Life, yet he had no qualms about tearing it down? Didn't he realize the illogicality of such praise?

Ian dipped his head. "We'll be in touch. Have a lovely meal, ladies."

Robin glared after him.

"It should be illegal," Amanda said.

"What?"

"That smile."

The heat in Robin's chest expanded. "Who cares about his smile? He wants to knock down my café."

Amanda tapped her finger on the profit and loss report. "Maybe it wouldn't hurt to listen to his offer."

NINE

Robin yanked off her oven mitts and threw them down on the counter. She closed her eyes and pressed her fingers against her temples. After Val's Diner, she'd baked an entire pan of strawberry-rhubarb muffins and two dozen of Caleb's favorite chocolate gingerbread cookies, and she still couldn't get the picture of Ian and his raised eyebrow out of her head.

Lord, why do I feel so unsettled about this?

Caleb's little fingers grazed her forearm. "Are you taking a nap, Mommy?"

She opened one eye and found the face of her boy, head tilted up as he smiled his father's smile. "No, silly man, I'm praying."

"About my cookies?"

She opened her other eye and cupped his chin. "I'm praying for my sanity."

He scrunched his nose. "What's sanity?"

Robin laughed, then plucked the strawberry-rhubarb muffins from the pan and set them onto a large cooling rack on the prep table. The meet and greet had officially started, and as much as she wanted to avoid Kyle and whatever awkwardness their lackluster date left behind, it was time to get out there and mingle. As if hearing her thoughts, Bethany popped her head into the kitchen/supply room.

"We're filling up fast and everybody's raving about your lemon bars."

"Just as long as they don't have to pay for them."

The door swung on its hinges, breaking apart the chatter filtering inside the kitchen. Bethany stepped over the assortment of Tonka trucks Caleb had dug from the toy chest she kept in the kids' corner below the loft. "I'm the cynic, remember? Not you."

Caleb dropped to the floor and raced a truck in circles around Bethany's feet. Robin untied her apron and flopped it on the counter next to the oven mitts.

"Are you going to tell me what's bothering you?"

Concern whipped her insides into stiff, pointed peaks—sharp and overbeaten. Robin didn't want to give voice to her worry, but even after all these years, she could still hear her mother's words. *"Better out than in,"* she would say. "With the way news spreads in this town, I'm sure you'll hear about it soon enough."

"Hear about what?"

"Did Evan tell you who we ran into outside of church while you were getting Elyse from the nursery?"

"Who?"

"Remember the guy Amanda spilled coffee on?"

"The cute auditor?"

"Turns out he's not an auditor." And he wasn't *that* cute. Robin took a deep breath and let her fears whoosh past her lips. "He wants to buy Willow Tree so he can knock it down and build condos."

Bethany's eyebrows disappeared behind chocolate-brown bangs.

"I don't know why I'm getting worked up over it. It's not like he can force me to sell and I already told him no. So I should let it go, right?"

Bethany folded her arms and leaned against the counter.

"But he turned up at Val's with Mayor Ford when I was going over numbers with Amanda. Supposedly he's meeting with town council on Friday."

"Sounds serious."

Robin threw Bethany a withering glance. "That doesn't make me feel much better."

"Look, there's nothing you or I can do about the condos at the moment. Today is about extending hospitality to Kyle, right?" Bethany came to Robin's side and wrapped one arm around her shoulder. "So let's find that caring, eternally optimistic Robin everybody loves and adores so we can go mingle with the guests."

A smile poked at Robin's lips as Bethany led her to the door.

"You can nod in humble gratitude as everybody worships your baking skills. Maybe play the piano and hypnotize your guests with not one, but two amazing talents that, on occasion, wreak havoc on my self-esteem." Bethany squeezed her shoulder. "Everything will work out. You'll see."

Caleb popped up from the floor. "Can I play in here?"

"Unsupervised? I don't think so, dude." Maybe after ten years of no broken bones, she could forgive herself for letting him out of her sight yesterday.

With Bethany's arm around her, and Caleb's hand tucked in hers, she could let go of the uncertainty swirling like chaos. Taking a deep breath, she stepped into the crowded café. Groups of people huddled together over cups of coffee, munching on homemade goodies, filling the room with laughter. Her throat tightened. This was the dream she and Micah shared all those years ago, when Willow Tree Café had been nothing more than some sketches on paper. Not empty space. Not losses that outweighed profits. But this. People brought together over coffee and conversation. Her smile took full shape.

Bethany patted Robin's shoulder and joined Amanda at the espresso machine. Evan sat at a table near the door talking with Kyle, baby Elyse gumming his knuckles. With a tuft of fuzzy brown hair, big dark eyes, and a trademark pointy chin, the little girl was a miniature version of her mother.

Caleb moved toward them, but Robin tightened her grip on his hand, a reminder that he needed to ask permission first. He looked up. She nodded and he tore through the crowd. When he climbed onto Evan's unoccupied knee, a dull ache stirred inside Robin's chest. She closed her eyes and let herself imagine it was Micah sitting across from Kyle. Micah with his arms wrapped around Caleb.

Is a mommy and a loving uncle enough for my son, Lord?

She pushed away the pointless question. Micah was dead. It would have to be enough. She bypassed the counter and walked toward Kyle, eager to get their first postdate encounter over with. Halfway to her destination, the scent of rain traveled through her café and Mayor Ford stepped inside, followed by the man who was everywhere.

Something inside her sparked to life. Mayor Ford coming was one thing, but Ian? Huh-uh. No way. She wouldn't let them use this meet and greet to further their plans, especially when those plans were a threat to the very ministry everyone was gathered to support. She marched toward the front door with every intention of giving him a piece of her mind, but the Crammers intercepted her and all the words she had for Mayor Ford and Mr. McKay fell away.

She wrapped Carl and Mimi in a tight hug. "I'm so thrilled you came." She had tried numerous times to get the Crammers to utilize One Life's services, but the couple—Mimi especially—didn't accept charity easily. An occasional free scone or cup of coffee was one thing. Free meals, clothes, and job training services were something else altogether.

"We promised we would," Carl said. "We don't break our promises."

She beamed. "Does this mean you'll let me introduce you to Kyle?"

Carl glanced at his wife and rubbed the scruff on his leathery cheeks. "We'll meet him so long as it's understood we're not asking for no handouts."

"Of course."

A throat cleared behind her.

Robin wanted to swat the sound away. She knew who it belonged to. But Carl and Mimi stared over her shoulder, so she pivoted and sure enough, there he was. The condominium man.

"The place is hopping," he said.

Robin set her hand on Mimi's. "Why don't you and Carl get a cup of coffee? Maybe a cappuccino. I'll introduce you to Kyle in a minute."

Mimi looked relieved. Carl's shoulders perked. The two were obviously not in any hurry for the introduction. He led his wife toward Bethany and Amanda, her two baristas, and as soon as the couple fell from earshot, Robin turned to the man beside her. "May I ask why you're here?"

"Mayor Ford invited me. I couldn't turn down the invitation."

"Sure you could. Instead of saying yes, you say, 'Sorry, but I don't think that would be appropriate. Seeing as I'm not in town to support One Life or the new director.' See? That's not very hard, is it?"

Ian's lips twitched. "Well, when you put it that way..."

"I'm not kidding around."

His face melted into something serious. Almost sincere. "Look, Robin. I know we got off to a bad start. I didn't want the mayor to spring my plans on you like that, especially not outside of church. I was hoping to sit with you in private, where we could discuss our options like civilized adults."

"Then what was all that sneaking around yesterday? Why didn't you tell me your plans last night?"

"Because I was more than taken aback by your music. I've never heard anybody play like you, and I've been to my fair share of symphonies. I know music well."

"What's your point?"

"My point is, you're an extraordinary musician."

She took a step back. "Excuse me."

"Where are you going?"

"To my kitchen. We need more napkins." And she needed a proper breath of air. She swept past the people and her piano and the front counter. Only when she pushed through the swinging door did she realize she had a shadow. "No customers are allowed back here."

"I'm not a customer. But as great as the food smells, I'm tempted to be one." He sniffed the air. "Too bad you couldn't swap locations with somebody on the north end."

"And One Life? What about them?"

A shadow fell over his face, swallowing up any trace of a smile. "I am sorry about that, but we didn't choose the location. We're building where the city wants us to build."

"You should leave."

"Can I apologize first?"

"For what?"

"What I said at church. And at the diner. Sometimes I can get a little competitive. Not a bad quality when it comes to sports. Not the best when it comes to things that are more personal." He stepped farther inside her kitchen, bringing with him the smell of soap and wintergreen mints. "I can tell, when it comes to your café, that it's very personal."

She backed into the stepladder hanging on the wall.

"I didn't mean to put you on the defensive. I'd love to start over."

If he thought she would fall for this charming, nice-guy routine, he was sorely mistaken. She yanked the stepladder off its hook and swept wisps of hair from her eyes. "Are you still hoping to buy my café?"

"Yes."

"Then there's no reason to start over." She pried the ladder apart.

He placed his hand on the prep table, trapping her in the claustrophobic space. She clamped her mouth shut and raised her eyebrows at his arm. The kitchen was her sanctum and he was invading it.

"I don't like being so thoroughly despised. Can't we at least clear the air before you make your escape?"

"I don't despise you. I don't even know you…and I'm not escaping." She held up the metal contraption. "I'm only trying to get to the napkins."

"Oh." He stuck his hands in his pockets. "Then by all means."

She plunked the ladder down, stomped up a couple rungs, and flopped her hand around the top shelf, searching for the napkin packages. Her mind rewound to her last supply order. Did she forget to order napkins? Her cheeks puffed with air at her dismal inventory skills. Amanda was right. She really needed to improve.

"Do you need help?"

"No." The word came out like a whip. She rested her forehead on her arm. Just because Ian wanted to get rid of Willow Tree and One Life didn't mean she had a free pass for rudeness. "I'm sorry for snapping."

Her hand landed on something smooth and stiff. She pulled it back and found a brown package. "Look, Mr. McKay, I'm not one to play games. I understand you're just doing business and your plans to bulldoze this place to the ground aren't personal. But please know this café is very special to me. I'm not going to sell it."

Ian seemed to size her up, as if measuring the determination behind her words. She pulled her shoulders back, hoping the ladder made her look more intimidating. "Okay, then. I won't play games either. You're right. This condo venture is business. My father's business. There's a lot riding on this deal, which means I can't quit."

She hugged the package of napkins in the crook of her elbow. "Then it seems we're at an impasse. Because I'm not going to quit either."

The door swung open and Caleb came barreling through. "Mommy? Are you in here?" He stopped short of knocking into Ian's legs. Robin stepped off the ladder, only her foot did not touch solid ground. Her leg slipped out from under her. The napkins flew into the air, and so did her body. Her arms flailed. But before her bottom crashed against the hard floor, Ian snagged her around the waist.

Caleb's Tonka truck lay sprawled near the napkins. Belly up. Tires spinning.

ᵔᵕ

Ian held her still body for a shocked moment before her eyes widened and she jerked from his arms. He let go and stepped away.

Her son's mouth hung open like a dead fish. "You saved my mommy," he whispered.

Robin ran a trembling hand down her shirt. "He did not save me, Caleb."

The boy bobbed his head, a lock of hair springing from his scalp and bouncing like an overexcited pogo stick. "Uh-huh. You could have broked your arm." He held up his cast for Ian to see. "I falled off a tractor once."

Ian rubbed the back of his neck.

"Hey, Bug-man?" Robin crouched low and placed her hands on her son's arms, gathering his attention. The little boy looked into his mother's eyes, his own full of youth and innocence. "What did I tell you about putting toys away?"

"Sorry, Mommy. I forgot." The kid picked up his truck and peeked around his mother. "Do you like dinosaurs?"

"Um, sure," Ian said.

"The bad kind or the good kind?"

"I've always been partial to triceratops."

Caleb beamed. "'Ceratops is a good guy!"

Ian smiled at Robin. Her son was really cute.

For a brief second, it seemed like she might smile back, but before he could coax it out of her, she looked away. "You go put that truck in the toy chest. I'll be right behind you." She patted Caleb's bottom and scooted him toward the door. As soon as he was gone, Robin tugged at her shirt and screwed her face into the most unintimidating glare Ian had ever seen. He had to bite his lip to keep his amusement in check. Somehow, Robin didn't strike him as the glaring type.

"A simple 'thank you' would suffice," he said.

"For?"

"Saving you from a broken tailbone. I hear they are quite painful."

Her baby-blue eyes narrowed. "Mr. McKay, I think we've said all there is to say. I appreciate your apology for earlier today, but it hasn't changed my position. Which means our business together is done. I'm sorry it didn't work out for you."

The rich aroma of melted chocolate and brown sugar soured.

"If you'll excuse me, I need to get out to my family." She brushed past him and walked out the door, leaving him alone with the echo of her words.

My family.

Must be nice. A spouse. A kid. She didn't need a café too.

TEN

Y ou've got to be kidding me." Robin closed the oven door and laughed, because if she didn't laugh she'd cry. Or kick her oven and bruise her toe. She jiggled the temperature knob, then poked her head behind the large appliance to check the plug. Not the best way to start a Monday morning.

Joe, recovered from his stomach bug, swung the door open, his sloppy mop of white-blond curls preceding him into the kitchen. "What's wrong?"

"I put these soufflés in twenty minutes ago and somehow they're getting colder."

"I thought Lenny fixed the oven."

"I thought so too." She blew her bangs from her eyes. "I'll have to call him again. Do you know where the phone book is?"

"Under the front counter, but maybe you should put him on speed dial."

"Very funny, Joe." She pushed through the door and found Jed Johnson, her only customer, sitting in the far corner of her café, an unopened Bible on the table in front of him. Despite his forlorn posture, she couldn't help but smile. He was out in public, which meant he was making real progress. She had hoped a nice, hot egg soufflé and some music would cheer him up, but thanks to her oven, she'd have to make do with what she had. She ducked under the counter and dug out the phone book.

The door swung on its hinges. Joe and his hair appeared, a bag of coffee roast tucked under his arm like a football. Robin thumbed through the yellow pages until she found the circled number. "Hey, Joe, would you get Mr. Johnson a steamed milk with a shot of caramel?"

"You got it." He grabbed a cup near the espresso machine and went to work.

Robin punched in the number to Renegade Appliance on Old Town Avenue and tapped the counter. The line rang as a breeze of warm air ruffled wisps of hair around her face. She looked up and spotted Ian, strutting through her front doors in a pressed royal-blue dress shirt, a briefcase strap slung across his broad chest. He gave her an innocent wave and stepped up her staircase, metal clanging as he climbed to her second-story loft.

The phone hung limp against her shoulder.

"Better watch it, or you'll swallow a fly."

Robin closed her mouth.

Joe chuckled. "My mom likes to say that."

A voice recording picked up on the other line. She left a short message for Lenny and squinted at the underside of her loft. If not for the sound of Ian rustling around, she might not believe what she'd seen. Well. If this was his attempt to get under her skin, she wouldn't let him. "Joe, could you go see what the gentleman wants? I'll take care of Mr. Johnson."

"Sure thing." He handed her the steamed milk and made his way up the stairs.

Robin had the distinct feeling Ian was watching her from the loft, but she ignored the urge to look and brought Jed his drink. "I know I promised you a soufflé, Jed, but unfortunately my oven isn't cooperating. The good news is we have an assortment of goodies left over from yesterday's meet and greet."

Voices murmured from above, followed by a round of laughter.

Robin's jaw tightened. "Blueberry tarts. Chocolate gingerbread cookies. I think we even have some lemon bars left."

Joe came down the spiral staircase with a big goofy grin on his face. He poured coffee into a mug, added cream, and returned to the loft. Robin watched him go, then forced her attention back to Jed, who stared through his coke-bottle glasses with large eyes. The poor guy looked so lost without his wife, Robin wanted to wrap him in a hug and assure him that breathing would get easier. "I'm not sure," he finally said.

"Well, take your time." She squeezed his frail shoulder. When he was ready, she would join him for breakfast and see how he was holding up, maybe share some verses that held her together through the worst of her grief. "I'll be right over there. You let me know when you've decided, okay?"

Jed nodded at his milk.

Robin made her way to the counter and picked up a broom leaning against the back wall, the heat of Ian's stare boring into the top of her head as she swept. She refused to peek. He could come every day for all she cared, stare for as long as he wanted, just as long as he paid.

"Hey, Robin?" Joe plopped his hands on the counter and leaned over it. "That guy up there wants to speak with you."

"Could you please tell him I'm busy?"

Joe furrowed his brow at the crumbless floor. "He says it's important. Something about running a check on your title?"

Her title? Robin's attention snapped to the loft, where Ian rested his elbow over the railing. His smile was mischievous as he gave her a goading wave. She handed Joe the broom. "I'll be right back."

When she reached the top of the stairs, she found him sitting at a table with his laptop open in front of him. He double-clicked on his touchpad and the county's website displayed across the screen. "Aha!" He folded his hands behind his head and leaned back in his chair. The top two buttons of his dress shirt were undone, revealing a clean, white collar beneath. "If you can believe it, Bernie doesn't have Internet access."

"Shocking."

His eyes danced. "I was going to camp out at the library, but this was closer and your coffee is highly addictive." He took a long, slow drink. "Do you have any more of those muffins you were serving yesterday?"

She picked up his black bag and shoved it onto his lap. "I don't think so."

"What?"

"I'm not going to let you do business in my café."

"You're going to kick out a paying customer? In front of..." He looked over the railing. "That one person down there? Do you really think it's wise to turn away fifty percent of your clientele?"

She peeked over the banister, where Jed sipped from his mug of frothy milk. Bethany would kick Ian out without so much as a second thought. Why couldn't Robin do the same?

"How about a refill and that muffin? Or should I ask your employee?" Ian brought both hands to his head and waved them around his scalp. "The one with the big hair. He seems like a good guy."

"Fine. How do you like your coffee?"

"Hot with lots of cream. Hold the sugar, *por favor.*"

She picked up his mug, all too aware of his stare following her as she clunked down the steps. She slipped behind the counter, topped off his mug, added no cream, dumped in two packets of sugar, put a muffin on a plate, and clanked back up the staircase. In her absence, he had pulled up the title of Willow Tree Café on his computer screen.

"Now look who's spying."

She pressed her lips together and set the coffee and muffin on his table. She would return to the kitchen and ignore him. Hopefully, the less attention he received, the less inclined he'd be to come back. Especially after he tasted his coffee.

"You own Willow Tree outright."

"Yes, I do."

Ian scrolled down, then leaned back in his chair. "Hmm."

"What?"

"It says here that you're the sole proprietor."

"And that's weird because?"

"I assumed your husband would be on the title."

The words punched her in the gut. Her husband? On the title?

Ian examined her face. "Why do I have the feeling I just said something wrong?"

She inhaled. The oxygen collected in her lungs, then escaped like a slow leak out her nose. "I run a well-respected business in this community, Mr. McKay. I have no outstanding debt. And I own the café. Just me. Is there anything else you'd like to know? Because if not, I'd really like to have breakfast with that gentleman down there."

"You usually eat breakfast with your customers?" he asked.

"No."

He scratched the back of his head, his hair styled in that messy "I don't care but really I do" way. "So he's your grandpa or something?"

"He's not my grandfather."

"Great-uncle?"

"He's a friend."

He looked at Jed, who kept glancing toward the loft. Ian waved. Jed returned the greeting with an uncertain hand. "I don't get it," Ian said.

"There's nothing for you to get."

"You two don't seem like you have much in common."

Her irritation dulled. She and Jed had more in common than Ian might think. "He lost his wife recently and needs somebody to talk to."

Ian cocked his head, studying her like a stained page from a recipe book, like he couldn't quite make out that last ingredient. His steady gaze made her cheeks warm. "I thought you should know that I'm meeting with Mrs. Arton later this morning," he finally said.

Robin's nails bit crescents into her palms.

"Won't you at least listen to my offer?"

"No."

A slow grin turned up the corners of his mouth. "You're very stubborn."

"This isn't about me being stubborn."

"Hey, uh, Robin!" Joe stuck his head out from the back room, one side of his face squished into an odd contortion as he looked up into the loft. "The oven is making sounds."

She leaned over the railing. "Sounds?"

"Yeah, like this really weird grumbling noise."

Oh, goodness gracious. "Could you unplug it, Joe? I'll be down in a minute."

He gave her the thumbs-up and darted back into the kitchen. Robin brought her hand to the crown of her head. "You're welcome to do whatever you want. Talk to whomever you want. It doesn't matter to me. Now if you'll excuse me, I've got a café to run."

"Do you want me to take a look at your oven?"

"What?" This man was spinning her in circles.

"You need a working oven, right? Would you like me to take a look at it?"

She crossed her arms and raised her eyebrows. "You repair ovens in your spare time?"

"I grew up in my grandpa's restaurant. His oven was old."

"Even if I believed you could fix it, why would you?"

"Because I enjoy fixing things. I'm good at it." Something sad flickered across his brow. "At least I used to be."

"No, thank you."

"Look, Robin, since we both decided against any game playing, can I be straightforward?"

Her arms fell to her sides. She did not want to hear whatever straightforward thing Ian had to say. She'd rather he keep his opinions to himself and leave. Her café and her town.

"Mrs. Arton is going to sell. The antique store owner will sell too. People are going to want these condominiums. Are you really going to be the one sticking point that keeps this town from prospering?"

"Please don't waltz in here and pretend you care about Peaks. Or know what's best for it. I've lived here most of my life and we haven't missed having condos." One Life would not be shoved aside for a bunch of Fixtel employees who wouldn't care about people like Carl and Mimi Crammer or Molly and her three children.

"You're right. Peaks doesn't need the condos. It's fine without them. But maybe McKay Development and Construction isn't satisfied with fine. Maybe we'd like to help your town become something great."

"Oh, please. All you care about is making a buck." Heat surged up her neck. She clapped her hand over her mouth, shocked that she had actually spoken the words out loud.

Ian leaned back in his chair. "You have no idea what I care about."

"You're right. I'm sorry. It's just…" She nodded toward the front counter, her shoulders deflating. "You see that kid down there?"

"The one with the big hair?"

"His name's Joe. He started working here in high school. Every penny has gone toward his college tuition. He's the first in his family to attend." Her personal feelings for Willow Tree aside, there were people who depended on keeping the doors open. People like Joe and Molly.

"Trust me, I don't want anyone to lose their jobs."

"But people will if you do this."

"People will if I don't." He shook his head, a muscle ticking in his jaw. "Listen, I'll do everything in my power to set Joe up with a job elsewhere."

"Mary Poppins calls that a piecrust promise." Easily made, easily broken. Robin couldn't let the sincerity of his tone fool her. Ian didn't care about Joe. He was a developer and, according to Evan, developers only cared about money. "I think it's time to chalk your business venture up as one small failure and go home."

His posture stiffened, like her suggestion was as unappetizing as the coffee.

The front door opened and the delivery guy from Blay's Supplies wheeled in a dolly stacked with boxes. She needed to meet him in the supply room and make sure they remembered napkins. "Can you please let this go, Mr. McKay? Before we both go nutty from having the same conversation."

"Your mayor is set on this development. There are ways he can put pressure on you."

"Is that supposed to be a threat?"

Ian's eyes bore into her with an intensity that made her incredibly aware of her hands. "It's the truth. One I'd like to avoid."

∽

The sign hung on the door like a storm cloud, offensive black letters behind a pane of smudged glass. Robin stood on the cement walkway, blinking at the two-word reminder that all was not well.

Liquidation Sale.

Her abdomen flexed against the image of cascading dominoes toppling through her mind. Willow Tree and One Life would not fall. She'd hold up those two dominos with bare hands if she had to. Taking a deep breath, she pushed through the front door of Arton's Jewelers, cool air and tinkling bells singing a chorus of welcome. Cecile looked up from the magazine splayed in front of her on the counter, her grin stretching from one beaded earring to the next. "If it isn't one of my favorite people." She held out her hand, palm up. "What's the special occasion?"

Robin thumbed her wedding ring. "I'm not getting anything polished this afternoon."

"Just popping in for some shopping? Everything's fifty percent off. I think I've had more customers this weekend than the whole year combined." Cecile flipped a page of her magazine. A closeup of Angelina Jolie's face filled the page.

Robin ran her fingers over the glass top of a display case.

"No handsome little man with you today?" Cecile asked.

"I'm on my way to pick him up from Linda's." She stared at the diamond necklaces captured beneath her hands. "Was Ian here today?"

"He stopped by about an hour ago."

"Is he the reason you took your For Sale sign down?"

Cecile grabbed a bottle of blue liquid near the cash register, bustled to the front door, and removed the Liquidation Sale sign. Mists of cleaner shot the window and dribbled down the glass. She pulled a rag dangling from the back pocket of her pleated slacks and wiped circles into the pane. "He offered us a really fair deal. One we'd be foolish to turn down."

Robin closed her eyes, her heart thudding a slow, hollow beat inside her chest. "Can I ask you a favor?"

"Of course."

"Please reconsider."

The older woman frowned.

"You've only been on the market for three days. How do you know somebody in town doesn't want to open their own business?"

"Don't be silly, Robin. Nobody in Peaks wants this old place." Cecile returned the rag to her pocket. "I don't want to see anything happen to your café or One Life any more than you do, but it doesn't make sense for Richard and me to pass this up."

Didn't make sense? Cecile's words left Robin miffed, because if she really meant them, she wouldn't accept the first offer that came her way. She'd roll up her sleeves and fight. "Cecile, accepting his offer puts One Life in danger."

"I have all the faith in the world that these condominiums won't stop God from ministering to the needy."

Indignation crawled under Robin's skin. That kind of passivity drove her nuts. God ministered to the needy through His body—the church—and if they didn't do their part, then who would? "I'm just asking you to wait a few weeks. I know God can provide another buyer." Desperation stained the edge of each word, making her cringe.

Please, Lord. Please…

"You and I both know this is the only offer we're going to get," Cecile said.

A piece of Robin's hope crumpled. She tried to straighten it back out, but it was too late. Cecile had made up her mind.

"Robin, sweetheart, the last thing I want to do is cause you any more grief. Lord knows you've had enough. Lord knows we all have." Cecile placed her hand over Robin's and squeezed. "But Ian's a nice man. He'll offer you a fair deal and we'll figure out what to do with One Life. Things will work out. You'll see."

They were the same words Bethany used yesterday. Only Robin didn't know if she believed them anymore.

ELEVEN

R obin drummed her fingers against the steering wheel and pressed harder on the gas pedal. Her impulsive visit to Arton's made her fifteen minutes late and desperate to hug her son—his little body a tangible reminder that God could bring sweetness in the midst of pain.

She unbuckled her seat belt and pulled over to the curb. The smell of baked apples and the sound of Caleb's singing greeted her as soon as she stepped inside Linda's front door. So did her son's Crocs, neatly set atop a brightly colored and otherwise empty welcome mat. Evidence that the other two children had been picked up on time.

Mommy fail.

She slipped off her shoes and climbed the stairs into the living room where Linda hung finger-painted pictures over the television and hummed backup to a bare-chested Caleb's enthusiastic yet off-key rendition of "The Farmer in the Dell." He sat on the sofa sans shirt, bouncing his legs and bobbing his head to the beat. As soon as she peeked over the banister, his face lit with a grin. It was the best kind of greeting.

Linda turned from her task.

"I'm so sorry I'm late," Robin said.

"No big deal." Linda switched off the music player. "I put a bib on Caleb before he painted, but he managed to get a little on his shirt collar. And a bit on his cast. I washed his shirt, but he didn't want to put it back on again. He said it would make him melt."

Caleb held up his injured wrist, displaying a bright orange stain on the electric blue cast. "I painted a mommy tiger and a Caleb tiger."

Robin looked at the pictures proudly displayed on the wall. Caleb's was in the middle—two orange blobs with long tails—one larger than the other, no daddy tiger in sight. "I have a budding artist on my hands." She kissed the top of his head and shuffled him down the stairs. "I'm really sorry about being late."

Linda waved her hand. "It's okay, Robin. You have a lot on your plate." Single motherhood. A ministry to save. A struggling café. And a businessman all too eager to knock it down. Robin wanted to ask what Linda thought about Ian. She saw the two talking at the meet and greet yesterday. But she was afraid to broach the subject. Linda's opinion mattered and Robin wasn't sure she could handle it if she shared the same sentiment as Cecile. Caleb plopped onto the bottom step and stuffed his feet into his Crocs—always and forever the wrong way.

"Jed Johnson came to the café this morning," Robin said.

Linda handed over Caleb's John Deere T-shirt, neatly folded and still warm from the dryer. "That's great news."

"I think he's going to join us for our next meeting. He wanted me to tell you how much he enjoyed the casserole you made him."

"I'm glad I could help."

Robin knew exactly how the woman felt. It was precisely why Robin had started the grief group two years ago. Caleb ran up the stairs and hugged Linda's legs just as Robin's cell phone vibrated. She waved good-bye and led her son into the sunshine. He skipped to the car while she dug inside her purse and pulled the buzzing phone from the rubble. Her spirits lifted at the name on her screen. "Hey, Dad."

"Hey, sweetie, how's it going?"

Caleb climbed onto his booster seat and buckled himself in. Robin slid behind the wheel and listened for the click. "It's been better."

"Uh-oh. Things not going well at the café?"

"Not exactly." She stuck the keys into the ignition. "A developer wants to buy Willow Tree so he can build condominiums along the riverfront."

"Really?"

"Yes, really. And he's incredibly irritating. I tell him I'm not going to sell and he looks at me like he knows better." The heaviness weighting her limbs ever since leaving Arton's gathered and wound into a tightly spun ball right behind her bellybutton. "He can't force me to sell, can he?"

"I don't see how he could force you. Not when you don't have any outstanding debt." Dad paused. "How persistent is he?"

An image of Ian ran through her mind. His David Beckham looks, his tailored clothes. The way he seemed to charm everybody who crossed his path, even the people who should be charm-resistant—like Amanda and Joe. "About as persistent as a used car salesman."

Dad let out a short-lived hum.

Robin shifted into drive and pulled away from the curb.

"Have you talked to him about his offer?" Dad asked.

The question stole her wind.

"Robin?"

"Did you really just say that?"

"I'm thinking as your lawyer right now, sweetheart. And as your lawyer, I have to ask. After hearing his offer, is there a possibility you'd be interested?"

"Of course I'm not interested."

"Looking into your options doesn't mean you have to sell."

"If I looked into my options, Ian McKay would tear me apart like a hungry piranha. And anyway, I'm not interested." Robin frowned. He, of all people, should understand.

"How about we talk about it this weekend?"

"This weekend?"

"I was thinking about buying some plane tickets. I haven't seen that grandson of mine in entirely too long."

"Seriously?" She stopped at a stop sign and waved a car to go ahead. "You're coming to Peaks?"

"As long as you don't have any plans."

"Just the picnic, but you can come to that." Excitement soothed her growing unrest. With the youngest Price brother, Gavin, out of town for a photo shoot and the oldest unable to get away from his job in Arizona, maybe Dad's presence would fill up some empty space at their annual Price family picnic. They'd thrown one the Saturday before Memorial Day for as long as Robin had known the Prices. With Micah's parents flying in from Arizona and her father flying in from Ohio, maybe the picnic would be festive after all. She accelerated through the intersection. "Caleb's going to be ecstatic."

Her son perked in the backseat.

She winked at him in the rearview mirror.

"If it's okay, I'd like to bring Donna."

"Donna?"

"She hasn't seen you since Thanksgiving."

"Dad, that's the only time she's seen me."

"I'd really like to bring her."

Her excitement waned. She rewound to last Thanksgiving. Dad had introduced Donna as a friend. She even ate dinner with them. Robin had watched them through the evening, looking for any sign that he and Donna might share anything more than a platonic camaraderie. She hadn't found a thing. "Dad, isn't that a little awkward? Flying Donna to Iowa? You don't want her to get the wrong impression."

"Donna is important to me."

After sixteen years of it just being her dad, his words poked at something in her gut—a longing she didn't want to feel. Her brain yelled at her finger to hang up before he could say anything that would make the unwelcome longing expand, but she was too late.

"I love her, sweetheart."

∽

Sunshine heated the back of Robin's head as she slammed the car door and took Caleb's hand.

"What's a matter, Mommy?" he asked, trotting to keep up with her long strides.

The grass whispered in the breeze. A mocking taunt. *"I love her. I love her."* She quickened her pace until Caleb's trot turned into a run, but she didn't stop until the familiar willow tree towered in front of them, bending over the small pond as if checking its reflection in the water's surface. She stepped inside the embrace of the weeping branches and slid down the massive trunk.

Caleb sandwiched her face with his warm palms. "Are you sad?"

She placed her hands over his. "I just needed to visit our willow tree, Bug-man." She nodded to the pond in front of them, a resting point for Feather Creek, which wandered through town, keeping company with an old blacktopped bike path. "Do you want to throw rocks?"

"Can we go to the park too?"

There was a small playground around the bend with a swing set and a slide. It was the same playground she and Bethany used to visit when they were twelve. Not too far away was the house where Robin's mother died. After all these years, she could still picture the damask pillows on her parents' bed. The line of pill bottles standing at attention on the dresser like white-capped soldiers. The cool touch of the wisteria-patterned wallpaper in the hallway as Dad sang "Fly Me to the Moon" while cradling Mom's head in his lap. Even at the end, when Mom could barely open her eyes, the off-key rendition made her laugh.

"Sure we can." Robin cupped Caleb's chin and ran the pad of her thumb across the ridge of his jaw. "Just as soon as Mommy has a minute."

He nodded and ran a few paces ahead in search of rocks and pebbles he could toss into the water. Robin sank down the trunk until her bottom met the cool, shaded grass. She released a long breath and rested her elbows over her knees, thinking about the upcoming weekend. Would Dad hold Donna's hand? Would he look at her with the same love he'd lavished on Mom for so many years? Would the longing in Robin's gut grow stronger?

She leaned her head against the tree.

Whenever anybody commented on her single status, she would confidently point to her father. His longstanding devotion to Mom was always something that gave Robin comfort. But now, after all these years, he loved another woman. An ache she hadn't felt in a long time wrapped itself around her heart, making her so homesick she had a hard time breathing.

Why now, Lord? This is supposed to be over.

She was supposed to be done with the grief. So why did it come back now, on the heels of Dad's declaration? Robin twisted her wedding ring and slipped it off her finger. She let it sit like a dead weight in the center of her palm, as if removing Micah's gift could remove the burden of his death.

A loud splash jarred her from her thoughts. Caleb bounced on his toes, one small fist pumping beside his ear. The canopy of willows rustled in the wind, a hypnotic lullaby that did not match the chaotic churning inside. This tree held so much laughter. So much pain. It was the place she'd come as a teenager, when brain cancer grabbed hold of her mother. Sometimes alone. Sometimes with Bethany. They'd swing on the branches while Robin made a wish on each of the willows, a simple plea for the cancer to go away. And after, when the cancer had won and Mom was gone, Robin would sit beneath the canopy and give her grief free reign. She'd let it swing through her body like the weeping branches.

Years later, she'd brought Micah the day before their wedding. He held her beneath the tree while she listened to the thrumming of his heartbeat and dreamed about their future. Never once had she dreamt this.

Robin sighed. Most days she could handle the loneliness. Most days, she had only to play a sonata, or cuddle with her son, or bless somebody with a batch of hot-from-the-oven caramel butter bars and the ache would melt away. But sometimes, like now—watching Caleb struggle to lift a large rock with his healthy arm, his grunts of exertion stabbing the air—her loneliness grew too big to hold on her own.

She tapped the back of her head against the bark. Why did Micah have to die? Why did life have to be so hard without him? Why did the pain have to return now?

The *whys* came without warning. They came without relief, or answers. *I miss having a mother, Lord. I miss having a husband.*

Robin closed her eyes and let herself soak in the memories—Micah's strong arms wrapping her in a hug. The smell of his cologne pressed into the collar of his work shirts. Running her fingers through the thickness of his hair. The warmth of his skin when they made love on lazy Saturday mornings. His kisses. His laughter. The deepness of his voice. It had been over four years since she'd experienced any of them, yet at times like these, the memories were so clear and crystal she felt like she could reach out and gather them in her hands.

She blotted her eyes with the back of her wrist. This was silly. The troubles with her café had her turned around. Everything was fine until Ian showed up. His untimely disruption disturbed the rhythm of her life like a poorly placed note in the middle of a song, making her feel, more than ever, like an Israelite wandering in the desert. Because where was God in all of this?

Lord, You want me to fight for the café, don't You?

Robin tried to imagine life without Willow Tree, but the picture left a gaping hole in her heart. She loved serving Chief Bergman and his wife red velvet hot chocolate with whipped cream every year on Valentine's Day. She loved playing hostess to the Fiction Junkies book club on the third Thursday of every month. She loved serving coffee to the ladies who met for Bible study every Monday afternoon and she loved playing her piano for the Crammers every Saturday evening. Somehow she had turned a run-down flower shop into the dream she and Micah shared all those years ago. Bringing the place to life had brought her back to life. She couldn't let it go now.

Robin stood and brushed bits of grass from her jeans. She slid the ring back on her finger, picked up a smooth rock, and skipped it across the surface of the pond. It gave two pathetic hops and sank into the water.

Caleb looked at her with amazement, then picked up a smaller rock and imitated her throw, but the pebble only plunked near the bank and disappeared. He frowned at the ring of spreading ripples.

"You'll get the hang of it, buddy. It's in your blood. Your dad used to be the world champion rock skipper."

He smiled like he knew. Like he remembered.

"C'mon. It's time for the park."

Their joined palms swung as they walked along the pockmarked bike path.

"Grandpa's coming to visit," she said.

He smiled a big smile, one that showed all of his baby teeth. "Papa!"

"Do you remember Miss Donna?"

He scrunched up his brow. November was a long way back for a three-year-old.

"She was at Papa's for Thanksgiving. She's coming too."

"Why?"

"She and Papa are friends."

"Why?"

Robin chewed her lip. "Well, Papa loves Miss Donna."

"And she loves Papa too?"

Robin stopped, and so did their swinging hands. She peered down at her boy. "I think she likes him a whole lot."

The divot in his brow grew deeper. "Do you like somebody a whole lot?"

"I like you a whole lot." She tapped his nose, then poked his belly. "There's nobody in the world I like more than you."

He giggled and buried his face in her hip. She tickled his ribs, his laughter balm to her chapped soul. They fell to the ground, Caleb panting for air. Robin stopped her tickling and pulled him to her in a tight hug.

"I love you." His words patted her cheek with hot dog and ketchup breath.

"I love you too, Buggerboo."

"Mommy?"

"Yeah?"

He took her cheeks with his palms, his nose not more than an inch from her own, and gave her his most serious look. The kind she wore whenever she talked to him about strangers. "Is it time for me to have another daddy yet?"

His innocent question felt like barbed wire. It snagged and tore and scraped. "Do you want another daddy?"

Caleb's bobbing head fractured Robin's heart. It broke for Micah, because his son didn't know him. And it broke for Caleb, because giving him what he wanted felt utterly impossible.

TWELVE

My mother was a sucker for holidays—especially the overlooked ones. Because of her, I know that St. Nicholas Day is on December 6 and Flag Day is on June 14. Because of her, I can't get through April 1 without playing at least one harmless prank on somebody I love. Because of her, the first thing I do every second day of February is turn on the television to see whether or not Punxsutawney Phil saw his shadow. Because of her, I still get up early every single May Day and check my front porch.

Of all the neglected holidays, May Day was my favorite. We'd spend the night before weaving together small paper baskets, filling them with pastel-wrapped candies left over from Easter. The next morning, we'd wake up early, and as a special treat, Mom would let me have a cup of coffee—more hazelnut cream than anything else. Still, the warmth and the bitter aftertaste and the birds chirping outside the opened window turned the tradition into something magical.

When we finished our coffee, we'd race up the block, hanging the baskets on our neighbors' doors before the sun could make its full appearance over the horizon. Mom would start on one side of the street. I'd start on the other. Until every doorknob on our block had a special treat waiting for its owner. I remember every single May Day since I was five. They are catalogued inside my memories, tucked away in a file marked with a smiley face.

But there is one in particular that I remember more clearly than all the others. And that was in third grade. Spring came early that year. The leaves had long since budded and the once-barren branches overflowed with green. Flowers had grown up from the ground. The world had come back to life.

Dad tracked bits of freshly mowed grass into the kitchen while Mom and I wove baskets in the dining room. Anticipation and excitement kept me up late. I spent at least an hour lying in bed, hands folded behind my head, eyes squeezed tight, as if slumber might be more willing to take me if I wasn't looking. When my mom poked her head into my room the next morning, I sprang out of bed like an overeager jack-in-the-box.

Mom held her finger by her lips because Dad was still sleeping. She grabbed my hand and whispered, "You have to see this."

She led me through the hallway, into the kitchen, where the coffee was brewing, and out onto the back porch. My mouth fell open and the tiniest of gasps tumbled out. A fresh blanket of snow covered the very grass Dad had just mowed. The whiteness clung to the green leaves on our pear tree. A fascinating contradiction.

I looked at my mom, my eyes wide with wonder. Of course, we saw snow all the time. We lived in the Midwest. Snow and I were not only well acquainted, we were good friends. I just wasn't used to seeing it in May. We stood there, hand in hand, looking at our backyard, and for the life of me, I couldn't tell if the green poking up through the whiteness was beautiful or disconcerting.

"I don't like it," I finally said.

"No?"

I shook my head.

"Why not?"

"Winter is supposed to be over."

Mom squeezed my hand. "Don't worry," she said. "It won't last."

She was right. By the time we drank our coffee and gathered our baskets and raced up and down the block, the snow was already starting to melt.

THIRTEEN

An undercurrent of desperation swirled in the conference room. Ian's gum had lost its flavor twenty minutes ago, the moment his father sat down at the head of the table. Ian had hoped to swoop into the meeting like Santa Claus in May, with the Peaks project wrapped in a bow. He'd wanted to share a gift that would wipe away everyone's worry. Surely the news would make people forget, for a second, that he was the boss's divorced son. But his hopes had derailed—all thanks to a woman named Robin Price.

He spun a pencil around the tip of his thumb and tried to listen as one of the project managers shared updates and ideas. He pretended not to notice Dad's glances every time the conversation paused.

McKay's newest intern passed a second round of drinks around the table, then opened a can of ginger ale and set it near Ian's elbow. He scooted it toward his father.

Dad brought the green can of ginger ale to his mouth. "You're next, Ian."

All eyes turned in his direction.

He traced the condensation beading along the plastic of his bottled water. "Mayor Ford definitely wants us for the job."

There seemed to be a collective exhale of breath.

"That's excellent news," Dad said.

"I've checked zoning restraints. Switching from business to residential won't be a problem. Not on the south end of town anyway. I've been making some phone calls and have several early investors lined up. It's going to be a very lucrative project, just as we suspected."

The desperation settled. Eyes brightened and several smiles were exchanged. If only Ian could make the brightness stay. If only he could figure out a way to fan the pride in his father's eyes into something so much more than a flicker.

"Next steps?"

"I have a meeting on Friday with the town council, which will make our plans official. Then we'll have to win the support of Peaks. I'm hoping that won't be too hard, since the condominiums will be good for local business."

The hope grew into something palpable.

"And what about the businesses we'll have to buy out? Any problems there?"

Ian took a deep breath and let his answer escape on the exhale. "Potentially."

"What do you mean?"

"One of the owners doesn't want to sell."

The hope swooshed away. Its sudden departure had everyone in the room fidgeting in their seats.

Dad set his elbows on the conference table and rubbed his eyes with his pointer finger and thumb. "How reluctant are we talking here?"

"Substantially reluctant."

Dad seemed to consider Ian's news, as if it were a morsel he could roll around on his tongue. When he finished rolling, he clasped his hands beneath his chin. "What if we offer more money?"

"It's hard to say. She won't listen to my initial offer."

"Then you'll have to make her listen." Jim Harley stopped short of pounding his fist on the table. He had a gray mustache and a paunch and glasses that were always sliding down his nose. He also had four kids at home, a girl who was starting college in the fall, and a wife with multiple sclerosis. Without this deal, his territory would most likely be the first to go.

"I know," Ian said.

"There are ways you can pressure her." Jim looked around the table, as if waiting for somebody to jump in. "Who's her lender?"

"She owns the business outright."

"Well, does she have a line of credit? That might be a place to start."

Ian's grip tightened around his water bottle, the plastic crackling in the aftermath of Jim's suggestion. Ian had always taken pride in Dad's integrity. He refused to conduct business like so many of their competitors. It was one of the many reasons Ian harbored so much respect for his father. "I understand we're all feeling uneasy. But I don't think I like what you're suggesting."

"Desperate times call for desperate measures," Jim said.

"Making underhanded deals would turn us all into a walking cliché."

"I'll take cliché over unemployed any day."

Heat stirred in Ian's chest. "Look, I understand what's at stake. But I'm not going to do anything underhanded."

"Easy for you to say. You don't have a wife and children to take care of."

Jim's words were like a sucker punch to the gut.

Dad cleared his throat, effectively collecting the room's attention, giving Ian a moment to recover. "Is her business doing well?"

"I don't believe so."

"If she's a smart woman, she's not going to hold on to a sinking ship. Especially not if Ian can get the town on his side."

Dad motioned for a notepad. The intern slid one over along with her pen. He jotted some numbers and made a clicking sound with his tongue. "Fixtel opens next spring. We need these condos up before then." He scratched a few more notes on the paper. "In order for this investment to work in our favor, we should have everything squared away soon. Mid-July at the latest."

Jim coughed.

"The timing is tight, especially with a reluctant seller. But Ian's up for the challenge." Dad picked up his ginger ale and studied Ian over the top of his can, fire burning in his eyes.

For the rest of the meeting, while two more managers relayed updates with much smaller projects, Ian jotted ideas onto sheets of paper. The first of which was to hightail it back to Peaks so he could get moving. Dad was right. The timing was tight. Somehow, he'd have to find a way to get Robin to see reason. Maybe if he spoke with her husband. Surely he had some clout over the decision, even if he wasn't listed on the title. He ignored the shards of guilt slivering his chest. Robin had a full life to invest in: a husband, a son, her music, and her church. She'd survive without a café. He, on the other hand, had no spouse, no kids, a sick mother, a disappointed father, and a company that was counting on him. She might love her café, but he had so much more at stake.

When the meeting ended, Ian stacked the papers in front of him as the rest of the development team filed out of the office.

Dad stood by the door. "I hope the deadline didn't rattle you."

"Maybe a little."

"Do you have a game plan?"

"Go back to Peaks, for starters. Stay there and make some waves."

"You think staying in Peaks is the way to go?"

"It'll be hard to get the town's support without being there." Never mind how much he enjoyed the time away from his house and the empty rooms and a past he couldn't quite bury. "To be honest, Dad, sometimes I think relocating permanently wouldn't be such a bad idea."

Dad laughed, like Ian had told a joke.

"Not all the project managers work out of Peoria."

"Not all the project managers are my son—the future president of McKay Development and Construction. I need you here. Especially now." Dad picked up his briefcase. "And don't forget your mother. I'm not sure she'd ever forgive me if I let you go."

Ian tried to return Dad's smile, but the effort didn't quite reach his lips.

"Speaking of, she'd like you to come over for dinner."

"I was hoping to head back to Peaks."

"What are you going to accomplish tonight that you can't take care of tomorrow?" Dad clapped his broad hand over Ian's shoulder. "Can't let business get in the way of family. If I've taught you anything, I hope it's that."

Ian gathered his notes and slid them into his briefcase.

"Running away from your mother's cancer won't make it go away."

The muscles in Ian's arms tightened. His mother, of all people, should not have to fight this battle. Not again. "Is that what you think I'm doing?"

"She wants to see you. And if getting you home for dinner tonight will boost her morale, then so help me God, I'll drag you by your ears if I have to."

Ian dismissed the threat with a short-lived laugh, one that fell from his lips and toppled into nothing. "I'm not running away from anything. You got Mom through this last time. You'll get her through it again."

"This is different than last time."

Ian shook his head and fought against the unease crawling through his insides. "Of course it's not."

"She's in a lot of pain, Ian."

He unfolded the notes and set them back on the table. The creased lines blurred out of focus. "I'll be over at six."

∽

The smell of oregano filled the foyer. Ian slipped off his shoes, made his way through the living room, and entered the kitchen—home away from home. Mom stood at the island, her head wrapped in a silk bandana, chopping onions and tomatoes while Dad leaned against the counter behind her.

As soon as she looked up from the cutting board, her face lit with a smile. One that did very little to erase the dark circles under her eyes or the hollowness beneath her cheekbones. She went to him with opened arms and hugged him fiercely. The thinness of her frame made Ian's Adam's apple swell. He met Dad's gaze over Mom's bony shoulder, but Dad just winked, like he had everything under control.

"Smells delicious," Ian said.

"Of course it does." She patted his chest and resumed her chopping. "I'm making your favorite. Baked ziti."

"Where's the garlic?"

Mom pointed the knife at the ceramic bowl in front of the window. He plucked out a fat bulb. Putting both hands over his head, he crushed it and the cloves popped apart.

Growing up, Grandpa Vin taught Ian his way around a kitchen. While Dad was busy ingraining a pocketful of timeless life lessons in Ian's young mind—like family first and nothing's worth doing unless you give it your best and failure's an option only if you think it's an option—Grandpa Vin had one simple piece of advice to impart. More garlic. As if all of life's problems could be solved by those two words.

Bland meal? More garlic! Hard day? More garlic! Runny nose? More garlic! At times, Ian would catch Grandpa popping a few minced pieces into his mouth, uncooked. He claimed it was the key to a strong immune system. Why get a flu shot when there was raw garlic to eat? Once, when Ian had a bad cough, he tried it for himself. He ended up with a stomachache.

"Any word from Bailey?" Ian asked. His kid sister tied the knot two weeks ago. Her husband was a trust fund kid who graduated from Brown and whisked her off on a six-week honeymoon across Europe. Ian had a hard time thinking about her as a married woman.

"Three postcards," Mom said. "Paris. Venice. Rome."

Ian grabbed a chef's knife from the block by the fridge and cut the roots off the cloves. After removing the skins, he crushed each one and started mincing. The fast rocking of the knife sounded like a woodpecker had taken up residence in the kitchen. His tension melted away. He could do this all day, for the rest of his life—a quiet kitchen, the soothing chop, chop, chop of knife against cutting board. Cooking stilled the chaos.

Mom came beside him—shoulder to shoulder—and watched. "It's like magic," she said,

"What?"

"Watching you cook."

He smiled and scooped the minced garlic into a small porcelain bowl.

"You missed your calling." The words must have slipped out of Mom's mouth by accident, because she flicked a look at Dad, then Ian, and quickly resumed her tomato chopping. "Did your father tell you he was nominated for employer of the year again?"

"No, he didn't." Every year, the chamber of commerce in Peoria held a banquet on behalf of local businesses. Employer of the Year nominees were selected by employees. Dad had been nominated numerous times. He'd taken the award home on more than one occasion. "That's great news, Dad."

"It's nothing."

"It's not nothing, Joseph. It's a wonderful accomplishment. We're very proud of you."

Ian rinsed the knife and set it in the sink. "When's the banquet?"

"Next weekend."

"Will you be bringing anybody?" Mom asked.

Dad frowned. "Who would he take, Maureen?"

The knife clattered to the floor. Mom sucked in a sharp breath and stuck her finger in her mouth. Before Ian could react, Dad was already by her side, taking her hand, surveying the damage. Blood seeped from a thin slice running across the tip of her pointer finger. "Do you think you need stitches?"

"It's just a cut." She pulled away and returned her finger to her mouth.

Ian stepped forward. "I can chop the rest of the vegetables."

"Don't be ridiculous. I'm completely capable of cooking dinner for my two boys." She rinsed her finger in the sink. "Joseph, could you please get me a Band-Aid so I can finish up without bleeding all over our food?"

Before Dad could protest, Mom shot him a look—her dark eyes melding into iron. Arguing with her when she wore that particular expression was futile. Ian knew it. Dad knew it too. Once he disappeared down the hall, Mom leaned against the counter, cotton shirt outlining her sharpened frame. "You and your father..."

"We're worried about you," Ian said.

"It's very obvious."

"I promise to be more subtle."

When Dad returned, he wrapped the bandage around her finger and kissed the tip.

Mom put her hand on his cheek. "You have to stop treating me like I'm an invalid."

"You have to stop pretending everything's okay."

"I have cancer, Joseph. A truth that hardly escapes me." She washed the knife and resumed her vegetable chopping. "The last thing I'm going to do is sit around and let fear have its way. If I can't fight the tumors, I'll fight for a little normalcy."

"Can't fight the tumors?" Of course she could fight the tumors. She had to fight them. Ian looked at his father, but Dad wouldn't meet his eyes. "You fought the tumors last time."

"God fought those tumors, honey. It's up to God if He's going to fight them again." Mom pointed her knife in Ian's direction. "I need you to be okay with that. You and your father."

Dad came behind Mom and buried his nose in the crook of her neck. "If you're asking me to stop trying to protect you," Dad said, "that's a promise I'll never make."

"Not everything is fixable, Joseph. It's a lesson you might consider teaching our son." She stopped chopping and looked at Ian, her smile haunted and worried. "Now go sit down and visit while I finish making the salad."

Maybe she should go sit down and they should fix dinner. But Ian knew better than to argue. If Mom wanted to cook dinner, then that was exactly what she would do, so he followed Dad into the dining room and took a seat in one of the high-backed chairs.

"You're heading back to Peaks in the morning?"

"That's the plan." Ian drummed his fingers into the oak. He peeked over his shoulder and leaned over the table. "Mom looks terrible."

"It's the chemo. She has her final round this Friday."

"Is it helping?"

"We'll find out in a week or so."

"Is there anything I can do?"

Dad knocked on the tabletop. "How about this? I'll take care of your mother and you close the deal in Peaks. That's the best thing you can do right now."

Ian fidgeted with a woven placemat. Mom wasn't the only one who looked unusually worn-out. Wrinkles that had once been barely noticeable carved deep trails around Dad's eyes. More and more gray crept through his hair. It was as if Mom's cancer had infected the entire house. Ian wanted to erase Dad's burden for a change. He was so tired of adding to it.

"I'll close the deal," Ian said. "You won't have to let anyone go."

Dad smiled. "I'm counting on it."

FOURTEEN

For eleven o'clock on a Thursday, the café was quiet. The creaking of the oven door filled the silence, and thanks to Lenny, a blast of hot air flushed across Robin's face. Golden-brown mounds rose in eager puffs, anxiously awaiting their union with the cream she'd whipped and stuck in the refrigerator. Inhaling the aroma of choux pastry, she pulled out the baking sheet. Parchment paper crinkled against her oven mitt as she pushed the cream puff shells onto a cooling rack.

Judy, the local librarian, was on an Alaskan cruise and Pastor Mike and his wife had left town that morning for their youngest daughter's wedding, which meant her usual lunch crowd would not be making an appearance. Robin removed her oven mitt and breathed in the stillness. She hadn't heard a peep about condominiums since her confrontation with Cecile three days ago.

Brushing her fingers over the smooth pages of her opened Bible on the prep table, she soaked in the words she'd clung to on Monday evening: "Fear not, stand firm, and see the salvation of the LORD, which he will work for you today.... The LORD will fight for you, and you have only to be silent."

The verses felt like a promise straight from God. And in this quiet moment, she could almost believe that Ian McKay had given up and left Peaks for good. She could go back to life before he came and provide for her town in peace.

∾

Mayor Ford greeted Ian at the door of the conference room with an outstretched hand. "It's great to see you again." He pumped Ian's hand and smiled. "Did everything go well in Peoria?"

A vision of Mom glued itself to the forefront of his mind. Sitting like a waif at the dining table, picking at her food, covering her pain with a disturbing smile. The picture turned his heart cold. He massaged away the tightness in his neck and forced himself to focus. Today's meeting was incredibly important. "It went very well, thank you. You've got a pristine town hall on your hands, Mayor Ford."

"Did you get a chance to peek inside the chamber?"

"I did. It's wonderful."

"You should have seen our old building. Nothing glorious about it. We're very pleased with this one." He turned around and motioned to seven others sitting in chairs around the table. Ian recognized Richard Arton, owner of the jewelry store; Brian O'Malley, the Irish beanpole; and Darrell Maddocks, the barrel-chested bulldog. The three men nodded their greetings. Four others—two women and two men—examined Ian with open curiosity.

"I've called together the council members and the planning commission. I didn't think the zoning board needed to sit in on such a preliminary meeting. Not this early in the game."

Once the mayor did his round of introductions, and Ian greeted each person with a handshake, he straightened his suit coat and took the only remaining seat—at the head of the oblong conference table.

"As you all know, I contacted McKay Development and Construction about doing business here in Peaks." Mayor Ford turned to Ian. "Why don't you start with an introduction? Explain what your company can bring to the table. Get us all on the same page."

Heads swiveled from the mayor to Ian.

"I'm a project manager for McKay Development and Construction." He flexed his fingers over the chair's armrests. If he could close this deal, he'd be more than a project manager. He'd be the company's hero. And perhaps he'd finally find the satisfaction so many others claimed to experience whenever they closed an important deal. "We target small to midsized towns in the Midwest that have experienced, or will likely experience, a substantial growth in population. We build condominiums and townhouses to accommodate the growth. When Mayor Ford contacted my father, we both agreed Peaks would be an ideal place to build."

Mayor Ford clicked the end of his pen. "Our town's economy has been sitting on a plateau for the past ten years. Fixtel opening its doors next spring will foster the kind of growth we've been wanting."

"Fixtel will undoubtedly provide a substantial number of jobs, but as of right now, Peaks doesn't have the residential appeal some of the surrounding towns do. We're hoping the condos will change that and corral potential taxpayers."

The mayor barked his laugh and raised his hand. "Sign me up!"

A ripple of laughter circled the table.

"All joking aside"—Mayor Ford's laugh lines disappeared—"this is a fabulous opportunity for our town. One I'd like to seize. Which is why I'm proposing we add McKay condominiums to our development plan.

"They align with our objectives and give us the means to accomplish many of our goals." Mayor Ford tapped his pen against the tabletop. "But we can't move forward without the town's support on the matter. And we're not going to get their support unless we are united."

Steve Milton, a narrow-faced man with a pointed nose, set his elbows on the table. "I'm not so sure I like this idea."

Ian clasped his hands and folded them over his knee. "I'd love to hear your concerns, Mr. Milton."

"You want to knock down three local businesses and a ministry that is near and dear to many people's hearts. I'm not sure your condominiums are worth it." Milton looked at Mayor Ford. "Does improving the south end of the district have to include tearing it apart? Shouldn't our loyalty be to the businesses already existing in Peaks?"

"Of course my loyalty is to the businesses and residents of Peaks. That's exactly why I'm proposing these plans. More people equals more business."

"But what about the antique shop? Or Willow Tree?" Milton motioned to Richard Arton at the opposite end of the table. "Or the jewelry store?"

Arton removed his chin from his hand. "My wife and I have already spoken with Ian. We're more than willing to sell to him. Quite relieved about it, actually."

Milton frowned. "What about One Life? They just hired a new director, and I hear he has big plans for the ministry."

Mayor Ford balked. "Steve, the ministry can find another spot to rent."

"My loyalty remains with the people of Peaks—"

"So you're implying my loyalty lies elsewhere?"

Ian raised his hands. "Gentlemen, I'm sure we can talk this out. I'm glad you raised these concerns, Mr. Milton. I would love the opportunity to address them."

Milton's frown deepened into a scowl.

Mayor Ford huffed. "That antique shop has been an eyesore in this community since I became mayor ten years ago. One Life...well, who's to say it will even be needed once our economy improves? And Robin will sell when she realizes how much the condominiums will benefit this town."

"She's a widow who's invested more than time and money into Willow Tree, Chuck." Milton removed his elbows from the table. "Or have you forgotten?"

In fifth grade, Ian's best friend had chucked a crab apple at him when he wasn't looking. It walloped him in the chest and knocked the wind right out of him. Milton's words might as well have been that crab apple. "Excuse me a minute. I don't think I heard correctly. Did you say Mrs. Price is a widow?"

"I assumed you knew," Mayor Ford said.

Robin? But that couldn't be right. He'd met her husband at church. Face to face. He saw him at the meet and greet. The man had Caleb's eyes and mouth. The same last name. Of course he was Caleb's father. "Then who's the gentleman you introduced me to outside Grace Assembly?"

"Evan? He's Robin's brother-in-law."

Ian's thoughts tumbled off some sort of invisible precipice. They flailed in a confusing free fall. He tried to catch up with this new bit of information before the conversation got away from him, but the determination he'd mustered over the past couple days fell to pieces.

It couldn't be helped.

This shifted everything. Robin Price, the woman who had it all—a business, a son, a spouse—didn't actually have it all. The woman with eyes the color of a winter sky, the one who created soul-stirring music, the one who poured her heart into her café…she was a widow?

"It's a sad story, to be sure." Mayor Ford folded his hands. "We all loved Micah."

Her nervous ring-twirling. The old widower sitting in her café, patiently waiting to talk. The reason she was the only one on the title. The insensitive things he'd said. Ian wanted to ram his head against the conference table.

"But we're getting off track here. That was a long time ago. I don't see why it should have any bearing on our decision today."

"I don't think she'll sell," Milton said. "No matter what we agree to."

Mayor Ford batted his hand. "Of course she will. Robin grew up here. She cares about this town more than most folks I know. We all wanted her café to do well. As much as it pains me, the fact of the matter is, it's struggling right alongside every other riverfront business. This town doesn't need a café. It needs condominiums."

"But what about One Life? People in this town do need that."

The debate floated around Ian's ears. He tried to pin it down, but all he could see was Robin, praising God with her music in church. It was as if somebody had pushed the pause button in his mind and stolen the remote.

FIFTEEN

The whirring of the espresso machine drowned out the woman's chatter. Amanda wished the cup would take longer than twenty short seconds to fill. She let the dark liquid come out in a slow drip, unconcerned about the burnt taste that would ensue. Blaire St. Claire—seriously her name—wouldn't notice the difference. She never stopped talking long enough to taste anything.

Robin was short staffed again and had to pick her dad up from the airport, which left Amanda here. Despite the lack of funds for it, her sister-in-law needed to hire another employee. Because as much fun as this might be, it was a constant reminder that Amanda did not have a life. At least not the one she was supposed to have.

She glanced at the clock. Thirty minutes before Molly's shift started. Amanda wondered if Blaire would stay and talk the entire time. As soon as she stopped filling the cup, the woman's voice came back to life—her whiny, high-pitched, too-fast voice.

"...I told Jeremy no way. I'm not pregnant. I'm just PMSing. But he had this dream that I was pregnant with twins. Can you believe it? So he goes and he buys me a pregnancy test and wouldn't you know it. I'm pregnant. I am pregnant! Insanity, right? I mean, we got home from our honeymoon two months ago and I'm already impregnated?

"So this whole time, I've been freaking out, trying to figure out how to tell my sister. I mean, she and her husband have been married for five years with no kids and now they're adopting." She put her hand over her stomach and shook her head, like adoption was some tragic backup plan. Amanda held onto the cup, afraid if she set it on the counter, she'd reach over and smack Blaire St. Claire upside the head. Not just for saying something so incredibly stupid, but for having the life Amanda had prayed for since Jason told her he loved her three years ago. "She never said they couldn't get pregnant, but I'm not an idiot. My sister's basically been depressed for the past three years. And here I am, pregnant as can be after two months of marital bliss. She's going to be devastated, I just know it."

Blaire waved her hand, as if to shoo the stench of her ten-minute monologue from the air. She picked up the cup and took a drink. "Anyway, enough about me. Tell me what's going on in your life. I haven't talked to you since the big breakup." She quoted the last two words with her fingers and made her eyes go so wide, she looked like a strangled frog. "I couldn't believe it when I heard. I mean, you two started dating before Jeremy and I even met. I thought for sure you were headed to the altar before us."

Amanda gritted her teeth and told herself to stay quiet. To not respond. Anything she said would simply go in one ear, zip through the cavern in the middle, and float right out the other ear. There was no use wasting her breath.

Blaire took another sip of her espresso and dug a credit card from her purse. "And for him to leave you the way he did. For Africa? What does he think he's doing in Africa? He's obviously a loser and you're better off without him."

Amanda's jaw tightened. "He went to Africa to do medical work in Nairobi. I hardly think that makes him a loser."

"But he left you. I mean, how could he just leave you like that? I swear, he's going to regret his decision. Someday he's going to wake up, and he's going to be sorry he chose Africa over you." Blaire handed over her credit card and her oversized wedding ring caught the light.

Amanda snatched the card out of her hand, a little too fast. "He's not going to regret his decision." She hated that Blaire was prompting her to defend a man who had broken her heart. She hated even more that Blaire's words sounded so blasted familiar. How many times had Amanda lain awake, hoping he'd regret the same thing?

Her mind wandered to the letter she'd folded and stuck in the sock drawer of her dresser. The one with his e-mail address written at the bottom. Last night she broke down and wrote him. This morning, when she checked her inbox, disappointment had settled in her gut at its emptiness. A disappointment that had yet to leave.

"If he's smart, he will. I mean, you're a catch, Amanda. You really are. Don't let what Jason did make you doubt that."

Amanda slid the card across the counter and pressed her lips together. Maybe Blaire's words would be sweet if she didn't look so condescending when she said them. The bell on the door jingled. Amanda looked over Blaire's shoulder and spotted Ian McKay strolling through the front door. A welcome relief.

Blaire put the card in her purse and slipped on her oversized sunglasses, oblivious to the fact that they made her look like a fly. She looked over her shoulder and the second Blaire's head was turned, Amanda waved theatrically at Ian, her eyes filled with an exaggerated plea—a signal that communicated *Rescue me, please.* Blaire turned back around. Amanda stopped her waving and scratched the back of her head. Fly lady tipped her glasses down her nose and leaned close. "Hubba, hubba."

Ian strolled toward them, wearing a moss-colored dress shirt and a slightly loosened dark chocolate tie, his eyes crinkled with amusement. Amanda's stomach fluttered, something it hadn't done since Jason. "If it isn't the coffee guy."

"That's me."

"You've been MIA the last few days."

He set his hands on the counter. "Duty called."

"Hey, I forgot to ask the last time our paths crossed. Did you ever get that stain out?"

"It's as good as new, thanks to Bernie."

Blaire let out an exaggerated cough. "Aren't you going to introduce me to your friend, Amanda?"

"Blaire, this is Ian McKay. Ian, this is Blaire St. Claire."

Ian's attention snapped to Amanda's as soon as she said the name. *Oh yes, I'm serious.*

"Well, if it isn't the developer man. I've been hearing the buzz. So nice to finally meet you." Blaire stuck out her hand. Not for Ian to shake. But for Ian to kiss. Amanda choked on her laughter, but Ian looked completely unfazed. He kissed her knuckles and shot Amanda a subtle wink across the counter.

"How do you know Amanda?" Blaire asked.

"Oh, we go way back," Ian said.

Blaire fingered the ends of her hair. "Do you?"

He nodded.

"Enjoy your coffee, Blaire," Amanda said. "I hope you don't get morning sickness, being pregnant with twins and all."

Blaire's cheeks turned pink. She pushed her sunglasses back into place and wiggled her fingers in a farewell wave. When she walked out the door, Amanda collapsed against the counter.

"Seems like a nice gal," Ian said.

"Oh yes. Super nice." Amanda pushed herself up from the counter. "So, Robin told me about your surprise visit on Monday. And the sale of Arton's."

"Is she doing okay?"

The concern was oddly placed. "Besides the fact that you're trying to tear down her baby, she's doing all right."

His eyes lost their crinkles and she wanted to bring them back. She enjoyed the light, swoopy feeling they brought to her stomach. "So, fancy man, you really think you'll get Robin to sell this place?"

"You don't know me very well, Amanda. I can be pretty persuasive when I need to be."

"I'll bet you can."

His attention wandered to the piano, to the loft, then stalled on the door leading into the kitchen. "Speaking of the owner, where is she? Shirking her duties on a Friday afternoon?"

"She's picking up my parents and her dad from the airport. They're flying in for the Price family picnic. It happens once a year, always on Memorial Day weekend." And just this morning, Amanda invited Kyle. Robin would kill her, of course, but Amanda was willing to bear the brunt of her wrath. Kyle was a nice guy. Robin needed to give him another shot. One awkward date was no reason to hammer all the nails in the coffin.

"Will she be working tomorrow?"

"Nobody will. She shuts this place down on holiday weekends."

Ian tutted. "Not good for business."

"Try telling her that. She never listens to me."

"Could you relay a message?"

"For a reasonable fee."

The crinkles returned. She would spout off a thousand quippy comments if it meant making them stay. "There's a town meeting next Thursday about the condominiums."

"Really?"

"I'd like to speak with Robin beforehand."

Amanda set her hands on the counter. Robin was incredibly attached to Willow Tree. Sometimes Amanda wondered if the attachment bordered on unhealthy. Ian deserved to know what he was getting himself in to. "You seem like a nice guy."

"I try my best."

"I wouldn't get your hopes up about this place. It means a lot to her."

He gazed at the piano. "Well, Amanda, these condos mean a lot to me. At least we're evenly matched."

She shrugged. He'd either figure it out and quit or beat the odds and convince Robin to sell. Weirder things had happened. Like Blaire finding a man who could stomach the sound of her voice. "Can I get you that free chai tea?"

"No, thanks. Just make sure Robin gets the message. I want to speak with her before the meeting. I really think she should listen to my offer before this gets out of hand."

An appealing idea wiggled into her mind. Just because Robin was afraid to give love another shot didn't mean Amanda needed to follow in her sister-in-law's overly cautious footsteps. She ducked under the counter and resurfaced with a pen.

"Why don't you tell her yourself?" She took Ian's hand and jotted an address across his palm. She invited Kyle for Robin. She'd invite Ian for herself. "At our picnic tomorrow."

He quirked his eyebrow at the address. "You really think she'd let me come?"

"Of course she won't. But I will."

"This might put you on Robin's naughty list."

Amanda dismissed his concern with a wave of her hand. "You two need to talk this out, right?" And she needed something to distract her from her empty inbox. Someone cute and flirtatious. "What better way to do it than over burgers and hot dogs?"

Besides, this wasn't about Robin. This was about Amanda. It was about distracting herself from Jason and his stupid letter. It was about forgetting her dreams and her plans for the future. For whatever reason, they hadn't been good enough—not for Jason. Not for God. Perhaps it was time to improvise.

SIXTEEN

The smell of charcoal and smoke and mowed grass scented the air—summer's perfume. Short stalks of corn sprouted from the land surrounding the farmhouse, evidence of Evan's hard work earlier in the month. Robin breathed the freshness deep into her lungs as Caleb raced toward Bethany and Evan beside the grill. Evan grabbed him by the waist and flipped him onto his shoulders to a round of Caleb's red-faced giggles. "How's my favorite little guy doing?"

"Good."

"You want to help me park the tractor before the party starts?"

He squirmed on his perch, his eyes widening.

Evan caught hold of his writhing body and set him on the ground. He darted to Robin's side and clamped on to her leg. Evan gave Robin a "what was that about" look, but all she could do was shrug. Caleb loved riding the tractor. It was one of his favorite things to do. She placed her hand on his hair and withdrew him from between her legs. "You don't want to ride on the tractor with Uncle Evan?"

"I wanna stay with you." Caleb mumbled the words to her thigh.

"Are you sure?"

He buried his face in her hip.

A string of worry tugged at her heart. Giving up his toy combine was one thing. Refusing to ride on a tractor with his uncle was something else altogether. She returned Evan and Bethany's perplexed stare and caught sight of Dad and Donna holding hands in the background. The sight had the same discordant effect now as it had at the airport. No matter how much Robin tried to prepare herself for the open signs of affection, each one pinched her with a twinge of longing.

The screen door squealed on its hinges and banged shut. A sandal-clad Amanda stepped out of the farmhouse and onto the grass, carrying a bag of chips and some condiments to the picnic tables. Ruth sat at one of them, holding Elyse on her knees. The little girl wore a pink bucket hat with a wide brim and sucked on a pacifier.

"My mom needs to support Ellie's head better." Bethany peered down the hill at them.

Evan wrapped his arm around her waist. "Relax, babe," he said. "Your mom adores Elyse. You need to cut her some slack."

Bethany melted into his side, as if his nearness unwound her. "I promise I'm trying."

Evan kissed her temple. "I know."

"Now can you please unhand me so I can very politely suggest to my mother that she put her hand behind our daughter's head?"

Evan chuckled and let go so Bethany could hurry down the hill after Amanda. Robin's heart stretched like pulled taffy. Not only did Bethany have a husband who could kiss her temple and rein in her neuroses, she had a mother too. Sure, the two of them had a strained relationship and years and years' worth of issues to wade through, but they were working through it. Robin didn't like feeling jealous of her best friend, but she would give anything for Caleb to know his grandmother.

"Mommy?" He tugged Robin's sundress, a residue of fear lingering in his eyes. "Can I play with the doggies?"

"As long as you stay where you can see me."

He shuffled toward one of Evan's Border collies, his walk devoid of its usual skip. Robin left Evan to his grilling and made her way toward the picnic tables, where Dad, Donna, Ruth, Micah's parents—Jim and Loraine—and an unidentified sixth person sat conversing. As soon as Robin recognized him, she stopped midstride. What in the world was Kyle doing at their picnic?

Amanda joined Robin where she'd stalled in the grass. "You're looking mighty pretty today. I love your dress."

"Why is Kyle here?"

A devilish grin slid across Amanda's face. "I invited him."

"Please tell me you aren't trying to play Cupid."

"You only went on one date. Would it kill you to try again?"

Robin pressed her fingertips against her hairline.

"What? Kyle's nice. He's good-looking. He's single. You're single. You both love the same ministry and he kept checking you out at the meet and greet."

"That's because I was handing out free lemon bars."

"Trust me. He wants to ask you out again. He's just too shy to do it on his own. I'm helping the poor guy along."

"There's one small problem, Amanda. I don't want to be asked out."

"Micah would want you to be happy."

Amanda's words chaffed. "How could you possibly know what Micah would or wouldn't want?" Especially when Robin didn't even know herself. She pressed a cool palm against her forehead. "And why does everybody assume I need to date to be happy? I've got Caleb and the café. That's more than a lot of people can say."

"The café can't keep you warm at night."

Robin held up her hand. Enough was enough. "I'm happy, Amanda, okay? I don't want to be set up with anyone. Especially not the director of One Life."

Something clattered against the picnic table. Robin covered her mouth, her ears flooding with heat. She hadn't meant to speak those words so loudly. Bethany righted the fallen mustard bottle, scooped Elyse off Ruth's lap, and joined Robin and Amanda several paces away from Kyle and the in-laws.

Robin grabbed Bethany's wrist. "Do you think he heard me?" Perhaps the sound of Elyse's pacifier sucking had drowned out her careless words.

"Well, I did. And last I checked, I don't have exceptionally keen hearing."

Robin groaned.

"I told her not to invite him," Bethany said.

Amanda rolled her eyes. "Oh, please. It's a picnic. Not the end of the world."

"You invited him," Robin whispered. "He probably thinks you're interested."

"I don't think so."

"Brace yourself for more." Bethany readjusted Elyse's hat and examined a patch of skin on the little girl's arm. "Kyle isn't the only man she invited."

Heat drained from Robin's face. She'd been looking forward to this day all week, but how was she supposed to enjoy it with Amanda hurling men at her feet? "Please tell me you didn't invite more than one potential suitor."

"As fun as that would have been…"

"Amanda!"

"Robin—relax. This other guy's not your type. He's more—"

"What secrets are you three whispering over there?" Loraine called from the picnic table, hands tucked beneath her chin. Kyle twisted his upper half to follow Loraine's entreaty and gave a tentative wave.

Robin smiled—the most friendly, unromantic smile she could muster. "Hi, Kyle."

"It was nice of you to invite me to your picnic."

"We're glad you could make it." Robin itched the back of her neck. "I'll be right back. The pies are in my car."

Kyle's lanky frame scrambled from the picnic bench. "Do you need any help?"

She shook her head, but Amanda nudged her with her elbow. "How nice of you to offer. I'm sure Robin would love your help."

Robin clenched her jaw. She would have words with Amanda later. Not-so-nice words. Until then, she was stuck. She waited for Kyle to join her, then led the way toward the gravel drive, blades of grass tickling her bare ankles.

"I've been meaning to thank you for hosting the meet and greet last weekend. It was a great way to get to know the people I'll be serving at One Life. The whole thing felt very welcoming."

"I'm glad. We all want you to feel at home. Like family." She studied him from the corner of her eye as they walked toward the farmhouse. Kyle was a nice-looking man. Taller and lankier than Micah with a pointy Adam's apple and flecks of gray peppering his hair. He was kind and considerate and a man of strong faith. Yet despite all the obvious assets, her heart did not stir—not on their date last Friday and not now. The observation had her teetering between disappointment and relief.

"I also wanted to thank you for your support. I can't tell you how relieved I was when I heard you wouldn't be selling to Ian McKay. It means the world to me, especially now."

Robin scrunched her brow. "What do you mean 'especially now'?"

"Well, now that Sybil's agreed to sell."

Robin stopped walking. "Sybil's going to sell?"

"Her sale is contingent upon yours, which means you are the only one keeping us from losing our space."

"When did this happen?"

"Yesterday afternoon. That contractor fella—Ian McKay—stopped by and spoke with Sybil, explaining his offer." Kyle squinted against the sun, his expression filled with concern. "I take it you didn't know?"

Robin shook her head, then forced herself to start walking again—one foot in the front of the other until they arrived at her car. Ian's weeklong absence had lulled her into a false sense of security. She'd let down her guard, assumed the Lord had indeed delivered her. Maybe she'd been too hasty in her assumptions.

"It's very comforting to know you're willing to fight for the ministry."

"Of course." She tried to think of something reassuring to say, but her mind raced in a thousand different directions, spinning into a tornado of worry. Sybil and Cecile had agreed to sell. What did this mean?

"So…" Kyle stuffed his hands in the back pockets of his jeans. A breeze rustled the hostas on the side of the house and lifted Robin's hair around her shoulders. "I heard your son talking to Evan at the meet and greet. Something about dragons and hot lava. The kid's got quite the imagination."

Robin smiled, grateful for the distraction. "More like overactive."

"He looks a lot like his uncle."

"You should have seen his father." She opened the passenger door of her car. "I have a picture in my purse." She fished through her bag and pulled out her wallet, removed the picture of Micah she kept tucked inside—crinkled and worn from Caleb's little fingers—and handed it to Kyle.

He took it gently, like he understood its value. "You weren't kidding. He's the spitting image of his dad."

Ribbons of warmth spread through her body. She couldn't imagine life without Caleb. His very existence had anchored her to the earth at a time when she'd wanted nothing more than to unstrap from gravity and float away. She might not have five children, like she once imagined, but she lavished all the love she'd have for those five on her one little boy.

She smiled and looked toward the elm tree, where Caleb had stood petting one of Evan's Border collies. But he wasn't there. She turned toward the mowed meadow, where Dad and Donna fussed over Elyse and Amanda chatted with Loraine and Jim. She cast a look across the horizon, head swiveling in search of her son.

Leaving the car door open, she hurried toward the picnic tables. This wasn't the first time Caleb had run off at the farm. He did it once before. On his third birthday party last summer, he'd moseyed to the white fence to look at the new calves while the adults washed cake-smeared plates. That's probably where he was now. Or maybe he followed Evan after all. Maybe he decided he wanted to ride on the tractor with his uncle. She lengthened her stride. That was it. Caleb went to the machine shed with Evan. Or was climbing on the fence behind the barn.

Kyle caught up with his long strides. "Everything okay?"

"I told Caleb to stay in sight. I think he's down by the fence." Robin stopped in front of the picnic tables. "Has anybody seen Caleb?"

The conversation died.

Bethany set her bottled water on the table. "Is he with Evan?"

"Dad, could you go check?" Robin didn't wait for his answer. Instead, she half walked, half jogged to the barn, Kyle trotting beside her. She pushed through the barn doors and found nothing but straw and sticky heat.

"Caleb, are you in here?"

Nothing.

She tried to take a deep breath, but the air was too thick.

"I'm sure he's with Evan," Kyle said. "Or maybe he went into the house to use the rest room or get a drink."

Yes. Of course. That had to be it. Caleb went inside to grab a juice box. She took off toward the house. Dad and Evan met her halfway. Robin didn't break stride. "He wasn't in the machine shed with you?"

"No, he never followed me."

"I think he's probably in the house," she said.

"Right. Of course."

Robin ignored the worry fraying Evan's words. He had no reason to sound that way. They were all blowing this out of proportion. She worst of all. Caleb would be inside and Robin would have to sit him down and talk to him about following directions. She opened the screen door.

"Caleb!" She walked through the still kitchen.

"Caleb!" Evan and Dad called behind her.

Robin hurried into the living room and took the steps two at a time. Nothing but the hallway stared back at her—dark and empty. She called Caleb's name, but she knew better. He would never hide up here alone. The upstairs frightened him. She rushed down the stairs. "Where are your dogs, Evan? Caleb has to be with them."

"They followed me to the machine shed."

Panic strangled her airway.

Oh, God...

"He was outside five minutes ago," Kyle said. "He has to be around here somewhere."

She flew out the front door and stood on the porch, peering down the drive that led to the road. The tire swing hung from its bough, still and untouched. She hopped past the stairs and cupped her hands to her mouth. "Caleb!" Hysteria swallowed his name.

"Caleb!" Dad called.

Their eyes locked. The fear growing in Dad's made Robin jerk back, as if burned. She ran past the porch. Rounded the corner. And stopped short. Ian McKay stood by the side of the house.

"I think this belongs to you," he said.

And there, at Ian's side, was her son.

She dropped to her knees and clutched him to her chest.

∽

A fault line shifted beneath Ian's heart. It was the first time he had seen her, knowing the truth—that she wasn't happily married, but a widow. She knew something of pain. Life had been messy for her too. He shifted his weight and tried to look away from the frenzied, relieved kisses she lavished on her son's face, but something about the mother and the boy and the kisses mesmerized him. It was as if the kid held her entire world in his small body.

Three men, one Ian recognized as the guest of honor at the meet and greet, and one as the man he'd assumed to be Robin's husband, hurried around the corner of the house. The third sported more wrinkles than the other two, a thick head of silver hair and the same pale blue eyes as Robin. He nearly collapsed with relief at seeing Caleb clutched in his mother's arms.

Ian pictured his own parents with a little one. A baby boy or girl who would make his mother melt and his father laugh. Surely a grandchild would have been able to shine a light through the dark shroud of cancer haunting his family.

Robin brought Caleb away from her chest and dug her fingers into his shoulders. "What were you thinking? You know better than to run off like that." She crushed him to her body before he had the chance to explain.

The fault line shifted again, giving way to a fissure that cracked through his chest. Curiosity bubbled from its depth like hot lava. What would it be like to have his own flesh and blood housed in a body? To worry about somebody so small? To be charged with raising and protecting a life so deeply connected to his own? Before the fissure widened into a canyon, he slipped his hands into his pockets and studied the side of the house. Neglected orange lilies grew over an air conditioning unit that rattled and hummed to life.

"I don't understand what you're doing here." Robin looked up at him from her crouched position in the gravel as if he'd kidnapped her son.

"Amanda invited me."

"What?" She looked over her shoulder, toward the picnic tables. "Why?"

"Because I told her I wanted to talk to you."

"And you think now would be a good time? During a family picnic?"

"You could say thank you," he said. "That would be the normal response."

"Thank you?"

"For returning your son. He was headed toward the road when I found him."

Robin rounded on Caleb, whose face looked two seconds from crumpling. "You were walking toward the road? Caleb, you could've gotten hit. Or hurt. Or—"

"I wouldn't be too hard on him. He seemed pretty down and out when I got to him. I was trying to get him to laugh when you found us, but I don't think he thought any of my jokes were very funny." The boy peeked out from Robin's embrace and Ian shot him a wink.

"I'll have a talk with him, Robin." The older man scooped Caleb into his arms and turned toward Ian. "Thanks for finding my grandson."

"I'm just glad I got to him before he found the road, sir."

The man squinted at the sky, as if trying to pull his thoughts from the clouds. "You wouldn't happen to be the gentleman who wants to buy my daughter's café, would you?"

Ian looked at Robin. She remained in her crouched position over the gravel, fingers propped against the ground. "That would be me," he said.

Robin's dad examined Ian over the top of Caleb's cowlick. "Do you have any idea what you're getting yourself into?"

"I think I'm beginning to realize."

The man chuckled, then made his way down the hill with Evan. Kyle stayed behind, scuffing one shoe against the ground, a glossy photo pinned in his hand. Ian had no idea what brought the director of One Life to the picnic, but his presence was convenient. Kyle should know about the town meeting too since its outcome would affect him just as much as Robin.

She straightened from her crouched position and dusted the gravel from her palms. "Thank you for finding Caleb."

"Enough that you'll listen to my offer?"

She and Kyle exchanged a look, one that seemed to bolster Robin's spirits, because when she turned her eyes on him, they were filled with the same fire he'd seen outside Grace Assembly a week ago. Despite the obvious problem her spirit posed, he couldn't help but admire its beauty. "I'm sorry, but it won't change my mind. Not about the café or One Life. And not about you."

"About me? But just last week you said you didn't even know me. When were you able to form an opinion?"

"I've learned enough."

Her words settled between them—an invisible barrier. She knew his name and what he did for a living. How could that possibly be enough?

Kyle shifted his weight, then held out the photograph. "I'm going to see if Evan needs help with the grill."

"Thanks." Robin took the photo and sandwiched it between her palms. Kyle turned and walked away, glancing once over his shoulder as he did.

Ian nodded toward her hand. "What's that?"

"Nothing." Her eyes dimmed. "Everything." She puffed out a breath and crossed her arms as if to ward off a nonexistent chill.

She was cracking. He could feel it. A little more pressure and she'd crumble. He convinced himself this was a good thing, a necessary thing. So why did he find himself battling the urge to hold her together? He looked at the small crowd gathered around the picnic tables. "I don't know about you, but I'm famished." He stepped toward the opened car door. "Are those pies in there?"

"You're not going to eat with us."

He picked up the two pans. "I am if you baked these."

SEVENTEEN

Caleb scooted to the edge of the picnic bench, ogling Ian like he wore a cape and might blast into the sky at any moment. Robin pushed him back in his seat for the third time and pointed to his half-eaten hot dog, unsure why her son was so taken with the developer, while Ian charmed her father with a story of a trip to Ohio gone wrong. Dad's laughter grated.

Amanda set her elbows on the table. "How long do you think you'll be here?"

"A couple weeks. Give or take."

Robin tightened her grip on the plastic fork and pushed potato salad around her plate. It would take him a lot longer than fourteen days to convince her to sell, especially now that One Life hinged on her resistance. She uncrossed her legs. Recrossed them. Then raised her eyebrows at Bethany in a do-something appeal. Bethany's forked pineapple paused near her lips.

"Are you going to the fish fry at the park on Monday?" Amanda asked.

"The mayor invited me."

Of course. The two were joined at the hip. Robin was surprised Ian hadn't invited the mayor to her family picnic. She stuffed a bite of potato in her mouth to keep from saying so.

"So"—Ian turned his caramel eyes on her—"I'll be at the town meeting this Thursday."

The potato turned gritty. Robin forced herself to swallow. "Why?"

"I met with town council yesterday. Most are in favor of the condominiums and want to give the rest of the town a say in the matter. That's why I came here today. To give you a heads-up and to see if you'd consider my offer. I think it would be best for everyone if we could have a conversation first."

Loraine set down her sweet tea while Jim made funny faces at baby Elyse on his knee. "A conversation about what?"

Loraine didn't know. Neither did Jim. Or Donna. But everybody else at the table, everybody else laughing and enjoying Ian's company, knew his intentions. Maybe they all needed a polite reminder. "Ian wants to tear down Willow Tree and build condos."

Loraine stopped chewing.

"If he succeeds, not only will I be out of a café, the town will lose One Life." She glanced at Kyle, who shifted food around his plate. Judging by its fullness, he wasn't having any more fun than Robin.

"Is there a reason One Life can't relocate?" Ian asked.

"It's not that simple." Kyle set his fork beside his plate. "We rent the space from Sybil at an incredibly low cost. We won't get that price anywhere else in town."

"Which means we'll have a lot less money to give to those in need." Robin tried her hardest to glare. "If they move, they'll have to cut back on programming."

"Couldn't you run the ministry out of the church?" Ian asked.

"A lot of the people we serve would never set foot inside a church. The whole purpose of the ministry is to be the hands and feet of Christ in the community, outside the church walls."

Robin had no idea how Kyle could speak so calmly, so patiently. Not when she was using every bit of her strength to temper the heat rising in her chest, partly on behalf of One Life, partly because of the remorse on Ian's face. He had no right to look so sorry about the news. Not unless sorry made him change his plans.

"This is ridiculous, isn't it? He can't force me to sell." The panic she'd tried so hard to swallow throughout the meal spewed from her mouth.

"Why don't you hear him out before making a decision?" Amanda suggested.

Robin turned on her with razor-sharp eyes. Inviting Kyle was one thing.

They were at least on the same side. But Ian? Before she said something she'd later regret, she snatched her empty cup and stood. "Excuse me."

Amanda clambered out of her seat and followed Robin's fast retreat. "Robin, wait."

But Robin didn't wait. She stalked up the hill toward the house. She didn't stop until she reached the screen door and Amanda grabbed her arm. "Robin."

She whipped around. "How could you invite him, Amanda? Don't you care about me at all? Don't you care about Willow Tree?"

Amanda took a step back. "Whoa, it's just a picnic. I had no idea you'd get so upset."

"It's not 'just a picnic.'" Robin flung her hand toward the gathering. "It's you and everybody else acting like what Ian plans to do is no big deal. You're taking his side."

"Okay, hold on a second. Nobody is taking his side. I'll go to bat for you over the café. And so will Bethany and Evan. You know that."

"It doesn't feel that way," Robin said. "Even my own son is enamored."

"Can you blame him?"

She gritted her teeth and walked inside the kitchen.

Amanda followed. "I've never seen you like this."

"Like what?"

"Like this." She pointed to Robin's tight grip on the underside of the counter. "You really hate him, don't you?"

"I don't hate anybody."

"Yes, you do. He totally gets under your skin."

Robin filled her cup with the filtered water from the fridge and took a long drink.

"Inviting Kyle was obviously a waste of time," Amanda said. "I invited Ian for me, but maybe I need to take a step back."

Robin yanked opened the refrigerator and put the water back. "What are you talking about?"

Amanda arched her brows. "Oh, please! You don't react that strongly to someone without sparks flying."

"Sparks?"

"Attraction. You were fighting it every time you stuffed your mouth with food."

"That's ridiculous."

"Sure it is."

"The only reason I'm upset is because I'm worried about my café."

Amanda set her hand on her hip and dipped her chin. "So if I asked him out on a date, you wouldn't care? Not even a teeny tiny bit?"

"No." Robin hurled the word from her mouth before she could think. "But as my sister-in-law and my roommate and my accountant, don't you think it's a little inconsiderate of you to go on a date with a man who wants to bulldoze my café to the ground?"

Amanda shrugged. "I can't help it. I like him."

"You don't even know him."

"I know when I'm around him, Jason's the furthest thing from my mind."

Robin looked away. Amanda's reference to her ex-boyfriend wasn't fair. "So what? You want my permission to date Ian?"

Amanda took the glass from Robin's hand and set it on the counter. "I'm sorry, okay? I shouldn't have asked Ian to come or invited Kyle without giving you a fair warning."

The screen door opened. Bethany stepped inside. "Amanda, really? Inviting him was over the top, even for you."

She threw up her hands. "I already apologized. Sheesh."

"Your dad wants to talk to you." Bethany gave Robin an apologetic smile and escorted Amanda out the door. Dad came in and wrapped Robin in a much-needed hug. She melted against him, thankful for his warmth and the familiar scent of pine pressed into his clothes.

"I know this is driving you nuts." His chest rumbled as he spoke. "But can I give you my honest opinion?"

She shook her head into his shirt.

"There's no harm in listening to his offer, getting the details."

Her body sagged. She didn't want to talk about this right now.

"As your lawyer, it's the smart thing to do. And as your father, I think it would give you a little peace. As I said before, he's not going to quit until you at least hear him out."

Robin pulled away and stared at her pink toenails, suddenly very sick of this conversation. She wiggled her toes beneath the leather strap of her sandals, trying to ignore the throbbing in her temples. Perhaps Bethany had some ibuprofen in her medicine cabinet. "Donna seems happy. She looks at you like a love-struck teenager, anyway."

"The feeling's mutual."

The words clinked like a penny tossed into a dried-up wishing well. She should feel happy for her father, not empty, but she couldn't help it. Seeing Dad and Donna hold hands and laugh not only made Robin miss Mom, it reminded her of everything she didn't have. She worked hard to push the negative thoughts aside and focus instead on all that God *had* given her. She had so much in Caleb and the café. What good did it do to focus on the one thing He'd taken away?

"Robin?"

She looked up from her big toe.

"I want to tell you something, in private, before we make the announcement."

A far-off humming came to life in her ears. "Announcement?"

"Donna and I, well"—Dad gave her a sheepish grin and brought his hand to the back of his neck—"we're getting married."

She tried to smile, but her lips felt all loose and tingly, like she'd just had work done at the dentist. *Dad had proposed...*

He stepped forward and wrapped her in a bear hug.

She forced her arms to hug him back. "Congratulations," she whispered.

"Thanks, sweetheart. Your support means the world to us."

Us. She had been an *us* once, with Micah. But even in their happiest *us* moments, Caleb had been missing. And now in her happiest moments with Caleb, Micah was missing. Why did something have to be missing?

"I really want you and Donna to be close." Dad tipped her chin and looked into her eyes. "I know you'll love her once you get to know her better." He let go and held out his elbow. "I'm going to announce the big news. Care to join me?"

Robin opened her mouth, but nothing came out. She pressed her palm against her collarbone and tried a second time. "You go ahead. I need to use the rest room first."

A hint of a frown flickered across his brow, but he nodded, wiped his hands down the thighs of his jeans, and left Robin stranded in the kitchen, scrunched and twisted, like a once-wet towel wrung out and left to dry.

∿

Ian pulled at his collar, searching for an opportunity to politely excuse himself. Now that he had delivered the news about the town meeting, he felt terribly uncomfortable about staying at what was clearly a family party. But he had a hard time following the conversation. Robin's vehement words about One Life had him distracted. Contrary to what she might think, he didn't want to see the ministry go. Especially not at the hands of his father's company. He glanced toward the farmhouse and spotted Bethany escorting Amanda back to the picnic tables.

When they arrived, Amanda straddled the bench, wrapped her arms around Caleb's chest and set her chin on top of his head. Bethany slid next to her husband. She and Evan exchanged a hidden look—a wordless language carved from years of intimacy. One that watered Ian's growing discomfort.

"How's your job going, Bethany?" Kyle asked. "Evan was telling me about it at the meet and greet."

"She's getting referrals left and right. Pretty soon I won't have to farm anymore."

Bethany gave Evan a playful nudge. "You'll quit farming the day I learn how to bake."

"You bake okay."

Bethany raised her eyebrows at Loraine. "Your son's a liar."

Loraine smiled. "I know I've said it before, Bethy, but every time I see that café, I'm amazed. You really made it into something special."

"I'm always wondering where she got her talent," Ruth said.

Ian sat up straighter. "You designed Willow Tree?"

"Bethany's an architect." Amanda dug her hand inside an opened bag of chips. "Any of the new or renovated buildings on the north end of Peaks are in her portfolio."

"Really?" Ian pondered this new bit of information. He didn't have to be a genius to figure out Bethany had more clout with Robin than any other person at the table. "Our company is always looking for talented architects. Have you ever designed condominiums or townhomes?"

"A couple."

"Would you mind if I took a look at your portfolio?"

"She's got a really great website," Amanda said.

Evan and Bethany shot her a look.

"What?" Amanda popped a chip in her mouth and crunched it between her teeth. "I was paying you a compliment."

Ian chuckled. He liked Amanda.

Robin's father returned. He stepped behind Donna and squeezed her shoulders. "If I could have everyone's attention, we have an announcement to make," he said.

Everybody turned.

"Would you like a drumroll?" Amanda asked.

Donna laughed. "I think a drumroll would be most appropriate."

Amanda drummed her pointer fingers against the picnic table. Caleb joined. Robin's dad took a deep breath, his eyes dancing as he looked from one person to the next. "Donna and I are getting married."

Amanda and Loraine and Ruth jumped up from the table and descended on Donna with excitement and hugs. Jim stood with baby Elyse and pumped the man's hand. And in the midst of the jubilation, Ian spied an uneasy look pass between Bethany and Evan before they joined in the congratulations.

Ian peered toward the farmhouse, then back to the celebration unfolding before him. The family party had become even more intimate. Capitalizing on the moment of jubilee, he made his exit, walked up the grassy hill and knocked on the screen door. Before he left, he wanted to check on Robin. Despite what she might think, he didn't like causing anyone grief.

When nobody answered, he walked around the house and spotted her still, slender frame sitting on the top step of the wraparound porch, the sun shimmering against her hair. She tucked a loose strand behind her ear, giving him access to her silhouette, her features sketched with warmth and sorrow. How had he missed it before? Passion and joy had filled the notes of her music...but something else had given it depth. The chord that had touched his soul? It had been a chord of sadness—a sound he wished he didn't know.

Despite his quiet approach, she looked up, away from whatever she had been examining in her hand. Ian closed the gap between them and sat beside her on the stoop. A strong breeze rustled through the tree towering in the front yard. The chain of the tire swing groaned as the treaded rubber swayed back and forth. "You okay?" he asked.

"I've had better days."

Ian peeked at the photograph in her hand. The man in the picture looked like a younger version of Evan. "Do you usually carry a photograph of him?"

Robin clasped the photo to her chest. "Don't you have anything better to do? Like woo my family?"

"Consider them wooed."

"You're very cocky."

"Confident is such a nicer word." He placed his hands behind him on the warm floorboards, bleached white from years of sun.

She leaned so far away that her back hugged the banister.

"You're not happy about your dad's news?"

Robin cocked her eyebrow. "On top of fixing ovens and child-rescuing, you like to play Dr. Phil too? Any other hidden talents I should know about?"

He smiled at his shoes. "So what, you don't like Donna?"

"Of course I like Donna."

"You want your parents back together?"

"My mother's dead."

"Oh." The breeze returned. It whispered through the branches of the tree until the boughs bent back and forth, like Mother Nature wagging her finger at him. "I'm sorry."

Robin twisted her wedding ring. "It was a long time ago."

"Time doesn't always make things easier."

She looked at him, then. Full in the face. Tangles of dark hair framed her cheeks, and the sadness in her eyes tugged at something deep in his chest. "No, it doesn't."

Staring straight at Robin's loss reminded him of his mother. If the cancer won—something he refused to believe possible—he couldn't imagine all the time in the world would dull the ache she'd leave behind. Setting his elbows on his knees, Ian spotted a penny lying on the dirt between his shoes. He picked it up, rubbed his thumb over the dull copper. When he looked back at Robin, a deep divot had etched itself in between her eyebrows and her lips were twisted to the side.

"Penny for your thoughts?" he said, holding out the coin.

She didn't take it.

"I'd love to know what you were just thinking."

"I was thinking about One Life. Last fall, they helped my employee, Molly, secure a new apartment after the bank foreclosed on her home."

He flipped the penny off his thumb, where it landed in the grass, a piece of treasure waiting for Caleb to discover. "Believe it or not, I'm sorry about the ministry."

"Just not enough to stop."

Ian pulled at his jaw, then gripped the back of his neck. He didn't choose the location. Robin blamed him for things outside his control. "If it were up to me, I'd build the condos elsewhere. Far away from your café and far away from One Life."

Robin looked down at her feet. A soft, pale pink painted her toenails.

"Do you really think I want to go to battle with the town saint?"

She jerked her head up. "Town saint?"

"I believe that's what Cecile Arton called you. Saint Robin, caretaker of the hurting and lonely." At the time, he assumed Robin was a typical do-gooder, helping the less fortunate so she could feel less guilty about her own good fortune. He had no idea she belonged to the very population she served. "Has a nice ring to it, don't you think?"

"I'm only doing what anybody else would do."

"That's not true. Otherwise every widow and orphan in this world would have full bellies. Last I read in the paper, that's not the case."

A blush the same color as her toenails painted Robin's cheeks, but her posture stiffened. "Why are you still here?"

"I'm waiting for you to listen to my offer."

"Fine. What is it?"

He blinked, then quoted his price.

The rosiness in her cheeks faded to chalky white.

He and his father had discussed it. They'd offer her as much as they could if it meant getting her to sell. "The mayor wants these condos. He's thrilled about them. Come Thursday, I'm willing to bet the rest of the town will be thrilled as well."

"Your overconfidence will be your downfall, Mr. McKay."

"Ian."

"You're underestimating Peaks." She lifted her chin. "And you're under-estimating me."

He took her in—from the blazing blue of her eyes, to the stubborn set of her jaw, to the determined slant of her narrow shoulders—and smiled. "Is that possible?"

"After losing my husband and single parenting and getting that café up and running, I've discovered something about myself."

It was his turn to cock his eyebrow.

"I know how to get back up after being knocked down. I'm a fighter, especially for things that matter to me, and let me tell you, Mr. McKay, that café matters. Despite the broken appliances and being short staffed and every other headache that comes with running a business, I love Willow Tree." Robin pushed herself up to standing and sandwiched the photograph between her palms. "So thank you for your offer, but no, thanks. I've listened, and I'm not interested."

Ian looked up at her, careful to keep his face neutral. He couldn't let her see how much her words shook him, not just because they boded ill for his plans, but because he couldn't help coveting her passion. "I guess I'll see you at the town meeting, then."

"I guess so." She walked away.

"Hey, Robin?"

She stopped and turned.

"I don't want to fight you on this."

"Then don't."

She said it like it was so simple. But if he gave up, the mayor would simply find another developer. Robin would still lose her café. One Life's ministry would still be shoved aside for condominiums. And Dad would be left to pick up the pieces of Ian's failure once again. "I don't have a choice."

She shoved the picture in her pocket. "There's always a choice," she said, and continued on her way.

Ian scuffed his shoes against the ground, the untruth of Robin's words scraping against tender scars.

EIGHTEEN

People used to warn us that the first year of marriage was the hardest. At my wedding shower, my great-aunt Ingrid, who was deaf in her right ear, told me very loudly to enjoy the honeymoon because lovemaking would eventually turn into a chore. Several of my older cousins nodded, like Aunt Ingrid had offered up a golden morsel of wisdom. People would look at Micah and me holding hands like they knew something we didn't. Like the minute Micah and I said "I do," our love would spoil and we'd stop touching.

It made me nervous.

So much so that on the plane ride home from our honeymoon, I braced for the change. I readied for a shift, mentally preparing myself for a souring that never came. Micah and I settled into married life like perfectly poured cement. As far as Aunt Ingrid? She couldn't have been more wrong. It was as if God had created Micah for me, and me for him. Living with him, sharing my life with him, was as easy as breathing.

Marrying Micah made me a believer in soul mates.

Then on our five-year anniversary, we decided to have a baby. The first time I took a pregnancy test, I was almost shocked at the single line. Micah and I did everything so well. I assumed pregnancy would be the same.

But it wasn't.

Getting pregnant became the thorn in our flesh. The one thing we couldn't get right. I remember sitting on the edge of our bed, twelve months of negative pregnancy tests littering our past, gripping the stick in my hand after the three minutes had expired, as if that second line was late in coming. Micah rubbed circles into my knee and I wanted to tear his hand away. I wanted to yell and scream and blame him for this thing that wasn't happening. Instead, I sat there—my heart cold and empty.

"This is going to happen. I know it will."

"It's been a year, Micah." A year of taking my temperature every morning. Charting my cycle. Swallowing vitamin B pills and knowing way too much about my cervical fluid. I'd even started drinking whole milk and forbidding my husband to wear anything tight around his manly parts. And Aunt Ingrid's long-ago prediction? It was coming true. Trying for a baby had turned sex into a chore.

"We should go see a doctor," I said.

"If that's what you want."

I nodded at the carpet. Never in a million years did I think I'd have to go on Clomid. Never in a million years did I imagine our future would involve fertility testing. But here we were, at the twelve-month mark and my womb remained barren. I felt like a failure.

Micah took my hand and squeezed my palm gently until I looked into his eyes. "Someday you are going to be a mother. A beautiful, amazing mother. We're going to be parents, Robin. I can feel it right here." He moved our hands to his chest and beneath the desperation, beneath the despair, I felt the faintest glimmer of hope. Micah could be so convincing. "We just have to be patient. God's timing is perfect."

Six months later, I had my positive pregnancy test. And Micah was in the hospital—brain dead.

NINETEEN

Dad and Donna took Caleb to a River Bandits baseball game. Enjoy a night off, they said. Relax and do something fun. Over the past four years, the words *something fun* entailed Chuck E. Cheese's or squirt gun fights or tents as big as a T. rex in the basement. Robin no longer knew what fun meant apart from her son. Which is why, after Dad and Donna and Caleb left, she sat in the kitchen, tapping her nail against the table, with no clue what to do with herself.

Bethany was at home with Evan and Elyse. Amanda was out with friends. And she—Robin Price—was Caleb-less for the night. Most mothers might find it refreshing. Robin found it unnerving. After thirty minutes of table-tapping, she grabbed her keys, drove to Willow Tree and attempted to fill the empty space with music. She played several of her mother's favorites—all the while thinking about Dad and Donna and the happy way they kept smiling at each other.

Robin's hands fell from the keys, her thoughts turning to Ian and One Life and Kyle and her town and Bethany and Evan and Amanda and Jason, and somewhere in the silence, a knock sounded against her window. She turned, expecting to find the Crammers, unaware that the café was closed for the holiday weekend. Instead, she saw Ian.

Swallowing the dryness in her throat, Robin walked to the entrance, unbolted the locks, and opened the door halfway. He stood on the other side with his hands in the pockets of his slacks, eyes twinkling, wearing the same blue-and-white checkered button-up and gray undershirt he'd worn at the picnic, except it was untucked and a five o'clock shadow had replaced his smooth shave.

"I'm closed," she said.

"So says your sign."

"Then what are you doing here?"

"Asking you the same thing."

She opened the door wider. "Were you spying again?"

"*Again* implies I spied a first time." He stepped inside, only she hadn't invited him in. "I was at the park across the street when I saw a light come on in your café."

"What were you doing in the park across the street?"

"Collecting my thoughts. Enjoying the swings, but then your light came on and I was curious. So here I am." He smiled, like this little encounter was entertaining.

"And here you go." She swept her hand toward the night outside.

But he stepped around her, scanning the loft overhead and the canvases on her walls. "It's nice like this."

"Like what?"

"Empty."

"You are quite the comedian."

He pivoted on his heels, his eyes wide with innocence. "Oh no. I'm being totally sincere. I always loved my grandpa's restaurant after close. It was peaceful."

"How nice." Her voice came out flat. Being alone in her café with the attractive condominium man was not how she pictured her evening. The day's events left her zapped of energy, almost to the point of delirium. She couldn't afford to be delirious in front of Ian McKay. "No offense, but I'm not really in the mood to talk about your offer or the condominiums."

"That makes two of us." He picked up a stray sugar packet from one of the tables and tossed it into his other hand. "Where's your little guy?"

"At a baseball game with my dad."

"Have you eaten dinner?"

"No."

Before she could object, he walked toward her kitchen. She hurried after him. "What do you think you're doing?"

"Making you dinner," he said, pushing through the door.

She slid in front of him, trying to ignore his warmth and the growingly familiar scent of wintergreen. "No, you're not."

He grabbed an apron hanging on the wall behind her and tied it around his waist.

"I'm sorry, but could you please get out of my kitchen?"

"I'm an excellent cook."

"Yeah. Right." Cooking. Fixing ovens. Charming families. Dr. Phil. The guy was too much.

"You think I'm lying?"

"I think it's irrelevant." Seriously, they were not doing this.

He tossed the sugar packet toward the trash can by her refrigerator. It sailed through the air and landed in the center with a faint plop. "Let's make a deal. You let me fix you something to eat. If you honestly don't like it—and you have to promise you'll be honest—I'll wave the white flag and leave Peaks forever. One Life will be safe and so will your café, at least from McKay Development and Construction."

Robin's lips fell apart.

"But"—he held up his finger—"if you do like it, you have to stop calling me Mr. McKay and start calling me Ian."

"You're serious?"

"I never ever joke in a kitchen."

"It seems like a pretty lopsided deal." She crossed her arms and sized him up, from his tan loafers to the small white scar above his left temple. "I don't understand why you'd make it."

"Because I love to cook, I'm a very confident chef, and Mr. McKay is my father."

"You should know that I'm an incredibly picky eater."

"Challenge accepted." He stepped around her and washed his hands in the sink. He dried them with a towel and walked into the refrigerator. Robin stood there, blinking at the door, not entirely sure what had just happened. How did she end up alone, in the small confines of her kitchen, with Ian McKay? It was so ludicrous that she almost wanted to giggle—a definite sign of delirium. He came out with a handful of ingredients and began dicing a tomato on her prep table. Decisive, even strokes. Robin stared at the hypnotic movement. His fingers were long and tan, with wide, neatly-trimmed fingernails shaped like squares.

"Were you two alike?" he asked.

"Who?"

"You and your mom."

She swallowed and looked away from his hands. "In a lot of ways."

"Tell me something about her."

Robin picked up a towel—folded it, unfolded it, folded, unfolded. What something could she say that might convey the loveliness that had been her mother? "Listening to her play the piano was like magic," she finally said. "Every song made me want to grab someone by the shoulders and ask if they were hearing what I was hearing. She had this way of making everyone feel like they were the most important person in the room. She would have spoiled Caleb rotten." She shot him a pointed look. "And she would have loved this café."

"I have no doubt." He picked up a red pepper and began chopping. "What else?"

"What do you want to know?"

"I don't know. Something special." The knife made a soothing staccato sound against the prep table. "Like your favorite memory of her."

One came to mind so swiftly and suddenly that a smile captured Robin's lips. "A couple weeks after my mom had been diagnosed with cancer, we went to the grocery store. She was adamant about making a pumpkin pie. According to her, pumpkin pie made everything better. Anyway, somebody spilled an entire bottle of vegetable oil in aisle nine."

"How does that happen?"

Robin shook her head. "I have no idea. While we were trying to avoid the mess, Mom slipped and fell. She couldn't get a hold on anything to pull herself up…the shelving, brownie mix boxes, powdered sugar. For the life of her, she couldn't get up. I tried to help, but the oil spread like The Blob and we both ended up on the floor. Oh my goodness"—her smile grew so wide it took over her entire face—"we were just laughing hysterically. It was paralyzing. We were probably stuck on the floor for fifteen minutes."

For weeks afterward, even amidst a gloomy prognosis, Robin and her mother could not look at each other without bursting into laughter. A bubble of hilarity rose in Robin's throat at the memory, but she clamped her hand over her mouth to keep it in.

Ian stopped chopping, a smile of his own pulling up the corners of his lips.

"My dad called it The Great Grocery Fiasco of '95." The memory of the slippery tile and her mother's oil-permeated pants expanded until the bubble burst. Robin giggled. Which turned into laughter, and then, somehow, Ian was laughing too, and she couldn't stop. The more she laughed, the more he laughed, until they were doubled over, wiping their eyes, gasping for breath. She placed her hand over her stomach, trying to compose herself. Ian wiped his cheek and shook his head, and when the laughter adequately subsided, took back the knife.

Robin filled her lungs with air and dabbed at her wet eyelashes. Man, that felt good. "What are you making?" she asked.

"A very easy, very delicious omelet. You can add it to your menu, if you'd like."

She leaned against the oven. "So where did you learn to cook, Dr. Phil?"

"My grandpa Vin, who owned the restaurant. I spent a lot of time in his kitchen." The tenor of Ian's voice was low, almost intimate. The sound of it made her skin prickle, and then her muscles tense, because what was she doing laughing and chatting with this man? She raked her teeth over her bottom lip, suddenly eager for Ian to leave.

He finished his chopping and looked up. "Frying pan?"

She grabbed the one hanging on the wall and set it on the stovetop while he cracked three eggs into a bowl with one hand, seasoning them with spices she hardly ever used.

"When I was a kid," he said, "I used to pretend I was a famous chef."

"Then how did you end up in the development business?"

He poured the scrambled eggs and the chopped vegetables into the pan. The sound of sizzling filled her tiny kitchen. "Because I'm my father's son, the future president of McKay Development and Construction."

"You don't sound too excited."

Ian shrugged, and crumbled a handful of goat cheese over the omelet. "Not everyone gets to do what they love. You're lucky that way."

Lucky? She was a widow. People didn't call her lucky very often.

When he finished, he slid the omelet onto a plate and handed it over. "Remember, you promised to tell the truth."

Robin picked up a fork and took a small, tentative bite. She wanted to hate it. She wanted to make a face and spit it out. Tell him she didn't like it and insist he hold up his end of the bargain. But she couldn't lie. It was the most delicious thing she had ever tasted.

His eyes crinkled. "So?"

"So I guess I have to stop calling you Mr. McKay."

TWENTY

The smell of fried cod clung to the air as people stood beneath white tents, drinking cold beer over abandoned plates of fish and tartar sauce. The sun beamed overhead, casting short, fat shadows across the grass that flickered and jolted to the country music beat blasting from the band shelter. A sticky breeze tussled Robin's hair. Caleb bobbed up and down by her side, his hand clasped in hers as his head swiveled back and forth, from the inflatable bouncer on their left to the short line of porta-potties on their right.

"Do you have to go potty?"

He shook his head, but Robin knew better. Pulling Caleb with her, she made a beeline for the right and kept one eye open for the man who insisted on disrupting her life. The man who claimed he had no choice. The man who showed up at her café on Saturday night and somehow distracted her with belly laughs and a delicious meal. A tricky bit of magic. Well, today she would not be distracted. Today, she had a plan. Robin stepped in line and watched her son potty dance. "You can make it, buddy. We're almost there."

Caleb crossed one leg over the other and puckered his brow. Robin squeezed his shoulder in moral support. When they reached the front, she pried open the door and stepped forward, but Caleb stopped her with his hands. "I can go by myself."

Yeah, and fall in. "Can't I come in with you?"

"I can do it myself!"

"Okay, but don't touch anything." Robin kept the door cracked and peeked inside. She could just see Caleb using the opportunity to check whether or not the tiny plastic triceratops in his pocket could swim. She shuddered. Porta-potties gave her the heebie-jeebies.

"Everything okay in there?"

She jumped and spun around. The master of distraction stood behind her. He'd foregone his usual pressed garb for a pair of well-worn jeans, cross-trainers, and a Cubs shirt. Micah had hated the Cubs.

"A little jumpy today, are we?" he asked.

"That's because you spoke directly in my ear." Robin took a step back. "Where's your shadow?" As soon as she said it, she clapped her hand over her mouth.

Ian laughed—a rich, husky sound. "My shadow?"

She shook her head, hand still covering her snafu. She liked the mayor. At least she used to. She had no business calling him a shadow.

"You mean the mayor?"

"I never said the mayor."

"Oh, right." He rocked back on his heels and stuck his thumbs through the belt loops of his jeans. "To answer your question, my shadow—"

She shot him a look.

"Excuse me. The *mayor* is right over there, if that's who you meant."

Robin followed the direction of his nod and spotted Mayor Ford with his wife. The pair conversed with Roy Hodges, her banker. Not more than two feet to their left, Amanda, Bethany, and a baby-toting Evan stood in a small group—sans Loraine and Jim, sans Dad and Donna, all of whom had flown home earlier in the morning.

"Amanda looks nice today," Ian said.

She narrowed her eyes.

He opened his wide. "What?"

"Amanda's been through the ringer these past couple of months."

"And?"

"She's easily enamored. I don't want to see her get hurt."

He held up his hands, showing her his palms.

The door of the porta-potty opened. Caleb stepped out, a corner of his

T-shirt tucked inside the band of his Spider-Man underwear, his shorts twisted. "See, Mommy, I told you I could do it by myself."

Robin shuffled him to the side, away from the line, then untucked his shirt and straightened his shorts. She dug in her purse for a small bottle of hand sanitizer and found it hiding beneath a stack of flyers and coupons. She took out the bottle and the flyers and squirted a dollop of sanitizer into Caleb's hands.

"What are those?" Ian asked, nodding at the stack of colorful papers.

Robin tossed the sanitizer in her purse. She'd been praying last night when the idea popped into her head. If she wanted to save Willow Tree and One Life, she had to be proactive about it.

Caleb grabbed Robin's hand. "Can we go jump now? Please?"

"How about you help me pass these out first?" She handed one of the flyers to Caleb.

He thrust it at Ian, then grabbed Robin's hand with both of his and tugged her toward the bounce house. "C'mon, Mommy. Let's go."

She dug her heels into the ground while Ian scanned the advertisement and held up the paper. "Am I allowed to use this?"

She plucked it out of his fingers. "You most certainly are not. These are only for people who don't wish ill will on my café."

"I wish no such thing."

"You want to tear it down."

"I'm just doing my job." Ian tucked his hands in his pockets. "Are you sure handing out free coffee is going to help your predicament?"

"Of course it will."

"Come"—tug—"on"—tug, tug.

"Caleb, honey, I'm talking right now. You need to be patient." She kept a firm grasp on her son's hand and addressed the man standing in front of her. "It's Business 101. Get customers in the door by offering them a freebie, wow them with said freebie, and they'll come back for more. The more people who support Willow Tree, the less inclined Mayor Ford will be to proceed with these plans of his."

"Uh-oh, Robin's not talking business, is she?" Amanda folded her arms over Caleb's chest and attacked his ribs. He let go of Robin, giggling and squirming until Amanda stopped. She put her hands on Caleb's shoulders and examined Robin's flyer. "All your late-night work paid off. They look nice."

"Hopefully next month's profit and loss report will look nice too." Robin peered at Ian, searching for signs, for cracks that she was getting to him. He only raised his eyebrow at her stare-down. She looked away and found Mayor Ford and Elaine approaching.

"Good afternoon Robin. Amanda." The sun glinted off the mayor's bald head. "There's some people over there I'd love to introduce you to, Ian."

"Care to join us?" Ian asked.

Was he nuts? Join Ian and Mayor Ford while they schmoozed with the town commissioners and council members? "I think I'll pass."

He shrugged, then held out his elbow to Amanda.

Robin's heart pounded. Surely her sister-in-law would take his proffered arm and Ian would smile that irritating smile and the pair would walk off without her. But Amanda didn't move. "Thanks, but I promised this little squirt I'd watch him jump in that blow-up contraption over there."

"Maybe some other time, then. Hey, good luck with those coupons." Ian winked and walked away.

Robin glared after him.

"Will you admit it now?" Amanda asked.

"Admit what?"

"You have a crush on Ian."

Robin huffed. "Believe me. I do not have a crush on Ian."

"Fine, then. The next time he asks me to join him, I'm not going to say no."

"Do whatever you want. I don't care." But as they headed to the bounce house, she knew that some part of her did care. The question was—why?

༄

Ian took a bite of his sandwich and tried to reel in his waning attention. How many people had Mayor Ford introduced already? Ten? Fifteen? As hard as he tried to concentrate on the conversation and the people in front of him, his attention kept returning to Robin passing out those ridiculous flyers while her son had a field day in the bounce house. The kid was going to knock somebody out with that cast.

The woman with the contagious laugh and the fiery eyes was the belle of the fish fry. And no wonder. She radiated so much warmth when she talked with people—a trait she must have inherited from her mother—that even Ian wanted to stand closer. He watched as Robin laughed and talked with an older man. She had him sign something and they shared a friendly hug before he strolled toward the dunk tank. The fried cod lost its flavor in Ian's mouth. It wasn't the first signature she'd collected. He wanted to know what she was up to. As if sensing his stare, Robin glanced in his direction— the third time in the span of ten minutes. When their eyes met, she didn't look away. She stared back with a look of proud defiance on her face. He forced himself to swallow the seafood while somebody new joined their group.

"Ian, this is John Broughton, editor-in-chief of the *Peaks Gazette*."

"A journalist, huh?" Ian shook hands with the stocky man in front of him.

"John here practically writes the whole paper," Mayor Ford said. "He's on the front page of every single issue, and he's got a knack for making me look good, which means we get along well."

"You make yourself look good." John crooked his thumb at the mayor. "Not something you can say about many politicians these days."

Ian looked at Robin through the mass of people. She spoke with three ladies who clutched coupons in their hands. "Are you searching for stories to run this week?"

John pulled a small recording device from his back pocket. "I'm always looking for stories. Why? You have one for me?"

"Has the mayor mentioned the topic of discussion for the town meeting this Thursday?"

"I've heard talk."

"Would you care to discuss it somewhere a little less noisy?"

John swept his arm in front of him, an invitation to lead the way. Ian led him to a clutter of picnic tables crammed beneath a tent, Robin's stare following them the entire way. Ian eased onto one of the benches. John sat across from him and held up his recorder. "You mind?"

"Not at all."

He pushed the record button and set the device between them. "So what's this business about condominiums? I've heard some whispers, but it's all pretty nebulous right now."

"I'm hoping this article will clear things up and spread the word about the upcoming town meeting."

"What's the word?"

"McKay Development and Construction—my father's company—is in the process of acquiring a site for condominiums the mayor wants built in Peaks."

"So that's what the meeting will address?"

"The mayor needs the town's approval before he can add the condominiums to the development plan for the downtown area."

"Does Mayor Ford foresee a problem?"

"Potentially." Ian steepled his fingers beneath his chin. "The site we need to acquire is on the south end of the business district. Two of the businesses have already agreed to sell, but the other is not being as cooperative. The owner is making things a little tricky."

John's eyes sparked. The man seemed to like *tricky*. "Who's the owner?"

"Me," Robin said.

John turned before Ian did. Ian had seen her approaching from the corner of his eye ever since John hit the record button. "Good afternoon, John," she said.

The journalist turned off the recording device. "This other building is yours?"

"You two know each other?" Ian asked.

"John wrote a story on my café when it first opened. A very well-written piece about what a fine establishment it was. About how it added to the cozy, family-feel of this town." Robin crossed her arms and eyed the re-corder. "What story are you writing now?"

"Ian is telling me about these condominiums."

"His version is very lopsided," she said.

"Tell me your version, then. I could run a parallel story. Your take versus his take, give the town all the facts, and see who wins. News has been pretty dry around here lately. I think we're all getting sick of reading about this recession." John pressed record and looked at Robin. "What do you say?"

She bit her lip.

"I'm game if you're game," Ian said, nodding at her clipboard. "What do you have there?"

"A petition to save One Life. There are many in this town who depend on the ministry and even more who support its mission. They aren't going to want to see it shut down. And they're not going to want to see Peaks over-run by a bunch of Fixtel employees, either."

Ian smiled. He couldn't help it. Robin was cute when she was heated. "You have something against these employees?"

"I don't have anything against them, but they aren't Peaks. I don't want to see the character of this town change and I especially don't want to see people who depend on One Life shoved aside in the process. Neither do these individuals." She held the petition up higher. There were more signa-tures than he wanted to see.

"This is good." John moved the recorder closer to Robin. "What else?"

"The sale of Sybil's is contingent upon the sale of Willow Tree. Which means if I sell, One Life loses their space."

"How about apart from One Life? Why should Willow Tree Café mat-ter to Peaks?"

John's question seemed to stump her. She continued her lip-nibbling and glanced over her shoulder at Caleb and Amanda. "My café is a place of community. We have church functions there. It hosts the PTA fund-raiser at the end of every school year. We had the meet and greet for Kyle last weekend."

"Couldn't they hold those events somewhere else?" Ian asked. "Like the place I saw on the north end of town. Shorney's Terrace?"

Her forehead knotted and she twisted her wedding ring. As if so many spins would wind her up with more arguments. When none seemed to come, she closed her eyes for a moment longer than normal and expelled a long breath. "Remember last year, John? When we were afraid the river was going to flood again? Where do you think everyone came for a hot cup of coffee and a treat in the middle of all that sandbagging? Willow Tree is an important part of this town. It's the place mothers come to relax and catch up with girlfriends while their children play in the kids' corner. You can step inside my café and enjoy the food and the music and the atmosphere and somehow, life doesn't feel so crazy anymore." She paused and looked down at her petition. "I know I can't offer much in the way of tax revenue or boosting the town's economy, but Willow Tree Café represents what so many people love about this town. It would be a shame to see it go."

John waited, as if to make sure Robin had finished her speech, then scooted the recorder toward Ian.

He removed his chin from his knuckles. "So basically, your café represents the old, and my condominiums represent the new. I think we can agree that the old isn't working out so well."

The faintest of breaths toppled from her parted lips.

His chest tightened, but he forced himself to bat away the guilt and focus on the jobs he was saving. Dad had enough to worry about with Mom. He didn't need the added burden of laying off a bunch of employees. "Your speech was nice, but if what you're saying is true, if Willow Tree represents what people love about Peaks, then I have to say, not many people love this town. You don't seem to have very many customers."

She winced.

He squished his tongue against the roof of his mouth and refused to apologize. The quicker he could get her to surrender, the quicker he could stop hurting her. "I admire your passion, Robin, but Peaks needs revenue, not coffee."

She pulled back her shoulders, her lips thinning into a thin, straight line. "I guess we'll see what Peaks needs on Thursday." And with that, she spun around and stalked away.

John sighed. "It's really too bad."

"What?"

"All of it. That her café is struggling and the spot you want to build is the place where Willow Tree is located." John pocketed his recorder. "Like Robin said, I wrote that article when her place opened. It did okay the first year. Sort of a novelty, you know? But the novelty wore off and the economy got worse. Still, she kept it going. I've never met a woman so passionate about something."

The familiar pull returned, stronger this time. "What is it about that place?"

"She built it after her husband died. She and her friend over there." John pointed to Bethany. "I think it represents healing, maybe. Or hope."

Something uncomfortable squirmed in Ian's gut. And it wasn't the food.

TWENTY-ONE

The cash register dinged open, a glorious sound that repeated itself throughout the morning. Robin hurried to the kitchen and removed a batch of red velvet cupcakes from the oven. Hot and fresh. Her customers wouldn't be able to resist them. The tips of her fingers smarted as she scooted each cupcake onto the cooling rack. Taking one last whiff of cocoa, she pushed through the door to join Joe.

Her chest swelled. For the second day in a row, she had a line in her café. An actual line. Yesterday, for the first time in years, she had run out of food. If not for making a fresh batch of chocolate fudge brownies in the afternoon, she wouldn't have had anything to bring to the kids at One Life's afterschool program. Robin pictured Piper Greeley—a red-haired, freckle-faced girl with knobby knees and sticky fingers, not much taller than Caleb. She smelled like cigarettes and wore the same purple shirt with a stretched-out collar every time Robin saw her. As soon as she brought in the brownies, Piper squealed and flung her skinny arms around Robin's waist, jabbering about how much she loved chocolate.

Joe handed a woman change and a tall cup, then took the next woman's order. Robin swept past him and positioned herself at the espresso machine. After a stretch of several frantic minutes, with Joe taking orders and her filling them, the line disappeared. Her doors opened and closed. And except for one patron crinkling through a newspaper in a corner seat, her café emptied.

Robin leaned against the counter. "That was great."

Joe closed the register and held up a wad of multicolored papers. "Except most of them had these again."

The rush of busyness dimmed as Joe fanned the coupons apart like a hand of cards. "You sure gave a lot of them away."

"I thought they'd be good for business." She ran her hands down her apron. "We're building clientele. Those people will fall in love with our coffee and keep coming back."

Right?

She refused to let the pathetic squeak of a word escape. Of course she was right. She had a two-part plan. First, get people through her doors and remind them why Willow Tree did so well that first year. The second part— where they returned as loyal customers willing to fight against Ian and his condominiums—would follow.

Joe pressed his palm against the top of his head, momentarily flattening his flyaway curls. "If you're right, then you're going to need another employee. I can't work all those shifts you've got me scheduled for next week. Not with the classes I'm taking this summer."

Joe was right, of course. If this continued, and she prayed it would, she would need more workers. Between Joe and Molly and Amanda's willingness to step in from time to time, Robin had a hard time finding a schedule that didn't involve her working every minute the café was open. And that wasn't fair to Caleb. But how could she afford to hire another employee when, thanks to her ingenious coupon idea, her increased clientele wasn't bringing in much profit? She buried her face in her hands. Why couldn't life be easy for once?

"This probability and statistics course is kicking me in the rear. Math and I don't get along so well." Joe grabbed a stack of coffee cups wrapped in plastic, poked through the top and pulled the plastic away. "Do you mind if I take my break? I need to pick up a prescription at CVS."

"No, of course not." She pulled her hands away from her face.

The man in the corner rolled up his newspaper and came to the counter. Robin racked her brain, trying to recall his name. He worked at John Deere. An engineer. Married to Betsy, a constantly exhausted-looking woman with four boys under the age of four. Every time Robin saw her, she wanted to give the woman a hug.

"That coupon I got on Monday said free refills."

What in the world had possessed her to put free refills on a coupon? Robin forced a smile, filled his cup a little farther from the brim than she might have if worry wasn't burrowing its way beneath her skin, and handed him his drink.

"Thanks, Robin. I haven't had coffee this great in a long time."

"I hope you come back." *Man. What is his name?*

"You read this yet?" He flicked the paper. "Interesting article." Mr. No-Name nodded farewell and left the café.

Robin unrolled the paper and came face to face with a large picture of Ian McKay, just as annoyingly dashing in black and white, and beneath him, the logo of McKay Development and Construction. The headline blazed, "A Battle Ensues: Old Versus New."

She skimmed the article. Words about tax revenue and building the town's economy. Boosting local business and a picture of McKay condominiums. They looked classy and well built. Especially beside a current picture of the area. Finally she came to her side of the story. A paltry paragraph. Her concerns about One Life and the population boom and how much she loved her café. All of which sounded incredibly lame next to Ian's fancy statistics.

Heat pricked the back of her eyes. Crumpling up the paper, she shuffled to the wall and brushed her fingers across the surface of her favorite canvas, wishing, more than anything, she could crawl inside and return to that carefree time and space—when Micah was alive and their love was invincible and Robin wasn't a widowed mother trying to save a struggling café. She brought her fingers over her lips, as if touching them might connect her to her husband.

She and Bethany had printed these pictures on canvases and hung them as soon as the paint dried. Every pounded nail, every paint stroke, the polished floor beneath her and the tables in front linked her past and her future—pain and hope encased in the mortar of a building. She'd poured her broken heart into this café, her dreams, her sorrow and regret, until the walls pulsed with healing, pulsed with memories, pulsed with hope. Robin's hand fell to her side. She sat on the piano bench and stroked the keys.

Micah had been her middle C—his life, their marriage, his love had determined where all the other notes of her life fell. When he died, the café took his place. The café became her middle C, her grounding point. And now Ian wanted to take it away. He wanted to banish it from existence.

Lord, I thought You wanted me to fight. How can I possibly win if You don't help me?

Her eyes blurred the keys into an indistinct mass of ivory and ebony. She placed her hands over them and began to play. Phrasing, articulation, tempo adjustments. Everything her mother taught her fell from conscious thought, until the music ebbed and flowed inside her fingers. She depressed the soft pedal with her left foot and let the muted, mysterious notes pour out, an otherworldly tune that matched the churning in her soul.

∾

Raindrops landed on the newspaper in Ian's hand, melting into the words and pictures. He tucked it beneath his arm and trotted up the stairs, through the thick drizzle, until he stood beneath the awning of Willow Tree. He wanted to show Robin the article. She'd put on her boxing gloves at the fish fry, and it was his turn to do the same.

Running into John Broughton on Monday had been fortunate. Nobody would miss the front-page story. Tomorrow, the people of Peaks would show up at the town hall ready to listen. And hopefully, ready for change. Ian shook out his wet hair and peered inside the front window.

His attention traveled over the empty tables and landed on Robin, her hair gathered and swept over her shoulder, giving him an unencumbered view of her back as she sat straight and moved her hands over the piano keys. She wore a sundress the same color as the purple lilacs Dad planted on the side of their house when Ian was ten.

As soon he opened the door, her notes blew around him like a warm breeze. Slow and hauntingly beautiful. The music knocked on his chest, an irresistible tapping that beckoned him to sit and listen. To soak in the music the way his mother used to soak in the smell of those lilacs every spring. But he couldn't afford to get sidetracked now. So he blocked out the melody and spotted a crumpled newspaper on the floor.

She'd seen it. And obviously hadn't liked it. He took a few more steps inside and steeled himself for her anger. For the moment she would turn around and spot him in the doorway. Her eyes would flash. She'd dismiss the article, claim that the citizens of Peaks cared more about One Life than tax revenue, and then she'd probably try to kick him out again.

The music stopped in the middle of a refrain. The sudden quiet jarred the air. She didn't turn around. She didn't move a muscle. She sat in the thickening silence. Then dropped her head into her hands and wept.

The café lurched. Throwing his determination not just off balance, but away. His calf muscles twitched. One leg moved closer. The other wanted to step toward the exit. And in the midst of his indecision, Robin turned, tears glistening on her cheeks, those blue eyes filled with equal parts sorrow and desperation. All because of him. He'd placed that desperation there. With his stupid news article. He took a step closer.

"Please…" Her whispered word came out dry and cracked, like the desert floor, making him thirsty for something he couldn't define. "Please, leave."

Ian listened. He hightailed it outside, where the drizzle had turned into fat, wet drops that splattered against his eyelashes and hair. He punched in the office number on his phone, hurrying toward the parking lot of Willow Tree Café until the receptionist answered. "Good morning. McKay Development and Construction."

"Good morning, Sue. It's Ian. Can you put me through to my dad, please?"

"Hold on just a minute, Ian. I think Jim's in his office."

The rain soaked through Ian's shoulders and stuck to his skin. After a beat, Dad's voice came on the other line. "Ian? Everything okay?"

No, nothing was okay. He either crushed Robin's dreams or lost people their jobs—like Jim, who despite his suggestions last week, was a nice guy with a family to take care of and a wife who needed health insurance. There had to be a better way. "Listen, Dad, I wanted to run something by you." He ran his hand through wet hair. "I'd like to offer Robin Price first-floor ancillary use of our condominiums."

The rain fell harder. Dad's silence gave him too much time. Resentment built—for this job, for the position it placed him in. For the briefest of moments, he imagined leaving. He gazed at Arton's through the downpour and pictured a restaurant there instead, something like Grandpa Vin's Italian bistro. What might it be like, not living with his father's legacy weighing on his shoulders? Ian dismissed the idea. He had responsibilities. He couldn't ditch them because things were hard. That's not who he was.

"Where's this coming from?" Dad finally asked.

"She doesn't want to sell and she loves her café. It's a nice establishment. It could work with our condominiums."

"It's your call, Ian. Usually we rent out the space to a boutique or a chain. Something more established. But if you think renting the space out to Robin will get her to sell, then by all means, go right ahead."

Robin's face swam in his mind. Her tears and her sorrow. This was the best option. The only way to make them both winners.

"You can let me know how things go this weekend."

"Thanks, Dad. I'll see you at the banquet."

Ian powered off his phone and did an about-face, back toward the dryness of the café, and used the wet sleeve of his shirt to wipe away the drops of rain rolling down his temple. As soon as he walked inside, Robin looked up—her tears gone, her eyes red. She was no longer alone and the crumpled newspaper was gone. Joe, the young man with the crazy hair, wiped off one of the tables and stepped behind the register, but Robin intercepted Ian before he reached the front counter. She tucked her hair behind her ears, her attention sweeping over his wet shirt and even wetter hair. "What do you want?"

"I have an offer to make."

"We already did this."

"This is a better offer."

"I told you, I don't care about money."

"What if you could keep your café and I could build my condos?"

Robin hugged her middle and took a small step back. "Then neither of us would have a problem."

"What do you think about renting out first-floor space for Willow Tree? You'd have a built-in clientele. A brand-new space. It would be perfect. I know this is all coming out of left field, but it makes a lot of sense." The more he thought about it, the more he warmed to the idea. What might it be like, working alongside Robin, instead of against her?

"What about One Life?"

Ugh. In his zest to fix Robin's heartache, he'd forgotten all about the ministry. His mind scrambled for a solution. Maybe they could rent first-floor space too. But as soon as the idea formed, Ian had to dismiss it. That wouldn't work. Rent would be too expensive and the entire landscape of the south side of town would be different. If people like the Crammers already struggled to walk inside One Life's doors, how much less inclined would they be to do so with posh condominiums surrounding the place?

Robin shook her head.

Ian wanted to grab hold of her face and make her stop. "We can figure something out with One Life."

"I appreciate your offer, but I can't."

"You can't?" What kind of nonsense was this? Of course she could. All she had to do was sell him her deed and he'd ensure she got prime retail space on the first floor of his condominiums.

"I have a petition filled with signatures from people who care about One Life. One of those signatures is mine. I'm not going to sell them out."

Ian ran his hand through his hair. "Surely if we put our heads together, we can figure out what to do with the ministry."

"I'm sorry."

He couldn't believe it. She was throwing the solution in his face. "You're sorry?"

"What else do you want me to say?"

"A detailed explanation might be nice. Some insight as to why you just threw an excellent deal away without at least considering it first."

"What about you? Explain to me why you care so much all of a sudden. Where's all of this even coming from?"

He stepped closer. "Believe it or not, I'm not in the business of destroying a person's dreams. Especially not a good one like this."

Robin hugged her waist tighter, her eyes wide, as if his answer—or maybe his nearness—frightened her. "My dream isn't running any café. It's running this one."

"It will still be this café."

"No, it wouldn't."

"You're saying no because you've grown attached to some walls?" Ian brought his hand to the back of his neck and studied the lighting, the loft overhead, the high windows revealing a mass of gray clouds. "Look, Robin, I understand switching spaces would be a giant hassle. I understand it will make for a busy, slightly hectic season in your life. I understand change is a scary thing, but this is the best I can do. This offer is the only way I can see us both coming out on top."

She bit her lip.

He stepped closer, catching the scent of cocoa and nutmeg, as if the ingredients Robin used so often had soaked into her skin and hair. "We can come up with a solution for One Life. I know we can."

Robin looked left, right, up, down. Anywhere but straight ahead. Ian wanted to step into her line of vision and force her to see him. Convince her that this was the only way he could stop hurting her. But her chest rose and fell with an expelled breath and by the time she looked at him, stubbornness had settled in her eyes. "I'm sorry, but my answer is no."

TWENTY-TWO

Ian slammed the door of his car and strode toward the farmhouse, wet gravel crunching beneath black leather shoes. If Robin wouldn't see reason, maybe her friend would. Maybe Bethany could convince her to stop fighting what would surely become a losing battle.

He stepped onto the porch. The front door swung open and Evan clomped out in his work boots, holding a coffee mug to his mouth in one hand and a small wooden birdhouse in his other. He stopped short and eyed Ian over the top of the mug. "What are you doing here?"

Ian ran his hand down the front of his shirt, thankful he'd dried out since standing in the rain. "I was hoping to speak with Bethany."

"What do you have to say to my wife?"

"I wanted to talk to her about doing some work for McKay Development and Construction. We're always looking for talented architects." And he needed to figure out why Robin was so desperate to hold onto a building.

"You're a piece of work, you know that?"

Ian's hackles rose. "Excuse me?"

"There's something you should know about Bethany. She's loyal and she loves Robin. They're closer than most sisters."

"What does Robin have to do with it?"

"You're a smart guy, Ian. I don't appreciate you playing dumb. Especially on my front porch." Evan took a sip of his coffee. "I let you stay here for the picnic because I wasn't going to cause a scene in front of my nephew, who, for whatever reason, seems to like you. But don't mistake my family's politeness. Our allegiance lies with Robin. We don't want your condominiums."

"Amanda doesn't seem to think they're a bad idea."

Evan's posture didn't change, but his knuckles whitened over the handle on his mug. "My sister is friendly. And young and impulsive. But she loves Robin like the rest of us. When it comes to choosing sides, don't think it'll be yours. The same goes with a lot of people in this town."

"I'm not trying to turn your wife against Robin, Mr. Price. I'd just like to speak with her, if that's okay with you."

Evan studied him for a drawn-out moment, then pushed the front door open with his foot. Beside the couch, Elyse rocked in a swing, reaching her pudgy, dimpled hand toward the rotating mobile overhead. She had a fuzzy bear beside her and a tiny pink sock dangled from her toes. Ian looked away from the perfect picture the baby painted.

Bethany sat cross-legged on the sofa, a pencil tucked behind her ear and a laptop opened in front of her on the coffee table. Evan bent over his wife and whispered something. She eyed Ian through the opened door with one part curiosity and two parts suspicion. "We can talk on the porch," she said.

Ian wanted to laugh. Would he defile their home by entering it? He swallowed the retort and waited for the couple to step out into the soupy air.

"I'm going to take this over to Amanda." Evan held up the birdhouse and kissed Bethany full on the lips.

Ian blinked down at the faded welcome mat. His parents were exactly the same, forever reminding him of the mess that had been his own marriage. Bethany ran her hand through her hair and watched Evan go. When he climbed inside his old Bronco and pulled down the gravel drive, she folded her arms. "What can I do for you?"

She had an edge to her. Something professional. Or maybe reserved. She looked more informed, more savvy than the other town folk. As if she'd seen more of the world than the rest of them. "I looked through the portfolio on your website. You're very talented."

"Thank you."

"McKay Corporation is always looking for architects with an innovative vision. We'd love to have you do some work for us."

She crooked an eyebrow.

"Whatever your husband thinks, this isn't about choosing sides. You could be a stranger, no connection whatsoever to Robin and her café, and I'd still make you an offer."

"But I'm not a stranger, and I am connected to Robin and her café. So my answer is obviously no."

"Fine, then. What about after this all blows over? Could I contact you then?"

"That depends on how everything plays out."

"Can I have your business card, at least?"

She stood there, deliberating, then went inside and returned with a small white card.

He tucked it in his back pocket and held out his own. "Here."

"I don't want it."

"Just take it."

She took the card between her fingers.

"You and Robin seem close."

"We are."

"Do you mind if I ask you a question?"

"You just did."

He smiled. Bethany had spunk. "What is it with Robin and that café? Why is it so important to her?"

"It's not really my story to tell."

"Look, Bethany, despite what you and your husband believe, I don't want to bulldoze Robin's dreams to the ground. In fact, I tried to make her an offer today that would solve both of our problems, only she refused." More than refused. She acted as if his offer flat-out scared her. "I'm a little baffled by it."

"What was your offer?"

"First-floor condo space so she could keep her café."

Bethany's face softened.

"I understand her concern about One Life, but could you talk to her? Help her see reason? Otherwise, she's going to sink right alongside that ministry." Ian rubbed the back of his neck, a vision of a weeping Robin stuck on repeat in his mind. A familiar feeling of helplessness pressed against him. He was scrambling to fix things, only he couldn't do it. He could never do it. "This is the best I can do. It's this, or nothing."

"What I say won't make much of a difference."

"I think you're underestimating yourself. She values your opinion."

"Ian, you're underestimating what that café means."

"Tell me what it means, then."

She scratched her elbow and peeked over her shoulder, toward the living room, where baby Elyse was swinging off into nap-time oblivion. "Willow Tree was a dream they shared."

"They?"

Bethany looked at him, as if waiting for something to click.

"Oh." *They.*

"We built that café while she was pregnant with Caleb, right after she lost Micah. We renovated it from the ground up. Ripped out walls, put new ones in. Painted. Reconstructed the staircase. You name it, we did it. The project brought Robin back to life."

Ian bowed his head. How could he compete with that?

"That building means a lot more to her than brick and wood. It holds four years' worth of memories, most of which include Caleb."

He scuffed his shoe against the floorboard. Why did his heart have to twist for a woman he hardly knew?

"These condominiums of yours. Are they really that important?"

The question echoed inside of him. As much as he hated the answer, he couldn't bat it away. He might have failed in his personal life, but he had yet to fail in his corporate one. These condominiums were Ian's chance to do something right. He could save the employees of McKay Development and Construction from unemployment. Make Dad proud and prove that he wasn't a quitter. Ian couldn't walk away. Not even for a woman he didn't want to hurt.

∽

The house was quiet. Robin had taken Caleb to the theater to watch a Mickey Mouse throwback playing through next week. Amanda relished the silence. She loved Caleb, but living with a three-year-old didn't give her many moments of calm. It was good in a lot of ways. He didn't give her a chance to pout or sulk, not when there were trains to play with and forts to build and bad guys to fight.

His energy forced her to hurdle the pain Jason left behind, but sometimes she wondered if the hurdling had drawn out the grief. Sometimes she wondered if it wouldn't have been better to let herself experience it in the beginning—like a Band-Aid torn off quickly. A burst of intense pain that stung and went away. That had to be better than this slow peel of heartache she experienced now. Her rush to forget had left her with a residual sadness she couldn't quite shake.

Jason's latest e-mail only made it worse.

She crept into the two-car garage, crawled onto the hood of her Honda, and stood on her tiptoes. Batting away cobwebs, she pulled a fishing pole and a dusty tackle box down from the rafters, brought both inside, and got to work untangling the fishing line—an attempt to distract herself from the computer. She would not open her e-mail. She already reread Jason's reply at least a dozen times and every time she did, she wanted to smack herself with a pillow. Or something harder.

He wasn't coming back. As much as she searched for clues, he never alluded to that in his e-mail. He was in Nairobi and he missed her, but not enough to come home and propose and promise her the forever she used to think he'd promise. So what was she doing? She had no desire to spend her life in Africa. He hadn't even asked her. She tied a small weight on the fishing wire and brought the pole outside.

As a kid, tagging along with four older brothers meant spending a lot of time with a fishing pole in hand. Lately, she craved the mindless activity of casting out a line and waiting for something to bite. Perhaps she should teach Caleb. He'd probably scare away the fish with his dinosaur growls and constant motion, but at least she'd be out of the house. Amanda brought the pole back and cast out into the wet lawn when a familiar Bronco grumbled into the driveway.

Evan parked his car and hopped out. "Catch anything?"

"Nothing's biting."

He pulled out a small, cardinal-red birdhouse from the front seat. "I come bearing gifts."

She reeled in the line and cast out into the yard again. "You finally finished, huh?"

"It only took me two months." He stopped in front of her and held it up.

She traded—one slightly worn fishing pole for one gorgeous homemade birdhouse—then twirled it around to examine the creation. So far, Robin had let Amanda hang three different ones in various trees throughout the yard. She wondered if she could get away with a fourth. "It's beautiful, Ev. Thank you."

"Thank *you*. Not all accountants accept birdhouses as payment. It's kind of a weird fetish, but I'll go with it." He reeled in her line and examined the pole. "It's been a long time since I went fishing."

"I was thinking I'd take Caleb to the creek behind your farm." She set the birdhouse on the front stoop and took back the pole. "What are the chances we'll catch something other than floating bark?"

He didn't answer. Instead, he scratched at the scruff on his jaw and stared at a squirrel chattering beneath a forsythia bush. Not a good sign. That look was Evan-speak for "I'm about to give you a lecture."

"Why'd you invite Ian to the picnic?"

And there it was. "Because he's cute and because I like him."

"The guy's a developer."

"Sheesh, Ev, you're such a bigot. Not all developers are evil, you know."

"They are if they're trying to tear down Robin's café."

She rolled her eyes. Sometimes having older brothers could be such a pain. Especially when said older brother wanted to reprimand her for something she was already regretting. Inviting Ian to the picnic hadn't been her brightest move. "So what? You came over to lecture me?"

"No, I came over to give you your birdhouse. I wasn't planning on lecturing you until Ian McKay showed up on my front porch, asking Bethany if she'd like to do business with him."

"Seriously?"

"The only reason he knows to ask is because you invited him to our picnic and started yapping about all the buildings Bethany renovated downtown."

She cast the line toward the squirrel. The weight dropped in the bush and the critter scurried away. "She can thank me for the referral later."

"This isn't a joke, Amanda."

"I'm not laughing, *Evan*." Thunder rumbled in the distance. The forecast called for spotty showers throughout the day. She reeled in the line quickly, picked up the birdhouse and went inside. She didn't want to get wet. And maybe Evan wouldn't follow. She wiped her bare feet on the rug and set the birdhouse on the couch beside her laptop. The one she wasn't going to open.

"It was a tactless move," he said, stepping in behind her.

"Tactless?"

"Yes, tactless. So was inviting Kyle."

Her muscles tightened. "He likes Robin. Sue me for wanting to give the man a second chance."

"She doesn't want you throwing men at her feet."

"I didn't throw anyone. And even if I did have the strength to pick up a full-grown man and throw him at Robin's feet, she would step right over the guy. In case you haven't noticed, big brother, she avoids men like the plague. I think they scare her."

"Robin's not afraid of men."

Now she did laugh. "I swear, you are blind. Did you not see her at the picnic? Her avoidance of Kyle bordered on artistic. I almost started clapping."

"Would you be serious?"

Amanda propped the fishing pole against the sofa table. "Okay, fine. You want to get serious? Let's get serious. I've been living in this house for two years and I'm officially creeped out by that picture of my brother." She pointed to the framed photograph from Robin and Micah's wedding perched on the mantle. "There's one in Caleb's room too."

"Your point?"

"My point, Evan, is that Micah died when Caleb was a baby bean."

"So you think she should forget about our brother? Pretend he never existed?"

"I didn't say that. Please don't put words in my mouth."

"Caleb deserves to know his father."

"Caleb deserves to *have* a father."

"He has me."

Her heart softened. "You're just an uncle, Ev. A really great uncle. But you have a farm to run and a wife and a kid and, judging by the way you and Bethany look at each other all the time, more on the way. You can't be Caleb's father. No matter how hard you try."

"So according to you, Robin's obligated to get married so Caleb can have a dad?"

"Don't be stupid."

"This whole conversation is stupid."

She crossed her arms, probably to keep herself from picking up the birdhouse and chucking it at Evan's head. "You started it."

Evan glared.

Amanda eyed her computer. Maybe it would be better if she chucked that at her brother's head. Two birds, one stone.

"Robin's going to need your support on Thursday," he said.

"She'll have it."

"I hope so." Evan pushed open the door and walked to his car.

She stomped over and stuck her head outside. "Thanks for the birdhouse, jerk!"

He threw a dismissive wave over his shoulder. She gritted her teeth as he reversed out of the drive. She wanted to take his birdhouse and throw it out the window. She wanted Evan and Robin to let go of the past. She wanted Jason and her dying dreams to combust into flames and float away like ash.

That wasn't too much to ask, was it?

She plopped onto the couch and did the one thing she promised she wouldn't do. She opened her laptop, let out a long, defeated breath, and re-read Jason's words.

TWENTY-THREE

Most sixteen-year-olds spend their time behind a wheel, driving just because they can. In a small town like Peaks, that meant teenagers circled a well-traveled loop, stopping at places like the old movie theater on Seventh and Val's Diner on Main, drinking milkshakes and shooting spit wads across checkered flooring. Or taking the occasional back road to see if cows really could be tipped.

That was my plan.

Bethany, however, had no interest in the well-worn loop. And she knew cows didn't sleep standing up. She wanted to ditch Peaks and drive to far-off cities like Los Angeles and New York. So we spent our freshman year of high school planning and plotting everything we'd do the minute I stepped out of the DMV with my driver's license.

We had no idea that instead of driving with my dad to the DMV, we'd be riding in a limousine to a funeral. We had no idea cancer lurked in my mother's brain, eating it from the inside out. We had no idea that instead of fun and friendship meeting behind the wheel of a new car, solace and grief would meet beneath the branches of our willow tree. The very branches Bethany and I had spent entire summers swinging from, splashing into the water. Clueless that one day, the same willow that brought so much laughter would cradle my tears.

I leaned my head against the rough bark, lifted my wrist to my nose, and inhaled the scent of my mother's perfume. It seemed impossible that only yesterday I'd sat in a fold-up chair at the funeral, wondering what to do with my hands, my heart, and the now empty space at our kitchen table.

A car door slammed in the distance.

"That's the fifth one today," Bethany said, twirling a long blade of grass between her fingers.

"Six if you count repeat visits." Ever since Mom's death, a constant stream of visitors showed up on our doorstep, bearing warm meals and sad faces. I was tired of seeing them. Tired of the constant reminder that Mom was gone, and I was still here. Bethany must have known, because this morning, when the doorbell rang twice in the span of a single hour, she rolled her eyes and brought me here—to our tree.

"Do you want to go to a movie tomorrow night?" she asked.

"Tomorrow's Sunday."

"So?"

"So we order pizza and play Scrabble on Sundays." Bethany and I had been eating pizza and playing Scrabble with my parents every Sunday since we first met at Peaks Laundromat four years ago. My mother was a Scrabble queen. All four of us liked to make up words.

"I thought you'd want to do something different."

I sat with her suggestion, letting it soak while a bullfrog croaked to the waning daylight, until I decided I couldn't do that to my father. I couldn't leave him alone at our house. I couldn't throw a last-minute change into our well-established routine. "I think we should keep it the same," I said. "For my dad."

Bethany shrugged.

And that's what we did. For the next three years.

We ate Mom's favorite pizza and played Scrabble every Sunday night. Until Bethany went away to college. The very next Sunday, Dad ordered Chinese. He poked at noodles with his chopsticks and sat in his recliner while the television flickered with football. He looked happy. Or maybe relieved.

I spent the evening in my room, moving Scrabble squares across the board.

TWENTY-FOUR

The parking lot was so full, cars lined both sides of the street, making Robin's nerves wind tighter. When was the last time so many people had shown up for a town meeting? She squeezed Caleb's hand and hurried across New Town Avenue. Her son had to run to keep up.

"Mommy, do the bad guys want to steal our café?"

"They're not bad guys, honey." Not really.

"Are they good guys?"

Caleb lived in a world where people were either good or bad. In between did not exist. At times, she coveted his simplistic outlook. "They're just guys doing what they think is best."

Caleb's brow furrowed. He obviously didn't think that answered his question. She glanced at her watch and lengthened her stride.

"Can you tell me the café story again, Mommy? The one about me and you and Daddy?"

Her son loved that story. She told it so often that he adopted the memory as his own. "I'll tell you tonight, okay, buddy?"

Nodding, Caleb made an imaginary gun with his pointer finger and thumb. "Well, I'm gonna get those bad guys with my shooter."

Robin set her hand on Caleb's shoulder and pushed him along. She could not miss any part of this meeting. "You're not going to get anyone with your shooter."

"My shooter's only for dinosaurs?"

"And really mean dragons." She entered the hall and turned toward the council chambers. Propped oak doors led into a room bursting with people. She took a deep breath and guided her son inside.

Mayor Ford and five council members sat up front, atop an elongated dais, and off to the side, Ian stood, looking completely at ease in a power suit while he conversed with a group of local business owners. Robin's knees trembled. Last time she saw him, he'd swooped into her café like some would-be knight in shining armor, soaked from the rain, throwing out solutions to problems he'd caused. As if her pain meant something to him. As hard as she tried, Robin couldn't get the things he said and the way he looked when he said them out of her mind. The memory turned her fingers cold.

"Mommy, I'm hungry," Caleb said.

"Do you see Aunt Bethy or Uncle Evan anywhere?" Robin stood on her tiptoes, frantically searching until she spotted Amanda's ponytail up front, where she stood beside Kyle. She weaved through the crowd and squeezed in between them, her teeth chattering. It had nothing to do with the temperature in the chamber and everything to do with her jittery nerves.

"Cutting it a little close, don't you think?" Amanda asked.

"Baby-sitter canceled." Robin pulled some homemade granola bars from her purse and handed one to her son. "Where are Evan and Bethany?"

"Beats me. I was beginning to think I'd have to go to bat for your café all by myself."

Robin glanced at Kyle. His face stretched thin with anxiety. It wasn't exactly reassuring.

A *tap, tap, tap* sounded from the microphone on the dais. The chamber eased into silence.

"As you all know, we only have one issue on the agenda this evening, and that is the development plan for our downtown area." Mayor Ford smiled at the crowd. "We've been ironing out the details and there's a particular component we're interested in adding, which would be condominiums on the south end of the business district. Before we make this official, we wanted to engage in an open dialogue with the public. See where everybody stands."

Robin eyed the entrance, then glanced at her watch. Where were Bethany and Evan, her biggest supporters? She opened her purse, rummaged through flyers and crumpled coupons, a sticky tube of raspberry lip balm, a bottle of hand sanitizer, and her keys before finding the smooth solidness of her phone. She pulled it out and checked to see if Bethany or Evan had sent her a text—something that might explain their absence. No messages. She placed her hands on Caleb's shoulder.

Ian nodded at the council members, then the crowd. When his attention wandered toward her, she looked away. "Before we open this up to discussion, the mayor has graciously allowed me to say a few words."

Caleb squirmed. "Ouch, Mommy, you're hurting my shoulders."

She unclenched her fingers and straightened Caleb's collar.

"I want to thank you all for welcoming me into your town. It's been a pleasure getting to know so many of you." Robin felt his eyes on her, but she kept her attention glued on Caleb's cowlick. "I've worked as a project manager for McKay Corporation for six years and I can confidently say that we work our hardest to ensure every town benefits from our developments. So far, we've been successful in our intentions."

Robin frowned. Why did he have to sound so sincere?

"We'll start by voicing our opinions and concerns," Mayor Ford said. "Ian or I can address them one at a time."

Robin stepped around her son. "Our biggest concern is One Life."

"She's right," Joe's father called from the back. "It helped so many of us get back on our feet after Alcoa issued cutbacks last year. Seems a shame, after all it's done, to shove it aside for condominiums."

Robin looked at Kyle and the two of them exchanged hopeful smiles.

Gene Bradley, a local attorney, spoke up from the front. "There are plenty of spaces for rent on the north side of town, aren't there?"

"You're right," Kyle said. "There are some spaces. However, one of the reasons One Life has been so effective over the years is because Sybil has allowed us to rent the space for an incredibly low price. Moving would greatly diminish our capabilities. We'd have to cut back on many of the programs we currently have in place."

"Not to mention the location. The elementary school is two blocks away, which means One Life doesn't have to pay for bussing for their after-school program." Robin thought about Piper Greeley. Without the after-school program, that little girl would be all alone in her house while her father bartended at Shorney's.

"Better than losing the ministry altogether, isn't it?"

Several people frowned at Gene's comment.

"That's an easy thing to say when your welfare doesn't depend on those programs." Robin's words came out hot and indignant. Gene's ears turned red, but Robin didn't care. How could he speak so flippantly about something that impacted people's lives? She pulled a sheet of paper from her purse and brought it up to the dais. "I have a petition. Signatures from people who all agree that One Life matters more than these condominiums."

"Oh, but wouldn't they look so much lovelier than what's there now? The area's so run down." The woman's voice was familiar, but Robin couldn't place it. Nor did she want to. Otherwise the next time Robin saw her, she might give the lady a piece of her mind. She laid the paper before Mayor Ford and returned to her spot. Kyle's face didn't look so drawn anymore.

Mayor Ford furrowed his brow at the signatures. "I understand One Life has been a very important ministry to this town for many years. I'm no more comfortable with it going away than anyone else. But I think it's important to point out that without these condominiums, the employees of Fixtel Software Systems will choose somewhere else to live and our town will not only miss out on some much-needed tax revenue, but many of your businesses will not see the boost in sales that would make One Life's ministry less necessary."

"I have to agree." The owner of the local Piggly Wiggly stepped away from her spot against the wall. "Mr. McKay was gracious enough to pay me a visit yesterday. We talked about what these condominiums would do for my store. For all of our businesses. I think we'd be stupid not to vote in favor of them."

Dr. Bremms, the superintendent of Peaks's school district, raised his hand in the front. Besides Ian and the men on the dais, he was the only other man wearing a tie. "You all know our school system has suffered from statewide budget cuts. I don't want to lay off teachers, and I most definitely don't want to shortchange students. If these condominiums will bring in tax revenue, then perhaps we ought to be more open to the change."

"But, Dr. Bremms," Robin said, "some of your students have dinner at night because of One Life. How can you take away their meals, but expect them to thrive in school?"

Several comments arose from the crowd.

"How much revenue can these condominiums really bring in?" someone shouted.

Mayor Ford set aside the petition and spoke into the microphone, listing off a series of statistics. Robin tried her best to pay attention. She knew she should care about tax revenues in her town, but Peaks was so much more than figures and data. "I think it's also worth mentioning that they are extremely well built and aesthetically pleasing. Elaine and I took a road trip to look at some that have already been built by McKay. They will look quite charming downtown."

"The municipality of Alchew swindled five hundred acres of farmland to set up a big box store outside their town." The man who spoke was a local farmer—a friend of Evan's—and his expression scrunched with disapproval. "We've lost enough farmland already. Agreeing to this development will lead to more. I vote we leave Peaks alone."

Robin beamed at the man. If not for the crowd between them, she'd walk straight over and plant a kiss on his forehead.

"I understand and appreciate your concern, Mr. Noldt." *Hold up.* Ian knew the guy's name? Did he have a cheat sheet behind the podium? "But with Fixtel opening, the surrounding area is going to grow regardless. Peaks can either embrace these changes and reap the benefits, or resist them and miss out on revenue and progress."

The crowd began to whisper.

"If people want to move to Peaks, why can't they move into the housing developments on the northwest side of town?" Carl Crammer asked.

Ian bent his head toward the microphone. "The housing developments on the northwest side of town aren't conducive to the population that will be moving in to take jobs at Fixtel. I've done my research. I know what type of living these people will be looking for."

Robin's toes fidgeted in her boots, her nerves pulsing and twitching. She had to say something more. Fight harder.

"Think of what these developments will do for your business. Ryan and Kim"—Mayor Ford held out his hand toward the married chiropractors— "how many more clients will your practice see if we experience a population boom?" The mayor smiled at Hank, the local barber, and Jim, the owner of the golf course on the outskirts of town. "And so many others who've been struggling since this recession hit."

The whispers morphed into chatter.

"This town's economy has idled for the past five years," a woman said from the left of the crowd. Robin could only see the top of her head. "We're ready for a change."

The chattering grew louder.

Robin cleared her throat. "I don't think tearing down three local businesses and an important ministry is the best change to make."

Mumbled arguments erupted throughout the room. Robin tried to form more words, articulate some sort of point that might silence them, but Carl Crammer beat her to it.

"I don't hardly see how any of this matters." He twisted his hat in grease-stained hands. "If Robin doesn't want to sell, then ain't we all wasting our breath?"

"Let me remind everybody here," Mayor Ford said. "This hearing is about adding condos to the development plan. It has nothing to do with Willow Tree Café or One Life."

Robin couldn't believe it. How could Mayor Ford dismiss such an important point? The condominiums had everything to do with Willow Tree and One Life. "Of course it does if that's where you're planning to build them."

The hall erupted. Disagreements and heated opinions spilled into

Robin's ears and filled the space inside her head, swirling together into one giant, matted tangle. But before she could comb through any of it to find something coherent to say, her phone buzzed.

Bethany's number lit the screen. Robin's heart stuttered. In her fervor to win the crowd's support, she had forgotten all about Evan and Bethany and their strange absence. The chatter in the chamber turned into a distant hum. She gripped the phone and stared at Bethany's name, half of her wanting to stay and fight, the other half wanting to hightail it out of the chamber and make sure everything was okay.

Mayor Ford tapped his microphone and waited for the room to quiet. "Thank you, everyone, for caring about our town, for coming tonight and expressing your opinions. Does anybody have anything else to add?"

The room spun. Her mouth burned with half-formed ideas, reasons why her deep-rooted love for Willow Tree should matter to Peaks.

The mayor motioned to the superintendent. "We've heard how it will help our schools. We've heard how it will help local businesses. I apologize to those of you concerned about One Life. I apologize to anyone who doesn't want to see Peaks change, but change is a part of life. I'd like to see our town embrace it."

Change is a part of life…

How well Robin knew that truth.

"All right then, I'd like to see a simple show of hands. The municipality of Peaks will move forward based on majority. Who's in favor of adding McKay condominiums to the town's development plan?"

Arms rose into the air. Not all. Not even most. But more than half.

Robin's phone vibrated. She took Caleb by his arm and rushed out into the night, where there was quiet and space. With her heart pounding, she hit talk and pressed the phone to her ear. Elyse screamed bloody murder in the background.

"Bethany? What's wrong?"

"I am so sorry."

"Don't worry about it. Tell me what's going on."

"Elyse woke up screaming and she wouldn't stop. We tried everything, but she kept crying. We were going to take her to the ER, but Evan thought it would be smarter to rush her over to Dr. Dotts. You should have heard the way she was screaming. It was awful."

Robin could hear her now.

"I guess she has a double ear infection. My little girl is miserable. I'm so sorry we weren't there tonight. How did it go?"

A lump of heat lodged itself in Robin's throat. It didn't matter how hard she fought or that others had joined her. They still lost.

TWENTY-FIVE

Bits and pieces of Mayor Ford's words slipped into Ian's brain. He tried harder to listen, but he couldn't erase the image of Robin's face as she made a beeline for the exit. He stared at the oak doors, where she had disappeared with her son.

Benches groaned. People stood and started arguing and talking and speculating. The excited humming vibrated the air. He stepped away from the podium and turned toward the exit, wanting to find her, to get her to reconsider his offer, but Mayor Ford hopped off the dais like a young kid and pumped Ian's hand. "I'd be a liar if I said I wasn't a little worried. It's sort of like an election. You never know until the vote is out."

Ian returned the mayor's enthusiastic shake and smiled. The proper response. He should, after all, be thrilled. One step closer toward the condos. So why did the room feel so claustrophobic? And why had Robin worked so hard to avoid looking at him throughout the meeting? O'Malley and Maddocks joined the conversation, but Ian listened with only half his heart.

"Don't you think so?" the mayor asked.

Ian tugged at his collar. "Sorry, what was that?"

"I was just saying how exciting it will be to see you bring our vision to life."

"Oh yes, of course."

"Will you be in town during the construction phase, or will you hand the project off?" O'Malley asked.

"Once I have everything squared away for the groundbreaking, I'll hand the project over to the construction manager." The thought of leaving

Peaks emptied him out. It was refreshing to stay in a place that didn't carry the weight of messy memories. Nobody here expected Ian to become his father.

He enjoyed eating breakfast at Bernie's cherry-finished dining table. Getting that woman to smile had become a challenging game. He was up to two a day. Mayor Ford's enthusiasm was contagious. Val's Diner served the world's best iced tea and he got a kick out of Megan's novelty T-shirts. And Robin...well, life would be easier if he didn't think about Robin.

"I'll stop in now and again to check on things," he said.

"That's a relief." The flirtatious purr belonged to Amanda. She stood behind him, her hair swept into a ponytail, hazel eyes brightened by sun-kissed cheeks. "We'd hate to have you leave and forget all about us."

Ian slipped his hands in his pockets. "Not possible."

"So I guess congrats are in order. Your condos are looking more and more feasible every second." Amanda's words were meant as a compliment, but somehow they left him deflated.

The mayor clapped his hand over Ian's shoulder. "I think we should celebrate. What do you say? Dinner and drinks this Saturday, on me."

"I'm afraid I have a prior engagement," Ian said.

Amanda raised her eyebrows. "A hot date?"

"My father was nominated for employer of the year. A local thing in Peoria. I'm leaving tomorrow so I can attend the banquet." He looked at the mayor. "I'll probably stay a few days to take care of some business. When I return, we should get together and discuss the best way to move forward."

"I'll have that arranged." Mayor Ford nudged Ian with his elbow. "So this banquet. You have a special lady friend back in Peoria you'll be taking?"

Ian raised a brow. "No, Mayor. Just myself."

"A handsome man like you?" The mayor bounced on his toes. "That's ridiculous. You should take someone. Like Amanda. I bet she'd love to go with you."

Mayor Ford's attempt at Cupid was painfully obvious, but maybe it wasn't such a bad idea. It might be nice to take Amanda. She was young, attractive, outgoing. Perhaps escorting her would get his mind off Robin, a woman who had no business preoccupying his thoughts. Especially when she wanted nothing to do with him. He looked down at the blushing accountant. "Would you like to accompany me?"

Loyalty and desire waged war in her eyes. Ian stood with his hands in his pockets and waited to see which side would win. Just how well did Evan Price know his kid sister? Ian didn't have to wait long.

"Well, actually, there is this dress I've been wanting to wear…"

❧

Robin set *Where the Wild Things Are* on Caleb's nightstand and swept his bangs from his eyes. Her boy loved Max and his wolf suit. "Somebody needs a haircut. You're turning into a shaggy dog."

"I'm not a shaggy dog. I'm a wild thing."

"Oh, well, I'm sorry, Mr. Wild Thing." She tickled his belly and laughed with his laugh, then brushed her lips across his forehead. Soft skin and Johnson's shampoo.

Caleb tucked his favorite blanket under his arm and rolled to his side. "Will you tell me the café story now?"

Robin sat on the edge of Caleb's bed and ran her fingers through his hair. "Once upon a time, you had a daddy who was the best guy ever, better even than Spider-Man."

His eyes went wide. Because Spider-Man was a pretty big deal.

"He knew that Mommy loved cafés. So every single day he told me we should open one together. It was Daddy's dream for us. But then he went to be with the angels. So while you were growing in my belly, Aunt Bethy and Uncle Evan and I built Willow Tree Café."

Caleb smiled with droopy eyelids. Robin kissed his cheek and tiptoed to his dresser.

A John Deere tractor lamp painted a yellow circle of light on the ceiling and spotlighted a framed picture below. A photograph of Micah and Evan—smiling from inside the cab of a combine—mounted on top of the dresser like a first-prize trophy. She ran her fingers down the metal frame.

"Mama?"

"What's up, Buggerboo?"

"Is Leesey sick?"

"She has an ear infection, but she'll get some medicine that will make her all better." If only life could be as easy—a spoonful of medicine to chase away the loneliness, to fix the broken parts.

"Are you gonna leave when I fall asleep?"

Her hand paused over the picture frame. She only left on Saturdays, when the café stayed open through the evening. She didn't think Caleb noticed when she left. She made a point to tuck him in before the babysitter came and she slipped away. She didn't miss good night kisses. She didn't miss before-bedtime baths or his animated stories about robots and T. rexes and evil dragons. She made a point to be there for all of it. "Not tonight."

There would be no music. No baking. Just sleep. And lots and lots of prayer, because from where she stood, she sure couldn't see God in any of this mess. She curled her fingers around the lamp's pull cord.

"Why? It's not Saturday?"

"Nope, it's Thursday, Love Bug."

"Are the bad guys taking Daddy's dream?"

Daddy's dream. Mommy's dream. Maybe she never should've told Caleb that story. "Would it make you sad if we didn't have the café?"

"Mm-hmm. And you sad too."

She looked over her shoulder. Caleb was curled on his side, one small hand and one casted hand tucked beneath his chin. He yawned wide and closed his eyes. Her heart pulled tight as she watched him nod off to sleep.

I wish you knew him, Micah. I wish you knew our little boy. But you don't. And I'm so tired of doing this on my own.

Caleb's breathing turned rhythmic. She stared at Micah's face, frozen in time with a smile, unaware that he had a son who was growing up without a father. Unaware that with each passing day, he faded a little bit more. Unaware that sometimes, Robin didn't fight the fading.

She pulled the lamp cord and the room went black.

❧

"*Mommy? Who's that?*" *Caleb stood in the middle of Willow Tree, pointing at the canvases hanging on the wall.*

Where were all the chairs? And the tables? She crouched low and pulled him close. "*Honey, that's Daddy. You know Daddy, right?*"

"*Where did his face go?*"

Her breath stumbled. She stood and spun in a circle until the pictures blurred into streaks of black and white. Every single one had a white blotch over Micah's face. Who would do this? Who would erase her husband?

She ripped a canvas off the wall and slammed it against the ground. Then another and another, until Caleb cried. She turned around to go to him, but he wasn't there. Somebody else was. A man standing by her piano. Tall and handsome and familiar, even from the back.

A guttural sound tore through her. She lurched forward and clutched his shoulders. "*Look at me, Micah. Let me see your face.*"

He pressed a key. The haunting note reverberated through the café.

"*You made it happen, Robin. You brought our dream to life,*" *he said.*

His voice melted over her, covering her in honey, wrapping her in warmth. She breathed it in, saturating herself in its perfect pitch.

"*It's everything we wanted. It's beautiful,*" *he said.*

She gripped his jacket between her fingers and pressed herself against him, desperate for the warmth of his skin and the smell of cologne. A sob bubbled up from her stomach. Her husband was alive! She didn't have to be alone anymore. His death was nothing more than a horribly long, drawn-out nightmare.

He turned around, brushed his lips across her hair, and looked into her eyes. "*You're beautiful.*"

Robin's heart dropped dead in her chest.

"*What's wrong?*"

She stepped back. Shook her head.

He reached out. "*Robin, what's wrong?*"

It was her husband's voice.

But it was Ian's face.

Robin jerked upright in bed, chest heaving. She sucked in mouthfuls of air, swallowing oxygen into her burning lungs. Micah. His name echoed from her dream. And for one horrifying moment, she couldn't picture his face. She couldn't remember the exact shape of his eyes or the slant of his jaw or the curve of his smile. Only the sound of his voice.

She threw back her comforter, stumbled across the room, and opened the bottom drawer of her dresser. With trembling hands she took out the photo album buried beneath her jeans and let it fall open over her knees. Night filtered through her window, ruffling the drapes. A beam of pale moonlight crept across her floor and cast a glow upon the pictures splayed across her lap.

Micah.

But the name only elicited an echo of the longing it once did.

TWENTY-SIX

Ian escorted Amanda inside the banquet hall, her fingers curling around his bicep as music and conversation filled the opened room. His attention jumped from one table to the next, bypassing the floral centerpieces as he looked for his parents.

"Do we have a spot where we're supposed to sit?" Amanda asked.

"We usually have a reserved table up front."

"How many times has your father been nominated?"

"I've lost count." Ian craned his neck and looked around a pair of old men. Was that Dad in the back? "He's been nominated at least ten. I'm pretty sure he's won half of those."

"Sounds like an impressive man."

Ian's father was more than impressive. He had started with nothing. No money. No parental support. Got a full-ride scholarship to Loyola. A flawless 4.0 in graduate school. His first bank loan and business deal. With determination, integrity, passion, and a whole bunch of hard work, Dad had accomplished all of it on his own. It was one of the reasons Ian admired his father, one of the reasons he aspired to be like him.

"This is exciting. I haven't gotten dressed up like this since senior prom." Amanda leaned toward his ear. "When do I get to meet your parents? Are they as fancy as you?"

"They're around here somewhere." He looked at Amanda in her sparkly black dress and something uncomfortable squirmed in his stomach. He didn't want to give her the wrong impression. And she deserved to be more than a distraction. "Thanks for coming. It's nice to have a new friend along."

She tilted her head back and laughed, black beads glinting over her neck.

"Did I say something funny?"

"You're just being a guy."

"Being a guy?"

"I give you credit for setting me straight before I could get my hopes up. That was very gentlemanly of you."

The knots of tension tangling his muscles unraveled, as if her words found the string tying them all together. Amanda understood him, and she wasn't angry. In fact, she had laughed. "I'm curious about something," he said.

"And that would be?"

"Why did you come tonight?"

"Why not come tonight?"

"I can think of a whole list of why nots. Starting with Robin, your sister-in-law, who hates me." His body temperature warmed and it had nothing to do with Amanda's arm looped through his. Ever since Robin escaped the hearing, he could think of little else. Despite his best efforts to distract himself with business, the desperation in her eyes haunted him, especially since he was responsible for placing it there.

"...so really, it's not a big deal. Wouldn't you agree?"

Ian blinked. "I'm sorry, what was that?"

"I told her where I was going tonight. It's not like I'm being sneaky or anything."

"How did she react to the news?"

"Pretended not to care."

"You think she does?" The question jumped out of his mouth. Too quick and eager.

Judging by the arc of Amanda's left eyebrow, she noticed.

He looked away, mortified by the heat in his cheeks.

"Of course she does."

He waited for her to elaborate. Only she didn't. She tilted her chin, her hazel eyes sparkling as if his painful silence amused her. Ian pressed his lips together and led her through the crowd before he could incriminate himself any further. He ushered her past a young couple and almost collided with a platinum blonde, a familiar apple martini in her hand.

Ian stepped back.

The woman's ruby-red smile froze in place.

"Cheryl?" He followed the length of her arm, entwined with another. A muscular gentleman with a receding hairline and a neatly trimmed goatee. Ian blinked several times, trying to register the fact that his ex-wife was standing in front of him. "What are you doing here?"

"I worked for your father for eight years. Of course I was going to come."

She was also his daughter-in-law for four. Funny how she left that part out. "Can I speak with you for a moment?" He turned to Amanda. "Would that be okay with you?"

"I'll keep your date company while you two catch up." The man with the goatee didn't look at all intimidated or perturbed that another man wanted a word with his date. He actually looked rather bored. After taking Cheryl's martini, he offered Amanda his elbow. "We'll be at the bar."

Amanda took the offered arm and snuck one last glance at Ian before being led away.

Cheryl crossed her arms. Not in a way that suggested annoyance, but in a way that suggested she needed protecting. The gesture reminded him of Robin. His insides revolted against the comparison. Cheryl and Robin were nothing alike. Ian stuck his hands in his pockets and clenched them into fists.

"What did you want to speak with me about?" she asked.

"Why are you returning my alimony checks?"

"Because I don't want your money."

Right. She didn't want anything. At least not from him. She'd made that crystal-clear. Nothing he had to give was good enough. He couldn't fix what had broken since… No. He wouldn't go there. Not tonight. "So I'm just supposed to stop sending them?"

"Every time I get them, it's like this barbed reminder of something I don't want to remember." Something in her eyes died—they turned cold and hard, like two stone pebbles. "I don't want to remember any of it."

Neither did he. But as hard as he tried, he couldn't forget. Not all the way. It lurked in dark corners, crouching in all its unpleasant truth, pouncing at unexpected, inconvenient times. And all he could do was get on his knees and pray. Ask for forgiveness. Offer forgiveness. Again and again. Until the lurking thing no longer choked him.

"I want to move on with my life. What's done is done. We can't change it."

"Ian! There you are!" Dad emerged from the shuffle of bodies, flanked by two men dressed in suits. He looked from Cheryl to Ian and a bit of hope sparkled in his eyes. Ian wanted to blot it out. "I was wondering when you were going to get here."

"Congratulations on the nomination," Cheryl said.

Dad shrugged, like it was no big deal. "Thank you, Cheryl. It was very kind of you to come."

She squeezed Dad's hand, gave Ian a "let's just drop it" look, and disappeared into the crowd, probably in search of her martini. Dad introduced Ian to the two men—the chamber president and a fellow CEO. Ian joined in the small talk with half his attention. The other searched for Mom. He'd like to sit next to her and talk. Unload the burden pressing so heavily against his shoulders. Cheryl. Dad's looming deadline. Robin's frustrating refusal to accept a draw. All that would be lost if Ian couldn't close the deal in time. And this vague, unsettling sensation of dissatisfaction that grew bigger and bigger every time he saw Robin in her element. Mom always listened.

The two men shook Ian's hand again and left to go find their seats.

Ian rounded on his father. "Did you invite Cheryl?"

"She was a part of our family for four years and one of the best employees I've ever had. Of course I invited her."

"Dad, she's my ex-wife." He had divorce papers to prove it.

"And I'll never understand why."

Heat gathered around Ian's collar. When would Dad let this go? "Cheryl came with a date. So did I. You should have warned me you invited her. I don't appreciate being blindsided."

Dad watched him like he might unravel. Right there, in front of everybody, in the big, fancy banquet hall. Like Ian was fragile and weak. "Are you okay?"

"I'm fine. I just wasn't expecting to see her." He tugged at the knot of his tie, beyond ready to forget Cheryl and the past. "Should we go find Mom?"

"Your mother's at home."

"Yeah, right." Mom wouldn't miss this event in a million years. She was Dad's biggest cheerleader. She was with him when McKay Development and Construction was nothing more than a dream. She supported him through every success, every setback. The company was as much hers as it was Dad's.

"She was feeling too unwell to come."

The words set off alarms. A cavern of ringing, echoing alarms.

"It's the chemo that's getting to her. Not the cancer."

Cancer. Ian didn't know it was possible to feel such loathing toward a word.

"So tell me, what's this good news you were talking about on the phone? Did you acquire the site?"

"I'm getting closer. We had a town meeting on Thursday. Majority's in favor of the condominiums."

"That's excellent news."

Yeah, except for the giant roadblock that is Robin.

"You said you brought a date?"

"Amanda!" Ian turned on his heel. What kind of man left his date unattended when she didn't know anybody? He looked from table to table until he found her standing next to the bar, stuck between a stiff-shouldered Cheryl and her bored date. She caught Ian looking for her and gave him and his father a wave.

Ian waved back. "That's her, right there."

"Nice-looking woman. Are you going to introduce me?"

Ian held out his hand. "After you."

His father parted the crowd like the Red Sea. Everybody stepped away with a look of admiration, like Dad was a modern-day version of Moses. Like he had a staff that could do miracles.

∾

Ian stared at the empty chair—the place Mom should have been—and let the banter float around him. The dark cloud shadowing McKay Development and Construction had temporarily lifted. Ian's coworkers seemed determined to set aside their worries over an uncertain future and celebrate Joseph McKay—their fearless leader. Ian had a harder time grasping the lighthearted mood, holding, as he did, those uncertain futures in his hand.

The table erupted in laughter. "You sure do know how to tell a joke, Joseph," Bob said, dabbing the corners of his eyes.

Ian reached down deep for a chuckle, but came back void. How could Dad carry on like normal? How could he tell jokes and laugh when Mom wasn't there? She never missed any award dinners in the past.

Jim Harley slid his arm around the back of his wife's chair. She looked much healthier tonight than she had at the company Christmas party. "You're unusually quiet tonight, Ian."

Six pairs of eyes turned in his direction.

"Just enjoying the conversation."

Jim wrapped his fingers around the stem of his wine glass and lifted it toward Amanda. "How did you two meet?"

Amanda chewed a bite of steak and wiped her lips with a linen napkin. "Peaks isn't a very big town. I think everybody knows Ian at this point."

"Do you know this café owner? This lady who's giving us such a hard time?"

The cloud returned.

"She's my sister-in-law." Amanda popped a bite of buttered potato in her mouth.

"Really?"

"And I'm her accountant," Amanda added.

Jim's muddy eyes studied Ian over the rim of his wine glass, a pinch of disapproval etched in the corners of his mouth. "An ironic choice for a guest. Especially tonight."

Amanda speared some asparagus. "Why's that?"

"Your sister-in-law is threatening the very company we're gathered to celebrate." Silverware stilled around the table.

Ian's jaw tightened. He didn't like the way Jim talked about Robin. "She's a widow who's devoted to her café. I hardly think that makes her the bad guy."

"I just hope you're as devoted to this company."

Jim's wife put her hand over his. "Jim, please," she murmured. "Now's not the time."

He threw his napkin over his food and scooted away from the table. "Excuse me while I get some fresh air."

Any hint of the jovial mood from earlier slunk away with him. Ian could feel Dad studying one side of his face, Amanda the other. Bob clinked his spoon against his glass, his cheeks rosy. Whether from the wine or the awkwardness, Ian had no idea. "I, for one, have every confidence in you, Ian. You're made out of your father's stock. And he's a man worth toasting." Bob picked up his drink. "To Joseph. Not only an exceptional boss, but a mentor, a leader, and role model for all of us."

Everyone lifted their glasses. "Hear, hear."

Ian raised his as well, but Dad wasn't smiling. He was too busy examining Ian, as if trying to put together two puzzle pieces. Ian shifted in his seat and pulled his attention toward the front as the chamber president started the ceremony.

It really shouldn't have surprised him when Dad walked on stage to accept his award. It really shouldn't have surprised him when he received the longest round of applause. It really shouldn't have surprised him when he thanked Ian. "For not only being a wonderful son, but for being an exceptional employee. I know the future of this company will be in good hands."

None of these things should have surprised Ian at all. And that feeling he got—one part admiration, two parts suffocation? That shouldn't have surprised him either.

∾

Raindrops splashed against the windshield in a steady drumbeat. Amanda glanced over at Ian several times during the short drive from the banquet hall to her hotel, and each time she caught him strangling the steering wheel with a white-knuckled grip. She'd counted on tonight being a distraction, and it most certainly was, just not in the way she'd expected. The whole evening had turned into an intriguing riddle. Amanda loved a good riddle.

Approaching headlights sliced through the dark as Ian steered his car into the parking lot of the Marriott. As soon as he pulled beneath the hotel's front awning, the patter of rain against the roof of the car went silent. He stepped outside, walked around the front, opened Amanda's door, and led her toward the lobby, stopping short of the automatic doors.

"Thanks for coming." He stood with one hand in his pocket, the other massaging the back of his neck, as if to squeeze away whatever tension festered there. "Sorry I was such lousy company."

"You were a bit distracted, weren't you?"

He pinched the air with his thumb and forefinger. "A little."

"Ian?"

"Yes?"

"What was Jim talking about at the dinner table before he left?"

Ian resumed his neck-massaging. "Jim had no business saying what he did. I'm really sorry he put you in that position. I promise he's not normally such a jerk."

She scuffed a rock with the ball of her shoe and peeked at Ian through her eyelashes. "I doubt Jim and I will ever cross paths again, so I don't care if he's a jerk. You didn't answer the question."

"Jim's worried about his job. Peaks isn't the only place hurting from this recession."

"And Cheryl?"

He laughed. "A little nosy, are we?" His words were lighthearted. The tone, however, came out short and stiff.

The riddle grew more and more interesting.

"I'm sorry. I promise my frustration has nothing to do with you."

"So what? She's an ex-girlfriend?"

"More like ex-wife."

Momentary shock stole her voice. She stood with her mouth slightly ajar, trying to adjust her impression. So Ian McKay was not the handsome and charming bachelor so many women in Peaks thought him to be. He was the handsome and charming divorcé.

He peered out into the wet night, a muscle ticking in his jaw.

"You still love her? Is that where the tension comes from?"

"I don't know if I ever really loved her."

"Ouch."

"If you asked Cheryl, I'm sure she'd say the feeling was mutual." He took a step back, as if to escape the conversation, but Amanda stepped with him. Her simmering curiosity had turned into a full-out boil. Ian sighed. "She was an ambitious intern. One of the best my father ever had. And gorgeous. She was passionate about the industry and enamored with my position in the company. I was jealous of her passion and she made work more exciting for a while. My dad didn't approve of our relationship at first. He's not big at mixing business and pleasure. But I didn't listen and we ended up with a big mess on our hands."

"If you weren't in love with each other, where'd all the tension come from?"

"It's complicated."

Her thoughts turned to Jason and Africa. "Isn't everything?"

He took a deep breath. The air puffed up his chest, then swooshed past his lips. "The short version? She wanted a divorce but I didn't. I fought her, but she got it anyway."

"I thought you didn't love her."

"Despite its prevalence, divorce isn't exactly something everyone smiles upon, especially when they don't understand why it happened. My dad refuses to accept it. He thinks I gave up too early." He closed his eyes. Amanda couldn't tell if he was trying to press something away or conjure something up. She simply knew that in that moment, Ian looked incredibly vulnerable and devastatingly handsome. She couldn't imagine why any woman would leave him. "I didn't take my vows lightly."

"That's an admirable quality."

"Yeah, well, sometimes I don't feel so admirable." He shook his head, as if the movement might shake away the memories too. "I'm not normally so morose. I apologize for the poor behavior."

"I know a way you can make it up to me." She wasn't ready to let the riddle go yet. And despite Ian's frankness—despite his obvious feelings for Robin—Amanda enjoyed spending time with him.

"Yeah?"

"Let me take you out. A night on the town." She held up her hand in a Girl Scout pledge. "Just as friends. I promise."

"I'm not sure why you'd want to."

"Because I think you're a good guy, Ian. And you look like you could use some fun." Plus, Robin would never own up to her feelings unless somebody stood behind her and gave her a good shove.

"I'm going to be here for most of the week."

"When you get back, then."

Uncertainty danced in his eyes.

"Come on! It'll be fun."

"If you can put up with me for another night, then I can put up with you."

"Good. Consider it a friend-date."

"Thanks for coming tonight," Ian said.

"It was fun." She kissed his cheek. "I can see where you get your charm. And your fancy looks. Your dad's quite the guy."

She meant the words as a compliment. Yet Ian looked at her like they'd rubbed against painful places.

TWENTY-SEVEN

Robin whacked the ball of dough on the prep table with a wooden rolling pin. It had been over a week, eight whole days since the town meeting, and all anybody could talk about was Ian and his condominiums. The only upside was a substantial increase in clientele. Between her two-part coupon plan and an outcry from a passionate minority, business at her café was booming. Mayor Ford's dissenters seemed to believe purchasing coffee was the best way to fight back.

Some came to her café expressing their condolences as if she'd already lost. Others encouraged her to keep fighting. A few were so offended they picketed outside Sybil's Antique Shoppe until Kyle kindly asked them to stop. Despite their good intentions, the marching and signs scared people away from One Life, and since Sybil didn't get any customers anyway, the whole thing was counterproductive.

A good chunk of the town, however, seemed eager. Everywhere Robin went—Piggly Wiggly, Val's Diner, CVS, the post office, even the barber shop for Caleb's haircut—buzzed with gossip and speculation and an excited sense of anticipation. More people than she hoped spoke about the south side renovation as if it were a done deal. As if she'd already agreed to sell her café. Well, she hadn't agreed and maybe she could clarify that important morsel of information if she could find Ian, but he'd left town and had yet to return. What kind of person touched off a grenade and left without watching it explode?

"Are you angry with that dough?"

Robin turned around, brandishing her rolling pin. Joe had his upper half wrapped around the door frame, his lower half hidden behind it.

"Just venting," she mumbled.

"Do you mind pausing for a quick second? Amanda's out here asking for you."

Amanda, the traitor. Besides an annoyingly brief text—*in Chicago w/Kelly, c u on Friday :)*—Robin was completely in the dark on Amanda's activities, including her fancy banquet date. "Why didn't she just come in?"

Joe shrugged and disappeared.

Robin wiped her hands on her apron and followed Joe out of the kitchen, where Amanda stood by the cash register, tapping a thick envelope against the countertop. "Payroll for my favorite client."

A week's worth of questions pricked inside Robin's head. How was the banquet? Did Ian accompany her to Chicago? Did they return to Peaks together? But Robin swallowed them. Amanda would only mistake her reason for asking, blow everything out of proportion. "I didn't know if you'd be back in time."

"I didn't have any meetings this week. And since I was already halfway to Chicago, I took the opportunity to visit Kelly. It was great. We spent the entire time scrounging through every sales rack along the Magnificent Mile. I got a killer pair of jeans for fifteen dollars."

A warm gust of humid air swept through the café as Judy, the town librarian, came through the front doors. "Joe," Robin said, "could you get Judy a whipless soy latte? Unleaded, and eighty-six the cinnamon."

Joe set aside a pair of metal tongs and stepped behind the espresso machine. Judy came to the counter, flashing a mouthful of horse teeth. "I go to Alaska for a few weeks and I come back to a tornado of excitement. I heard about the meeting and the condos. This is the most interesting thing that's happened since the last mayor decided to build a new library."

Interesting? More like a giant, ear-splitting headache.

"And that man who wants to buy your café?" Judy covered her lips, as if self-conscious about her teeth. "I don't know how you talk to him without getting all tongue-tied."

Amanda bent over the counter, set her chin on her fist, and nodded emphatically. "I completely agree, Judy. How *do* you talk to him without getting all tongue-tied, Robin?"

The residual anger from her sister-in-law's betrayal moved to Robin's foot. Just like usual, Amanda thought everything was a joke. At times it drove Robin so nuts, she wanted to give Amanda a swift kick in the rear. Right now was one of those times. Judy pulled a twenty from her purse and slid it across the counter. Joe handed over the lidded cup while Robin counted out the woman's change.

Once Judy left, Robin returned to the kitchen to finish her dough-whacking. Unfortunately, Amanda tossed the envelope next to the register and followed, the corners of her mouth tiptoeing into a smile. "I give you permission to ask."

"I just hope you aren't telling him anything about Willow Tree."

"What? Like insider secrets? C'mon, Robin, don't be ridiculous."

"You leaving town with him in the first place is a little more than ridiculous."

"I asked and you said you didn't care."

The intercom buzzed, indicating another customer. Joe would take care of it. "Of course I cared."

"Aha! So you are attracted to him."

Attraction had nothing to do with it. Robin picked up the rolling pin and brought it down on the dough. "I care because you're supposed to be on my side. I really don't understand why you want to date the one man in town bent on undoing all we've done with Willow Tree."

Robin hit the dough again. She would bake until her hands cracked with flour. Until her counters spilled over with blueberry crumb coffee cake. *Dulce de leche* cheesecake squares. Maybe even peanut butter cupcakes frosted with chocolate glaze. And when she finished, she would play the piano until the music swept her away to someplace calm, someplace peaceful, someplace where Ian McKay did not exist.

"First of all," Amanda said, "I will always be on your side. Second of all, if you cared, you should have said so when I asked. Third, I like spending time with Ian. I'm sorry if that upsets you." She sat down on the stepladder and examined her nails. "And fourth, Ian is hardly the enemy you're making him out to be. He's actually a pretty nice guy if you'd get to know him."

"I know him plenty well, thanks. Standing there all the time with his crinkly eyes and his hands in his pockets." Robin gave the dough a couple more whacks and set the roller down.

"Come on. It's not like he thought, *Whose life can I ruin today?* then picked your name out of the phone book and started plotting. These plans he has for condominiums, they would actually be good for the town."

Robin wiped her palms against her apron. "I'm not convinced Ian's condominiums are going to do half the things he claims they will. I think he's leading everybody on." Including the woman sitting on Robin's stepladder.

Amanda looked up from her nail, a bored expression on her face, as if she was done with this conversation. "What movies are playing at the theater tonight?"

"I…I have no idea." The last grown-up movie Robin had gone to in the theater was *Enchanted,* more than five years ago. She'd dragged Micah against his will. He'd moaned and groaned, pretending not to like it, but Robin knew better. She caught him smiling pretty big when Giselle and Robert twirled around the dance floor. "Why?"

Amanda picked off some of her raspberry-colored polish. "I'm taking Ian out tonight. We're going to Val's and probably a movie afterward."

Robin poked the tip of her finger into a corner of the dough. Throwing unsuspecting men at her was one thing, but dating Ian? This pushed past annoyance. It was hurtful and humiliating. "He's trying to buy my café."

"I know." Amanda stood from her perch. "Stop taking it so personally." She walked out of the kitchen, leaving Robin alone, rolling pin dangling by her side, door swinging on its hinges.

When the swinging stopped, she attacked the dough with short, frantic movements until it spread across the floured prep table in a thin, misshapen circle. She snatched the tin of cookie cutters, cut and plopped the uniform shapes onto a metal sheet, stuffed them in the oven, and grabbed a loaf of sourdough bread from the cooling rack. She sawed at it with the bread knife, cutting off chunks in angry slices. *Stop taking it so personally?* How could she not take it personally? Of all the—

Pain seared through her pointer finger.

She jerked her hand back and hissed. The knife clattered to the floor and blood gushed from the injury. The blade had sliced into her finger deeply. Really deeply. She grabbed a nearby towel, wrapped it around her hand, and cradled it to her chest. She hated blood. Cuts made her squeamish. And the mental image of that flap of separated skin… She shuddered and forced herself to breathe and blink away the dancing spots darkening her vision.

She needed Joe.

She pushed through the door and knocked right into him.

He caught her shoulders. "Whoa, Robin, that's a lot of blood."

She looked at the towel. Big mistake. Big, big mistake. The floor tilted beneath her.

"She needs stitches. I'll take her to the doctor." That voice…it didn't belong to Joe. She squeezed her eyes shut and tried to force away the spins. When she opened them back up again, Ian McKay stood in front of her.

∽

Robin's cakey skin beaded with sweat. "Joe can take me."

"Don't be stupid." Ian stepped closer, much more unsettled by Robin's blood than he should be. "If Joe takes you, you'll have to close down your café before noon. Do you really want to do that?"

Without giving her time to protest, he placed his arm behind her back and ushered her out of the café and into his car. Somehow, the entire towel wrapped around Robin's hand had gone from white to red.

"This is absurd. You can't just kidnap me."

"Buckle your seat belt." When she didn't respond, he reached across her and snapped the seat belt into place, ignoring the warmth of her body and the brown-sugar smell clinging to her skin.

"I'm not a little kid," she said.

"Then stop acting like one." He pulled the car out of the parking lot and glanced at the blood-soaked towel cradled in her lap. How much could one finger bleed? "Are you in a lot of pain?"

She squeezed her eyes shut, chest puffing up and down in an uneven rhythm, her face whiter than chalk. She looked two seconds away from passing out.

"Do you need to put your head between your legs or something?"

"I hate blood."

He wasn't a fan of it either. Especially hers. Ian curled his fingers around the steering wheel and pressed harder on the gas pedal.

∾

Dr. Dotts finished the last stitch on Robin's finger. The tugging sensation nauseated her so she pressed the knuckles of her good hand against her abdomen and kept her eyes closed. Of all the people in the world to sweep in and rescue her, why did it have to be Ian? And why had she acted like such a lunatic? An absolute raving lunatic. All because of a stupid cut.

Dr. Dotts wrapped the injury in gauze, then patted her knee. "All better."

Robin held up her hand and stared at the clunky bandage. "How am I supposed to do anything with this?"

"It'll be tricky." The doctor jotted something on his clipboard. "You came very close to severing the tip of your finger. You must have been cutting something pretty hard."

The nausea came back. Along with a horrible realization. How could she play the piano? She brought her wrapped hand onto her lap. "When will I get the stitches out?"

"I'll have you come back in ten days. We'll take a look and see how things are healing. Until then, I need you to be careful with that finger, which means no piano. I know how much you enjoy playing, but you're going to have to wait until you're healed." Dr. Dotts handed her a plastic bag filled with gauze and a small tube. "Clean it every night, but very lightly. When you're finished, dab on a generous amount of ointment and wrap it back up, at least for the first couple days. After that, you might want to let it breathe a little. Tylenol should help the throbbing once the Novocaine wears off."

Robin tried to listen to his instructions, but ten days? With no piano?

The doctor said something, but Robin didn't hear. She wanted to get home, away from this disaster. When Dr. Dotts finished talking, Ian held open the door. She frowned and walked past him. Joe should have taken her. So what if she had to close her café? At least she wouldn't be with Ian.

Once they reached his car, he opened her car door too, that crinkly-eyed smirk on his face. "Do you need me to buckle you in this time?"

She grabbed the belt and clipped it into place, then clutched her hands in her lap while Ian got in the driver's side. She examined his profile from the corner of her eye. Thick lashes. Straight nose. Strong jaw. Tan skin, with crow's-feet that somehow added to his attractiveness in that annoying man-way. He wrapped his hands around the steering wheel and pulled onto the road, his fingers reminding her of his cooking and the deep, rich sound of his laughter that night in her kitchen. Her heart thudded against her eardrums.

Lord, what is going on?

Ian's lips curled into a slow grin, like he knew she was staring. She turned toward the window and thumbed her ring finger. Only instead of smooth platinum, her thumb met warm skin. She looked at her hand. Where was her ring? She put it on this morning. She knew she did, so where was it? She pulled out her pockets and found nothing but lint.

"What's wrong?"

"My ring is missing." She leaned forward and scanned the floor, trying to remember the course of her day. Had she taken it off before she started baking?

"Relax."

"Don't tell me to relax." Panic stirred in her gut. She knew she was over-reacting, but she couldn't seem to control herself. Being banned from her piano was bad enough, she had to lose her ring too? Everything felt too big, too important. She needed to get out of the car, away from this man who made her feel things she didn't want to feel.

Ian pulled over to the side of the road. "Robin, I have your ring."

Her frenzied searching stopped.

"Dr. Dotts took it off before he examined your hand. Don't you remember?"

No, she didn't remember at all.

He reached inside his pocket and pulled it out. The ring sparkled on the tip of his pinky finger, speckled with blood. Her heart drummed against her sternum. He reached across the console, took her bandaged hand in his, and slid the ring in place. "There. Everything's right with the world again."

She pulled away from his touch, pressing herself against the door.

"You might want to get it cleaned."

"I will." She fiddled with the bandage wrapped around her finger, embarrassment replacing the empty space the panic left behind. "I'm sorry for freaking out. It's just…"

"Your husband bought it for you. Trust me, I get it. You don't have to explain."

But he didn't get it, not completely. Robin opened her mouth to clarify—that the ring belonged to her mom long before Micah ever put it on her finger. It was one of the reasons she rarely took it off. But the explanation didn't come and the two of them sat there in Ian's car, sandwiched between the park where Micah had proposed and the café Ian wanted to buy. She couldn't decide if she should fling open the door and leave, or stay and talk to this man who looked so defeated. "Ian?"

"Yeah?"

"Why did you come to my café this morning?"

"Honestly?" He looked out the window, past the streetlamps and the railroad tracks and the Mississippi River, as if whatever he searched for lay beyond the horizon. "I'm not sure."

TWENTY-EIGHT

Micah was supposed to propose in Chicago at the Navy Pier. He had it all planned out. We were going to ride the Ferris wheel at twilight, that romantic hour in between day and night, when everything looks beautiful and calm. We would ride to the very top, and while I was mesmerized by the darkening Chicago skyline, he would take the small, velvet box from his coat and wait for me to turn around.

That was the plan, anyway.

But when it came to Micah, plans burned holes through his pockets. So did my engagement ring. Which is why he showed up on my doorstep several days before our weekend trip, the night before he was supposed to fly to Florida over spring break with Habitat for Humanity.

"Let's go to Chicago," he said.

I was wearing pink checkered flannel pajamas, an oversized St. Ambrose University sweatshirt, and fleece socks striped like rainbows. "Right now?"

"Yeah, right now." He took my hand and pulled me out on the porch, so close that our bodies touched.

My insides went all soft and warm and fluttery, like they always did anytime I was close to Micah. I breathed in the familiar scent of his cologne, wanting to commit it to memory. We had reached that point in our relationship where being apart was physically painful. I wasn't looking forward to being separated from him.

"You have no idea how much I want to kiss you right now," he whispered.

"I think I do," I said.

He wrapped his arms around my waist, the warmth of his breath tickling my neck. "If I start, I'm not sure I'd know how to stop."

"Me neither."

He stepped away and jerked his head toward his car idling in the driveway. "Let's go."

I laughed. "This late? Micah, we can't go to Chicago right now."

"We'll go someplace else then."

"Where?"

He paused, as if considering, then took my hand and tugged me to his car. "It's a surprise."

I should have guessed then. Or maybe I should have guessed the moment I saw him on my doorstep. But I was only a sophomore in college and Micah seemed too good to be true. Too good to be mine. I dug my heels into the cement, but not very convincingly. "Micah, I'm in my pajamas."

"And you look very cute." He opened the passenger door and swept his hand toward the seat. I scrunched my nose at him. He was acting funny. Almost giddy. I wanted to know why, but he just folded his hands behind his back and smiled.

Five minutes later, we were at the park—the one overlooking the Mississippi River. The one with an old statue, a squeaky swing set, a paint-chipped merry-go-round, and a teetertotter I never quite trusted. The first time Micah brought me, I had chipmunk cheeks and a bottle of pain meds and a mouth devoid of wisdom teeth. We sat on the merry-go-round, but we didn't spin. It was the first time Micah held my hand. The official beginning of us as a couple.

As soon as he pulled into the small parking lot, I gave him my best suspicious look. He unstrapped his seat belt and told me he'd race me to the swings. I chased after him, an excited feeling stealing through my body. An inkling—a hope—of why he was dragging me here, to this place of all places. But I pushed it away, unwilling to put expectations on the eve of his departure.

We sat in the swings, digging our feet into the gravel, listening to the river splash against rock, talking about everything and nothing and all the stuff that fits in between as the last of the sun's light sank deeper and deeper below the horizon. A train whistled in the distance and I looked out at the water—its surface like rippled glass reflecting the sky.

When I turned around, Micah was no longer in the swing beside me. He was kneeling on one knee, a small velvet box opened in his palm. I released the rusted metal chains and my hand moved to my chest. Tears welled in my eyes as I looked from the ring to Micah, the ring to Micah, the ring to Micah. "Is that…?"

He nodded.

It was my mother's. I hadn't seen it since the day she died. I assumed it was still with her.

"Your dad thought you might want it someday."

My chest flooded with joy. So, so much joy. But sadness too. Because I wanted my mother to be there for that moment. A moment we used to talk about together, when I was a little girl. I wanted to race home and tell her all about this man who made my heart do funny things. This man she didn't know.

"I love you, Robin. I want to spend the rest of my life loving you. Will you be my wife?"

When I said yes, Micah slid my mother's ring onto my finger, then came to his feet and pulled me into his arms. He swung me in a circle and kissed me as the final vestiges of twilight melted into darkness.

TWENTY-NINE

W hat happened to your finger?"

"Oh, it's quite the story." Robin craned her neck to look past Bethany and searched the booths of Val's Diner.

"It looks like you amputated an appendage."

"Dr. Dotts said it was close."

"Who are you looking for?" Bethany stepped in front of Robin's hopping eyes. "The guys aren't getting here for another half-hour."

Heat crept up Robin's neck. She wasn't looking for Evan or Gavin. "C'mon. Let's sit down." She pulled her friend to a booth in the back corner, heart thwacking her breastbone like a meat mallet, and shimmied her way into the seat facing the door. What in the world was she doing? When she called Bethany to go out to dinner, she could've picked Shorney's or someplace in a neighboring town. She didn't have to choose Val's.

"Is something wrong with you?" Bethany asked. "You're acting all jumpy, like the pain meds are making you loopy."

Robin opened her menu. "The doctor didn't give me pain meds for a cut on my finger."

"Yeah, before we get to that, what's with the last-minute dinner date? Don't get me wrong. The night out is much appreciated, especially after the worst ear infection in the history of all ear infections—it was seriously awful—but usually you plan everything five months in advance."

"I thought it would be fun. We haven't hung out like this since Elyse was born. Who's watching her—your mom?"

"Yes. And I keep having these horrible thoughts that she's going to drop her on her head or give her too much medicine." Bethany pulled her cell phone from her purse and checked the screen. "Do you think I should call?"

"Bethany, your mom knows what she's doing. She never dropped you or David and I'm sure she had to give you medicine when you were babies."

Bells tinkled and the front door swung open. Amanda stepped into the restaurant, black beaded tank top hugging her curvy figure. Robin examined her own willowy arms, then looked up just in time to spot Ian. She ducked behind her menu.

Bethany's eyebrow shot up, like two marionettes attached to an invisible string.

"When are the guys getting here?" Robin asked. "I feel bad that we haven't had the chance to sit down with Gavin since he got back into town. I bet he took some amazing pictures in the Caribbean."

"I just told you. Evan's finishing up on the farm. Then he's meeting Gavin over at his place. They should be here…" Bethany twisted around to look at the place Robin's attention kept hopping.

Robin grabbed her wrist. "Don't stare!"

When she turned, she wore a knowing look. "You've got to be kidding me."

"What?"

"Spying? Robin, you invited me to dinner so you could spy on Amanda and Ian?"

"What? No! Of course not."

"You're a terrible liar."

"I'm not spying on *him*." The pronoun escaped like a disgusting word.

The invisible puppeteer tugged on Bethany's eyebrows again.

"I'm not. Seriously." Robin peeked over the top of her menu just in time to see Ian pull out Amanda's chair.

"You do realize Amanda's never going to let you live this down," Bethany said.

Megan shuffled to the side of their table. She wore a black T-shirt with Edgar Allan Poe's face printed on the front and tucked a frizzy flyaway behind her ear. "What can I get for you tonight?" Her voice came out duller than usual.

"Water for me, thanks," Bethany said.

Robin smiled. Unlike Amanda, Bethany knew the difference between real coffee and the cheap imitation. She also knew when a pot had been brewed too long. "Me too," Robin said.

"Are you ready to order?" Megan asked.

"We're waiting for two more."

Megan nodded, her attention fixed on Ian and Amanda. Robin wanted to tell her to stop gaping. "Are they an item now?"

Ian looked over, as if he'd heard Megan's question, and caught the three of them staring. Robin ducked behind her menu. Great. Now he knew they'd been talking about him. As if the man needed any more confidence. "It's not like he's sticking around that much longer," Robin said. "Whatever's going on between them won't last."

Bethany's eyebrow shot up again. Robin wanted to chuck the menu at her friend's head.

"I guess you're right." Megan's shoulders deflated and she stuck her notepad in her apron. "I'll be right back with your drinks."

"So tell me about that bandage." Bethany pulled a disinfectant wipe from her purse and wiped her side of the table. "You said it was quite the story."

"Amanda came to the café this morning to drop off payroll. When I told her I was upset about her leaving town with Ian, she told me I was taking things too personally."

"So you took your frustrations out on your poor finger?"

"A loaf of bread. My finger just got in the way. Anyway, guess who was there to rush me to Dr. Dotts?"

"Is he sitting across the diner?"

"Yes." Robin thumbed her ring, remembering the feel of Ian sliding it on her finger. She'd taken it to Cecile as soon as she finished work. The woman made it sparkly and new, and although dried blood no longer stuck to the diamond, the memory remained. "I can't believe he asked Amanda out."

Bethany set her chin in her hand. "I like your pearl necklace."

"Somebody really ought to tell her to be careful. I mean, she's my accountant. As soon as Ian figured that out his eyes lit up."

"You never wear pearls."

"And what's she doing dating him anyway? We're related. Doesn't that mean anything to her?"

"I like your shirt too. Makes your eyes really pop."

Robin stopped her one-sided interrogation and stared at her friend. "What are you talking about?"

"I think you look extra nice tonight, that's all."

"Stop being weird."

"*I'm* being weird?"

Across the diner, Ian leaned over the table and whispered something to Amanda. Robin pressed her lips together and glared at her menu.

"Remember Binky?" Bethany asked.

"Your cat?"

"Yeah. Grandpa Dan gave him to me for my thirteenth birthday."

Megan clunked two glasses against the tabletop. Ice clashed together, splashing water over the edge. The waitress muttered something about Amanda and tight clothes and left them to their conversation.

"We used to dress her up in our old doll clothes. Remember that? Binky would sit there and purr and let us put dresses on her."

Robin furrowed her brow.

"She used to sleep on my feet every night. Get them so toasty-warm I thought they'd melt off. And then I'd wake up and she'd be wrapped around my face. I think she was the only cat that snored."

Bethany was acting like Robin's great-aunt Agnes, who turned ninety-seven last week and suffered from advanced dementia. "Why are you talking about Binky?"

Bethany shook her head, a faraway, nostalgic look in her eye. "Then she ran away. And Mom found her on the road leading into the trailer park."

Robin remembered. Somebody had flattened Binky into road kill and Bethany had been distraught. They'd shoveled the cat into an old shoe box and buried her behind Bethany's trailer home.

"I refused to pet another cat for an entire year."

Annoyance licked up Robin's spine. "What's this about? Do you want another cat or something?"

Bethany shrugged. "I was just thinking that if I did, there wouldn't be anything wrong with that." She flipped open her menu. "It's not like it would be disloyal to Binky or anything."

◛

Ian snuck a glance at Robin. Their gaze connected and she ducked behind her menu. A smirk tugged at the corners of his mouth. She was checking up on him. If only he knew why…

"Is something funny?"

He set his elbow on the table and shifted forward in his chair. "No, sorry." He was determined to make up for his lousy behavior last weekend. Sneaking glances at another woman would not help him accomplish his goal, despite Amanda's Girl Scout pledge to keep things platonic.

She clasped her hands and propped them beneath her chin. "I'd love to know what you were just thinking."

He skimmed the menu. "I was thinking about how horribly I behaved at the banquet. I'm really sorry about that."

"You already apologized."

"I know, but I'm still ashamed," he said.

"Can I ask you something?"

"Be my guest."

She pulled out a sugar packet from the condiment rack. "Were Cheryl and Jim the only reason you were distracted, or was something else going on?"

Too many something elses to count, and if he started talking about them now, their conversation would never recover. "Just stressed out about the condominiums."

"Your dad seems to have confidence in you."

"Yeah, well, my dad has confidence in a lot of things."

"Like?"

"Me taking over the family business someday."

The sugar packet crinkled in her hand. "You don't want to?"

Ian looked around Val's Diner and thought about Arton's Jewelry store. The layout, the dimensions. He imagined replacing the display cases with tables and chairs, maybe a bar. "My dad is passionate about developing. That's his thing."

"What's yours?"

He remembered Robin's expression when she tried the omelet he made a couple weeks ago. She'd wanted to hate it. He could see the desire on her face, but she couldn't lie. By the time she took her third bite, she was smiling. "Restaurants."

"Really?" Amanda folded a corner of the sugar packet. "Then why are you a developer?"

"It's complicated."

"I'm sure I can keep up."

Ian fiddled with his napkin. "I enjoy working with my dad. He's a good guy, you know? I don't want to disappoint him." He'd done enough of that already. Besides, Ian had a stable future at McKay Development and Construction. He couldn't say those things about the restaurant business.

"Take him out of the equation for a minute. Do you like your work?"

"Do you like being an accountant?"

She shrugged.

"See, it's a weird question. How many people honestly love what they do?" His attention wandered to Robin. So did Amanda's.

"But the idea of owning a restaurant. You think you'd love that?"

"I know I would."

Megan dropped two chocolate milkshakes on the tabletop, tossed them a couple straws, and slunk away. Ian tapped one against the table to remove the paper wrapping and squinted after the waitress's retreating backside. He'd never seen her so glum. "Is something wrong with Megan?"

"She thinks we're dating."

Megan took an order from a group of teenagers off to the left. The poor girl looked like a kicked puppy. "Love stinks."

"Tell me about it."

"Perhaps the experience will be good fodder for her poetry."

Amanda dipped her finger into the cap of whipped cream floating over her shake and came away with a white dollop covering her nail. She put it in her mouth and closed her eyes, as if savoring the velvety sweetness. "All the women in here are dying."

"Sounds serious. Should we leave before the epidemic spreads?"

Amanda smiled.

"Do I get to know what they're dying of?"

"Half from curiosity, and the other from jealousy. This is a small town, you know. Right now you're the most eligible bachelor."

Ian looked over at Robin. "Do you know…?" His question trailed off. How could he ask it without sounding like a complete idiot?

"What half Robin is on?" Amanda dunked her straw up and down in her shake, mixing whipped cream and chocolate. "Of course. Don't you?"

"She's not exactly easy to figure out."

"Let's just say I told Robin about our date and she doesn't make a habit of coming to Val's on a Friday night."

"She's part of the curious half, then."

Amanda took a sip through her straw, cheeks pulling in with the effort.

The front doors swooshed open. Evan walked inside, followed by a man—slightly taller, with shaggier hair and an easy, laid-back swagger. They walked to the far end of the diner, to Bethany and Robin's table. Robin stood, hugged Evan before he slipped into the booth next to his wife, and then wrapped her arms around the other guy's neck in an all-too intimate squeeze.

Ian nodded toward the foursome. "She's obviously not jealous."

"Are you?"

He let out an uncomfortable laugh just as his cell phone chirped in his pocket. Saved by the bell. He fished it out from its hiding place, thankful for the distraction. His mother's number lit the screen. "Mind if I take this real quick?"

"Go right ahead."

"Thanks." He slipped outside and pressed talk on the fourth buzz. "Hey, Mom."

"I wanted to check in. Make sure you made it to Peaks okay." Even through the receiver, her voice sounded weak.

"I made it here all in one piece." He looked at the sky, dark blue melting into dusk, inky smudges of pinks and oranges trailing through the clouds. "How are you feeling?"

"Glad I'm done with chemo."

The memory of her wasted body gnawed at him. How could Dad pressure her to continue when it caused her so much pain? Especially when Mom made it sound like the whole thing was unnecessary. "Me too."

"Have you thought about coming home tomorrow?"

"I just got back." And Peoria was the last place he wanted to be. Maybe that made him a coward, but he couldn't stick around and watch her decline. He just couldn't.

"Is everything okay, honey?"

"Yeah. Everything's great."

"You seemed so out of sorts at dinner last night."

That's because last night had been altogether disturbing. Watching Mom pick at her food. Watching Dad watch Mom pick at her food. His father might have put up a great front at the banquet on Saturday, but his mother's ailing health was taking a major toll. Ian could see it in every line on Dad's face.

"I told your father not to invite Cheryl to the banquet. I don't know why he insisted."

"I'm sure Dad had his reasons."

"It was uncalled for."

"Mom?"

"Yes."

"I brought a date too, remember?"

"And I heard she was lovely." Mom's sigh whispered in Ian's ear. "I'm praying for you, honey. Every morning. All day."

Ian leaned against the brick façade and crossed one leg over the other. He wanted to tell her to save her prayers for herself. He wanted to tell her to stop worrying. It wasn't helping anything. Not her. Not him. "I'm fine."

"You sound like your dad."

"He'd tell me I sound like you."

The rise and fall of her laughter unclenched some of his muscles. "I love you, sweetheart," she said. "More than you could possibly know. So does your father."

"I know. I love you guys too." They said good-bye. Ian slipped his phone into his pocket just as the door opened and Robin stepped outside. He cleared the gruffness from his voice. "Leaving your date early?"

She startled and pressed her palm against her collarbone.

"Sorry, didn't mean to scare you."

Robin pointed toward the street. "My purse is in my car."

So the guy wasn't paying? Interesting.

She stepped around him, but Ian took her elbow. Her attention flitted from his hand to his eyes before she pulled away.

"You're not very appreciative, are you?"

"Why should I be appreciative?"

"First, I saved you from falling off the ladder. Second, I found your runaway son." He ticked them off on his fingers. "Third, I ensured you'd be able to play the piano with ten digits, fully intact."

Her eyes narrowed. "I know what you're doing."

"What's that?"

"You're using Amanda to get under my skin."

Ian stepped closer. "That's a bold accusation."

"Is it true?"

Anger simmered beneath the surface of his emotions. Mom's worry.

Dad's disapproval. His growing exasperation with this woman in front of him. Why, of all things, did she have to be a beautiful widow? Why couldn't she be a grumpy old man? "What about you?"

"What about me?"

Ian pictured her in his car, frantically searching for her lost wedding ring, and his anger grew. "Somebody should warn your date."

"I don't know what you're talking about."

"He doesn't stand a chance, Robin. Nobody does. Not when you're still in love with your husband." The words tumbled out before he could take them back. Before he could stop and think.

Her cheeks paled, but she didn't say anything. She pressed her lips together and stalked toward the street, leaving him alone with his regret and the last vestiges of pink receding from the sky.

THIRTY

The quietness inside Robin's living room screamed. She jiggled her leg and stared out the picture window, waiting. Always and forever waiting. Her life had turned into one giant interim. This temporary allotment of space and time and breath that she didn't know what to do with anymore. The wait tonight at least had a focus—headlights. Any minute now, Ian's car would pull into her driveway and release Amanda.

Robin crossed her arms and her legs, as if attempting to hold herself together. She'd watched Ian escort Amanda from the diner with a sickening sense of dread, and every minute after had her nerves closer and closer to unraveling. She hurled herself off the couch and began a short-routed pace, wondering if Ian would walk Amanda to the door. Would she have to listen to them whisper and flirt on the front porch? Robin imagined him kissing Amanda good night and her pacing grew more frenzied.

"When you're still in love with your husband…"

He'd spit the words out like an accusation, like there was something wrong with loving the man she'd married. Like death should make her stop. She fell back onto the couch and fingered her ring, wishing she could erase the memory of Ian sliding it on her finger. Squeezing her eyelids tight, she waited for darkness to blot it out. But it didn't work. The memory had turned into a stain.

Where are You, Lord? Because I could sure use Your wisdom right about now.

She took a deep breath and waited for something, anything. But nothing came. Robin felt abandoned, wandering in a desert with no escape. Pushing the air out of her lungs, she picked up Micah's Bible from the end table and flipped through the thin pages of Deuteronomy, drawing comfort from the underlined passages until her nerves settled and her eyelids grew too heavy to hold up.

Dreams came, fuzzy and disorienting. One minute Amanda was home, on the porch, kissing Ian. The next, a breeze filtered through her window and she was sleeping on the couch. Then Caleb was awake, running through the house, but she couldn't catch him. Bethany was showing her a positive pregnancy test while Robin cried and cried and cried. And then she was in the desert and she was kissing Ian and Micah was pulling her away...

Robin jolted upright, her heart pounding. A car door had slammed. The house was dark and quiet and she could hear the car idling outside. Footfalls sounded up the walkway. Porch light spilled onto the carpet. Robin leaned forward, straining to hear voices. Instead, the headlights backed out of the driveway and a key jiggled in the lock and Amanda stepped inside.

Robin clutched Micah's Bible and stood. "Where have you been?"

Amanda stopped on the threshold and held up her hands, her purse swinging from the crook of her elbow. "Whoa, major déjà vu. It's like I'm in high school all over again."

"Be serious, Amanda. It's almost midnight."

"Be serious, Robin. I'm not a little kid. Last time I checked my license, I was a full-fledged twenty-four-year-old adult." Amanda came all the way through the door and slipped off her heels.

Robin swallowed. If she didn't say it now, she'd never say it. "I wanted to talk with you about something."

"Speak freely, my friend."

"I'm concerned about you."

"What, specifically, is your concern?"

"You just got out of a long-term relationship. I don't want you to get hurt again." Even if Ian was interested in Amanda and his attention had nothing to do with Willow Tree Café, the man was leaving. As soon as he realized he was fighting a losing battle, he would return to his life and his home in Peoria. It would be Jason all over again.

Amanda's eyes darkened. "What makes you think Ian will hurt me?"

"You're my accountant and he's looking for dirt on my café."

"Dirt on your café? What is this, CSI?" Amanda tossed her purse on the sofa table and headed toward the stairs.

"Would you wait? I'm trying to have a conversation with you."

Amanda clutched the banister and turned around. "About what?"

"Ian."

"And your concern for my heart?"

"Yes."

"This doesn't have anything to do with your concern for me or any of my organs."

"Of course it does. You're vulnerable right now and—"

Amanda held up a flat palm, like a traffic cop directing the flow of Robin's voice. "Why don't you admit it?"

"Admit what?"

"You're jealous."

"That's ridiculous!"

"Any more ridiculous than you staying up until midnight to tell me what you think about my involvement with Ian? Or any more ridiculous than you spying on us tonight at Val's?"

"Okay, fine. You're right. The spying was messed up. But I'm worried."

"Well, don't be, because Ian and I are only friends."

The relief was immediate and disturbing. "But I thought you liked him."

Something clattered upstairs. It sounded like one of Caleb's toys falling from his bed. Most likely a dinosaur. Robin held her breath and waited for her sleepy-eyed son to come out of his bedroom, but only stillness filled the stairwell.

Amanda lowered her voice. "It's kind of hard to like a guy when he has feelings for somebody else."

"Somebody else?"

"Yeah. You."

Heat slashed Robin's cheeks. No, Amanda was mistaken. Ian did not have feelings for her.

"The feeling's obviously mutual. So..." The unspoken words settled between them. They turned Robin's mouth dry and rested like a cold lump in the pit of her stomach. It took her several seconds to realize she was shaking her head.

"Why not?" Amanda asked.

"Because..." Robin fumbled for an excuse. For a reason. "I don't want Caleb to get hurt."

"Oh, come on. You mean *you* don't want you to get hurt."

Robin's heart thudded like a bass drum. It beat inside her chest and her ears and her knees. "I had the love of a lifetime with Micah. I know how blessed I was. That sort of thing doesn't come around twice."

"How do you know?" Amanda stared into Robin's eyes, her expression filled with compassion and pity. "Listen, I'm not going to deny that what you and my brother had was special. And I won't tell you that love isn't risky. But it seems a shame that you'd shut yourself off from the possibility just because you're scared." Her posture deflated. "Fear is not from the Lord, Robin. You've read your Bible enough to know that."

∾

As hard as Robin tried to fight it, the yawn came. It pried her mouth wide open. She covered the offense with her hand and hoped nobody noticed. Jed Johnson had finally joined the support group and she didn't want him thinking her yawn had anything to do with the length of his prayer request. Especially when she was thrilled to have him there.

Thanks to the clunky bandage wrapped around her finger, she jotted the truncated version of Jed's concerns in a sloppy scrawl and glanced at the counter. Throughout the entirety of their Saturday morning gathering, a steady trickle of customers had kept Joe busy.

The leaning tower of blocks Caleb built in the kids' corner clattered to the floor, followed by his laughter. It was a good sound. A much-needed sound. Robin covered another yawn and waited until Jed finished. After last night's quarrel with Amanda, she hadn't been able to fall asleep until two in the morning. She lay with eyes wide open, Amanda's words flip-flopping in her stomach. So she'd opened Micah's Bible and read the Psalms until sleep finally took her.

"Are you finished now?" A not-so-subtle hint of annoyance colored Bernie's words.

Jed tore off bits of napkin and bunched them between his fingers. Cinnamon roll crumbs and white napkin flakes decorated his plate. He peeked at Bernie, his overlarge ears tingeing with pink. "My grandkids tell me I ramble. I guess it's a hard habit to break."

Bernie harrumphed.

Robin smiled. The woman was all bark and no bite. Hopefully Jed would pick up on that sooner rather than later. "Do you have any prayer requests for us this morning, Bernie?"

"My cat broke her tail."

Robin scrunched her nose. Since when did Bernie have a cat?

"Oh, the poor dear," Linda said.

"Bill's very upset. I'm not sure I should have left her."

Cecile set her mug on the table. "Who's Bill?"

"My cat."

Cecile made a face. "You named a female cat Bill?"

"It's a perfectly fine name."

Robin hid her smile behind her hand. *Oh, Lord, thank You for these people.* They were a bright spot to her week.

"The B and B felt empty after Ian left so I bought her at the farmer's market."

"They sell cats at the farmer's market?" Linda asked.

"Lyle Noldt was selling them for the 4-H club. But now Ian's back, and supposedly, he's allergic to cats. So on top of Bill's broken tail, I'm trying to lint-roll all her hair to make Ian's stay less miserable."

"It's not actually the fur that causes the allergies." Jed tore off a few more napkin pieces and looked at Bernie through thick eyeglasses. "It's dried saliva and protein particles. A good HEPA filter would help."

"And where in Peaks would I get a HEPA filter?" Bernie asked.

Jed ran his hand over thinning wisps of white hair. "I have some extras at my house. If you'd like one, I could bring it over."

Bernie harrumphed again, but Robin caught her eyes softening.

"Speaking of Ian," Cecile said. "Rumor has it he went on a date with a certain someone last night."

The same heat from last night bit at Robin's cheeks. How had the conversation landed here? She could feel Cecile's stare boring into the side of her face, probing for details. But Robin had nothing to say. She was still unable to fully process Amanda's declaration from last night—the one about Ian having feelings for her. Anytime she started to think about it, she lost her appetite.

"Val said they came to her diner last night looking awfully cozy."

"That makes me a little sad," said Linda. "She and Jason made such a good couple."

"How do you feel about it, Robin?" Cecile asked.

"What do you mean?"

"She's your sister-in-law."

"So?"

"He wants your café."

"Amanda is free to befriend whomever she wants to befriend." Robin set her pencil down and closed her notebook. She had recorded everybody's requests. It was time to wrap up with a prayer and spend the day with her son, not thinking about Ian. "Thanks for coming, everyone. If you don't mind, I'd like to close us in prayer."

The jingling of the front bell cut Robin off and Ian walked inside. Cecile Arton made a funny humming noise in the back of her throat. Robin excused herself from her table and made her way to intercept him. She did not want him talking to her support group, nor did she want to discuss her café. She'd rather not have anything to do with a man who made it sound like loving her husband was a bad thing. She met him halfway between the front door and the counter. "Can I help you?"

"Good morning," he said.

She pinned her gaze on his shoulder. Safer territory than the brownish-amber warmth of his eyes. "If this is about the café…"

"I'm not here to talk about the café."

"Then what are you here to talk about?"

"I couldn't sleep last night." He dipped his chin and caught her attention from the tops of his eyes. "I kept lying there, thinking about what I said to you. Sometimes having a conscience can be really inconvenient."

"Imagine that."

"I'm sorry. It was completely unfair and uncalled for."

"Which part? When you brought up my husband or when you accused me of leading on my brother-in-law?"

"Your brother-in-law?" Ian cocked his head. "You have *another* brother-in-law in Peaks?"

She nodded.

"I'm an idiot." He jerked his head in the direction of her piano. "And we have an audience."

Robin glanced over her shoulder. Four pairs of watchful eyes looked away, toward the drinks and empty plates in front of them. Robin swallowed. If Ian was going to be polite, she had no reason not to return the sentiment. "I'm sorry too."

"For what?"

"My accusation about you and Amanda. That wasn't fair. She's a big girl who can handle herself, and even though I don't like what you're doing in Peaks, I don't think you're that kind of a guy."

Ian's eyes crinkled. He slid his hands in his pockets and leaned close. "Did you just pay me a compliment?"

"Don't get used to it."

"Hey, I'll take what I can get."

She fiddled with the gauze on her finger, her stomach entirely too swoopy. "Is that all?"

"Unless you're in the mood to serve me some coffee?"

"Not particularly. Given the circumstances."

"Understandable." He looked as if he might say something more. Instead, he flashed his smile and walked out of her café. Robin stared after him, partly to avoid Cecile's inevitable interrogation. Partly to process his visit. Surely Ian had a next move. Guys like him carried checkmates in their pockets.

THIRTY-ONE

Ian straightened his tie with one hand and made his way toward the town hall. He'd spent the entire week paying a personal visit to every viable business along Main Street, meeting with owners about investing in the condominiums. He knew many of them were struggling, and even though McKay had several investors lined up in Peoria, he wanted to give the local business owners of Peaks an opportunity to benefit from these condominiums in a more personal way, no matter how small. And he needed the distraction.

From the problem that had become Robin Price.

Despite meeting with the zoning board, checking the property for easements, and having a mile-long list of investors, Ian still had not secured the site. For the first time in his career, he had no idea what to do. So he ignored the problem. He didn't return Dad's messages and he avoided thoughts about the weekend that lay before him—one that sheltered an anniversary he wished he could blot from existence.

The soles of his polished shoes padded against the ground as he buttoned his lapels with one hand and shouldered open the front door of the town hall. Ian greeted an auburn-haired woman sitting behind a long, polished desk. She smiled kindly and told him to go on back. He made his way down the hallway, where familiar laughter filtered through the open doorway of the mayor's office. Ian stopped short. Not only was the mayor there... so was his father.

"Come on in, Ian." Mayor Ford waved him inside, his cheeks filled with color.

Dad sat with his elbows propped on the armrests of his chair, as if his presence in Peaks, as if his presence here—in Mayor Ford's office—was nothing out of the ordinary.

"You never mentioned your father would be joining us today," Mayor Ford said.

"I wasn't aware of it."

"It was a last-minute decision." Dad clasped his hands. "I had an appointment cancel, so I thought I'd come check on things here. Get an update and make sure everything's going as planned."

"I think you'd be proud to know, Mr. McKay, that this son of yours has charmed most of the town."

Dad looked at Ian. "What about the resistant café owner? Have you charmed her?"

The muscles in Ian's shoulders tightened. Why was Dad checking up on him?

Mayor Ford centered his pencil cup. "Robin's not easily charmed, I'm afraid. And we're racing time—which is why I'm glad you and Ian are both here. I have an interesting proposition to make." He clapped his hands and rubbed his palms together. "Let's get right to it, shall we?"

Ian's skin prickled. He wasn't sure he wanted to hear whatever interesting proposition Mayor Ford had to make, but he set his briefcase beside the empty seat and settled into the chair.

"If we're going to turn Peaks into a bedroom community, not only do we have to offer the best, we have to offer it first. We're convinced you build the best, but none of that matters if your condominiums go up *after* Fixtel opens. The employees will already have moved elsewhere, perhaps buying in Le Claire or across the river in Port Byron."

Tightness rippled from Ian's jaw down into his neck and shoulders. He knew exactly what Mayor Ford was going to suggest.

"You probably have experience with eminent domain." Mayor Ford scratched his earlobe. "Basically, we'd force her to sell."

Dad crossed his leg and clasped his hands over his knee. "Yes, we know what eminent domain means, Mayor Ford."

The mayor chuckled, but as soon as he realized he was the only one laughing, the sound curdled. "The municipality of Peaks would condemn Robin's property. We'd pay her fair price for the land and we'd sell it to you. I know this sort of thing is usually reserved for state highways and the like, but a few of the council members and I have done our research. We think we're in a favorable position."

Ian couldn't believe it. He promised Robin it wouldn't come to force, but that was exactly what Mayor Ford wanted to do.

"It's a pretty bold move," Dad said.

Mayor Ford picked up a pen and gave it a few taps against his desktop. "Yes, well, I'm confident we won't end up in court over this."

"You do realize," Ian said, squishing the words between his teeth, "that eminent domain is a court procedure."

"The threat of it will be enough to get her to sell."

"She's a lot more determined then you're giving her credit for."

"Robin's a great gal and I understand that she's emotionally attached. She's had a nice run with her café, but I'm convinced these condos are exactly what this town needs." The mayor pulled a pocket calendar from the top drawer of his desk and flipped through the pages. "We have another town meeting scheduled in a few weeks. The fourteenth of July, I believe. We'll discuss condemnation then and move forward from there. That is, if you're still interested in building."

"I'm not sure—"

"Of course we're still interested." Dad's words sliced through Ian's objection. He stood and shook the mayor's hand.

Ian blinked several times, then exited the town hall behind his father. As soon as they stepped into the sun, Ian stopped. "Do you mind telling me what in the world that was about?"

"You've been MIA for a week. You haven't returned any of my messages, which means I had nothing to report at our Wednesday meeting. If you were any other employee, I'd call you into my office and we'd have a serious discussion about the future."

But Ian wasn't any other employee. He was the boss's son, which meant his future was secure, whether he wanted it to be or not.

Dad stepped closer. "This is the most important deal in the history of our company. I gave it to you because I thought you were the best man for the job."

"Maybe you thought wrong."

Dad's eyes filled with disappointment. "Please tell me you're not letting things get personal between you and this café owner. If you've learned anything from the divorce, I hope it would be that messes are usually created when we mix business with pleasure."

Ian ran his hand across his jaw, steam building in his chest.

"I heard the way you talked about her at the banquet."

"She doesn't want to sell."

"Then we brainstorm ways that will get her to reconsider." Dad's face turned red. "You don't give up. I didn't raise a quitter."

"Oh, and what's that supposed to mean?"

"You gave up on your marriage when it got hard and now you're giving up on this too."

"You have no idea what I'm giving up. And you have no idea about my marriage."

"You're quitting too soon, just like your mother!"

The words punched a hole straight through Ian's anger. All the heat swooshed right out of him. "What did you say?"

"The doctors found a new mass yesterday." Dad's shoulders collapsed. He took a seat on the curb and dug his hands through his hair. "She's refusing to do any more chemo."

The café and the condemnation became something far away, something distant.

"I can't lose her, Ian. She's my entire world." Dad's voice cracked. "I don't know what to do anymore. Lord God, tell me what to do."

In all Ian's life, he'd never heard his father say those words.

༄

It was Friday afternoon. Chief Bergman and his wife were finishing their coffee up in the loft. Professor Lofton—the man who taught Robin behavioral psychology at St. Ambrose—ate a three-cheese soufflé and prepared lecture notes at a table near the back. Robin had just sent Lyle Noldt's wife off with an entire box of oatmeal raisin cookies and now she stood behind the counter, staring at her piano. Her yearning filled the entire room. Seven days without music and the edges of her soul were turning brittle.

Kyle walked through the front door, his face creased with more lines than usual.

"Is everything okay?" she asked.

"Carl Crammer passed away last night."

Robin blinked several times, positive she'd heard wrong.

"He had a heart attack. Mimi couldn't get him to the hospital in time."

Her limbs went cold. Carl Crammer? The man who always clapped for Robin's music? The man who couldn't hide the twinkle of pride in his eye whenever he complained about his only son running off to Chicago? The coldness in her limbs leaked into her stomach. She'd seen Carl two days ago and now he was gone. How was it possible? Robin shuddered. Life could change in a snap. Without warning, everything could flip upside down and inside out. Just like that.

"Mimi doesn't have any family around here. From what I've gathered, they've lived alone in that trailer home for the past fifteen years. I believe their son might be on his way." Kyle dragged his hand down his tired face. Poor guy hadn't signed up for this. Moving to a town that split itself in two, taking over a ministry that landed itself in the center of the conflict.

"Who's with her right now?" Robin asked.

"Nobody. I just made sure she got home safely from the hospital. I met them at the meet and greet, but they never really came to One Life. I think I made her more uncomfortable than anything else."

"I'll go over to see her as soon as I'm done." And Caleb? Who would pick him up from day care? And why was he always getting the short end of her busy stick? Her schedule was too cramped. She had no margin. "I can help with the funeral arrangements, and I'll ask my support group to fix some meals."

"Thanks, Robin." Kyle squeezed her hand. "I'll give you a call later tonight to see how Mimi's holding up."

She grabbed a to-go cup from the stack. "Can I get you a coffee before you leave?"

"No, thanks." He smiled and left the café.

Robin put the cup back on the stack, tears welling in her eyes. Carl Crammer was dead and Mimi was still here. Left to pick up whatever pieces remained of life without her husband. She did not envy what that woman had ahead of her. Chief Bergman and his wife clanked down the steps, waved good-bye, and stepped out the door, oblivious to the fact that not too far away, a woman's life had shattered to pieces. Before the door closed, Ian McKay, the man she hadn't seen since last Saturday—the one who'd spent the week talking to every business up and down Main Street—slipped inside her café and headed toward the front counter. She turned around and pressed her hand against her middle.

"No Joe or Molly today?"

"Nope, just me." Robin blinked away the moisture in her eyes and faced Ian with a smile that felt lopsided and stiff. "You're not going to talk to me about investing too, are you?"

He cocked his head. "Is something wrong?"

The question almost undid her, but the jingle of the doorbell distracted them both. A woman came in with her son. Ian stepped to the side while Robin took the lady's order. The entire time she made the iced coffee, she could feel Ian's stare. She counted out the woman's change with shaky hands, thanked her for coming, and watched the mother-son duo exit.

"Robin?" Ian studied her beneath a concerned brow.

"Carl Crammer passed away." Robin cupped her forehead with her palm and shook her head. Even when she said it, she still couldn't quite believe it. "I need to go visit Mimi, which means I have to call Bethany and see if she can pick up my son. I'd like to bring Mimi something warm, and somehow, I'll have to make time to help arrange the man's funeral."

The front door swooshed open. For once, Robin wished away the customers. How was she supposed to call Bethany or make a meal for Mimi with a line at her cash register? She got the man a coffee to go, but as soon as he left, somebody else came in.

Ian came around the counter. "What's Bethany's phone number?"

"What?"

"Your friend's phone number? I'll call her and ask if she can pick up Caleb."

Robin handed a woman her change. "You don't have to do that."

The door opened again.

"C'mon, Robin, you can't do it all," he said. "Let me help you."

His words brought a lump to her throat. She hesitated for a moment, then scrawled the number on a napkin. Ian disappeared inside her kitchen while Robin served her customers. Four in total, two of whom gave her the thumbs-up for supporting One Life and fighting against Ian McKay. If only they knew the man was in her kitchen. A good twenty minutes passed before her café emptied of customers—including Professor Lofton—and Ian had yet to resurface. What was he doing back there? She looked at the clock. Five to three. Close enough. She flipped the sign on the door from Open to Closed, then stood frozen in place, nerves playing leapfrog until she smelled fried onion and garlic.

When she pushed open the door, she found a very familiar scene. "You're cooking?"

"Lasagna. I figured it's a safe bet. I've never met anybody who doesn't like it."

The muscles in Robin's chest constricted. Ian was cooking a meal for Mimi?

"Bethany said not to worry, she'd pick up Caleb at three thirty sharp."

Robin stepped all the way inside her kitchen, the door swinging behind her. Ian let her lean against the prep table and pray for Mimi while he navigated the small space. When he finally broke the silence, he did so with a simple request. "Do you have a pan?"

Robin grabbed one off a shelf and handed it over.

He began layering in the ingredients. "Do you mind if I ask why you do it?"

"What?"

"The support group. The funeral. All of it. If anybody has an excuse to sit those things out, it would be you."

"I can't sit any of it out."

"Why not?"

Because I know what it feels like." She picked up the chef knife and rinsed it off in the sink. "I've worn those shoes. So how can I not be there for someone who's going through the same thing?"

Ian shook his head.

"What?"

"I'm fighting Mother Teresa."

Despite Kyle's somber news, she laughed. "I am a far cry from Mother Teresa, trust me."

He pulled several lasagna noodles from the box and met Robin's gaze. "I've never met anybody like you."

Her stomach did several somersaults. "You're giving me too much credit. My reasons are not entirely selfless."

"No?"

"Helping people who are going through what I've been through makes me feel like Micah's death wasn't in vain. It gives the pain I went through a sense of purpose." Robin placed the knife on the bottom of the sink. "I just wish Caleb didn't have to suffer for it. Being a single parent isn't easy."

"For what it's worth, I think you do a great job." Pain peeked out from his eyes, bringing a shadow to his face that had nothing to do with the light. At that moment, she'd give anything to know what he was thinking. What pain did Ian McKay carry? But it left before she could inquire. "You're a wonderful mother," he said.

"If you can believe it, I used to want five."

Ian coughed. "Kids?"

"I know. Crazy. And it's impossible." Robin wiped her fingers off on a towel, the diamond of her ring catching the light. "It is now, anyway."

"You're still young." Ian smiled. "Anything's possible."

Robin wanted to tell him no, not that. But then she remembered Mimi and those dark days after Micah's funeral. If it was possible to get through such suffocating grief, then maybe Ian was right. Maybe anything was possible. She wanted to believe that. More than he could know.

Ian sprinkled mozzarella cheese over the lasagna and whistled. Watching him cook was like watching her mother play the piano—magical. Robin wanted to give him something in return for all his help. He couldn't possibly know how much it meant. But what? She studied her injured finger, remembering the lost look on Ian's face that day she sliced it open. When he slid her wedding ring back in place. "You know that day in your car, after you took me to Dr. Dotts?"

Ian stopped his sprinkling.

"I let you assume something that wasn't one hundred percent accurate."

"Oh?" He leaned toward her.

"You assumed Micah bought my ring."

"He didn't?"

Robin shook her head. "My dad did." She twirled it with the pad of her thumb and let out a shaky breath. "Part of the reason I freaked out is because I'm sentimental and it's my wedding ring. But I also freaked out because it belonged to my mother first. She wore it for twenty years before Micah ever put it on my finger."

The two of them stood inside the small kitchen, surrounded by the smell of onions and garlic and browned meat, Robin's intimate confession nestled between them.

"That's kind of sad," Ian finally said. "But romantic too."

She smiled down at the sink, charmed by this man who thought her mother's ring was romantic. "Yeah. I guess it is."

"Hey, Robin?"

"Yes?"

"I have to tell you something."

The air in the kitchen hummed with energy, but when she looked up, the crinkle was gone from his eyes. It made her stomach turn into a ball of lead.

"The mayor is going to speak with the town about condemning your property."

"Condemning my property?"

"It's when the government forces you to sell."

The quivering in her knees spread until both of her legs quaked beneath her. "That doesn't sound legal."

"Unfortunately, it is." He stuck his hands in his pockets and had the audacity to look tortured, as if this turn of events troubled him as much as it troubled her.

THIRTY-TWO

R obin knocked on the screen door of the double-wide. When no-
body answered, she craned her neck and looked over her shoulder.
Mimi and Carl's rusted-out pickup sat in the gravel driveway. Nearly every
Saturday evening at eight thirty, Robin would hear it thunder down Main
Street and rumble to a stop outside her café. Without its muffler, the thing
coughed and hacked like an old man with bad lungs.

Carl and Mimi would sit at the same table, sip coffee—black and pip-
ing hot—listen to Robin's music, and split a cinnamon roll, courtesy of
Willow Tree. Maybe Amanda thought it was poor business, but at that
moment, not one ounce of her regretted giving the Crammers anything for
free. She brought the warm lasagna pan to her side and knocked again.

The older woman shuffled to the door, her eyes puffy and bloodshot.
The familiar signs of grief hurled Robin into the past, back when those
puffy, bloodshot eyes had been her own. Mimi pushed her hand against the
screen door. It squealed on its hinges, a helpless cry for some WD-40. When
Robin stepped inside, the scrap of metal whapped against the door frame
and the stale smell of cigarette smoke greeted her. She shifted the lasagna to
the other side of her body and enfolded Mimi in a one-armed hug. The
woman crumpled, her body chugging like a silent steam engine. Robin held
on tight. She knew the long days the woman had ahead of her. The even
longer nights.

When Mimi resurfaced from her shoulder, Robin plucked a tissue from
her purse and handed it over. "All I keep thinking is that Carl will never get
to hear Jake play," Mimi said, blotting her face.

Robin led her to the tweed sofa and placed the lasagna on the fold-out table in the small kitchen. The tear-soaked cuffs of Mimi's oversized, tattered flannel shirt reached past her fingertips as she stared off into nothing. Robin sat next to her, the couch springs squeaking beneath her weight. "Do you mind if I pray?"

Mimi sniffed and closed her eyes.

Robin gathered Mimi's cold hands in her own and prayed the only thing she knew to pray. The same prayer she'd clung to when her own grief had threatened to consume her. A simple, heartfelt prayer that reminded her of her need and God's faithfulness to meet it. "Wrap Mimi in Your strong arms, Lord. Wipe away her tears. Carry her through this pain."

In the cocoon of that tiny trailer, with Mimi's hand in hers, Robin's problems with the café shrank into something very small and very distant.

∽

Caleb's face peered through the kitchen window of the farmhouse, twisting Robin's heart. She'd spent a much longer time with Mimi Crammer than she'd planned. She jogged the rest of the way toward the farmhouse and walked inside the kitchen. Caleb hugged her waist. She swept him into her arms and groaned. How was her baby boy so big already? "You are a giant!"

"I'm not a giant, silly."

"Fee-fie-fo-fum."

Caleb giggled and sandwiched her cheeks with his small hands.

She kissed his nose and hugged him tight, as if the tighter she held on the less time would slip away. She wanted to snuggle him to her chest and hold him there forever. Instead, she inhaled the scent of leftover shampoo and little boy sweat and looked over the top of his head. "Is Elyse asleep?"

Bethany held up the baby monitor. "Finally."

"Rough day?"

"She's been super fussy. Barely ate anything all evening. Running another fever. I called Dr. Dotts, but he didn't seem too concerned."

"Another ear infection?"

A tiny cough sounded from the monitor. Bethany held it up. "Is that normal for a four-month-old?"

"The cough?"

Caleb pulled her face toward his. "Look at me, Mommy."

He didn't give her much of a choice.

His bottom lip pushed into a pout. "You're late."

"I'm sorry, but Mrs. Crammer needed Mommy's help." She looked at Bethany. "Thanks for picking him up at Linda's."

"You look dead on your feet." Bethany pulled out a bottled water and a carton of milk from the refrigerator. She set them on the table, then rummaged through the cupboards and removed a package of Oreos. "Sit. Both of you."

Robin frowned.

"I know. Prepackaged cookies. The hail should start pouring from heaven any minute."

"I can't believe Evan lets those things in the house."

Caleb didn't seem to mind. He took a cookie and dunked it into the milk with his uninjured hand. Robin ran her fingers through his hair. "Only two, sweetheart. I don't want you to spoil your dinner." Maybe they'd go to Subway on the way home. It was one of two fast food restaurants in Peaks, squished between the interstate and the gas station on the north side of town.

Bethany took a cookie and twisted it apart. "How's Mimi?"

"Not good." Joe had called on her way to the farmhouse. His family decided to make a last-minute road trip to visit his brother in Texas. Molly couldn't work an entire Saturday on her own. So somehow, Robin had to find time to work on her day off, visit Mimi, and take care of Caleb. She'd ask Bethany for help if her friend wasn't dealing with a sick baby. Or Amanda if she wasn't going to a bridal shower.

Robin rubbed her temples. Caleb tried to twist his cookie apart like Bethany had, but it crumbled in his hands. He giggled. So did Bethany, and Robin's heart twisted tighter. She missed too many of Caleb's giggles, and tomorrow she'd miss more.

He took a long swig of milk and smacked his lips, a white mustache painted beneath his nose. "Mommy, are you happy or are you sad?"

"A little sad, Bug-man." She kissed his forehead and looked at Bethany over the top of his hair. "Do you mind if I make a quick phone call?"

"Sure. We'll have a dunking contest." Bethany reached for Caleb's milk. He laughed and pulled it away from her hand.

Robin went into the living room and sat on the couch, speed dialing her father. Time to get to the bottom of this condemnation business. The phone rang twice before somebody answered. "Helloooo? Is this Robin?"

"Yes. Who's this?"

"Donna, silly. Or is there another woman in your father's life I should know about?"

"Oh, sorry. Is my dad there?"

"He's sitting right next to me, as a matter of fact. But before I hand you over, I wanted to ask you a couple questions."

"Uh-huh."

"Did your father tell you we set a date?" Donna's high-pitched soprano grated against Robin's nerves. It sounded nothing like Mom's soothing contralto. "August 27! Can you believe it? Less than three months to put together a wedding."

Her tongue suddenly felt heavy, too big for her mouth.

"We've got a lot to do. I'm hoping you'll be my bridesmaid, of course. And Caleb the ring bearer. I wanted to get your opinion on color themes and flowers. And oh, the cake! Do you think you could make it for us?"

Donna's chattering mingled with the faraway giggles of her son and Bethany in the next room. "…I was thinking burgundy and white. Or maybe something closer to purple. What do you think?"

Robin had fidgeted her way to the armrest without noticing. She knocked into it, then dug her nails into the fabric. She didn't have the energy or time to talk about this right now. She had a hungry son eating Oreos in the kitchen and a support group to call so they could organize dinners for Mimi. A funeral to help plan. And a condemnation to fight. The last thing she needed to think about right now was Dad's wedding. "Sorry, Donna, could we talk about this another time?"

"Oh. Sure." She twittered into the phone. "Sorry for rambling. I'm just so excited. We can chat later. Here's your father, dear."

Dad came on the line. Robin skipped the platitudes and got right to it. "Hey, Dad, what do you know about condemnation?"

"Condemnation? As in your property?"

"According to Ian, the mayor is threatening me with it. He says the town could force me to sell."

Her father paused for a moment. "Technically they could."

She closed her eyes. Robin wouldn't let this be Ian's checkmate. She'd find an escape route. A move that would remove her café and One Life from danger. "I don't understand how this is legal. I own the café."

"If the municipality decides Willow Tree is a threat to the town's well-being, then I'm afraid it's legal."

"The town's well-being? You're making it sound like I'm out to destroy the place." When that couldn't be further from the truth. She loved Peaks. If she thought for one second her café was harmful to its well-being, she'd never have built it in the first place.

"Honey, maybe it's best if you sell to Ian."

She scooted to the edge of the sofa. "What?"

"Fighting this condemnation will be a huge investment of time and resources. I'm not sure either would be good for you or Caleb. There's only so much stress you can take."

"That's your answer? You think I should give up?"

"Not give up, sweetie. Move on to something new. A new location for Willow Tree."

Move on? Like he was with Donna? Robin wanted to pick up his words and throw them away. He said them like they were so simple. Like doing so was as easy as choosing between lemon bars and lemon scones. Like she only had to make up her mind and that would be that. But it wasn't simple, and besides, she had One Life to consider.

Caleb poked his head into the living room, a cookie-crumb smile spread wide across his face. A face with Micah's eyes and Micah's nose and Micah's chin. She crooked her finger in an invitation. He raced across the living room and snuggled into her lap.

"The condemnation isn't a sure thing yet. Mayor Ford has to call for a vote at the next town meeting on July 14. There are people in Peaks who don't want me to give up." She thought about Kyle and all the others who'd come to her café, encouraging her to press on. Robin pulled Caleb closer, wrapped her arms around his chest and squeezed him tight, as if the simplicity of his existence might seep from his skin into hers. "I need your support, Dad."

"What do you want me to do?"

"Come to Peaks for the meeting. As my lawyer. And as my father."

"If that's what you need. I can fly in that morning."

Robin thanked him and hung up the phone. Bethany leaned against the doorjamb. "Is everything okay?"

"You know that story about *Alexander and the Terrible, Horrible, No Good, Very Bad Day*?"

"Yeah?"

"I think it's time to move to Australia."

THIRTY-THREE

Caleb woke up on the wrong side of the bed. So did Robin. As soon as the alarm blasted, she wanted to pull the covers over her head and go back to sleep, where thoughts about Ian McKay and condemnation could not follow. But a busy morning awaited. So she got herself and her unhappy son brushed and dressed and in the car, his whiny voice scraping against her eardrums the entire drive to Willow Tree Café.

When they arrived, he pouted and scowled and even stomped his foot. She wanted to stomp her foot right back. Instead, she made phone calls for Mimi and baked for Carl's wake and thanked Linda for leading the grief group and helped Molly with the breakfast rush, all while keeping her grumpy son from making a scene in front of the customers. By the time the café emptied, exhaustion threatened to take over and it was only ten in the morning. She needed a break.

Caleb crouched on the floor behind the counter, crashing a plastic pterodactyl into his Tonka truck. Over and over again. Loudly. Robin tried to shave orange peels for her orange-cranberry tarts at the front counter, but her injured finger kept getting in the way. Molly walked from one table to the next, wiping away crumbs and filling empty canisters with sugar and sweetener packets.

Robin glanced at her son. His scowl was noticeable even from her bird's-eye view. Fingers of guilt wiggled around in her stomach. This was supposed to be one of their days together, but instead of playing outside at a park, her son was stuck here. She sighed and set down the peeler as Molly stepped over the traffic jam of toys and snuck into the kitchen.

"Caleb, honey, I told you to put some of those toys away."

His Tonka truck rammed into several dinosaurs and sent them flying.

The muscles in Robin's jaw tightened. She pressed her knuckles against her eyes and prayed for patience. "Do you want to watch a video in the back room? Maybe *The Land Before Time*? Or *Mary Poppins*?" Evan had installed a television. One with an attached DVD player. She had a basket full of Caleb's favorite movies in a drawer for times such as these.

"No!" The word came out like an accusing finger. Robin had the fleeting urge to snap it off, followed by an intense desire to wrap him in a hug and force him to understand that she loved him more than anything, but right now life was busy and she needed his help.

A wave of anger threatened to capsize the modicum of patience Robin had left. Being a single mother with a café was hard enough. Trying to save that café from a bulldozer was too much. The whole thing set her teeth on edge. She didn't understand how Mayor Ford could call himself a Christian yet knock down one of the town's biggest outreach ministries. How could he justify condemning her property and how could Ian stand by and support it? Robin pressed her fingers against her forehead, as if the pressure might push away her darkening thoughts and the headache throbbing in her temples.

"Fear is not from the Lord, Robin. You've read your Bible enough to know that."

Despite the truth of Amanda's words, that four-letter word coiled like a snake in Robin's belly, its venom seeping into every crevice of her body. She was afraid of disappointing Piper Greeley and every other person who depended on One Life. She was afraid that after everything, she would still lose Willow Tree. But most of all, she was terrified of the way Ian McKay made her feel.

I don't know what to do with these feelings, Lord.

They swirled together in a mass of confusion and fear and guilt. The piano called out her name, but she couldn't play because of her stupid finger. What a silly, pointless injury.

"Uh, Robin"—Molly stepped out of the kitchen—"the oven's making that sound again."

"Saturday is 'posed to be our day!" Caleb shot Robin a look he reserved for the baddest of bad guys and crashed his dinosaurs into the wall.

Molly stumbled over them and nearly fell.

"Caleb, clean those up before somebody breaks a leg!" And before she could swallow the word or pray for patience, a curse flew from her mouth and hung in the air—harsh and portentous.

Caleb had never heard such ugliness before, at least not from his mother. His bottom lip trembled. Tears gathered in his eyes. Robin shook her head and backed away. She couldn't do this anymore. Not right now. She looked at Molly. Grabbed her purse from beneath the register. "I just... I need...a minute."

Molly's head bobbed, fast. Maybe afraid. "I'll watch him."

Without saying a word, Robin hurried outside.

∽

The branches swayed and tickled her face. Droplets of rain took shape and fell from the clouds, painting ripples across the surface of the pond. The rain found its way through the canopy overhead and kissed her cheeks. What was she doing? How could she leave her child with one of her employees?

Lord, what is wrong with me?

Thoughts, images, words coalesced in her mind, gathering into a morbid song. The patter of rain against Micah's casket as they lowered him into the ground. A wrecking ball knocking her café into scraps of plaster and drywall. Mimi Crammer's shattered expression before she crumpled in Robin's arms. The confident, sure movements of Ian's hands as he cooked in her kitchen. Dad's words about moving on. Amanda's words on the stairs.

"Fear is not from the Lord..."

The song rose to its crescendo until all that remained was Micah, but with gaps. His form without substance. His face without any lines. His body without warmth. She scrambled to fill in the holes. To plug them up with memories and love and devotion. But she couldn't, and fire burned in her lungs. She heaved out her breath.

Get out.

Micah was gone. She wanted to move on. More than anything, she wanted to let go. To step forward and grab on to happiness and love and whatever might lie ahead if she could be brave enough to take it. It would be so easy to forget. So easy to let the memories seep through the cracks in her mind. But what would that mean for him and for her and the life they'd shared? And who was to say that step wouldn't lead to more loss, more heartache? The burning moved to her eyes and her arms.

Enough!

She clawed at her finger and pried off her ring. She gripped it in her hand, the metal indenting her palm with a circular welt. She was so sick of holding on, of watching others leave the wilderness while she remained stranded on the bank of the Jordan. She was tired of the waiting and the loneliness and the fear and the guilt and the half-empty closet in her bedroom. She didn't want it. She didn't want any of it. With a cry, she heaved the ring as hard as she could. It landed in the center of the small pond, broke through the crest of water with a glint of diamond, and disappeared, tiny ripples spreading to the shore.

Her breathing stopped.

Everything stopped.

What had she just done?

She squeezed her eyes shut and prayed for the feel of crisp linen sheets against her toes. Prayed she would open her eyes in bed and find that ring, her mother's ring, in its proper place. But the willows brushed her cheek and her finger was naked and the heat in her lungs had turned cold and panicky.

She hurled herself from the cover of the willow, branches snarling against her face, catching against her hair, and ran into the pond. Like a mad woman, with water up to her thighs, she high-stepped through the pond, toward the disappearing ripples.

THIRTY-FOUR

The date filled the bank sign across the street from Bernie's Bed-and-Breakfast—significant numbers in flashing orange. Ian stood outside on Bernie's front lawn, as still as her garden gnomes, staring at the numbers for at least thirty minutes, until his phone buzzed in his pocket.

The scrolling temperature pushed the date aside. Seventy-eight degrees. Sunny with a blanket of gray clouds escaping toward the horizon. He woke up to rain, and now he stood outside in the sun. Not even a trace of the cloying humidity remained. The brief morning shower had swept it away. If only he could say the same about the heaviness inside.

His cell phone buzzed again. Louder somehow. He surrendered to the inquisition and slipped the device from his pocket. "Good morning, Mom."

"I was beginning to wonder if you were ever going to answer."

He scuffed his shoe against the grass.

"I thought you'd be coming home this weekend. It is Father's Day tomorrow, you know."

Of course he knew. The holiday mocked him.

"It would probably cheer your dad up. He's been a bit melancholy around here lately. I think it's because he hasn't seen you in a while."

"He was here yesterday."

"He was?"

"And he was pretty upset."

Mom sighed into the receiver. "This is something your father can't fix, love. He's having a hard time with that."

A bolt of anger flashed through him. At Mom and the cancer and this entire blasted day. "He said you were done fighting."

"I didn't say I was done fighting. I just said I was done fighting that way."

"What other way is there?" Acupuncture? Herbs and spices?

"Oh, Ian." Her voice sounded so soft. So far away. "You know."

He squeezed his eyes shut and shook his head. He wanted to tell her that prayer didn't always work. It was something he knew firsthand. Despite all those nights he spent on his knees over his marriage, he still ended up divorced. He opened his eyes. The bank sign advertised high interest rates on CDs. A brown Mazda pulled out of the parking lot, splashing through a puddle, spraying up rainwater that landed at the grass by Ian's shoes.

"Will you please come home?"

Home. That word no longer fit with Peoria. "I'll think about it."

"I guess I'll take it." She paused. "I love you."

He returned the sentiment and powered off his phone, a deep weariness seeping into the marrow of his bones.

The date flashed in front of him. Big orange digits that screamed.

Two years.

Two years.

Two years.

The words repeated with every blink of the sign. Two years ago today, Cheryl had stolen Ian's hopes and future. She hadn't even given him a say in the matter. He came home after work, a small stuffed animal in his hand, as if the gift might erase her concerns. Instead, he found her curled up in bed. She couldn't do it, she said. She wasn't ready. So she made a choice she couldn't take back. And she left him with a ghost for a child.

෴

Ian had officially lost it. It was the only viable explanation for the fuzzy creature gnawing at his passenger side seat belt. He drove around a curve in the country road, green stalks of corn whizzing past his windows. What in the world had possessed him to buy a puppy?

"You better not pee on my leather," he said.

The small black Lab let out a playful yip.

Ian tightened his grip on the steering wheel. His mind was like a pendulum, swinging from one extreme to the next. Remember. Forget. Remember. Forget. Until he'd snapped, driven off to the nearest breeder, and purchased a three-hundred-dollar animal. His only reason? He grew up with a dog. Tucker had been his best friend in grade school. And it was something he might have done for his own kid if life had turned out different. If Cheryl hadn't stolen his choice away.

There was just one small problem. One small flaw to his logic. What was he going to do with a ten-week-old puppy?

∾

Robin's feet squished inside her shoes, leaving a trail of footprints that led up to her café. Her wet pants swished between her thighs in a slow, whispered chant as she climbed the cement steps.

It's gone… It's gone… It's gone…

Her ring was gone. She stepped inside, where Molly handed coffee to an unfamiliar man over the counter. When he turned around, his mouth fell open. No doubt at Robin's appearance—her hair a mess, mud caked beneath her fingernails, clothes soaked. She stared back, unapologetic, and he hurried out the door.

Molly blinked.

"Where's Caleb?" Robin needed to hug him. Ask his forgiveness—for leaving, for yelling, for making him stay at work on Saturday when Saturdays were forever and always one of their special days.

"You got your hand wet."

She looked at the pond-soaked gauze wrapped around her finger. Somehow, losing the ring made her forget all about the injury.

"Do you need a fresh bandage?"

The only thing she needed was to find her son. She pulled the wet gauze off her finger. "Is he in the back?"

Molly nodded. "I put a movie in for him."

Robin's shoes squeaked against the tiled floor. She stopped in front of Molly, hurdled the shame heating her cheeks, and looked the young woman in the eyes. "I'm sorry for leaving like that. It was inexcusable." Robin's brief lapse of sanity might lose her an employee. She wouldn't blame the woman for quitting.

But Molly smiled—shy and hesitant. "Everybody has their breaking point. I know I've reached mine a few times before. You were bound to reach yours eventually."

Some of Robin's hollowness filled with warmth.

Molly wrapped her fingers around a cup sitting beneath the espresso machine and handed it to Robin. "I figured you might need this when you came back."

Robin tipped the cup to her lips and closed her eyes as the foamy, coffee-flavored drink slid over her tongue. "Thanks, Molly."

"You're welcome."

Robin's shoes resumed their squeaking as she crept to the back door and cracked it open.

Her son's small form sat on a stool in the middle of the room, sniffling, his head tilted back so he could see the television screen. His casted arm rested in his lap while the other wiped his face. Her heart tore down the seam. She closed the gap between them in two long strides, wrapped her arms tight around his small chest, and buried her face in his neck. "I'm so sorry, Caleb. Mommy's so, so sorry."

He turned into her arms. She scooped him up and hugged him so tight against her body that she couldn't tell where he ended and she began. "I shouldn't have yelled or said that word. I shouldn't have left. And I shouldn't have made you stay here today. Can you forgive me?"

He released his vice grip around her neck and took a strand of her hair between his fingers. "Why are you all wet?"

A simple question with a not-so-simple answer. How could she explain to Caleb that she'd spent the last hour searching the pond, looking for her wedding ring? How could she explain the horrible, sinking feeling in the pit of her stomach? It was the ring Dad gave Mom and Micah gave her. And now it lay somewhere at the bottom of the pond.

"Did you go swimmin'?"

"Sort of."

He held up his cast. "I wish I could go swimmin'."

Her son, the fish, forced on land during the best swimming days of the year. She'd take him home. Fill up the plastic pool out back, wrap a bag around his cast, and let him splash around a little. Maybe that would make up for the rotten morning.

Molly poked her head into the kitchen. "Um, Robin?"

Robin's head turned in tandem with Caleb's.

"That guy's out here. And he's got something with him."

That guy. Robin didn't have to ask Molly who she meant. Caleb squirmed from her arms and rushed out the door. Robin ran a shaky hand over her tangled hair and actually pulled out a twig. She tried to smooth out her shirt, ruined from pond water, and looked longingly at the back door exit. But she'd already abandoned Caleb once today. She couldn't do it again.

So she took a deep breath and followed her son out into the café. Caleb sat on his haunches, tears forgotten, laughing as a puppy attacked his cheeks with its tongue. Ian stood over them, hands in his pockets, a smile spread across his face. The puppy pounced with its front paws and licked Caleb's nose. Robin cupped her hands over her mouth. Having the tiny fur ball inside her café had to break some sort of health code violation, but it was hard to care. Puppies were her kryptonite—draining her ability to do anything but pick them up and cuddle. She kept a wide berth from the Humane Society because otherwise, she'd bring everything home.

"Is this your little puppy?" Caleb's voice came out in whispered awe as he came nose to nose with the man bent in front of him.

"Well...that depends." Ian glanced at Robin and did a double take.

She tucked a wet lock of hair behind her ear, despising the heat that rushed to her cheeks.

"On what?" Caleb asked.

"On whether or not I can find a better home for him. I made a rather impulsive decision and now I'm not sure he'd get along too well with Bernie's cat. Bill's kind of ornery."

Caleb's eyes went wide. "Can I have that little puppy?"

Ian paused, his attention flitting to Robin, then back to her son. "I'm not sure, buddy. You'd have to talk to your mom about it first."

Caleb let out a whoop and hugged Ian's leg, a gesture he reserved for Evan or Gavin. Never ever a stranger. He ran to Robin. "Can we bring the doggie home, Mommy, please?"

Robin was a goner. Seriously, how could she resist her son *and* a puppy? She let Caleb tug her over and scratched the dog behind his ear. It let out a playful yip and nipped her knuckle. She laughed. "I don't know. Do you think you're ready to take care of a pet?"

Caleb bobbed his head. "Yes, I am. He can be my best friend."

She grabbed the puppy's face and kissed its wet nose. Was it weird to love puppy breath? When Robin looked over her son's head, she found Ian staring, obviously puzzled by her disheveled appearance. "Can I talk to you for a minute?" he asked.

Her stomach dipped. "Sure."

He swept his arm toward the back room, an invitation for her to lead the way.

She slipped past Molly and through the door. When she turned around, Ian stood directly behind her. She took a step back and knocked into a pan on the counter. Molly had remembered to take out the cookies.

He looked around her kitchen. Pans of all shapes and sizes filled every surface. "You having some sort of baking extravaganza?"

"They're for Carl's wake."

His line of vision moved from her toes, up her wet pants, paused over her dirty hands, and landed on her hair. The hair she'd pulled a twig out of a moment ago. "Did you get in a fight with some wet trees?"

"Sort of." Her hand fluttered to the tangled mess. "You said you wanted to talk with me?"

"Are you sure you have the time to take care of a puppy with everything else going on? Because I can figure out something else. I only brought the dog over because I thought Caleb would like to meet him." He took a step toward her. "You don't have to take him."

Robin thought about the puppy's floppy ears, its oversized paws. She *had* been thinking about getting Caleb a pet for his birthday. Sure, she'd planned on starting with something easier, like a goldfish or a gerbil, but a dog would be so much fun. "Did you see Caleb's face?"

"He was definitely excited." Another step.

Her airway pressed in on itself, like the walls of this shrinking room.

"If you're worried about being the bad guy, I can break the news to him. We can take a walk and then I'll figure out a plan."

Robin cocked her head. "How'd you end up with a dog in the first place?"

But Ian didn't answer. Instead, he took her hand. Held it up. And she stopped breathing for a second. "What happened to your ring?"

She brought her arm behind her back, heart thumping inside her chest.

"You always wear it." His voice was so low and he was standing so close. And her head was spinning and her thoughts were tangling. "You're always fiddling with it," he said.

She swallowed. "It's a long story."

He scanned her again, from her wet head to her wet shoes. Why, of all days, did she have to choose this one to go jump in a pond? A high-pitched bark slipped beneath the crack of the kitchen door, followed by Caleb's laughter. She didn't want to say no to something that produced such a wonderful sound, but Ian made a good point. Did she have time to take responsibility for a living creature right now? "How about we make a deal?"

"A deal could be good."

"We take the puppy home and see how it goes. If it ends up being too much, I have your permission to call and you will take him back."

"You're sure?"

A fresh round of Caleb's giggles sounded from the café. "Positive."

Really, now hard could it be?

THIRTY-FIVE

Robin chased after the dog, Caleb close on her heels as the little terror skidded around the corner of the hallway, a ribbon of tissue trailing behind him. The fur ball bounded down the stairs, paws slipping against the hardwood, and dashed toward the kitchen. Robin caught up with the animal, scooped it up in her arms, and gave the puppy a firm shake.

"No." She pried the ruined roll of toilet paper from its mouth.

Sharp puppy teeth nipped at her knuckles. Only this time, Robin did not laugh.

"No," she said again.

The dog let out a playful yip. Caleb tugged on her shirt and held out his hands. She handed the critter over. "Take him to the backyard."

He hugged the puppy to his chest, its legs dangling past his hips, and giggled while the animal showered his face in puppy-breath kisses. Unlike her, Caleb relished in the chaos.

"Make sure the gate is closed," she called after him.

She placed her hand on top of her head and surveyed the disaster zone. In a matter of three hours, the tiny beast had ruined a shoe, peed twice on her Persian rug, and crashed into an end table, toppling over one of her mother's blown-glass vases. The heirloom had fallen to the ground and shattered. She could only lose so many of her mother's things in one day.

She sank onto the sofa and blew out a breath. Her bangs billowed out from her forehead. She checked her watch. How much would Ian laugh if she called him three hours after striking that deal in her kitchen? Swallowing her pride, she took out the scrap of paper folded inside her pocket and pressed each number on the phone's keypad. He answered after the first ring.

"Not working out?"

"Now I know why the Bible says looks are deceiving. That thing is a heathen."

Ian's laugh was just as rich through the phone line. "It can't be that bad."

"Marley has nothing on this dog."

"Are you relinquishing the puppy?"

"Unless I want everything in my home destroyed, I'm afraid I'm going to have to. You can meet us at…" Her thought fell away. Amanda's car was at the farm while Evan replaced the starter and Robin had let Amanda leave with her car an hour ago to have dinner with some friends in Iowa City. Which meant Robin was stranded.

"Robin? You still there?"

"You know where I live. If you're not here in ten minutes, I'm calling animal control."

Ian laughed again. "I'll be there in five and don't call anyone."

She dropped the receiver onto the cushion and rested her head against the sofa's backrest. Ian was coming to her home. The thought made her feel as though a roller coaster were zooming around in her stomach. She hurried to the kitchen and poked her head out the window. Caleb ran in circles while the puppy chased after his flyaway shoelaces.

She spent five frantic minutes racing around the house, picking up toys and shoes and stray socks. Caleb was already a tornado on his own. What made her think she could add a four-legged monster to the mix? Robin stopped in front of her mantle and picked up the framed picture from her wedding day. She looked so young and invincible in her husband's arms, as if their love could conquer the world, as if it would last forever.

I'm sorry, Micah.

Brushing her fingers over his face, she walked the picture frame into the bathroom, laid it gently on the bathroom counter, and checked her reflection in the mirror. At least she no longer had pond water soaked through her clothes or dirt beneath her fingernails. She straightened her hair and her hand stopped. She blinked at her finger.

"It's really gone."

When the whispered words finally sunk in, Robin pulled back her shoulders and met her gaze in the mirror. "It was just a ring. There are more important things."

The phone rang in the living room.

She hurried to the couch and plucked the receiver off the cushion. "I thought you said five minutes."

"Robin? Is that you?"

A man's voice, but not Ian's.

"Oh, Evan. Sorry. I thought you were somebody else."

"We're on our way to the emergency room."

Her posture went stiff. "What?"

"It's Elyse."

"What's wrong with her?"

"She's having a really hard time breathing."

Robin's hands turned clammy.

"Bethany wants you to come."

"Of course. I'll meet you there." With the phone clutched between her ear and shoulder, she raced toward her shoes. She hopped on one foot while shoving the other into her boot. A bark floated inside the kitchen window. Caleb! What was she supposed to do with Caleb? Her son couldn't go to the NICU with her. And her car. Amanda had her car in Iowa City.

The doorbell rang.

She jogged into the living room and threw open the door. Ian stood on her front stoop with his hands in his pockets, rocking back and forth on his heels.

"Elyse is sick," she said.

The rocking stopped. "Who?"

"Elyse. Evan and Bethany's baby. I told them I'd meet them at the hospital, but Amanda has my car and I don't have anyone to watch Caleb. Or the puppy." Robin cupped her forehead with her hand. "Evan said she isn't breathing right."

"Take a deep breath. It's going to be okay." Ian stepped inside her home. "You get your other shoe on. I'll go get Caleb. Do you have an extra car seat?"

"A booster in the garage."

"Okay then. The puppy can hang out in the backyard, and I'll drive the three of us to the hospital."

∾

Caleb slurped the rest of his drink through a straw until the leftovers rattled. Ian examined the little boy's eyes, his face, and chin. He looked nothing like Robin and everything like Evan. Caleb pushed the drink away and smacked his lips. "Mommy never ever lets me have pop."

"Consider this a special treat." Ian wanted to make the kid happy. Keep him distracted. He didn't want him worrying about his baby cousin, who had been admitted into the NICU forty-five minutes ago.

"Can we go look at the babies now?"

Ian reached for his billfold. "How about I buy you another pop?"

The little boy held up two fingers. "I already had two ones."

"What about a candy bar?"

He shook his head. "I want to see the babies."

Ian closed his billfold. Caleb wanted to leave the hospital cafeteria. Not for the waiting room or the halls or the elevators. Of all places, the boy had set his mind on the nursery. Ian sighed. "All right. We can go see the babies." Chances were, they wouldn't even be allowed up there.

Caleb jumped off the chair and pulled Ian toward the elevators. The warmth of Caleb's hand inside Ian's large palm filled him with a longing he'd never quite conquered. He always wanted to be a father. Growing up with a dad who took him to the batting cage and let him pretend to shave at the sink made Ian excited to do the same with his own kids someday.

The little boy hummed a tune Ian didn't recognize inside the elevator and bounced on his toes. He pushed the button for an elderly couple who joined them on the third floor and got out on the fourth. The bell dinged and the elevators slid open on the fifth. Caleb tugged on his arm, but Ian didn't move. Caleb tugged harder, his cheeks puffing up with exertion until he stopped and hugged his cast. "Does your tummy hurt?"

Ian shook his head.

"Can we go see the babies now?"

He could do this. It was just a hospital nursery. Taking a deep breath, he stepped out of the elevator and led them both toward the nurses' station, half hoping the curly-haired lady dressed in scrubs would stop him. She only smiled warmly as they passed. Ian would have been content standing near the wall while Caleb smudged his face against the window, but the window was too high. The boy jumped on his toes, trying to see, until Ian lifted him beneath his armpits and a very happy Caleb pressed his hands against the glass.

A young nurse swaddled a newborn with a pink hat. She caught sight of him and Caleb and waved. Ian could imagine what they looked like. He, the proud father. Caleb, the big brother. He shook away the thought and focused on the other baby lying in a bassinet, his tiny, wrinkled finger poking out from the top of the receiving blanket.

Something about the sight of that blue cap unleashed two years' worth of suppressed questions. Ian tried to push them away, but they came too fast, too forcefully. Had his child been a boy or a girl? Would it have had his detached earlobes? Cheryl's upturned nose? His crooked pinkies? He bent his head toward the glass and let himself imagine what he never let himself imagine. A button nose and the curve of two tiny ears. A head of baby-soft hair that matched the color of his own. The child would be walking by now, maybe even running. They'd read books together and go to the park and a couple baseball games every summer. Ian pressed his forehead against the thick pane and watched the nurse tuck the baby girl inside her bassinet.

"There you are." Robin's breathless voice broke through his thoughts.

He set Caleb down.

"I was looking all over." Her eyes sparkled, like the sun reflecting off the ocean. "Elyse is going to be fine. They have her hooked to oxygen and she's already doing much better."

He tried to say something like "that's good" or "I'm glad." But the words got stuck, trapped behind the questions he let himself ask and the picture he let himself create. Questions that would never be answered and a picture that was lost two years ago.

"I guess she has RSV, but Evan and Bethany got her here early." Robin ran her hand through her hair. "Thanks for watching Caleb, Ian. Thanks for bringing us. I'm not sure what I would've done without you."

He settled on a nod and looked away. From her and Caleb. From the babies behind the glass. And when the knot in his throat only grew bigger, he shoved his hands in his pockets and stepped away.

"Hey. You okay?"

"Yeah. Just need some air." He turned to leave, but she grabbed the sleeve of his shirt.

"Ian?"

He twisted his arm from her grip, suddenly very eager to escape. He didn't want to be here anymore. Not next to all these babies on this particular day. "I'm fine. I... Will you be all right if I leave?"

"Sure. I can take Bethany's car home. They're staying the night."

"Okay, good." He turned and strode to the elevators. He didn't say good-bye, and he didn't look back.

∽

What had just happened? Was Ian angry at her for leaving her son with him while she disappeared to the NICU? Robin crouched beside Caleb, who stood on his tiptoes, fingers clasped to the ledge of the nursery window, nose poking over the top. She looked too, her heart pinching at the sight of the two little ones on the other side.

She kissed the crown of Caleb's head, pressing her lips against his flyaway cowlick. It was hard to believe, but almost four years ago one of those little ones had been him. Time moved at such an odd, disorienting speed—stalling in place, then lurching forward in spurts and stammers. Back when the pain of losing Micah had been fresh and sharp, she'd prayed for time to hurry. To drag her away. But somewhere along the line, as time pulled her further and further from the life she'd dreamed, her prayers had changed.

Had it really been four and a half years since Micah's death? Was her baby boy really going to start preschool in the fall?

A nurse walked around the corner. When she saw Caleb, she bent over her knees and tucked her clasped hands between her thighs. "This handsome fellow looks familiar. Weren't you peeking in the window a little bit ago?"

Caleb smiled his shy smile, the one that poked at his lips but didn't come out all the way.

"Looks like somebody's ready to be a big brother." She winked at Robin. "He was just here with his daddy looking at the babies."

His daddy?

The woman ruffled Caleb's hair and disappeared around the corner.

Robin's confusion lifted and she took a step after the nurse to clear up the misunderstanding, but a picture flashed in her mind and held her in place. An image of Caleb on Ian's shoulders, looking into the nursery at a baby swaddled in pink, with Ian's eyes and Robin's dark hair. Ian pointed at the tiny bundle, a gold ring circling the finger on his left hand. Robin jerked, as if the picture had eight legs and scurried up her arm.

She pushed the image away and convinced herself it came because she'd seen Ian holding Caleb a few minutes ago and these babies did funny things to her heart. That's all it was. She touched Caleb's shoulder. "Do you want to go say good-bye to Uncle Evan and Aunt Bethy before we go?"

He gave an enthusiastic nod. "Is Leesey all better now?"

"The doctors are giving her medicine."

She led him past the nurses' station, down the long corridor, and turned into room forty, where Evan wrapped his strong arm around Bethany's waist as she bent over the crib and stroked Elyse's cherub face. Evan rested his chin on Bethany's shoulder and whispered something into her ear. She turned her face toward his, and he kissed the worried crease between her eyebrows. A soft, tender kiss while Elyse slept below them. A three-part family wrapped in a posture of intimacy. Robin's chest squeezed. Evan and Bethany were a complete family, while Robin scrambled to fill the missing hole in her own. No husband. No Daddy tiger.

THIRTY-SIX

Exhausted from its day of terror, the puppy slept in Robin's arms. Her four-legged, furry excuse. Caleb wouldn't be happy when he woke up, but what else was she supposed to do? She couldn't keep it. And for whatever reason, she had to see Ian. She had to know why he left the hospital in such a hurry. As soon as Amanda got home and Caleb was asleep, she got in her car and drove to Bernie's, where apparently the front door was left unlocked after hours.

Robin glanced at her watch and pressed her ear to Ian's door. It was silent inside, but light flickered from the thin strip of space between the door and the floor, as if he had the television on mute. She stepped back, reconsidering. This was stupid. Showing up on Ian's doorstep so late at night. She clutched the sleeping puppy to her chest and turned toward the staircase. If she left now, nobody would have to know about her strange visit. But a handle clicked and the door groaned open behind her.

She glanced over her shoulder.

Ian stood in the doorway, his carefully pressed shirt now rumpled and untucked. A tuft of hair stuck up from the back of his head, as if he'd been lying on his pillow for too long, and a shadow lined his jaw, hinting at the thick beard that could grow should he ever allow it. His eyes were big, wide, and somehow lost. She'd never seen him so completely disheveled or so completely attractive.

"I wanted to bring back—"

He held his finger up to his lips. "Bernie's a really light sleeper," he whispered. He nodded toward his room and walked inside. A nonverbal invitation. Trapped between his door and the stairs, Robin stood very still, the safe and the uncertain going to battle. Half of her itched to follow him, the other grasped for an escape. She took a deep breath and scratched the itch.

The room was small, barely big enough to hold an armoire, a full-sized bed, and a desk. No nightstand. Not even an extra chair. She deposited the puppy on the mattress and Ian clicked the door softly behind her. "It's not the Marriott, but it works."

She stayed where she was, standing at the foot of the bed. If she stepped any closer, he'd hear the pathetic sound of her hammering heart.

"Did she put you in the smallest room?" she asked.

"She claims it's the biggest." The puppy turned in a circle, then curled into a ball. Ian brought his hand to the back of his head and smoothed down his hair, but it sprung back as soon as he took his palm away. "Sorry it didn't work out."

"To be fair, you did warn me."

He smiled. The effort stopped short of crinkling his eyes, reminding her why she came. She couldn't get the look he'd given her at the hospital out of her head. And now he wore the same one.

He scratched the dog's scruff. "I could have picked him up tomorrow."

"I'm not sure either of us would have survived."

He laughed an empty laugh.

"What will you do with him?" she asked.

"The breeder seemed like a nice lady. I'm sure she'll let me take him back."

"That's good." She watched him pet the dog's ears, thumbing her naked ring finger. "Hey, Ian?"

"Hmm?"

"I wanted to thank you again. For looking after Caleb." She stared down at the fuzzy carpet. "I also wanted to apologize."

"For?"

"You don't like hospitals very much, do you?"

"Was it that obvious?"

Robin bent her ankles out, so that her weight rested on the outside edges of her unlaced tennis shoes. "Is it because of your mom?"

Ian looked up from the floor. "How do you know about my mom?"

"Amanda's my roommate and she's not exactly the type to keep things to herself." When Robin told Amanda about Ian's odd reaction at the hospital, Amanda suggested it might have something to do with his mother's cancer. The news rocked Robin to her core. She had no idea his mother was sick. Then she felt selfish for not knowing. Ian had gone out of his way to ask about her mother and all this time, Robin hadn't inquired once about Ian's family.

He walked to the opened window, the thin drapes lifting from the breeze. Robin stepped closer, until the night settled over the tops of her shoes. As if sensing her nearness, he turned and looked at her with eyes so lost she felt a little lost herself.

"She's not doing well?"

"No."

"I'm really sorry."

He shrugged. "It's not your fault."

"I know, but I'm still sorry."

"I'm determined to take your café and you come here to express your sympathy about my mom." He shook his head, like he couldn't make sense of her apology. "You're a hard woman to figure out."

"Not that hard."

He touched the drape. "She had cancer when I was in high school. But my dad got her the best treatment and it went into remission for a long time."

"Do you have any siblings?" After her own mother died, she'd longed for a sister or a brother, somebody to share her grief, somebody to help her understand it, somebody who could shape her sorrow into words. Bethany grieved, but it wasn't the same. "Maybe talking to one of them would help."

He let go of the drape and sat in the cove of the window. "I have a younger sister."

She took a step closer.

"Bailey got married last month." He rubbed his eyes with the heels of his palms. "To this wealthy trust-fund guy from Brown. I wasn't sure about him at first, but he's pretty solid. Right now she's finishing her honeymoon in Europe." He wrapped his hand around the back of his neck. "Even though she's married, she still seems like a kid, you know? I don't want her to worry about this."

It was peculiar. Listening as Ian unveiled this piece of himself. Envisioning his human side. Not as a businessman trying to buy out her café, but as an older brother and a son. Hearing Ian talk about his family made him so…real. Her fingers twitched. What would it feel like to place them on his shoulder? She tucked her hand deeper into her pocket, keeping it safe from temptation.

"My mother isn't the reason I was acting weird at the hospital."

"It wasn't?" She took another step closer, her insides wobbling.

"Tomorrow's Father's Day."

"Yeah."

He looked up from the ground. "I was supposed to be a dad."

Robin tripped over the hollow sound of Ian's voice. He was supposed to be a dad? When? How? She replayed the statement several times, trying to figure out what it meant.

"Did Amanda also tell you I'm divorced?"

She tried to put his words together, but they kept slipping from her grasp. Ian was divorced. Which meant… Robin thought about the scare she had with Caleb. She'd come so close to miscarrying her son. It had been absolutely terrifying. Had Ian and his ex-wife lost a baby?

He set his elbows on his knees and massaged his palms. "Two years ago, my wife got pregnant. When she told me, I was thrilled. I always wanted to be a dad, you know? And I thought it might fix whatever was wrong in our marriage. But she kept telling me she wasn't ready to be a mom."

Robin's heart stilled. Ian's wife didn't miscarry.

"But I thought they were just words. I thought she'd get over it. I never suspected…" He stopped his palm massaging and dug finger paths through his hair. "She didn't want to tell anyone about the pregnancy until the second trimester. Not even our parents. So we kept it a secret. And one day, on my way home from work, I bought this silly little stuffed rabbit at the gas station, thinking it might cheer her up. When I got home, the baby was gone."

Pain drew her closer. It was as if God had flipped over the fabric of his life and showed her the underside, where everything was twisted and reversed. A father without a child. A child without a father. She sat beside him.

"I should have seen it coming."

"It wasn't your fault." She'd spent too much energy thinking the same thing. That maybe if she'd called Micah at work that day, she would have noticed something funny in his speech or tone. Maybe he would have complained about a headache and she would have insisted he go to the hospital. It didn't take long to drown in the maybes.

"My father wouldn't have let it happen."

"Ian…" But what was there to say? What words could she possibly offer? That nobody—including his father—had that much power? That his child was in heaven? That they lived in a fallen world and things like this happened? Those things, no matter how true, had offered her little comfort back then, and would offer him no comfort now.

"The kid would be close to a year and a half. And today, all I could think was that we'd probably have a puppy by now. I always had a dog growing up."

She reached out and touched his knee.

He looked down at his leg—at the place where her palm touched his jeans—and took her hand, like he did earlier in her kitchen, only this time she didn't pull away. Her breathing turned shallow, uneven. He turned toward her, so close she could see specks of honey floating in the brown of his eyes. "What happened to your ring, Robin?"

"I threw it in the middle of the pond." Her heart thudded in the hollow of her clavicle. She wanted to cover it up, but she didn't want to take her hand away from his.

"Why?"

"I don't know." Nothing made sense anymore. She only knew that in this moment, sitting in the nook of Bernie's window, she understood Ian. Or at least a part of him.

"But it was your mother's."

"It's okay," she whispered. "Really."

He traced her knuckles with his thumb and goose bumps danced up her skin. She started to pull her hand away, but he circled her wrist and turned up her palm and rubbed his thumb over the frantic tapping of her pulse. And before she could think, before she could reconsider, she kissed him.

Attraction and fear and longing burst and pinged and pecked at her heart. She was kissing a man. He was kissing her back, and her pulse was pounding. He drew her closer and she let herself be drawn. But then he stopped. And her senses flailed.

A light tapping broke through her confusion. Robin jumped up and pressed her hand against her lips, her cheeks flooding with heat. What was she doing, kissing a man she was supposed to be fighting? What was she doing kissing a man at all? She hurried to the door and flung it open. Bernie stood on the other side with rollers in her hair, nightgown stopping short of her bony ankles, a scrawny black cat clutched under her arm.

Robin brushed past the old woman and took the stairs two at a time. When she got to the bottom, she heard Bernie's voice. "I thought I heard the television."

THIRTY-SEVEN

Early-morning dew pressed into the balls of Robin's feet. The lid to the mailbox creaked as she pulled out the lump of mail she'd neglected over the past two days. She frowned. People weren't supposed to deal with mail on Sundays, but then again, people didn't usually wait until Sunday to check it. With her coffee in one hand and the mail in the other, she padded across the walkway and sat down on the front stoop.

The quiet calmness of a June morning surrounded her. The sun hid in the east, a pink ball hovering over the horizon. Cool humidity hinted at the impending heat. She set her elbows on her knees and buried her face in her hands.

Lord, give me peace.

She'd repeated the same prayer over and over last night, like counting sheep, until sleep came sometime past midnight. Six hours later, she awoke with the same prayer on her lips. But peace eluded her. Fear kept her thoughts hyped up on adrenaline. They refused to rest, and so, too, did Ian's face, the story of his mother, the child that was taken away from him.

The memory of that kiss...

Robin rubbed sleep from her eyes and stared at the ground between her toes. Several times last night, she'd considered flinging off the covers and going into Amanda's room. Waking her up and telling her everything. But once she told Amanda, there'd be no going back, no retreating to safety.

She pressed her knuckles into her eyes and shook her head. She was a giant idiot. How could she fall for the man who wanted to tear down her café? How could she fall for a man, period? But as hard as she tried to fight it, longing oozed out of control like the fizz from an uncorked champagne bottle. She wasn't sure she'd ever be able to put it away again.

Lord, what's going on? What am I doing?

Some could have turned away from God after losing a husband so young. Some might have rejected Him after such loss, but Robin hadn't. She'd clung to Jesus with a tenacity she didn't know existed. And somehow, she'd found peace—an unexpected blossom watered by her own tears. What she had now felt familiar and safe. It felt...enough.

At least it used to.

She grabbed the handle of her coffee cup and brought the brew to her lips. Fresh, Columbian coffee. Dark and rich with a strong, wake-me-up aroma. She let the steam curl around her face. The sun turned from pink to orange and outlined her pear tree, ripe and swollen with fruit. She was scheduled to sing at church, which meant she needed to get Caleb up and ready for Sunday school. She also needed to call Dad and wish him a happy Father's Day. Then after church, she'd take Caleb to the cemetery to put flowers on Micah's grave. Time pushed her to get moving. Always and forever marching her forward.

She picked up an envelope from the top of her stack, slipped her uninjured finger beneath the flap, and opened it with a clean tear. She shook the letter open with one hand and took a sip of her coffee. The mug paused in front of her lips and her heart came to a screeching halt over one word.

Termination.

Robin clamped the letter in her hand and brought it inches from her face. It was a notice. From Roy Hodges, her banker. They were cutting off her revolving line of credit.

∽

The ring of the doorbell silenced Caleb's milk slurping. His head perked up from his bowl of Cheerios, the handle of a spoon gripped in his fist. Robin stopped her deranged pacing and ran her hand down the back of his messy hair. "Mommy needs you to go upstairs, Buggerboo. I have to talk to someone in private, okay?"

"But I'm still eatin' my cereal."

She looked into his bowl. Three meager rings floated near the edges of the plastic. She scooted out his chair. "Go brush your teeth. And when you finish, you can play quietly in your room."

Caleb stuck out his bottom lip. Ever since breaking his arm, brushing his teeth had turned into a battle of epic proportions. A battle she didn't have time for right now. Not when Ian stood on her front stoop, ringing her doorbell. She gave her son a stern look. His lip jutted out farther, but he got up and shuffled out of the kitchen. She scooted him along, hurrying his slow pace, and waited until he disappeared around the corner of the second floor before opening the door.

Ian stood on her stoop, a far cry from the rumpled, vulnerable version of himself from last night. A boyish grin crept into place. "Good morning."

She held the folded letter in front of his face. "Explain."

He peeked around the paper. "What am I explaining?"

She shoved the notice closer. "Read it."

"May I come in first?"

She crossed her arms and stepped back. He came inside and plucked the letter from her fingers. To his credit, his face paled as he scanned the contents.

"Did you do this?" A floorboard creaked overhead. She swallowed and stepped closer. "Did you ask Roy to cut off my line of credit?"

"What? Robin, no. Of course not."

She hugged her middle, wanting more than anything to believe him.

"I swear, this wasn't me." He scanned the floor, like answers were ingrained in the hardwood. "It had to have been Mayor Ford."

"I called him this morning. As soon as I opened the letter. It wasn't him."

"He's lying. Robin, he has to be."

"Mayor Ford may be a lot of things, but he isn't a liar. And Mr. Hodges wouldn't up and cut off my credit for no reason."

A shadow fell over Ian's face. "So you think I'm the liar?"

"No, I don't think you're a liar. But I do think your father might be behind it."

He laughed a humorless laugh. "There's no way."

"Who else wants to run me out of business, Ian?" Robin paced to the couch. She needed space from him and the memory of last night. She turned around and startled. Ian stood closer than she expected, his gaze fierce.

"My dad is a good guy. He might be ambitious, but he would never do this."

"It's the only explanation that makes sense."

"I'm telling you he didn't do it."

Robin pressed her fingers against her forehead, her fear so palpable she felt as though she could pick it up and measure the physicality of it. "This is a mistake."

"What?"

"Us. This." She motioned from her to him and took a step back. "The idea that we could ever…be anything. It could never work."

He stepped closer. "Why not?"

"Because I'm the owner of Willow Tree Café and you're a developer for McKay Development and Construction." She shook her head and took another step back. Impossible, impossible, impossible.

"Would you stop shaking your head?"

Her heels ran into the baseboard of the couch. She couldn't move any farther away unless she hurdled the sofa. And he was so close it seemed like he might kiss her again, with the notice of her credit termination in his hand.

He dipped his head.

She put her hand on his chest to keep him away, but the beating of his heart against her fingers made her longing return. It went to battle with everything she'd just said. Despite it all, she wanted him to kiss her. But before he could, the telephone rang.

Robin jumped. So did Ian. They stood, staring at one another with matching breaths until the phone rang again. She stepped around him and picked up the receiver, her voice cracking over her greeting.

"Robin? It's Cecile Arton."

Robin couldn't get away. The panic was everywhere. In Ian's nearness. In Cecile's voice. When would it end? "What's wrong?"

"There's been a fire in your café."

❧

The roof of her café was visible over the top of Arton's. Robin squeezed her hands in her lap and took calm, even breaths. *Lord, let it be okay. Let my café be okay.* She blinked at the lone fire truck blocking the road and the stragglers who stopped to watch the show.

Ian, who'd insisted on driving despite her insistence that she was okay, parked her car behind the bright red vehicle. Robin's fingers trembled as she undid the clasp of her seat belt and stared up the small hill to the signpost out front. She looked past the walkway, through the flowers bursting up from the ground on either side of the cement, her attention stopping at the front doors. Everything looked the same. Surely the damage couldn't be that bad.

The fire chief rapped on her window. She rolled it down while Ian got out of the car and opened the back door. He helped Caleb unbuckle. Her son scooted out of his seat and took Ian's hand. Robin massaged the tightness in her neck. "What happened?" she asked the fire chief.

"Mrs. Arton called as soon as she smelled smoke. Your oven seems to be the culprit. We put it out before it could spread much further than your kitchen."

Her stupid, good-for-nothing oven. "Am I allowed to go inside?"

The fire chief opened her door and she stepped out into the sunlight.

"The building's all clear, but I wouldn't let your son go in." He led the way up the cement steps. Robin followed, with Caleb and Ian trailing behind. They stopped at the door. Glass and debris decorated her flower beds. Somebody had broken the windows. The fire chief handed over his hard hat. Robin placed it on her head and pushed the door open.

Sunlight filtered across the floor and flooded the room, revealing the damage. Behind her front counter, black smoke stains danced up her wall, charring her canvases beyond recognition. She shuffled inside, the ground wet, the smell of smoke heavy and binding. The chairs and tables, metal and marble, stood like proud soldiers refusing to fall. She hurried to the counter. Somebody had ripped the door leading to her kitchen away. She stepped through the open doorway and pressed her palm against her chest.

Charred ashes. That's what her kitchen—the heart of her café—had turned into. The outside of the building might look the same, but the inside had crumbled into a ruined heap. She had a hard time breathing.

Why, why, why? Why did this happen?

She spun away from the wreckage, toward the front doors. Ian stood over the threshold, Caleb peeking through his legs. Both were staring at something in the far corner, off to her right. She followed the direction of their stare and the heaviness in her chest gave way. Her piano, once polished and proud, tipped at a slanted angle, standing on a broken leg. She stumbled over and ran her hand over the ashy, damp surface. The wrath of the fire's heat had warped the cabinet into something foreign. She pressed a finger to one of the keys. The haunted note echoed through the room. If the kitchen was her heart, the piano was her soul. And the fire had destroyed them both.

"This was my mother's." Her lips trembled over the words.

And then he was there, wrapping her in a tight embrace as she wept against the steady thrumming of his heart.

THIRTY-EIGHT

A phone call with Mayor Ford and a ninety-minute drive with nothing but scattered thoughts blaring in Ian's mind landed him in Peoria. He didn't want to believe Robin's accusation, but he had to find out for himself. A hangover pounded in his temples, only he hadn't had anything to drink. At least nothing alcoholic. But thoughts of Robin? Last night he'd knocked those back in enormous gulps until he was drunk with indecision.

Ian pounded on the front door of his parents' home, then twisted the knob and threw it open. Bailey stood inside, long blond hair hanging in a loose braid down her back, a healthy, younger version of their mother. Her eyes lit up when she saw him. "Surprise!" she said.

"What are you doing here?"

"Chad and I came home a little early. I wanted to surprise Dad on Father's Day." She hurried over and threw her arms around him. "Did you miss me like crazy?"

He hugged her back and spotted his parents over her shoulder. Mom stood in the entryway of the kitchen, a paring knife in one hand, an apple in the other. Dad towered behind her. All the anger, all the disbelief that had built during the ninety-minute drive gathered together and pointed directly at him.

Bailey let go of his neck. "You should hear how good I am at accents now. Hollywood will be calling any day. And the words! Do you know how fun Irish slang is? I'm going to start calling all my friends *shams*. Or asking where's the *craic*." Her smile faltered. "What's wrong with you?"

Ian took the notice from his pocket—the one Robin showed him this morning—and held it out to Dad. "What's this?"

Dad scooted around Mom and gave the paper a cursory scan. "A notice of credit termination."

"Were you behind it?" He waited for Dad to say no. To deny the accusation. His father might be ambitious and determined, but he wasn't underhanded. He needed Robin to be wrong on this one.

"Your mother's making apple pancakes. Why don't you take off your shoes?"

"Why don't you answer the question?"

The room went still. Ian could feel Bailey gawking at him in her frozen state, but he refused to look away from his father's deadpan expression.

"Yes."

The simple answer made Ian's ears ring. Robin was right—McKay Development and Construction was responsible. He flung his arm toward Dad's office down the hall. "What are all those awards for then? You won them because of your integrity."

"I won them because I care about my employees. If making a suggestion to a banker is going to save ten of my workers from unemployment, then that's what I'll do."

"I can't believe you."

Dad set his jaw. "What did you expect me to do, Ian? Not fight for my company? Lie down and surrender with Jim and Bob and everybody else's jobs at stake?"

"I expected you to be better than this." Ian crumpled up the notice. He tolerated working for his father because his father was supposed to be different than so many of the other developers out there. Turned out, Ian was wrong.

Dad puffed up his chest. "I don't think that's the issue."

"No?"

"I think you're starting to care too much about this woman."

"Since when is caring a bad thing?"

"You're letting your emotions get in the way of your responsibility. You're losing track of what's important."

"And what's important, Dad? Since you've always been the one to decide, why don't you refresh my memory?"

"Family—that's what. Or how about giving loyalty and commitment a try? Or maybe for once, finishing what you start."

The words were like a punch to the gut. "This is not about my marriage."

"You're right. It's not. It's about this company and your obligation to it."

"Did you ever think for a second that maybe I don't want that obligation?"

The stillness returned, hugging the end of Ian's outburst.

Dad looked stunned, pale even.

"That's enough, both of you." Mom stepped between them. "I won't have you two fighting like this, especially not on Father's Day."

Ian closed his eyes.

"Bailey and I will finish making brunch. You two finish your conversation out on the porch. Once you're done, come inside and we'll enjoy a meal together. As a family." She kissed them each on the cheek and disappeared with Bailey into the kitchen.

Ian stepped outside, his muscles tied into knots.

Dad came out behind him and stood in front of the porch railing. He grabbed on tight to the banister, like the wooden boards might rise up and pitch him over. With the truth finally out, Ian had no idea what to say. "How long have you felt this way?" Dad asked.

"I don't know, Dad. Always?"

"Always?"

"You never asked me what I wanted to do with my life. You had it all planned out the second the doctor said, 'It's a boy.'" Dad never gave him a choice. Neither had Cheryl. He was so sick of not having a choice.

"Ian, when you were a little kid, you used to ask to come to work with me."

"That's because whenever I asked, it made you smile." Ian looked across the expanse of the yard, a place where the two of them used to toss the foot-ball. Play catch. Practice batting. As a kid, Ian swung as hard as he could, every single time, just to see the pride in Dad's eyes. That little-boy piece of him still wanted to see it.

"If I pressured you to follow in my footsteps, it's because I love this company. And I love you. I wanted it to be something we could share." Dad's face looked stretched and old. "I had no idea you've been miserable all these years."

"I haven't been miserable." There was a comfort in having life planned out, a safe predictability. But maybe God didn't want him to play it safe anymore. Maybe there was freedom to be found in the uncertain. "But I haven't been happy either."

"So where does this leave us?"

Ian stared at the grass. "You paved your own way. You found something you were passionate about and you went after it. Maybe it's time for me to do the same."

Dad let out a long, slow sigh. "Could you do me a favor before you do?"

"Of course."

"Finish strong. We need this deal."

∾

Ian stepped inside his home, a place that was somehow empty and crowded all at the same time. He trudged up to the master bedroom and pulled out a shoe box from beneath the bed. He tucked it under his arm, grabbed a shovel from the garage, and started digging a hole in the backyard while birds chattered in the lilac bushes on the side of the house and bees buzzed around the hydrangeas growing up around the deck and cotton-white clouds polka-dotted the blue sky overhead.

"Finish strong…"

Unlike the way he finished with his marriage. Ian's parents had no idea. He took another chunk out of the ground, memories that died from neglect resurrecting themselves.

After Cheryl did what she did, she turned catatonic, slipping into a depression so deep and miry, it left no room for Ian's anger, so he bottled it up for the sake of his marriage. When Cheryl finally resurfaced, she claimed Ian's anger as her own. Somehow, he was to blame. It was his fault she got pregnant and terminated the pregnancy. He was to blame for her guilt. Ian tried everything to fix what she broke, but how much could he do when she wouldn't let him tell anyone? Not a counselor or their pastor. Nobody. So while his marriage disintegrated, his parents scratched their heads, wondering what in the world had happened.

Ian stuck the blade of the shovel into the earth and sat cross-legged in the overgrown grass, cradling the box in his lap, so sick of feeling shame and guilt and anger over something outside of his control.

A cold hand pressed against his shoulder.

Ian twisted around and looked up. The blinding sun outlined the frail shape of a woman, a wisp of a smile tracing her features. He scrambled from his spot in the grass, but Mom pressed her hand against his back and eased herself down beside him. She looked at the hole, then at the box. "What have you got there?"

He let her take it from his lap. She opened the lid and pulled out the contents one by one. A tiny stuffed rabbit, bought at a gas station two years ago. A pink Cubs onesie, for a girl. A small Cubs hat, for a boy. She laid them out on the grass, side by side, her eyes glistening with moisture.

"You would have made one incredible grandma."

"We didn't know," she whispered.

"Cheryl didn't want to tell anyone."

She folded the onesie into a small rectangle and returned it to the box. Followed by the hat and the rabbit. She set the cardboard container on the grass. "Life is messy, isn't it?"

They sat in silence, letting that truth soak and settle, until one of the neighborhood dogs started to bark in the distance—a high-pitched yipping that enticed several others to join in the conversation.

Mom patted his knee. "You know what I'm learning, though?"

"Hmm?"

"Grace comes in all different shapes and sizes. Even the messy ones."

"Oh yeah?" Ian quirked his eyebrow. "What shape and size have you been experiencing lately?"

"Cancer."

The two syllables thumped him in the chest. He blinked at Mom as she plucked blades of grass from the earth and let them fall on top of the box. What grace was there to be found in something as horrible as cancer?

"There can be grace in there too, if you want," she said.

A lump pushed against his Adam's apple. "Cheryl had an abortion."

"And she'll have to live with that for the rest of her life."

"So will I."

"I know you will, Ian." She stood and gently placed the box in the hole. "Even after you bury this."

"That's not grace, Mom. That's pain."

She picked up the shovel and handed it over. "Sometimes, love, grace *is* pain."

Confusion knotted his soul. Where was grace in the loss of his child or Robin's husband, his mother's cancer, or even his divorce? "I don't understand."

"If that pain brings us to the throne of God. If it brings us to our knees before the King of Kings." She placed her fingers beneath his chin and tipped his face to look up at hers. "Oh, honey, there's amazing grace in that."

༄

The high-powered dehumidifier filled her ruined café with a loud humming that drowned out the man's words. Robin cupped her hand to her ear and leaned forward. "What did you say?"

"We'll run these for the next couple days. It's really important we get this place dried up. Don't want mold growing behind your walls."

Robin nodded, desperate to get away from the droning. She had no idea a fire could bring about so much busyness in such a short time. Boarding up broken windows. Calling the insurance company. Filling out paperwork. And now a strange, heavyset man roamed around Willow Tree, turning on loud contraptions, knocking on the walls, removing ruined pieces of furniture, writing notes on a clipboard. Thank the Lord for Gavin, who offered to take Caleb for the day. Robin had no idea what she'd do with her little boy running around.

The man jabbed his thumb toward her piano. "What do you want to do with that?"

She bit her lip and looked away just as the front doors opened and Amanda burst inside. The man turned on a second dehumidifier. The droning doubled, along with her anxiety. As if sensing her distress, Amanda guided Robin outside and sat her on a cement step. The loud humming faded. Fresh air touched her cheeks and fluttered her hair around her shoulders.

"I heard Cecile Arton talking at church about a fire. As soon as she said Willow Tree, I ran here." Amanda wiped at fine beads of sweat breaking out along her hairline. "And I mean it. I literally ran."

"Fire restoration contractor," Robin mumbled.

"What?"

"That man's a fire restoration contractor." She picked at the rubber lining of her shoe. She still couldn't fully process what had happened. One minute Ian was about to kiss her, the next they were zooming across town to her ruined café. "I didn't even know they existed. But they do. Fire restoration contractor. Have you ever heard of that before?"

Amanda shook her head.

"They work on Sundays too. The guy said there are lots of fires on Sundays. He has movers coming later to take away all the ruined furniture. I can't decide what to do with the piano."

Amanda set her hand on Robin's shoulder.

"Lenny warned me about the oven. I don't know why I waited so long."

"You had other things on your mind."

Yeah, like Ian McKay. A man who should not be on her mind. Robin wrapped her arms around her knees.

"I know this all feels overwhelming right now, but we'll get it fixed. That's why you pay that expensive insurance premium every month, right?"

"Ian and I kissed."

"What?"

"I have no idea how it happened. One minute we were talking, and the next..." Robin's fumbled attempt at an explanation trailed off. "Why are you smiling?"

"You and Ian kissed?"

Robin buried her face in the crook of her elbow. "I don't want you to be happy about it."

"Why? It's a good thing."

"No, it's not."

"You're attracted to Ian."

"No, I'm not."

Amanda whistled the tune to the Oscar Mayer song. Robin could practically hear her sing-song thoughts. *My bologna has a first name, it's R-O-B-I-N...*

Robin shook her head in her elbow, as if her denial could make everything untrue. "But I can't be."

"I can keep whistling if you want."

Robin removed her face from her arm and looked at her friend. "I can't be attracted to him, Amanda."

"Why not?"

"For a thousand, million reasons."

"You can't spend the rest of your life being afraid of love."

"That's not what I'm afraid of." At least not all the way. Not completely.

Amanda set her elbows on her knees. "What is it, then?"

Robin took a deep breath, unsure if she could put words to her thoughts. Unsure if she wanted to say them out loud. "I don't want to look back on my life in twenty years and feel happy with the way things turned out."

"You don't want to be happy?"

Robin let out a ragged breath and thumbed her naked ring finger. "If the roles were reversed, I'm not sure I'd want Micah to move on. Maybe that makes me the most selfish person on the face of the planet, but I wouldn't want another woman kissing my Caleb to sleep. I wouldn't want another woman making love to my husband."

The thought made her physically ill.

She tugged at a weed growing up from a crack in the cement and looked at her sister-in-law as if she possessed the words that might set Robin free. "Where am I supposed to go from here? Micah and I never had this conversation."

Amanda didn't answer right away. She gazed at the black lampposts and the mulberry trees lining the empty street for such a long time, Robin worried she didn't have an answer at all. But then a fly landed on Amanda's arm and she swatted it away and looked at Robin with eyes the same shape and color as Micah's.

"I don't know what my brother would or wouldn't have wanted, but I do know you, Robin. I see the way you love people. It's full and unwavering. It would be a shame for you to withhold that gift from someone who might embrace it, who might need it in his life. I can't imagine Micah would want you to."

∽

The buildings lining Main Street corralled the sunlight. Yellow rays tunneled down the road, reflecting off storefront windows, making Ian squint. He shook his head, forcing himself to wake up. The short hand barely crept past five—not even dinnertime—yet he felt as if he'd lived an entire life in a single day.

His foot tapped the brake as his car rolled past Willow Tree. A man stood on a ladder, nailing boards over one of the windows. Two others wheeled Robin's damaged piano down the lawn toward a bay truck. Ian pulled over to the curb and hopped out of the car. There were a lot of things he couldn't fix, a lot of things he couldn't change, but this wasn't one of them.

The two men grunted and strained as they wheeled the piano onto a metal loading dock.

"Excuse me, fellas."

The men stopped.

"Where are you taking this?"

One guy mopped sweat from his brow. "Junkyard."

"Can I have it?"

"Why?" The guy kicked at a half-broken leg. "It's a hunk of junk."

"A really heavy hunk of junk," the other said.

Ian ran his hand along the charred surface. Some of it had to be restorable. He thought of the instrument repair shop across the street from his office in Peoria. Surely they could do something. "I'd like to have it."

The two men exchanged looks.

Ian reached into his back pocket and pulled out his debit card. "How about I pay you two hundred bucks apiece and you help me get this hunk of junk to a repair shop?"

Their suspicion melted. They turned to Ian with matching grins. "Lead the way."

THIRTY-NINE

Two months after we moved to Peaks, Dad had to go away on business and Mom decided to get rid of his recliner. I invited Bethany over after school and as soon as we stepped inside, we caught sight of Mom grunting and straining, trying to shove the mammoth chair toward the door. She swiped at the beads of sweat forming across her brow and blew strands of hair out of her eyes. "Oh, hi, girls," she said.

Bethany and I exchanged looks.

"Wanna give me a hand?"

"Where are we moving it?" Bethany set her backpack by the door.

"To the curb."

I'm pretty sure my mouth fell open. Dad loved that recliner. So much, in fact, that he lovingly referred to it as Old Pete. I have no idea where the name came from. Regardless, Old Pete was the centerpiece of almost all of their arguments. Mom wanted the recliner to go. Dad was adamant that it stay, even though it smelled like feet and showcased several unidentifiable stains. Old Pete had been a part of our family for as long as I could remember.

I looked out the large picture window. Swollen storm clouds rolled overhead. The forecast called for severe thunderstorms, possibly even flash flooding. If Mom got Old Pete out on the curb and the sky unleashed, there would be no going back. The thing would never survive. "Mom?"

"Come on, Bethy, you grab that end and I'll grab this end. A couple of strong women like ourselves ought to be able to lift this thing."

Bethany grabbed underneath the left armrest.

"Make sure to lift with your legs. On the count of three. One...two..."

"Mom?" I said again.

She stopped counting. "Yes, dear?"

I pointed at the clouds. "It's going to rain."

"Which is precisely why I want to get this thing outside."

"Dad's going to kill you."

"Your father might be many things, but a violent man he is not." She rubbed her hands together. "Now, are you going to help us?"

I stared at Old Pete. Sad, pathetic Old Pete. I think maybe he used to be blue, but time had worn him into a faded gray. Nothing about him matched our new furniture. Nothing about him fit in with the rest of our house.

"Your father has had this abomination since college. Trust me, the parting is long overdue."

"Okay, but if he gets mad…"

"I shall take the brunt of his wrath. Now come on, my darling daughter."

It took the three of us forty-five minutes to drag that thing to the curb. As soon as we finished, the sky unzipped and buckets of rain soaked us straight through. We laughed like maniacs and sprinted up the long driveway. I tore open the door and we spilled inside. Burger, our bulldog, lifted his head from his spot near the piano but didn't bother getting up.

Once we finished wringing ourselves out, Mom fed us peanut butter and honey sandwiches while thunder crashed outside and wind pummeled the side of the house. It was a fierce storm, but short-lived. When the rain stopped, Old Pete's ruin was complete.

Mom clapped. "Who wants to go to Sofa Mart?"

Bethany and I raised our hands.

We piled inside Mom's van and spent two hours trying out new chairs. When Dad came home three days later, the garbage man had taken Old Pete away and a nice new leather recliner sat in his place. I waited for Dad's face to turn red. I waited for an explosion. Instead, Dad set his briefcase down and scratched his chin. He gave Mom one of those arched-eyebrow looks.

"It was time, babe."

He sat down and reclined back, a reluctant smile tugging at the corner of his mouth. I couldn't believe it. Dad liked the new chair.

Mom bent over and gave him a kiss. "I promise not to say I told you so."

He grabbed her wrist and pulled her into the chair with him. She giggled and that was that. Old Pete was a thing of the past.

FORTY

D r. Dotts removed the last stitch and patted Robin's elbow. She held her hand in front of her, fingers splayed. The wound looked tender—more red than pink.

"I'd still wait a good week or so before playing that piano of yours," he said.

That shouldn't be a problem, seeing as she no longer had one to play.

"I want you to be gentle with it for a while, and make sure to clean it every night."

"Thanks." She mustered a smile and blinked at his bow tie. He had always worn one, even when she was a teenager and he still gave her safety pops. Something about the tie's familiarity—its consistency—bolstered her spirit. Some things did stay the same.

"How's Caleb doing?"

"Great." A genuine smile tugged at her lips. With her café in disrepair, they would have a lot of time to spend together. The one silver lining to this fiasco.

"He's healthy?"

"As a horse."

"When does he get his cast off?"

"A couple more weeks."

"And how's your gentleman friend? The one who brought you in when you cut your finger."

Her stomach knotted. "Ian?"

"He was a nice fellow. Seemed to treat you well. How's he doing?"

Robin bit her lip. She wouldn't know. She hadn't seen him since yesterday morning, when she cried into his chest. "I think he's okay."

"That's good." Dr. Dotts patted her knee. "You take care of that finger. If it gives you any trouble, come on back and I'll give it a proper scolding."

Robin slid off the table and brought her purse strap over her shoulder. She waved farewell and left the office, digging for her keys as she went. Halfway to her car, she found them and something else too. Her fingers slid over the smooth surface of the letter. She pulled it out of her purse and unfolded the note with great delicacy—as if it were an ancient relic about to fall apart—and stared, for the hundredth time, at Ian's handwriting.

She'd found the note in her mailbox last night, after returning from a very long day at the café. A patch of clouds glided past the sun, dimming the paper in her hand, but she didn't need the sunlight to read the words. She didn't even need to open her eyes.

Dear Robin, I'll be away taking care of some business. I'm not sure how long it will take. Would you call me, please? Below, he'd jotted his number and signed his name. Something about the neat, slanted shape of his letters made her stomach quiver. Robin's arm fell to her side. She hadn't made any phone calls, at least not to him.

What good would it do? He wasn't going to quit. And even if she wanted to give in, One Life depended on her.

∽

Ian pushed the door open to the smell of varnish and pine. He followed Mom inside the piano restoration shop and ignored the question twinkling in her eyes.

A tall woman with flyaway hair met them at the door. "May I help you?"

"I'm Ian McKay. I brought in a piano a week and a half ago."

The woman clapped her hands together. "Ah yes, Ian. How are you doing?"

"I wanted to stop by and check on the progress."

"We've been working on it day and night and nothing else. It's a gorgeous instrument. Do you mind if I ask how old it is?"

"I'm afraid I don't know."

Mom stepped closer and looped her arm through his. He could feel her staring at the side of his face.

"Is it almost finished?" he asked.

The lady laughed. "Oh, goodness, no. Even with everybody working on it, it will still take us another couple weeks, at the very least. We've had to replace some of the wood, but we're trying our best to keep it as uncompromised as possible."

"Could you make sure it gets delivered to this address when it's finished?" He handed her a folded slip of paper with Willow Tree Café's address and Robin's phone number scrawled inside. "I'd sure appreciate it."

"Yes, of course. We'll call as soon as we're done."

"No need to call me. You can call that number, there." He pointed at the paper. "And charge the bill to my credit card, please."

"We most certainly will. Thanks for your business, Mr. McKay."

Ian tipped his head and led Mom out of the shop, counting backward from ten. He'd be shocked if he reached one before she voiced the questions flickering in her eyes. He didn't even get to five.

"That was an odd little detour."

He nodded and helped her over the curb.

"Whose piano are you fixing?"

"Robin's. Where do you want to go for lunch?"

He escorted her to the passenger side of his car and opened the door. She squinted at him before slipping inside and pulling the seat belt across her chest. Ian shut her in. He'd just returned from a business trip to Wahlberg. Rather than hightail it to Peaks and force Robin to speak with him like his heart begged, he'd opted to take Mom out for a bite to eat. See how she was feeling. Checking on the piano was a temptation he couldn't resist, and now he needed to answer her questions. He got in the car and started the ignition.

"Robin's the owner of the café."

He nodded.

"Why are you fixing her piano?"

"The fire ruined it and it's important to her." He tightened his grip on the steering wheel. "How about that new Italian restaurant downtown?"

Mom rolled down the window. Her bandana rippled as she tilted her head back and smiled at the sunlight. "How long are you staying in Peoria?" she asked.

"I have to help Jim close the deal in Wahlberg. Then I have to go to Peaks for a couple days to wrap up some stuff before the town meeting in two weeks." He needed to return the mayor's phone calls. Iron out the details. He told Dad he was leaving the company at the end of July and was determined to show his father that he could, in fact, finish strong. But focusing was hard, especially when all he really wanted to do was knock down Robin's door and ask her why she hadn't called.

"Your father's proud of you, you know."

Ian gave Mom a look. "He's disappointed."

"Sad, yes. Disappointed, no."

He brought his foot to the brake as his car approached a set of stoplights.

"Don't forget, Ian, that your father didn't follow in his father's footsteps either. He admires you for stepping out to find your own way."

"Yeah, well, what if I fall flat on my face?" The restaurant business was a risky one, especially when he had no idea where he would start.

"You won't, honey. I've tasted your cooking."

"But what if I do?"

"Then you do. And you take heart that failure doesn't define you. Neither does your past or your divorce." Mom fingered the silver cross hanging around her neck. "When that truth sinks in, you dust yourself off and get back up again."

The light turned green. Ian pressed the gas. Mom rested her head against the headrest and closed her eyes.

"Mom?"

"Hmm?"

Ian dragged his teeth over his bottom lip. "What do you think about this condemnation thing?"

"I think Mayor Ford is doing what he thinks he needs to do."

"And Dad?"

"I think your father has a good heart. I think his son does too." Mom reached for his hand on the console. "Nobody will discredit you for following it."

Ian's grip tightened around the steering wheel. Perhaps he could follow it, if he knew what direction it was leading. Robin's silence was messing with his head, as was that kiss. Part of him wanted to erase it. The other part wanted to grab her by her shoulders and kiss her again. He spent half his time trying to figure out how to convince her to give them a chance, the other half trying to convince himself that she was right. It was impossible.

"I'd love to meet her."

He looked at his mother. "Who?"

"This woman who has you so distracted. Robin. She must be special."

A vision sprang to life in his mind—Mom and Robin, sitting out on his parents' deck with their feet up, sipping iced tea. The two would get along, he knew it. He merged onto I-55 and welcomed the wind. Robin was everywhere. No matter how hard he tried, he couldn't stop thinking about her. He'd left her a note and his phone number.

Her silence spoke volumes.

∾

Robin carried the box of muffins with both arms while Caleb opened the door to One Life. Willow Tree might be out of commission for the time being, but that didn't mean she wasn't going to bring Piper Greeley and all the other kids their after-school snack.

As soon as they stepped inside, Kyle was there. As if he'd been watching them make their way from the street. "Here, let me get that," he said, taking the box. His eyes were bright, an odd combination of excited and nervous.

No doubt the threat of condemnation was making him just as antsy and riddled with adrenaline as it was her. He handed the box off to the woman who coordinated the after-school program, then clapped his hands and smiled a smile that seemed unnaturally large. "Do you mind if we talk in my office?"

"Um…sure." They didn't have very much time. As hard as it was to believe, Caleb's birthday was tomorrow. Which meant she wanted to get back home so she could start on his cake. She took Caleb's hand and followed him down the cramped hallway, into a dimly lit, doorless office—one that couldn't be much bigger than a supply closet.

"I have some really good news," he said, walking behind his desk.

"I'm always up for hearing good news."

"It's an answer to prayer." Kyle rubbed his jaw, then tapped the desktop with his knuckle. "I'm not sure I've wrapped my mind around it yet."

Robin shifted her weight. "Well, are you going to tell me or keep me in suspense?"

"We found another space. On the north end of town."

She blinked several times, staring at tall Kyle in this cramped space, positive she heard wrong. "But I thought that was too expensive. I thought you didn't want to cut any programming."

"That's the good news. Thanks to an elder at Grace Assembly, we won't have to."

Caleb wrapped his arm around Robin's leg and leaned against her hip. "Can we go now, Mommy?"

"Just a second, sweetheart." She swallowed the dryness in her throat. "I don't understand."

"One of the elders thinks One Life is an incredibly important ministry. He hates seeing the town torn apart over it and now that your café is…well, so damaged…he and his wife have offered to cover the extra cost of renting the new facility each month."

Robin gaped.

"Isn't that great? What an answer to prayer, right?"

She tried to nod or say yes, but nothing came. And by the time she finally forced something out, it wasn't what she'd intended. "But what about the location? How will the kids get all the way to the north side of town after school?"

"You're right. The location is a bit inconvenient, but the facility is so much more accommodating. I'm sure I can apply for some sort of grant that would cover the cost of bussing the children over."

"Wow. I'm not sure what to say."

"I know. It's a lot to process." Kyle scratched the back of his neck. "I wanted to thank you, Robin. For everything you've done. I can't tell you how much I've appreciated your support."

Robin didn't respond. She couldn't find her voice.

◈

"Is it at the bottom?" Caleb asked.

"I think so."

"Aren't you gonna look for it?"

"I already did."

"Do you think I'll get another puppy for my birthday?"

"I don't think so, buddy."

Caleb sat at the edge of the pond and dipped his toes into the water. His socks were tucked inside his shoes and his shoes sat next to the trunk of the willow tree. The sun threw sparkles across the water's surface. Somewhere beneath all that glitter was Robin's wedding ring. Or maybe it had already become fish food. Maybe some lucky fisherman would discover a diamond on his plate after frying up his latest catch. A light breeze rustled through the drooping willows. Caleb jabbered about sea monsters and Robin rested her head against the bark, trying to process the bomb Kyle had just dropped on her.

She was thrilled that God had provided for One Life, but what did that mean for her café? A parade of memories marched through her mind—starting with that very first day, when she stood on the lawn of Sunshine Daisies, a run-down flower shop for sale, listening as Bethany planted a seed of life in Robin's weary soul.

Heat welled inside her chest, pulsing in tune with her heart. She wrapped her arms around her legs and tapped her head against her knee caps. When it came to fighting or fleeing, she had always been the type to stand and fight. But now that One Life no longer depended on her, could she justify dragging her town through the battle?

Lord, what am I supposed to do now?

No more credit line. All kinds of fire damage and the threat of condemnation. Fingers of abandonment gripped her spirit, leaving her cold and numb. Robin didn't know if God wanted her to put on her boxing gloves or throw them in the ring. Bad news heaped on top of bad news, dragging her back to a time when she'd waited for test results from the doctors. Back to a time when she'd sat in the corner of Micah's hospital room, clinging to hope, praying for one of the tests to come back with a promise of brain activity. But every test came back worse, confirming what she didn't want to hear. Micah was gone. His brain had no activity. And as much as she'd wanted to fight for him, she couldn't. There had been nothing to fight for. Was history repeating itself?

Are You asking me to give up, God? After everything, is this Your answer?

Caleb plopped down in the grass beside her. She wrapped her arm around his shoulder and drew him close, as if her little boy possessed the answers she needed. Taking a deep breath, she looked through the willows, out to the sparkling pond, and as the wind rustled the leaves, an answer stirred in her soul.

Be still, and I will fight for you.

Only instead of comfort, the words brought fear and doubt. Because as much as she wanted to believe them, the Lord did not fight for Micah when she'd begged Him to more than four years ago. She knew firsthand that her definition of deliverance did not always match up with God's. A small part of her thought maybe she was better off fighting for herself. But the words whispered over and over again.

Be still, and I will fight for you.

Robin closed her eyes, trying to escape that same sense of helplessness she felt all those years ago, when the doctors told her Micah was as good as dead.

FORTY-ONE

The current of the Mississippi slapped against the short wharf, gently rocking Amanda as she stared into the muddy depths of the river and waited for the fireworks that would cap off another Fourth of July. Families sat in clumps along the bike path, lounging on chairs and blankets. Little kids raced around with sparklers and the air snapped and squealed with firecrackers and bottle rockets—a prelude to the big show.

But Amanda couldn't get into the celebratory spirit. Not with a box filled with cards and pictures and mementos sitting on her knees and Jason's letter clutched in her hand. A letter that had led to some e-mails that led to a phone call—an hour-long conversation that went nowhere. Enough was enough. She tore it into tiny shreds and let them float away. They bobbed along the water's surface and disappeared.

Jason was in Africa and she was here. Neither of them were getting on a plane anytime soon. Which made her hypocritical. How many times had she urged Robin to move on? How many times had she felt annoyed with her sister-in-law's inability to let go of the past and grab onto the future? When all this time, she was engaged in the same battle.

She needed to get over it already. Build a bridge. Make lemonade. All that cheesy bumper-sticker stuff. She needed to accept that the dreams she dreamed and the future she hoped for had been her plans, not God's. And although it hurt, although she didn't understand the whys, perhaps His plans were bigger than her dreams. Amanda held her phone out in front of her, her thumb hovering over the button that would delete Jason's phone number. She jabbed it, set the phone beside her fishing pole, and took the box with both hands.

"You're not going to litter that too, are you?"

Amanda twisted around. A man stood on the bike path behind her, his elbows propped on the black railing. Dark shaggy hair, swarthy enough to be Italian or Greek, with a crooked nose, a V-necked white tee, and cargo shorts.

"Not sure it'd be good for the fish," he said.

"Have you been watching me?"

"A little."

"That's not creepy or anything."

He walked down the wharf and sat beside her. His eyes were almost black—like coffee without any creamer.

She leaned away. "And you would be...?"

"Joel St. Claire. I'm in town visiting my brother. Technically, this is his dock and I was hoping to watch the fireworks here."

"St. Claire, huh? You wouldn't, by any chance, be related to a girl named Blaire, would you?"

"She's my sister-in-law."

Poor guy. "Want to do me a favor, Joel?"

"Possibly."

She handed him the box. "Find a garbage can and toss this for me?"

"Is there something wrong with your legs?"

"It's better if you do it." She didn't want to know where it was. If she did, she'd probably go back and fish it out again. She needed a clean break. He started to open the lid, but she clamped her hand over the top. "You can't look in it."

"If I'm going to do your dirty work, don't you think I at least deserve to see what I'm disposing?"

She kept her hand in place and shook her head.

"How do I know it's not something illegal? Like drugs or body parts?"

"Do I look like a druggie or a serial killer?"

"The good ones never do."

She picked up her fishing pole. "Except for some not-so-flattering pictures, there is nothing incriminating in that box. Cross my heart and hope to die."

"Stick a needle in your eye?"

"If that is what it will take."

Joel chuckled as a barge made its way down the river. The wharf rocked harder in its wake. "Okay, fine, I'll do your dirty work. On one condition."

She baited the hook. "I might be able to handle one condition."

"Once I ditch whatever this is, you let me join you for the fireworks."

Amanda sized Joel up. Outside of his relation to Blaire St. Claire, she couldn't find anything wrong. "You have yourself a deal, Joel."

He nodded at the pole. "Don't you think the fireworks will scare the fish away?"

"I'm only looking to catch the brave ones."

"I'll be back then." He stood and held the box in the crook of his arm. "I'm glad I ran into you...?"

"Amanda."

Joel smiled. "I hope you catch something."

She cast the line out into the water. "Me too."

∽

"We talked about kids again last night. Evan is convinced bigger is better."

Robin smiled wanly, then ran her hand over the shiny surface of an older, but well-kept piano. "You're still having doubts?"

"One daughter is making me neurotic enough. Can you imagine me with two?"

Robin smiled. Bethany didn't give herself enough credit. She was a wonderful mother. "You're only saying that because of your recent trip to the ER."

"I'm saying it because the thought of giving birth to another child is terrifying."

Bethany's labor had been long and grueling. Unlike Caleb, baby Elyse was in no hurry to leave her mama. A week and a half past her due date, the doctors finally induced, and the little girl wasn't so little anymore. Twenty-four hours of hard labor that ended in a C-section made the entire thing pretty traumatic. "Give it a few more months, and you'll forget the pain."

"The memory's pretty much seared into my neurons."

"Even if it is, you have to admit, the pain's worth it." Robin thought about her son. The kid was a living, daily testament to that truth. She smiled at Bethany, but her friend was giving her an odd look. "What? You don't agree?"

"Oh, I agree. In fact, I think it was a pretty astute observation."

The irony sunk in, slow motionlike, and Robin's cheeks burned. She turned around and scrambled for a subject change. She didn't want to talk about Ian. "So…Amanda's dating somebody new."

"I heard."

"She's pretty smitten."

"I think she's still in rebound mode."

Robin examined a nine-foot black grand piano. "Donna called yesterday."

"Oh yeah?"

"She wants me to bake their wedding cake."

"That's right up your alley, isn't it?" Bethany stopped in front of a cherry-finished upright—brand-new and freshly polished. "What about this one?"

Robin pulled herself from the grand and came to her friend's side. She pressed a few of the keys, her heart tugging at the sound. Three weeks of no café or piano had taken their toll. All the idle time gave her unoccupied mind too much space to wander. And wander it did—to things she'd rather not think about, like her increasing restlessness over Ian's absence. So when Evan offered to spend a Sunday afternoon with the kids so Bethany and Robin could go piano shopping, Robin pounced on the offer. Anything was better than sitting around thinking about Ian, the town meeting, and her café.

"It reminds me of the one you play at church," Bethany said. "Do you like it?"

Robin lifted her shoulder. "It's pretty."

"Okay, what gives?"

"I didn't think it would be this hard. Looking for a different piano."

"Robin, of course it would. That old one was your mother's and you learned to play on it. She learned to play on it. It had memories."

"Are you trying to make me feel worse?"

Bethany took Robin's arm and pulled her to the side of the store, away from a young couple examining one of the instruments. "But Caleb's young. Teach him how to play on a new piano and make more memories."

Robin did her best to rally, to find that silver lining she was usually so adept at grasping, but her insides only drooped. Why was rebounding so hard these days?

"Where's your mind right now?" Bethany asked.

"Nowhere productive."

"That's what I thought." Bethany handed her purse to Robin. "Could you hold this? I have to use the rest room. When I get back, let's skip the piano shopping and get ice cream."

"Do you have gum in here?" Lunch had left Robin with major onion breath.

"Somewhere. Go ahead and dig." Bethany turned toward the ladies' room.

Robin opened the purse and dug through the contents—so completely different from her own. No Band-Aids. No extra pair of Spider-Man underwear. Obviously, Bethany didn't have to worry yet about Elyse having some sort of four-year-old emergency. Robin moved aside Bethany's keys, her cell phone, several business cards and stopped. She blinked at the name typed across the top of one of them. Ian McKay. McKay Development and Construction.

What was this doing in her friend's purse? With the card in one hand and the purse in the other, she followed Bethany's fresh trail and pushed through the bathroom door. "Bethany?"

Bethany's Ann Taylors were visible beneath the stall. One of her Ann Taylors disappeared and the toilet flushed. Bethany had an odd habit of flushing public toilets with her foot. "What's up?" she asked, opening the door.

Robin held out the card.

Bethany stepped in front of the sink and pumped two squirts of foamy soap into her hands. "That reminds me. He was in town the other day."

She hated what that bit of news did to her heart. "He was?"

"Evan said he saw him talking with the mayor and the superintendent outside Val's. Did you see him?"

"No."

"Do you wish you would have?"

Robin ignored the affirmative answer jumping to the forefront of her mind. She didn't want to admit it, but she missed him desperately. "Is he still in town?"

"I don't know." Bethany rinsed away the lather and dried her hands. "Why don't you just call him?"

"I can't."

"Why not?"

"If he's talking with the mayor and the superintendent, his plans haven't changed and as far as I know, neither have mine." Despite her reservations and uncertainty and the niggling doubts, the same phrase kept repeating through her mind. *Be still, and I will fight for you.* So Robin was doing her part and trying her best at stillness.

"If your plans haven't changed, why haven't you started fixing your café?" Bethany took back her purse.

"I already told you. I'm waiting until after the town meeting." If the town voted condemnation, then what was the use? She was not going to take the city she loved to court. "Out of curiosity, how did you end up with his business card?"

"He came to the farm several weeks ago. The day that article came out in the paper."

"Why?"

"He was trying to figure you out. He didn't understand why you re-fused his offer about renting first-floor space from him. After we finished talking, he insisted we swap cards. I wasn't going to follow through with anything."

"What did he say?"

"That I should call him when everything was over and—"

"No. Not that. What did he say about me?"

Bethany smiled.

Robin rolled her eyes. "Please don't turn into Amanda right now."

"He cares about you. He wanted to understand you better."

Robin's stomach didn't know whether to swoon or twist. Bethany's words shouldn't matter so much. And anyway, if that were true—if Ian did really care—wouldn't he have come looking for her as soon as he returned to Peaks? Half of her wanted him to disappear, the other half wanted him to chase after her and make her another offer. She held out her hand. "Can I borrow your phone? Mine's in the car."

Bethany dug through her purse and handed it over.

Robin walked out of the bathroom, past the rows of pianos, and out into the humidity. She settled herself on the curb, turned the business card over in her hand, and wondered if his work phone had caller ID. For some reason, calling him at work from Bethany's phone felt so much safer than calling his cell phone. Sunlight glinted off the white surface as she punched in the numbers typed at the bottom. A friendly-voiced woman answered on the second ring.

"Good afternoon. McKay Development and Construction."

Robin's airway tightened.

"Hello? Is anybody there?"

She scraped her tongue over the dryness sticking to the roof of her mouth. "Is Ian McKay there, please?"

"I'm sorry. Ian's out of the office all day."

"Do you know where he is?" If she drove back to town, past Bernie's, might she see his car parked in the street?

"He's in Wahlberg. Then he'll be in Iowa next week. Soon after that, Jim Harley will be taking over his accounts. Would you like me to put you through to his voice mail?"

"Excuse me, what was that?"

"Jim Harley will be taking Ian's position at the end of the month."

"Why?"

"Ian will no longer be working for our company at that time."

Robin's ears hummed.

"Would you like Ian's voice mail or Jim's?"

"Neither, thanks." As soon as the friendly voice said good-bye, Robin's thumb hit the end button. Ian wouldn't be working for his father anymore? He was leaving the company? She stared—in a daze—at the cars passing in front of her, wondering what all of it meant.

FORTY-TWO

People spilled out the chamber doors of the town hall, huddled in groups, a hum of excitement filling the air. Robin stopped and wiped the slick of sweat from her palms onto her slacks. Dad squeezed her shoulder. The gesture did little to alleviate her jumbled nerves.

This was it. The outcome of tonight would determine the course of her future. So why, in the midst of such an important moment, were her thoughts more consumed with Ian? The three and a half weeks since she'd last seen him stretched into an entire lifetime. The news of his departure from McKay Development and Construction would not leave her head. It kept popping into her thoughts at odd moments, like in the middle of the night, when Caleb padded into her room. Instead of pulling him close and going back to sleep, she'd lie there thinking about how comfortable Ian had been in her kitchen and the things he said about his grandpa Vin's restaurant.

Robin spotted a flash of blond hair, and her arm muscles clenched. The man turned around and she let out her breath. It wasn't him. Pressing her hands against her stomach, she faced her support group. Dad, Evan, Gavin, Amanda. They'd all met in the parking lot. Bethany was at home, keeping watch over Caleb and Elyse.

Gavin patted her upper arm. "Don't worry, Robin. We have your back."

Her eyes twitched at the swarm of people intent on condemning her property.

"Not everyone is on Ian's side," Evan said. "A lot of people at Grace Assembly support you and I've talked to some farming buddies. They don't like the plans any more than I do."

She gave them a weak smile and led the way into the chamber. She weaved through the crowd, ignoring the growing chatter. By the time she reached the front, a cold dampness pressed against the back of her neck and crept underneath her arms. Evan squeezed her hand and Dad brushed up against her shoulder. Her personal bodyguards.

Her insides sloshed. This was it: Robin versus the development plan. She gathered the nerve to peek across the chamber, where Ian had stood last time, but he wasn't behind the podium. Her eyebrows bunched together. She glanced at the dais, where Mayor Ford conversed with the council members, all looking equally perplexed.

Ian was late.

Robin scanned the rest of the room, a bubble of emotion expanding inside her chest. Dr. Bremms, the superintendent. Hank, the barber. Ryan and Kim Dolzer, married chiropractors. Judy, the town librarian. Lyle Noldt. Chief Bergman. Cecile Arton, bedecked in her usual mass of jewelry. Bernie, her face a roadmap of wrinkles and age spots. The old woman fanned herself with a folded up sheet of paper while Jed Johnson prattled into her ear. All people Robin had served at her café through the years. If God would truly fight for her, she'd gladly serve them for as long as people kept coming through her front door. Robin checked her watch—five minutes past seven and still no Ian.

Mayor Ford was scratching the top of his bald head, clearly unsure whether or not to proceed without the developer present, when the murmuring stopped. The crowd shifted and there he was, standing across the room. His suit coat unbuttoned, his tie askew, his face sporting more than a five o'clock shadow. Except for that night at Bernie's, she'd never seen him so...rumpled.

He buttoned his suit coat and strode to the podium. She waited for him to find her, to see her. After so much time, she expected him to at least look. But he straightened his tie and bent his head toward the microphone. "I'm sorry I'm late."

∽

"I don't understand what we're arguing about. These condominiums will be good for business."

"Exactly! This is a waste of everybody's time."

"If we condemn her property, then we lose One Life."

"That's not true. One Life found another space to rent."

Robin stared at Ian. Surely he had to feel it. But he just stood there, gripping the podium, his gaze fixed on some unknown target before him. The pounding in her heart picked up speed as the crowd split itself in two. Those in favor of condemnation. Those against it. She waited for Ian to join in and use his charm and his smooth speech to tip the scales in his favor.

"This is about forcing a person out of business, and I say we have no right to do that."

"We do if it's for the town's best interest!"

"Isn't the café ruined? It's been closed for the past two weeks."

Seats groaned as the occupants swiveled to face Robin. She addressed the crowd with a voice much steadier than her emotions. "A fire destroyed the kitchen, but the damage isn't irreparable."

"Willow Tree Café is a fine establishment," somebody chimed. "We have no right to shut it down."

"Was a fine establishment. It's charred now."

She stepped forward. "Yes, but I can fix it."

Several people stood to speak. Robin lost her focus. Familiar face after familiar face stared at her from the crowd, and so did the memories…

Sitting like a rolled-up pill bug in the corner of a hospital room, begging God for a miracle. Whispering news of her pregnancy to Micah's still body, hoping beyond hope that somehow it would pour into his ear and heal the broken places in his brain. She'd believed, with absolute certainty, that God could accomplish the impossible. He could have healed her husband. Nothing was beyond His power.

But God didn't heal Micah.

And now Willow Tree was slipping through her fingers, the place she had poured so much of her love into over the past four years, the place that had given her so much purpose and hope and joy, and she found herself in the exact same place as before. Certain God could save it, unsure if He would.

First Micah. Now the café. And Caleb—her heart and her life and her breath—would keep having birthdays. Last week he turned four and the next year, he would turn five. Before she knew it he wouldn't climb into her bed at night. He wouldn't want her to give him kisses and tickle his belly anymore. He wouldn't want to play dinosaurs and dragons or good guys and bad guys. Instead, he'd be going to high school dances and football games and then he'd leave to college and meet a woman and get married.

Voices escalated. Arguments banded together. Not all, but enough. Ian didn't have to say a word. He didn't have to fight. The town fought for him. She closed her eyes.

Is this the way You fight, Lord?

The mayor called for order. He stood from the table and waved his arms for quiet. Mouths stopped moving. Silence hovered.

"Before we call for a vote"—Mayor Ford directed his attention to the podium, where Ian stood like a sentry—"I'd like to hear from Ian. Do you have anything you'd like to say?"

Robin clasped her fingers together. The crowd waited, expectant, and Ian did something he hadn't done since stepping foot inside the chamber. He looked at her, his eyes darker than storm clouds.

He looked at her and dipped his chin toward the microphone. "I can't do this."

Benches creaked. People shifted in their seats. Robin's ears rang.

An uneasy chuckle escaped the mayor's lips. "What was that?"

Ian's eyelids fluttered, as if emerging from a fog. He let go of the podium. "I can't take away Robin's choice."

"What?" The mayor's voice rose above the whispers.

"If she doesn't want to sell, I don't believe in forcing her."

The mayor's chest puffed out, his face filled with bewilderment and indignation.

"If you want to build the condominiums, you'll have to find a different developer."

And as if that comment ended the hearing, the hall erupted. Amanda and Gavin and Evan and Dad patted her shoulder and wrapped her in hugs. People jumped from their chairs, chatter growing louder with each passing second.

"Can you believe it?"

"What would make him do such a thing?"

"That's horrible of him. Getting this town's hopes up and quitting like that."

Robin couldn't breathe. The air was too thick. She excused herself from the throng of congratulators and pressed through the bodies, winding her way toward the exit, her heart beating like a caged animal. Ian forfeited. He was a move away from checkmate, yet he knocked over his own king. She pushed through one last crowd, so close to the exit, when somebody grabbed her arm. It was him. The man she couldn't stop thinking about.

"Robin..."

She pulled away and hurried out the door.

∾

The low sound of an approaching train whistle crept through Robin's open window and filled the cab of her Volkswagen. Potholed pavement with faded parking lines gave way to patches of weeds that sprouted between iron tracks and sloped downward to meet the river. Robin took a deep, rattling breath and blinked at the sun sinking toward the horizon, casting pink and orange along the river's surface.

The train whistle grew louder, sharper, vibrating the steering wheel gripped in her hands, until the cargo train passed in front of her, slow and steady—so unlike the exhaustion and shock rumbling through her body.

God had fought for her after all. He'd brought her deliverance in the form of Ian McKay. Her mind prodded his motivations with uncertain fingers. Why would he surrender after he'd already won? She fingered the edges of understanding, afraid to look beyond its border. The last freight car rolled past and the train's whistle receded in the distance.

Maybe when she hugged Caleb, everything would finally sink in.

Maybe the joy, the relief she should have felt upon Ian's forfeiture, would come in the arms of her son. She shifted her car into Drive, crept out from the abandoned parking lot, and drove to Evan and Bethany's.

Dusk settled over the farm as she pulled up the gravel drive. She turned off her car and stepped outside. The sound of laughter floated in the air. It mingled with chirping crickets and the occasional spark of a firefly. Robin walked around the farmhouse, where Evan threw a tennis ball and Caleb jumped on his toes. The two Border collies chased after it, yipping at each other's heels.

The screen door opened and shut. Dad came out and stood by her side.

A lump wedged itself in her throat, but she didn't understand it. She should be overjoyed, ecstatic, ready to toss up the confetti and celebrate. So why, after such a victory, did she feel so much like crying?

He wrapped his arm around her waist. "It's been quite a night."

She rested her head against his shoulder.

"How are you holding up?"

She had no answer, but Dad didn't seem to mind. The two of them stood, looking out over the farm as Evan threw the tennis ball one last time. The dogs barked. Insects buzzed. Cattle lowed in the distance.

"Dad?"

"Hmm."

"Do you still love Mom?" The question escaped small and childlike. And while it took her by surprise, Dad didn't pull back from the misplaced inquiry.

Instead, he tightened his grip around her waist. "I'll always love your mother."

Her head rose and dipped with his deep breath. "But you're marrying Donna."

"I am."

A tractor engine rumbled. Evan steered the powerful machinery away from the fields, toward the shed. Caleb stood beneath a large tree, watching his uncle man the tractor, while the dogs panted at his sides like two furry bookends.

"The LORD our God said to us in Horeb, 'You have stayed long enough at this mountain. Turn and take your journey.'"

Robin's skin prickled. She looked away from Evan and blinked at her father. It was an odd memory verse.

"The Israelites spent such a long time wandering in the desert that when the time to enter the Promised Land finally came, they were scared. Those Philistines were awfully intimidating."

She wrinkled her forehead. What was Dad talking about?

"They were familiar with the desert. What lay ahead was uncharted, frightening territory. I have to imagine it was tempting to stay put." Dad chuckled. "Sounds kind of silly, doesn't it?"

Robin shook her head.

"I was reading all this in the Bible around the time I met Donna, and I realized that maybe it wasn't falling in love again that scared me. Maybe it was letting go."

"Of Mom?"

"Your mom was already gone, sweetie. There was nothing to let go of."

"What, then?"

"The familiar." Dad sighed. "Fifteen years after your mother's death, and my life as her husband was still very comfortable. Like that old recliner I used to fall asleep in when you were a kid."

Robin smiled. "Old Pete?"

The scent of gravel dust and hay wafted across the farm. The tractor's engine growled, and her son's small frame stood beneath the whispering leaves of the tree, watching the approaching machine, posture etched with longing and fear.

Caleb took a step forward and stopped.

The tractor idled. Evan looked at her tentative son. The one with a tractor bedspread and John Deere wallpaper. The one with an abandoned toy combine, worn with play and love. Robin wanted to go to him and help him get back on.

You can do it, Caleb. You love tractors, baby.

But Dad stopped her. "He'll do it on his own."

Robin wasn't sure he would. Caleb stood there, paralyzed, torn between the safety of the ground and his yearning. Until Evan waved. A simple invitation. And that's all it took. Even across the distance, Robin could see her son's shoulders square. He took a step closer. Then another. And another. Until he broke into a sprint, little legs pumping beneath him. Evan reached out his arm, scooped Caleb into the seat, and snuggled him in front of his chest.

The delight, the victory, the relief Robin had been waiting for—it finally came. She clasped her hands in front of her mouth.

Dad kissed her temple. "It was time for me to get back on the tractor. It was time to turn and take my journey."

Turn and take your journey.

The words rolled through her mind, again and again, until the last of the sunlight waved farewell and her phone rang. She dug into her pocket and spoke a garbled greeting.

"Is this Robin Price?"

"Yes. Who's this?"

"Doug Hanning. I was given this address for a delivery, but there's a Closed sign hanging in the window and I don't think you'd want me to leave it outside."

"What delivery?"

"Your piano, ma'am. It's all finished."

FORTY-THREE

Ian clutched the flashlight and strode through the grass, toward the only pond in Peaks. He'd spent the entire day praying and pacing, begging God for clarity. His coworkers' livelihoods were at stake and he didn't want to put an extra burden on his father's plate, especially now that he was leaving. But no matter how hard he prayed, the unrest in his soul would not leave.

His feelings for Robin aside, he could not condone the condemnation. His mother told him to follow his heart and this is where his heart had led him. He couldn't stand by and be a part of something that didn't feel right. Ian would always struggle with Cheryl for what she did and he'd die before he became that person to somebody else—especially Robin. He couldn't steal her choice.

Stopping in front of a massive willow tree, Ian turned on his flashlight. A beam of yellow light sliced through the encroaching darkness and shot over the small pond. Robin said she was okay with losing the ring, and while he believed her, he couldn't help but think that someday she'd wish she had it back. He removed his shoes and stuffed his socks inside, took off his suit coat and rolled up his sleeves. He'd failed in love once before. He was terrified of failing again. But Robin was worth the risk. She was worth any mess that might result. He just needed to convince her that he was worth it too.

He waded into the pond and pointed the flashlight into the water, careful not to stir up too much silt and sediment. When he'd made lasagna in Robin's kitchen, he told her that anything was possible. She'd looked at him as if he'd thrown her a lifeline. She wanted to believe it just as much as he did, he had seen the hope and the desperation in her eyes. If he managed to find that ring tonight, then maybe they both finally could.

∾

One of the men waved as soon as Robin's foot hit the first step, his hand on top of a piano-shaped tarp buttressed between two dollies. Her momentum froze. This had to be a mistake.

"Evening, ma'am," he said.

She forced herself to move. "I never bought a piano."

The man squinted at his clipboard. "Your name's Robin? Robin Price?"

She nodded.

"This is the right address. And this here number called your phone." The man flicked the sheet in front of him, as if the phone number should explain everything.

"But I don't understand. Who would buy me a new piano?"

"This piano isn't new, ma'am. We picked it up from a repair shop this afternoon. A gentleman paid us extra money to deliver it as soon as it was finished."

"A gentleman?"

He gripped both sides of his clipboard and held it in front of his nose. "Yep. A Mr. Ian McKay. I guess it got burned up in some kind of fire."

This couldn't be… She touched the tarp with trembling fingers.

"You okay, ma'am?"

Robin bit her lip, unsure.

"Mind if we get it inside? It's getting pretty late."

She dug her keys from her purse, unlocked the doors, flipped on the lights, and blinked against the flood of brightness. The damage had been gutted. All that remained were charred walls and her catastrophic kitchen.

∾

The tarp rustled and fell to the floor. A slow gasp tumbled from Robin's lips. She stood, transfixed, taking in the shape, the color, the familiar perfection of the keys. It was Mom's piano, as good as new. She laid her cheek against the smooth finish, inhaling the scent of pine and lemon.

How could this be? When had he done it?

She sat at the bench and brought her hands over the keys. She played several scales. Mom used to call them finger stretches. Musical training. A practice in discipline, only it never felt like discipline. Not with Mom's vanilla plum lotion kissing the air and her hands dancing over the keys.

The scales turned to a song—a rich serenade flowing from her fingertips, swirling with the quiet, filling her body. Mom had always reminded her not to let her fingers get ahead of the music, but Robin never listened. She couldn't then and she couldn't now, especially when she hadn't played for so long.

Her fingers raced ahead of conscious thought until all that existed was the music. It melted into her hands and carried her away. Song after song poured out, one after the other. Songs Mom had taught her, songs she played in church, songs she'd written while Caleb slept in his crib. She closed her eyes and surrendered to her hands.

Sadness and joy. Longing and fear. Desire and loyalty. All of it coalesced into a terrifying hope wrapped within a thousand what-ifs. All this time, she'd been living as if the days between Micah's death and her own were nothing but a drawn-out interlude. But what if they weren't? What if God wanted more for her life than filler music? Life with Caleb and the café *was* enough. But what if God, in all His generosity and love, wanted to give her more than enough? Perhaps giving her heart away didn't have to be such a scary thing when He was holding it in His palm. Maybe it was time to turn away from this mountain of fear and her past and the man she once loved bigger than the moon so she could take whatever journey God had for her.

I'm done with the desert, Lord. I don't want to die staring at the mountain.

Something niggled between the crevices of her mind. Sharp and soft. Dark and light. Micah and Ian. Two men. One gone and one very much alive. Fear and hope went to war, as one by one, God removed the familiar tentacles that kept her rooted in place, afraid to step, until the desperate cacophony of notes morphed into a joyous melody of new beginnings and fresh starts. A melody of healing and hope.

She didn't stop when her finger throbbed. She didn't stop when blackness crept into her windows. She played until a sharp tapping interrupted her personal concert. Her hands stopped and Robin turned. Mayor Ford had his face pressed against her window, knocking on the front doors. She looked at her watch, then went to the front and unlocked the dead bolt, inviting the night air across her empty café floor. Mayor Ford stepped inside, his face lined with wrinkles she'd never noticed before.

"I was driving past and saw your lights on."

Her finger throbbed. She clasped it in front of her. Dr. Dotts would not be pleased.

Mayor Ford wrung his hands. "After the crowd cleared, the council members and I discussed our options."

"And?"

"I'm sorry, Robin, but these condominiums are part of our development plan. We really do think they will be good for the town."

She closed her eyes and waited for the pain, for the heated emotions of defeat to sweep her away. Only they didn't come. Memories marched in their place. They reeled through her mind like scattered lyrics from a song. Ian's smile. The confident way he navigated her kitchen. The depth in his eyes when he told her about his mother and the child he never knew. The gentleness of his hands when he held Caleb up to the nursery window. The faint scent of wintergreen pressed against his shirt as he held her in his arms. And her son. Getting back on the tractor. If he could do it, so could she.

"We've decided to move forward with condemnation."

She opened her eyes. The walls that she and Bethany had built and painted. The walls that had brought her a sense of healing. They had served their purpose. But when it came right down to it, they were just walls. "That won't be necessary."

Mayor Ford furrowed his brow.

"I'd like to sell."

"You would?" His tired face flickered with disbelief, then flooded with pleasure. "That's wonderful, Robin. I'll start looking for a new developer first thing tomorrow morning." His face split into that cherry-cheeked smile of his.

"There's just one thing."

His smile faltered.

"If it's okay with you, I'd really like to sell to McKay Development and Construction."

⌒

Robin raced through the gate leading to Bernie's and knocked on the door. Was Ian still here? Had he driven back to Peoria? She paced on the step, waiting for somebody to answer.

The door swung open. Bernie stood before her, dressed in a terrycloth robe and slippers, the same black feline clutched in her arms—the broken-tailed she-cat named Bill. "Robin?"

"Is he still here?" She craned her neck to see past the woman blocking her view.

The cat squirmed. "Who?"

"Ian. Is he still here?"

"He left an hour ago."

No.

Robin shook her head. She had to speak with him. She turned around and stepped off Bernie's front stoop.

"What's all this about?"

"Nothing, Bernie. Go back to sleep." She pulled her phone out of her purse and dialed Ian's phone number, but he didn't answer. Each time she went straight to voice mail.

⌒

Her headlights sliced through the darkness as she drove down Main Street. Caleb slept in the back and Dad sat silently in the passenger seat. Weariness dragged at her eyelids, a hint of hopelessness too. She wanted to drive to Peoria, find Ian, and explain all that had happened. But he wouldn't answer his phone and she had no idea where he lived. She couldn't just traipse off to Peoria when she had a little boy to think about.

Her stomach tightened. What if Ian never answered his phone? What if he never returned her phone calls? What if he decided she wasn't worth the drama and they never saw each other again? The idea made her heart hurt. Robin pulled down her cul-de-sac and turned into her driveway. Her chest physically ached. A familiar feeling, only this time, it wasn't Micah she longed for.

Dad patted her hand. "I'll get Caleb."

Robin unclasped her seat belt and coerced her body from the car. The sensor light flooded on and Robin stopped. A man sat on her front stoop.

Their eyes locked and held and the tapping in her pulse broke into a sprint. Ian's hair was disheveled, his tie gone, shirtsleeves rolled up to his elbows, hands clasped in front of his knees and his clothes...wet?

Robin tried to close her car door or pry her hand from the handle, but her body wouldn't work properly. Her heart beat too fast. Her lungs worked too slow. Dad straightened from the car with her son and stopped, his eyes sparkling as he looked from Ian to Robin. "I'm going to go put this guy in bed."

He kissed Robin's forehead and headed toward the house. Robin followed, her muscles tight as she watched Dad pat Ian on the shoulder and disappear inside the front door with Caleb. Ian stood and stuck his hands in his pockets.

"You fixed my mother's piano," she said.

He nodded.

"Why?"

"I wanted to give you something."

So he'd given her music, her mother, a lifetime of memories? "And tonight? The meeting? What was that about?"

He curled his hand around the back of his neck. Robin wanted to peel it away and trace her thumb over the defined line of his jaw. She wanted to erase the tension squeezing around his eyes. "I don't want to take your café," he said.

"No?"

He shook his head. "That's not what I want anymore."

She leaned forward, so close she could feel the heat from his body and smell…pond water. Questions jumbled in her mind—a thousand million questions. Like why did he quit his job? And what was he going to do now? But before she could get any of them out, he reached inside his pocket and pulled out something very familiar.

Her hand fluttered to her chest as she looked from the ring to Ian, the ring to Ian, the ring to Ian. "Is that…?"

"I thought you might want it back someday."

Ian had found her ring. Her mother's ring. Micah's ring. He'd waded into the pond and he found her ring. She'd accepted the fact that it was lost. Finding it would be impossible. But somehow, Ian McKay did it.

"I didn't know how else to show you."

Tears welled in her eyes.

"I don't want to replace Micah, Robin. I know he'll always be a part of your life." He took her wrist. Set the ring in her palm. Curled her fingers around it and brought her fist to his chest. "I would never ask you or Caleb to forget him."

Her heart thudded—a loud beat that pounded in her ears. He included Caleb. He couldn't possibly know how much that meant to her that he included Caleb. "Mayor Ford came to see me."

Regret rippled across his brow.

"The town is still going through with it. They're going to condemn my property."

He let go of her hand and ran his through his hair. "You can fight it. Mayor Ford doesn't want to take you to court. He thinks the threat will be enough."

"I told him I'd sell."

His hand froze on top of his head.

She took his arm and threaded her fingers through his. Ian's eyebrows furrowed as he looked down at their joined hands. They fit. Somehow. Someway. Robin didn't think it was possible for her hand to fit with anybody else's but Micah's. But she was wrong. "As long as I can sell to McKay Development and Construction."

"I can't let you give up your café."

"I'd like to build a new one. First-floor condo space, remember? You said something about a built-in clientele."

"Robin…"

"I'd like to build it with you."

His eyes widened. "Me?"

"Rumor has it you're unemployed. And I happen to know you're handy in the kitchen."

The doubt ebbed away, and he smiled that smile. The one that made his eyes crinkle and her knees go soft. "You like that idea?"

"I do."

He wrapped his arm around her waist, his hand spanning the small of her back, and buried his face in her hair. "I love you, you know."

She closed her eyes, imagining her feet treading into the water as God took her hand and led her across the Jordan. Toward a land filled with hope and second chances. A chance she never prayed for or even wished for. But God gave it to her anyway. She brought her lips to his ear. "You know what's kind of convenient?"

"What?"

"I love you too."

The whispered words came without fear or guilt or hesitation. They rang with honesty. She felt him smile against her cheek. And this time, he kissed her.

READERS GUIDE

1. This story follows three characters—Robin, Ian, and Amanda. How has life not turned out as expected for these three? In what ways has your life turned out differently than you expected?

2. Interspersed throughout the novel are short chapters told from Robin's first-person point of view. Which of these was your favorite, and why?

3. In this story, Ian and Robin have conflicting goals. Whose goal do you relate or empathize with more, and why?

4. Amanda is young and impulsive but means well. Do you agree with the way she handled things with Ian and Robin? Why or why not?

5. Do you think Robin and Ian are well suited for each other? Why or why not? What was your favorite Ian-Robin moment?

6. Robin often feels like an Israelite wandering in the desert. Talk about a time in your life where you felt the same. Looking back, what did you learn or how did you grow through that experience?

7. Ian has a hard time going to his church back home because of his feelings of failure and disappointment over his divorce. Have you ever felt this way? What verses, songs, or words of wisdom have you found helpful when you or a friend is battling feelings of shame or unworthiness?

8. Robin experienced two big losses in her life—her mother and her husband. Have you ever lost someone close to you? How has your grieving experience been similar or different from Robin's?

9. This novel explores the importance of fathers. Ian grew up in a home with an involved father, then Ian was denied his right to be a father, and Caleb is growing up in a home without a father. Discuss some father-child dynamics that you have found complicated. What role has your father played in your life?

10. Robin struggles with fear, especially fear of letting go of what's familiar and comfortable and stepping into the unknown. Can you relate to this? Talk about a journey you've thought about taking but haven't yet because of fear. What blessings might you experience if you were to step out into those uncharted territories?

11. Ian's mom says that sometimes "God's grace comes in a messy package." What do you think she means by this? Have you experienced this in your life? If so, please share.

12. Do you think Ian made the right choice in the end? What repercussions might his decision have on the people he cares about? In his position, would you have done the same thing or would you have chosen differently?

ACKNOWLEDGMENTS

A few years ago, when my agent called and told me that WaterBrook Mult-nomah was offering me a two-book deal, I was over-the-roof, can't-sit-still excited.

Once that settled and I found out what books were going to be published, I remember feeling uncertain about the first one, *Wildflowers from Winter*, but pretty confident about the second, *Wishing on Willows*.

Little did I know what a journey this book would turn out to be. If not for these people, I'm quite positive I wouldn't have survived...

Thank you to my husband, for not only loving and supporting this neurotic little writer, but for making this journey called life so much fun. You may take full credit for my sanity.

Thank you to my amazing editor, Shannon Marchese, for not only stretching my writing muscles, but for taking my hand and helping me scale walls that at times felt unscalable. Your ability to bring a story to life is nothing short of brilliant.

Thank you to the dream team at WaterBrook Multnomah: Amy Haddock, Lynette Kittle, the amazing sales team, and everybody else who has had a hand in getting this story on a shelf. I consider it a privilege to partner with such encouraging, classy folk.

Thank you to my agent, Rachelle Gardner, for talking me down off multiple cliffs; Lissa Johnson, for your attention to detail; and Tommy Woodsmall, for taking the time to brainstorm with me over the phone. Eminent domain was all you.

Thank you, Seth and Hannah Slay, for naming your female cat Bill and letting me use the idea. It was perfect for Bernie. And thank you Jeremy Hickman, Becky Houk, and the rest of the junior high crew. Your support is more encouraging than you know. It is an honor serving alongside you.

Thank you, Mom, Dad, and Peggy for entertaining Brogan so I could meet my deadlines.

Thank you, Melissa, Holly, and Susan. I always wanted a sister. God gave me three.

Thank you, Jeannie Campbell, Erica Vetsch, Wendy Miller, Janice Boekhoff, Nichole Wagner, The Debs, the Yellow Rocket Writers, and all you other crazy writer peeps who make this thing called publishing so rewarding.

Thank you, dear reader. The uplifting e-mails and Facebook messages and Tweets always seem to come at the perfect moment. You are such a blessing to me. Thank you for reading Robin's story. I hope you have enjoyed your time in Peaks.

And last, but never least, thank You, Jesus. Beth Moore says pride takes credit. Glory gives credit. Oh, Lord, may my life and my talents forever and always glorify You—the giver of both.

ABOUT THE AUTHOR

KATIE GANSHERT is a Midwest gal who's passionate about Jesus, her family, adoption, writing, grace, Africa, and all things romance. When she's not plotting her next novel, she enjoys going on ice-cream dates with her husband, playing make-believe with her son, and chatting with her girlfriends over coffee and bagels. She could talk books all day and absolutely loves connecting with her readers.

∾

You can connect with Katie at
katie@katieganshert.com
www.katieganshert.com
Twitter: @KatieGanshert
Facebook: www.facebook.com/AuthorKatieGanshert
Pinterest: http://pinterest.com/katieganshert

Grief like winter may have its day,
but life comes back in springtime.

Architect Bethany Quinn is comfortable being the creator,
but not acknowledging one. So when tragedy takes her back
home, can she keep avoiding the God of her childhood?

Read an excerpt from this book and more at
www.WaterBrookMultnomah.com!